No Longer the Property of Hayner Public Library District

OVERDUES 10 PER DAY, MAXIMUM FINE
COST OF ITEM
ADDITIONAL $5.00 SERVICE CHARGE
APPLIED TO
LOST OR DAMAGED ITEMS

RECEIVED
MAY 1 5 2014

Praise for Suzanne Palmieri

On *The Witch of Belladonna Bay*

"With a profound understanding of the ties that bind us through the generations and beyond the grave, Suzanne Palmieri has created some of the most emotionally resonant characters I've met in a long time. An enthralling tale of murder, magic, forgiveness, and redemption, *The Witch of Belladonna Bay* casts its Southern spell on page one and hasn't released me yet."
—Brunonia Barry, *New York Times* bestselling author of *The Lace Reader* and *The Map of True Places*

"Suzanne Palmieri has crafted a riveting tale that will keep you up late at night guessing what will happen next. It is a story that will intrigue both male and female readers. Guys, don't let this one slip past you."   —Jason Mott, *New York Times* bestselling author of *The Returned*

"All of Suzanne Palmieri's novels cast a spell, and *The Witch of Belladonna Bay* is no exception. Palmieri delivers a rich and magical story about the two most powerful forces in life: family and love."   —Elin Hilderbrand, author of *Beautiful Day*

On *The Witch of Little Italy*

"Palmieri's enthralling debut will make adult readers nostalgic for beloved books from their childhoods. Abundant with secrets, hidden passageways, magic, and several enchanting mysteries, it'll keep you on the edge of your seat until the end. The magic and witchcraft elements are subtle, enhancing the overall effect of this clever, beautiful novel."   —*RT Book Reviews*

HAYNER PLD/ALTON SQUARE

HAYNER PUBLIC LIBRARY DISTRICT
ALTON, ILLINOIS

OVERDUES 10 PER DAY MAXIMUM FINE
COST OF ITEM
ADDITIONAL $5.00 SERVICE CHARGE
APPLIED TO
LOST OR DAMAGED ITEMS

No longer the property of
Hayner Public Library District

MAY 1 5 2014

HAYNER PUBLIC LIBRARY DISTRICT
ALTON SQUARE

"Charming and enchanting—*The Witch of Little Italy* drew me in from page one. A magical story of family, secrets, loss, and rediscovery written in beautiful prose and sprinkled with effervescent characters you won't soon forget. Palmieri nimbly blends the past and present to concoct a delicious spell of a story that will appeal to fans of Sarah Addison Allen and other fabulously entertaining novels." —Karen White, *New York Times* bestselling author of *The Beach Trees*

"*The Witch of Little Italy* is a warmly enchanting debut that will have you believing in magic and craving homemade bucatini alla matriciana." —Susanna Kearsley, *New York Times* author of *The Winter Sea, Mariana,* and *The Rose Garden*

"I was utterly enchanted from the first page, and found myself continually marveling over the effortless grace with which this story unfolded. *The Witch of Little Italy* is a complex, richly textured tale that practically sings with magic, and I know Suzanne Palmieri has a long and brilliant career ahead of her. In a word: I was charmed." —Donna Ball, award-winning author of the Lady Bug Farm series

"An enchanting debut, Palmieri's plot makes for a wickedly good read!" —Melissa de la Cruz, *New York Times* bestselling author of the Blue Bloods series

"*The Witch of Little Italy* had me spellbound from the very start. Suzanne Palmieri has created a poignant, beautiful tale of love, magic, history, and family where all are deeply connected and interwoven." —Joanne Rendell, author of *Crossing Washington Square* and *The Professors' Wives' Club*

Also by Suzanne Palmieri

The Witch of Little Italy
I'll Be Seeing You (as Suzanne Hayes)
Empire Girls (as Suzanne Hayes)

The Witch of
Belladonna Bay

Suzanne Palmieri

ST. MARTIN'S GRIFFIN

NEW YORK

This is a work of fiction. All of the characters, organizations, and events portrayed in this novel are either products of the author's imagination or are used fictitiously.

THE WITCH OF BELLADONNA BAY. Copyright © 2014 by Suzanne Palmieri. All rights reserved. Printed in the United States of America. For information, address St. Martin's Press, 175 Fifth Avenue, New York, N.Y. 10010.

www.stmartins.com

Excerpt from THE LITTLE PRINCE by Antoine de Saint-Exupéry, translated from the French by Richard Howard. Copyright 1943 by Houghton Mifflin Harcourt Publishing Company. Copyright © renewed 1971 by Consuelo de Saint-Exupéry. English translation copyright © 2000 by Richard Howard. Reprinted by permission of Houghton Mifflin Harcourt Publishing Company. All rights reserved.

Library of Congress Cataloging-in-Publication Data

Palmieri, Suzanne.
    The witch of Belladonna Bay / Suzanne Palmieri.
        pages cm
    ISBN 978-1-250-01553-2 (trade paperback)
    ISBN 978-1-250-01552-5 (e-book)
    1. Families—Alabama—Fiction.   2. Young women—Fiction.
3. Homecoming—Fiction.   4. Murder—Investigation—Fiction.   5. Alabama—
Fiction.   6. Mystery fiction.   I. Title.
    PS3616.A353W576 2013
    813'.6—dc23
                                                                    2014008058

St. Martin's Griffin books may be purchased for educational, business, or promotional use. For information on bulk purchases, please contact Macmillan Corporate and Premium Sales Department at 1-800-221-7945, extension 5442, or write specialmarkets@macmillan.com.

First Edition: May 2014

10 9 8 7 6 5 4 3 2 1

For Rosy, born a Cooper, just like me. My sailing, mermaid beauty with eyes the color of the Gulf of Mexico. You're magnificent and your mother loves you.

Acknowledgments

This novel was a journey for me. A test of sorts . . . its own magic spell. I needed to write a story that was linear and still layered, and I couldn't have done it without the help of Erica Olivier, who read *The Witch of Little Italy,* critiqued it, and noted things I still needed to learn about the craft. She helped me edit this novel, and made it shine. Writers who also read this book in its many incarnations: Loretta Nyhan, Heidi Shultz, Adriana Cloud, and Sarah Wylie. Thank you for your time and epic patience. A huge thank-you goes out to Grace McCrocklin for giving me a few Southern sayings that helped me place myself squarely inside many unruly moments.

Thanks also to John Valeri, the Hartford Book Examiner, and Casey Heyer Schwing, both of whom read advance copies and whose enthusiasm for the story made my heart soar.

Living in Alabama was the single most important part of the writing process. So, to the people of Baldwin County, Alabama, thank you. The residents and shop owners of Fairhope, Gulf Shores, Bon Secour, and, most of all, Magnolia Springs (especially the owners of Jesse's), this book would not exist without you. You welcomed me into your community and "took care" of me and my little witches while I lived there. To Bev Overton, Ellen McDonald, and Butch Mannich. To the mayor of Magnolia Springs, Ken Underwood, his lovely wife Miss Helen, and their beautiful children and grand-babies, especially their daughter, Carrie. To Stephanie Winkler who printed, posted, and took care of all my office needs while calming me down. And to Carla and her daughter McKenzie. Friends made on the Gulf Shore seaside remain friends forever.

The magic I found (not five minutes from our cottage) at the Swift-Coles house in Bon Secour, is a novel in and of itself. Many thanks to the Baldwin County Historical Society and to all the tour guides who painstakingly answered a million zillion questions. Special thanks to Harriet Outlaw and the indomitable Micky Blackwell McConnell, whose eyes sparkled even more than her stories.

To my literary agent, Anne Bohner, who loved this book right from its meager beginnings. To the entire team at St. Martin's Press for your enthusiasm, hard work, and your belief in me. Especially my Glitter Editor of All the Things, Vicki Lame. Look, Glitter! Another book, baby!

To Don Roy King, who delivered a eulogy I attended and allowed me to use the term "an oxymoron of a man." It was the best way to describe Jackson Whalen. I love you, Donny.

To my mother, Theresa Anne, and her mother (my gram), Philomena (Fay), for teaching me how to long for what *was* and still live in what *is*.

To my husband, William, and our three daughters, Rosy, Tess, and Grace, who helped me find my balance this year. To my northeastern family: Robert Mele (godfather extraordinaire), Uncle Michael Mele, Rita Palmieri, Margaret Palmieri, and the entire Palmieri and Mele/DePaul clans. Your support for this literary adventure has been one of my greatest joys.

Mostly, this book belongs to my Cooper family down South. To my father, James Sterling. Your generous love has overcompensated for any hurt. Thank you for moving me forward. My brother, Talmadge James. You are the Moon in my sky. To my "Bonus-Mama" and dear friend Kim Cooper for delivering me my past, present, and future. My Cooper cousins, Alex, Max, and his soon-to-be wife, Caitlin. And to my cousin Lana. You are the sister of my soul.

As my daddy once said: "You may be half Eye-talian, girl. But never forget, you're also half redneck cracker." I think that about sums it up.

"I'm a Lost Witch. Are you a Lost Witch Too?"

Belladonna: (deadly nightshade): A plant to be honored and feared. It grows up to six feet tall, has green leaves, violet flowers, and shiny black berries. Use perparations to dull pain and to assist with sleep. When prepared in conjunction with the poppy it induces astral projection, flying, and the easing of childbirth. An oxymoron herb.

—Naomi Green's Book of Shadows

Goin' Home

Seems to me, you're gonna get yourself lost, BitsyWyn.
And then I'll probably be the one to have to haul your sorry
ass back home.

—*Patrick Whalen, sixteen years old*

I

Bronwyn

My mother, Naomi, always told me not to worry about trouble, that it came up behind you like a thief in the night. "Nothing you ever worry over actually happens," she'd say. "It's the trouble you aren't expecting that gets you. And it's all around you, Bronwyn, it's all around you like the air."

She was right.

I found out my brother Patrick was going to prison for murder while sipping my morning coffee. And if you'd asked me a second before the phone rang what I was most worried about in my life, I'd have had a list of a million things before I even thought about sweet Paddy with blood on his hands.

I was so estranged from my family in Alabama that no one saw fit to tell me he was in trouble, much less on trial. And it wasn't just any murder. He was sentenced to life for killing Charlotte, my closest friend growing up in Magnolia Creek. Worse, the state was gearing up to try him for the murder of her son, Jamie, too . . . though his body still hadn't been found.

Such trouble. And no notice whatsoever. Not even a second of sibling sixth sense. Naomi was right, this whole mess came straight up from behind out of nowhere.

My daddy, Jackson Whalen, used to say, "Sugar, the things we hold closest to our hearts are the things we just can't seem to see."

That man must hold everything close to his heart because he's as blind as a bat when it comes to basic human understanding. The way he ignored my mother's condition, supporting her addiction. It was madness.

And part of why I left.

My mother was a strange woman, who I'd learned—early on—not to trust. But I loved her. Only . . . love lies. It doesn't mean much when it stands alone. You need trust. Respect. And those are the things Naomi's addiction robbed her of—the ability for her children, Paddy and me, to trust and respect her. Family can be such a foul business.

But it wasn't all lies.

Like when she told us she'd die before we were ready to lose her. That Jackson would slip from heavy drinker to functional alcoholic. And that we couldn't stop him and didn't need to try. She sure was right about those truths.

Late at night, Paddy and I would climb into our Yankee mother's great big four-poster bed, pretending we were prince and princess in one of those fantastical Hindu epics Naomi loved to read, while the sheer canopy curtains flowed around us. And we'd snuggle up next to her feeling safe, if only for a moment.

She'd weave stories about the strange northeastern town where she grew up, and about her family, the Greens. A lonesomeness rang in her voice as she explained her magical ways, and why she tried to shut them off, like a faucet turning from hot to cold.

She told us about how some people just had magic built into them. That her family firmly believed somehow, somewhere, at the very moment when the stars first erupted with a bang, stardust settled on only a few specks of life already forming in the sea. And how those few specks evolved into people who hold all sorts of unexplainable talents. When I was little I thought it was terribly romantic, being half stardust, half Southern magnolia.

Somewhere along the way I forgot anything that reminded me of that particular romance. It was only after the phone call that I began to remember things I'd hidden deep inside the recesses of my heart.

Like, each night, after Naomi's tales of adventure and magic, when she thought surely we *must* be asleep, our mother would hold us close, kissing us on our foreheads and whispering softly.

She didn't whisper, "Don't leave me," like most. No. Naomi sang us a very different lullaby. She whispered, "Run."

Later, when we were too old for bedtime stories, I wondered about that same secret, because she never gave us the chance to run at all. She'd held us so tight, so severely, that it suffocated and sometimes scared us.

"Why does she do that, Wyn? Want us close and then push us away?" asked Paddy, who was maybe five at the time. I'm only a year older, but was determined to be a grown-up. He'd come into my room after having another one of his nightmares and I'd make a fort for the two of us by securing a blanket from a window hinge, and letting it drape down over the grand old window seat next to my bed. Then we'd hold a flashlight between us, so I could read to him.

"Paddy," I said, "it's time for you to be a big boy and realize our mama isn't right in the head. Okay?"

He'd cry as he snuggled up next to me, letting the flashlight fall dark, leaving silvery moonlight to trace the shadows of our fear.

"I don't want to 'reeleyth' that," he said, with that baby lisp he didn't lose until he was seven. "If I do that, then who'll be my mama?"

"I will," I'd promised. And I tried. I really did. But at the end of it all I'd run, just like she told me to. Leaving my whole life behind, even my beautiful little brother.

I ran fast and far as soon as we put Naomi in the ground. I was seventeen and never looked back. Jackson was drinking too much to keep me home, and Paddy was only sixteen. I asked him to come with me.

"Patrick Simon Whalen, you best come with me. I made a promise to you, and I can't keep up my end of the bargain if we aren't together," I demanded, arms crossed defiantly.

Sweet Paddy just kicked at the dirt, right there at Mother's grave. "Mama *was* a loon. You were right, Wyn. But I'm over it now. So you go across the universe. Go'n find what you're lookin' for and then come on back. I'll be right here. Where we both belong."

"I don't belong here anymore, Paddy. I don't know that I ever did."

"Seems to me, you're gonna get yourself lost, BitsyWyn. And then I'll probably be the one to have to haul your sorry ass back home," he said, with a classic Paddy glint in his eye. I still haven't figured out how he could be so irritating and so damn charming at the same time.

"First of all, I'm Bronwyn from now on, you call me Bitsy-Wyn one more time and I'll scream. Second, my bags are already packed, Paddy. Last chance for a grand brother and sister adventure. . . ." I tried to keep my voice steady, but the pleading came right through.

He hugged me tight and wished me well, both of us being the crazy, stubborn asses we knew we were.

I didn't mean to stay away. I figured I'd get homesick and then just come crawling back to the Big House. To my handsome, laughing father, to my best friend Lottie and her brother Grant, the first true love of my life. I figured, once I'd been in the great wild world, I'd see the error of my ways and embrace Magnolia Creek with all its oddness, giving me a chance to grieve for Naomi properly.

I figured I'd miss the great Southern magnolias that grew reckless all over town. Hundreds of feet high, forty feet at their base, and older than time. Magnificent.

Now, fourteen years later, I still hadn't returned to the red dirt of Alabama. Still hadn't laid eyes on the Big House with its Doric columns and wide porches. Still hadn't walked back up the long driveway lined with live oaks dripping with moss, and a majesty that spoke of the old money my family inherited from a long line of successful lumbering.

Lumber had been good to the Whalens. Yellow pine, in particular. By the time Paddy and I were born, our father didn't have to work. He just lived off all the earnings. He was mayor and the big man around town. I've often wondered what would have been different if we hadn't been privileged. Maybe my mother wouldn't have died. At least not overdosing on an old-fashioned drug that no one could even get anymore. Opium.

It wasn't a problem for Jackson, though. He could find anything.

But we can't rewrite our past. Especially if we're running away from it. And running I was.

As it turned out, Paddy's been right all those years ago. He *had* been the one to "haul my sorry ass" home. Just not the way either of us had intended.

That morning, before the trouble came sneaking up behind me just like Naomi said it would, I was safely cocooned in my stable northeast life.

Ben looked calm and beautiful as he brewed yet another pot of gourmet coffee and with a large, generous smile set the mug down in front of me. His skin was smooth and dark, just like that coffee. I wanted to wrap my pale, freckled limbs around his, to let my blond curls fall down softly against his strong shoulders. Our contrasts always made my heart sing just like Coltrane's saxophone, the music we listened to every morning. The music that was playing the first time we made love. And if there's a word that truly means the opposite of awkward, something *more* than graceful, I'd use it to describe the day we met.

I'd been searching for a lot of things when I got to Manhattan, and I'd torn through my fair share of men on the way there, trying to find what I was looking for. The day I met Ben, I'd set my sights set on a different man altogether. A jazz musician who had a jagged scar running down his face, brow to chin. He showed up at my apartment that scorching July day, but hadn't come alone; he'd brought his bandmates. There were four or five of them, but the only one I remember is Ben. He stood out, not just because the color of his skin was different but because of that glimmer in his eyes. Some people just shine. And he seemed so at home in the heat. He reminded me of myself. Heat never wilts me. Instead, I flourish.

Don't get me wrong, even the Gulf Coast of Alabama sees snow once in a while. When we were growing up, an inch or so fell sometimes in December or January. When Paddy and I were little, we used to envy the children up north with their snow days and snow angels. We'd whine about it, but Jackson would say, "We Southern folks have sunshine in our bones. Cold weather makes a 'bama native cranky as a gator." But snow was an event, no matter how short-lived.

By the time May came around we'd be in an all-out summer assault of hot humid air. You just get used to the heat because you don't have any other options. That's why summers in New York City never bothered me.

Those men in my apartment that day stared at me with a look I knew well. One that stated, "She's too cool to sweat," but the only stare I cared about that day was Ben's. Even before I knew his name.

I've always been vain.

I've never wanted to look like anyone else, unless you count my mother . . . and I wasn't counting her, I was forgetting her. When I looked in the mirror, especially back then, I saw someone I was proud of. Wide, blue eyes that told stories of where I'd been and what I'd seen. A self-confident chin that told people to "shut up" before I had to say it. I was aware that I was wanted, and it made men want me *more*. Fact is, when you could care less about someone or something, that's when everything you thought you wanted falls right at your feet. What I didn't know back then, is that I was cold. I'd turned off the longing, knowing that if I let one bit of weakness in, I'd tumble down that rabbit hole of sorrow.

When I think of that fearless young woman I used to be, I see a refugee. I see her sadness and desperation. Hindsight can slap you humble sometimes. I started to change the day I met Ben. He quieted my soul and showed me the solid person I could grow to be. He gave me a path, and I walked down it gladly.

We drank a lot of wine that day. The windows were open, and smooth jazz drifted over us in a haze of hours that felt more like days. Then, half drunk on the presence of that beautiful man, I spread out my tarot cards, the ones my mother gave me when I was little.

"I can't use them anymore," she'd said, her voice soft and far away . . . Naomi under glass. "Maybe they'll work for you now. Maybe you'll have better luck with all that crap."

I was born with a touch of my mother's "shine." Just enough to make me believe the impossible and run away from the inevitable. I don't think any women born into the Green family can avoid it really. I only had a little and never used it much, except to make some money here and there. Truth be told, I've always thought it was instinct more than magic. Like how you can look into a person's eyes and tell what they want to hear. It's taken me too long to realize that instinct and magic walk hand and hand.

For the first seven years of my self-imposed exile, I'd set up card tables on the streets of whatever city held my interest enough to make me want to stay a while and read the fortunes of strangers walking by.

That day, when I read Ben's cards, he helped me turn the spread, his hands brushing against mine—sending a shiver down to my toes. Our eyes met, and his soul locked in on a certain kind of truth, making every chaotic thought in my head straight and steady.

Later, I would understand why.

That afternoon was one of those lucky surprises, where the unexpected becomes far better than anything you could have planned. As the day slipped slowly into dusk, I left the musicians in the living room to lie across my bed as a comfortable fog fell over me. I drifted away on the sounds of the music and the city. My mother and father were both addicted to that feeling. Naomi called it "living inside the walls." I thought it felt more like floating in a calm, private ocean.

At some point a hand touched one of my ankles, and Ben whispered, "Goddamn you are beautiful, don't open your eyes. Stay just like you are. I want to admire you."

He slowly kissed the length of my body, from my legs to my lower back to that sweet spot on the side of my neck. I could have stayed in that moment forever. Then his kisses moved across my shoulder and I turned to face him. He eased my second-hand 1960s sundress over my head gently. Soon, his body pressed against mine. The passion building inside of me was unlike anything I'd ever known. Calm and riotous all at the same time.

Then he kissed my lips.

It began with our faces brushing, hesitantly. Our mouths catching hold, as my arms looped around his neck. We opened slowly to each other, taming my unquiet inner ocean.

When it was over, he said, "I've been waiting for you, you

little lost thing," and I cried, because he'd acknowledged what my gypsy legs knew all along.

"Have you ever been in love?" he'd asked me a few days later in an Italian pastry shop called Rocco's in the West Village.

"Only once," I said, taking a bite out of a creamy, rich cannoli. I'd always had a soft spot for Italian food. Grant and Lottie's mother, Susan Masters, was the cook at the Big House. Their last name, Masters, was just the Anglicized version of La Maestra. Susan loved to tell us stories about how their people were around since the colonies. And Grant used to joke that it was probably the *convict* ships that sent them there. I didn't care what it was, because when I was growing up, and though they were Southern through and through, everything Susan made was Italian. From Sunday sauce to fresh cannoli cream. I knew it wasn't a coincidence that he asked me about love in that shop right when I was pushing Grant out of my head and heart.

Hindsight is something everyone falls prey to, even those of us with a little magic. Sitting in that pastry shop, I wondered if Ben had read my mind, had somehow seen Grant there. But in all my travels I hadn't yet met another person who shared the "ways" of my mother's people, so I ignored it.

He pressed me. "Who was it? How long? Do you still know him?"

"I don't talk about it," I said. "I don't talk about where I've been, only where I'm going. How about we pretend there's no past at all. We can be the present."

"And future," he'd finished, smiling. We kept that promise. It's easier than you think to put blinders on and move forward.

Humans have short, selective memories. If we tuck away something important, put it in a safe place . . . we always end up spending hours trying to find it. Let it stay out in plain sight, and you never have to look for it.

Add that to the things I wish I'd known back then.

And now, seven years later, we still lived together in the confines of the blissful domesticity we'd created that first July day in Manhattan. Ben was my safe haven. My protector. But most of all, my escape.

He stood in our kitchen that morning, comfortable and worry-free, with a dish towel carelessly thrown over his shoulder and his bare feet solidly on the wood floor. For a moment I thought I might say yes to his seven-year open-ended question: "Marry me?"

But then the damn phone rang, bringing me back to the life I'd left behind.

It was my father. I hadn't heard his voice since we said good-bye face-to-face. But every month, like clockwork since the week I'd left home, I'd gotten a letter and a check. No matter where my vagabond legs carried me, no matter how many years passed, those letters found me. They never asked me back, and though I'd long since stopped needing the money, he sent it anyway. But he *never* called, so I knew I had to talk to him.

Damn Southern manners.

And there it was, the trouble I'd never expected, all wrapped up in a little girl who shared my name but saw fit to call herself Byrd.

2

Byrd

Grown-ups never understand anything by themselves,
and it is exhausting for children to have to provide
explanations over and over again.
—*The Little Prince*

The Old-timers and Towners all think I'm crazy. They say I act too old for my age, and that my strange ways (even though the whole damn town depends on them) curdle up my thoughts. But that's not the thing that bothers me most. I swear, I'm kept up nights just thinkin' on how anybody could manufacture such an evil thought about a girl. You know what they think?

Everyone in this godforsaken town thinks I'm a *tomboy*.

Damn it. They don't know much about anything. When I grow up and get my woman boobies, they're gonna be surprised. Everyone but Jamie. He's always told me how pretty I am. Well, and Jackson (he's my grandpap). My daddy, too. They tell me I'm beautiful. But they have to because they're related to me, and I'm the only person they got in this whole wide world who loves them. Also, it don't hurt that I look just like the one true love of both their lives, the grandmother I never met—at least while she was alive and everything—Naomi.

And then, there's Minerva (or Minny, *"Minny with the red, red hair*," as Jackson used to tease her), she's sorta old now. I tell her she's *old as dirt*), but I can't *not* love her because she's Naomi's aunt who came down this way when Naomi and Jackson got married. So she's family too, and "blood is blood," my daddy always says.

Minerva's husband is Carter. He's like another grandpap to me, and another father for my daddy 'cause Jackson's mostly livin' in his own world. Thing is, they *all* live with me. They're my family, and they're supposed to love me and think I'm beautiful.

But Jamie? He ain't got no other reason to tell me I'm pretty. He's just my friend, plain and simple. And gone or not, he's still my Little Prince.

The night his mama, Charlotte, got killed, and he went missin', I'd seen him right before supper.

"Why don't you stay, Jamie? Minerva's fryin' up them catfish we caught." Minerva always acts like the help. She does all the cookin' and housekeepin'.

"Why don't you go on and hire someone else, Minny?" I sometimes asked her. She says, "Pay good money to a stranger to do something I like to do? Fiddlesticks."

(Yankees get all strange about things like that, wantin' what they don't want, and never even seein' that they don't want it.)

Anyway, that night Jamie said no to eatin' the catfish (which was downright odd).

"Nah, I gotta get back to Mama," he said. He could be *such* a mama's boy sometimes.

"Your mama sure is needy these days. She okay?" I asked. I wasn't a stranger to the drama over at their house. Lottie (that's his mama's nickname), she was nice to me. But she'd been actin' funny before she was killed. She'd cut her pretty, dark hair

short. Real short, like a boy. She called it a "pixie" cut, but she
didn't look like a pixie. She looked kinda lost and alone.
Haunted.

So, me and Jamie were sittin' on the side porch of the Big
House and the sun was just lazily dancing across his face. I could
just tell he was tossin' thoughts around in his head. "Spill them
beans, Jamie Masters, or I'll make mincemeat outta ya!"

That made him laugh. I knew it would. "You couldn't *even*
hurt me. You'd be like a no-see-um all bitin' at me, and I'd just
swat you back into the air."

"Well, see? You don't want to do that. So why not just tell
me? I ain't got nothin' but time and money." I sat back in one of
the old wicker chairs, letting Jackson's favorite phrase come rolling off my tongue.

"Damn, girl, can't I have any secrets?" he asked.

'Nope. Not from me."

He leaned against the railing and looked away, but I knew
he'd tell me.

"She's altogether torn up over that daddy of yours," he said.

I didn't want to hear any more 'cause I didn't like my daddy
mixed up with Charlotte. I didn't know why . . . then. Couldn't
use my strange ways to see into his mind.

They do that, you know. My ways get all wonky when I'm
learnin' something important that has to do with me. If I'm too
close, the sight plays tricks on me. Ain't that the way. I'm never
able to see things that are too close. Sometimes I wonder what
good it is to have 'em at all if they can't help me figure out the
things that need figurin'.

"See, I knew you didn't want to hear about this," said Jamie,
watching my face closely.

I got up from the chair and crossed my arms in front of my chest. "*No.* You *are* right. I do *not* want to hear about your mama whining over my daddy. Just run on home and tell her to find herself another man. She's pretty enough, I guess."

"Byrd, it ain't like that! *She* wants to end it with *him*."

That hit me hard. My daddy was always teetering on the edge of a great big sadness that could, and would, eat him up whole. I didn't like his relationship with Lottie, but it kept him happy enough. In fact, they'd been friends for their whole entire lives before they started lovin' on each other.

"Uh-uh," I said.

"Scout's honor! And you know what? I think it's good. Come on, Byrd, you and me ain't liked it from the git-go."

"All right then, if you're so happy about it, why sulk all around and skip supper?"

"That's just it. I can't figure her out. The whole mess has her screwed up in the head. Cryin' all the time. Disgusting is what it is. And . . ."

"And what, spit it out."

"And I think she's on some kind of drug. She's all loose lipped and weak-kneed."

I was quiet. *Drug* is the worst, most ugly word in the English language. Drugs killed Naomi.

My daddy meddled with all sorts of drugs, too. Not to mention drinkin' it up with Jackson. I was always scared he'd find Naomi's love for anythin' comin' from that poppy flower. Opium was her favorite, like the caterpillar on the mushroom in *Alice's Adventures in Wonderland*, which, by the way, is a silly book. (Who'd eat anything without knowin' where it came from? Shoot.)

You know what? I think those Old-timers and Towners are right. I think I do act too old for my age.

"And there's more," said Jamie, pulling me out of my worry over caterpillars and poppy fields.

I'd moved in closer. I was frightened of what he'd say, so I needed to be nearer. That way his words might fly right past me and wouldn't sink in. I hugged him tight. Let him feel the love come out of me. Not a sexy kind of love. A better kind. True love. It let me know things about Jamie. That weakness made him queasy. It's why he loved me from the start. I ain't afraid of nothin'. Well, almost nothin'. His next words, those words scared me.

"What Jamie, what else?" I asked, not wanting to hear the truth.

"I think she's been over to Belladonna Bay." He nodded his head sideways toward the back of the house and past the creek where the mist, which never broke, enveloped that horrible piece of land.

And that's when I knew things were gonna change. But I couldn't foresee, even with all my tryin' and scourin' in bowls of water. Even with laying out a million tarot cards in all kinds of spreads and combinations. I couldn't tell he'd be gone from me by morning. Or that everyone important, all the grown-ups all around us, would consider him dead. Or that they'd blame my daddy for his murder, too.

❦

Jamie'd been missing for six months when Jackson finally fired the last prissy nanny and called my aunt Bronwyn out of sheer desperation. Carter and Minerva were too busy to take care of me (even though they asked Jackson to let them), and Jackson was too drunk. I tried to explain that I was just fine taking care of myself, but he wouldn't hear of it. He said I couldn't just "run wild." And I gave him a look that said, *And just what do you think I've been doin' my whole entire life, Jackson?*

In the end, it took him a whole half a year to get up the courage to call his own daughter. And even though I can't look into his mind like with folks I don't know so well, I already knew he wasn't really lookin' for Bronwyn to come home to take care of me. He'd just had enough of her bein' gone. And with my daddy gone too, he needed his other kid around.

But *damn.* six months is a long time in a girl's life to wait for the inevitable. I could already feel those boobies growin'. Minerva tells me I'm crazy and flat as a board. Seems that having strange ways slows down the whole process of getting old. But I swear I can see 'em, I swear it.

Thing is, I ain't never even been sick. And I don't expect to. And I'm beautiful and therefore useful. That's a funny idea, ain't it? It comes from my very own bible. *The Little Prince.* It's full of all sorts of funny ideas that don't seem to make sense at first, until you sit and think on it for a bit. Those are the best kind of ideas, in my opinion.

The book belonged to Naomi. She brought it with her from some little crazy town called Fairview up north. Only the view wasn't so fair, as far as I've been told. That little town sits right across from its own misted island, one just as cursed as Belladonna Bay. Only Jackson told me that Naomi's island was rumored to have mermaids.

I sure wish Belladonna Bay had mermaids.

Anyways, *The Little Prince* belonged to Naomi, and she read it to my daddy and my aunt Bronwyn.

It's the story of a pilot and a little boy, and the pilot, see, he's stranded in the desert. But then the Little Prince comes along and helps him to understand all sorts of things. And that's when they become best friends. But mostly, it's a book about bein' practical and strange all at the same time. Which is exactly how I like to see myself.

When Bronwyn left, she tried to take the book with her, but Jackson wouldn't let her. The cover ripped a little when they were fightin', but I don't care. I like broken things.

Like my daddy. He's been broken since before I was born. It makes him more interestin'. Jamie used to say it ain't good, how much I love my daddy. But I don't think you can love anyone or anything too much.

So I said, "But I love you, Mr. Jamie Smarty-pants. I love you almost, if not as much, as I love my daddy."

We were sitting up in a tree, and his head was crowned with a wreath of leaves I'd made. The sun shone through his dark curls and the heat made his cheeks pink. He was more beautiful than any boy or girl I'd ever seen, except for me. But you couldn't compare me and Jamie because he's a boy and I'm a girl. Other than that, we got a lotta similarities. We're both dark and small with hair black like the night. Daddy tells me I'm just like Snow White. Dark hair and pale skin.

I know what I see when I see my reflection in other people's eyes. Like those Towners and Old-timers. They see my *potential.* But Jamie didn't ever need to live up to his potential. He's just plain beautiful. Born that way and stayin' that way. Even if only in my memory.

He laughed a little in the tree that day and snuck a kiss on my cheek. I moved from my branch to his and wrapped my arms around him, letting our black hair mingle. Our congruities always made my heart sing. Made me feel less alone, too. *Congruity* means bein' similar, and it's one of my very favorite words.

And because we were both so amazing, me and Jamie, most other folks let us be. And the whole town of Magnolia Creek just lived in the shadow of our usefulness. Because we were gonna be famous together. We were bright shining stars 'bout to shoot off this tired planet and into the sky. Then we'd rain stardust into the eyes of every living thing this side of Mobile. Or the whole world, if you wanna think big.

Now I'd have to rethink that particular dream, 'cause Jamie disappeared into the dark, velvet Alabama night. Leaving a whole lot of blood. Blood that sent my daddy to prison and brought my aunt Bronwyn home.

3

Bronwyn

I tried to hang up the phone, but I was shaking too much. Ben placed his hand over mine, and we hung the phone up together. Then he gently led me to the front porch, a place that always calmed me. I'm happiest outdoors.

After we left Manhattan, we moved upstate. I'd been working as a freelance photojournalist for about six years and had become well known enough to have a decent savings (not that I needed one, Jackson's checks kept on keepin' on). The subtle notoriety brought me more of what I *really* liked about my job. The running away part. I was called when anyone needed really good pictures of a place no one else wanted to go. War-torn nations were my specialty.

We decided to move to the forest, both of us inspired by the trees. And it was on the porch—the porch that sold us on the house before we'd even walked in—that I told him what happened to my brother. And told him how my father needed me to come back home.

Ben leaned back easily in the Adirondack chair and stretched out his long legs, cupping his hands securely around his coffee mug. "Why do you suppose he didn't call sooner? You've gotten letters, but no mention of any of this . . . ," he ventured hesitantly.

"That's not how Jackson works, Ben. And it probably wasn't in the news because Jackson wields a lot of power with his wealth."

"I can understand keeping it out of the news, but keeping it from you? Why?"

"Because he wanted me to come home on my own terms. Don't underestimate Southern pride. I bet he thought he could just fix it all up and I wouldn't have to know a thing. Remember, Ben—this man let my mother die. I love him, but he practically spoon-fed her drugs. Anything to make her happy. Anything to avoid conflict, to stay in control. He knows I'll come back now. That man knows I don't have a choice."

"Are you going to go?" he asked.

"I have to go."

"Why? Why do you have to go?" he asked.

Because I promised Paddy I'd try to be his mother, and now I have to face the fact that I've been a crappy, absent one, I thought. *Just like Naomi.*

But Byrd was easier to think about, and easier to explain.

"Because she needs me. Byrd needs me," I said.

My niece I'd never met. Byrd.

I tried to push away the questions that were tugging at my heart. Sure, I knew the basics from Jackson's letters: that Paddy'd gone and found himself a crazy, beautiful Italian girl from somewhere in Virginia. Turns out, she had magic in her, too. "I guess us Whalen men can't love no ordinary type of woman," he'd written. He said Stella came looking for bits and pieces of her own scattered family, and it brought her to Susan Masters, the one person of Italian descent in the whole town. Later, I'd find out that her searching led her to the Big House as well. The only thing I did know was that Stella died giving birth to Byrd. And I should've been there.

And why wasn't I? Why hadn't I gone straight home the second I heard? Why hadn't I at least called? For a second I felt myself panic, a childhood fear slowly lacing itself through my veins.

"The mist over Belladonna Bay is inside. . . . *It seeped into me, Mama, I can feel it!"*

"Hush, Bronwyn, Hush, darling, there's no mist inside of you. I promise."

That old, familiar boogeyman. That same feeling churned inside me now as if Jackson's voice was casting some sort of memory spell all his own.

I'd never even seen pictures of Stella or Byrd. Jackson never sent any, and Paddy never wrote. We were in a communication stalemate, my brother and I. First person to give in and contact the other would be the loser. "You two are competitive to a *fault,*" Jackson used to say.

But there, in the safety of Ben's gaze, I knew the truth. It was *me. I* should have called Paddy. *I* should have requested a photo of my niece. Damn, *I* should have gotten on the first plane back to Magnolia Creek when I found out she was born. I was the abandoner. It was my responsibility, and here I was just living my life and thinking it was *their* fault for not reaching out. Guilt sits uneasy in the belly, and mine was churning with all I'd missed.

Byrd. Paddy, Stella . . . Lottie.

"Why haven't you ever gone back?" Ben asked.

And Lord, if that wasn't the ten-million-dollar question.

The one I'd been worried he'd ask, at first, because I didn't have an answer. Then, after enough time passed, I didn't think about it anymore. Short memories, remember?

"I don't know. I guess, as cliché as it may seem, I was running away from everything, and I guess I never stopped," I said.

"Why?"

"That woman they say Patrick killed, she was my best friend. And her brother, Grant . . . I don't talk about him. And I won't. But my mother? I did something pretty bad the day she died." I sighed, looking away.

"What do you remember about that day? Bronwyn, if you remember it well enough, you could just stay here and we can send for Byrd. Raise her here, together," he suggested.

"So, you're suggesting we rip her away from everything she knows, right when she needs something real to hold on to. Sounds great," I responded, shaking my head.

"You didn't answer me about what happened to your mother."

"I don't want to answer that. Some things don't need to be remembered."

"Let's try together. Want to try?" he persisted.

Usually Ben's soft voice calmed the mean right out of me, but right then I was in no mood to be soothed.

"Why is this such a big deal? What do *you* remember from fourteen years ago?" I said.

Snotty was always my best defense when I was home in Magnolia Creek. The fact that it made its appearance at that moment should've been a warning sign of sorts. There she was, the old me . . . BitsyWyn Whalen rearing her ugly, vain head. Susan Masters had given me that nickname because I was so tiny when I was born. My mother hated it, but it sure stuck in Magnolia Creek. It's the name of a girl who makes trouble, and I lived up to it.

Names are so important.

"The day your mother dies is a watershed moment. Something you can't forget," said Ben.

"Well, I guess I'm not like all those *other* girls," I responded. I'm damn good at sarcasm too, when I need to be.

"Be serious," he said. My sharp words, though few and far between, never managed to cut into him. It's part of why I loved him so much.

"Fine. You win," I whispered, the edge leaving my voice as quick as it had come.

Ben leaned forward, fixed on me. His feet planted far apart, his elbows on his knees. Solid, solid Ben.

"All I know is we had a fight, and I was pretty hard on her. But I don't remember what I said."

"That doesn't sound like you."

"You didn't know me then. I was Southern belle mixed with rattlesnake. My venom hurt people."

"Venom?"

"I always managed to say exactly what cut the deepest, especially with Naomi. That's her name. Did I ever tell you that? Naomi."

"You didn't. It's a really beautiful name. Was she beautiful?"

"More than beautiful. And I loved her something fierce. More than anyone ought to have the right to."

"So what happened? How did that change?"

"I grew up and realized she was a junkie and I hated her for it. Then she died. The end."

"Don't go," he asked quietly.

We sat, a new, uncomfortable silence growing between us.

"But if you do? I should come with you," Ben added, breaking in before the silence began to weigh on us. When Patrick and I were little kids and we'd have a fight, it would last for days because neither one of us would give in first. Paddy would have called Ben an "easy mark."

But, easy mark or not, Ben couldn't come. He didn't know my people. He didn't know BitsyWyn.

"Oh, no. Nope. You will not come," I said.

"Why not, Bronwyn?" he asked with the frustration of many years boiling up and out inside the question. Ben was serious. He wanted to *know*.

"Because it's not safe for you down there. Especially not coupled with me."

"What do you mean?"

Dammit. He was going to make me say it. "Jesus, Ben! You and me? Here we're a kind of fascinating, open-minded progressive couple. Down there? Down there it's still called miscegenation and you could get yourself killed."

He laughed at me, put his mug down, and then looked me straight in the eyes. "I know you, Bronwyn. You're lying. And I can't understand it, but I'll play. It's silly; we've already had a black president. Hell, I bet you any money it's more racist up here in the back of people's minds than down there where at least it's out in the open."

He was right, I was playing the race card to push him away. But knowing that didn't make me back down. It's funny how mouths keep on running even when there's nothing else to say.

"This is no time to be idealistic, Ben. I won't lose you over some kind of Northern amnesia about the way the world really works. I've lived here long enough to get complacent, not stupid." I said those words and felt smart. But Ben was right. I was making up a good excuse for a feeling I couldn't quite put my finger on.

"You've never let on that your family was racist, Bronwyn. Are they?" he asked hesitantly.

"It's not my family I'm worried about. And besides . . . my *family* is now reduced to my drunken, eccentric father, a little girl named Byrd, and a great-aunt who thinks she's the maid. I'm worried about the rest of Magnolia Creek. The Old-timers and the Towners."

"Why? Do they still lynch black folks, these Towners of yours?"

"Well, Ben, I don't rightly know." My voice eased back into its comfortable Southern slur whenever I even mentioned Alabama. "And the reason I don't know for sure is because there *ain't no black people* for miles and miles."

I let him turn all the information over in his mind.

"This racist shit you're pulling is bull, and we both know it, so I won't play. But you do seem serious about wanting to go alone, for whatever reason."

"I'm dead serious, Ben."

"All right, I hear you. But I'm still going to come. Not right away, though. I think part of the reason you want to go alone is to make peace with Naomi. I think you want to see what you left behind without any outside influence. Am I close?"

"I guess," I said, but I didn't know for sure. Ben had a way of making sense, so why argue.

"I'll give you a week," he continued. "You won't change my mind about that. And there's one more thing . . ."

"Which is?"

"Promise you'll marry me when the whole thing is over."

"What?"

"Don't play with me, Bronwyn. We belong together. I want to get married, and have a family. Say yes this time."

Something had shifted between us, a tension we'd avoided from day one.

"Ben, is this some kind of ultimatum or something?"

"That's exactly what it is. And this is the last time I'm asking. If you don't say yes, I'll never ask again. We'd stay close forever, but I can't promise I'd wait any longer. I have a life to live, too."

I took a deep breath, completely intending to have the "I'm not ready" argument again. "Okay" fell right out of my mouth instead. If I emerged from the whole ordeal, I'd have no earthly reason left to deny him.

Ben's smile widened and he had that glint in his eye, the one he got when he was about to beat me at Scrabble.

"Wait here!" he said happily.

He reemerged quickly on the porch and got down on one knee.

I laughed. "Is this necessary?"

"Totally."

He produced a blue velvet case. "This ring has been in my family for generations. I want you to wear it and never take it off."

He cracked open the case. Staring at me was the most beautiful ring I'd ever seen. A crescent moon sapphire, with an emerald tucked next to it like a dangling star, set in silver. It sparkled in the morning sun.

"Ben, this is lovely. Almost . . . Celtic." The ring made me wonder about this man I'd lived with and loved for seven years. He'd had it in his family for generations? For all the years we'd been together, I really didn't know anything about Ben or his family. We'd stayed pretty true to the decision we'd made those seven years ago—the one to keep our past separate from our present. "What and where are you from, Benjamin Mason?"

"Why, what were you expecting? An African mask? I'm from Massachusetts for Christ's sake! Why do you white people all think every single black American is a direct descendent of Kunta Kinte? It's a disease or something. Really, Bronwyn, I thought you'd know better."

It was a funny thing to say, especially for Ben who didn't crack jokes very often, so we laughed together as he placed the ring on my finger.

We stayed quiet for a little while, until Ben finally asked the question I'd been turning over in my own mind since Jackson's call.

"Did he do it, Bronwyn? Do you think your brother killed those people?"

Those people.

Lottie, who wanted to be a ballerina. My best friend. Beautiful, dark-haired, sparkling Lottie. Me and my brother. Lottie and Grant. The four of us, together forever . . .

"No. There is no way on God's green earth that Paddy killed anyone." And I knew it, too. I knew it with the sight my mother passed down to me through magic DNA. That's when the panic started to rise: *Patrick was in prison for something he didn't do. How on earth did that happen?*

"But he was already convicted," said Ben. "They must have proof."

"I don't care what proof they think they have. I'm going to find out what really happened. I owe it to Paddy. I owe it to all of them."

I was going to have to use all my instincts, all the "shine" I could muster, to exonerate my brother. And maybe get a chance to redeem myself in the process.

But how?

◊

My plane was delayed and I had to call Jackson, who I knew would send a car to pick me up at the airport. He loves to flaunt his wealth. The phone rang too many times for any good to come of the conversation.

" 'lo?"

He was drunk.

"Hey, it's me. My plane is delayed."

Keep it informal, like you saw him yesterday.

"No worries, darlin', I'll let the driver know."

I knew it.

"You don't have to send anyone, I can rent a car when I get in."

"Nope. You'll come home in style, sugar." Sugar. I hadn't heard that in a dog's age. I broke out in a cold sweat right then. *Maybe I shouldn't go.* But there was Paddy. Who would fight for him if I didn't? Jackson's fighting power had to be depleted. And Lottie deserved retribution . . . and I had a niece who was growing up alone. I had to go.

Then there was Grant.

It seemed an age since I'd loved him . . .

"How's Byrd?" I asked abruptly, pulling myself back from the edge. I couldn't start thinking about Grant or I'd never get on the plane, period.

He cleared his throat. "Byrd? Well, now. What should I tell you about our girl? I suppose you should know she has strange ways. Not like yours or Minny's, more like your mama's were when I met her, strong. Only she likes 'em and uses 'em all the time. Oh, and don't let this one shock you. She looks like your mama, too. Sometimes I can't even look into those green eyes of hers."

She has strange ways. So much in one little sentence. Byrd had the Green blood coursing through her. That, mixed up with whatever Stella gave her, meant Byrd was destined to shine.

Paddy and I believed in magic. When you're little, everything around you is "normal." It's simply what you *know*. Besides, when my own touch of "shine" showed up, even the parts of our family history we thought were exaggerated seemed true.

When I was little, there was magic around me. The rising moon, the setting sun. I saw it hidden in Naomi's sea-green eyes and in Great-aunt Minerva's glowing palms. I felt it the first time Grant kissed me.

So hearing Byrd had strange ways didn't shock me.

It was the *next* sentence that threw me under the bus. *"She looks like your mama, too."* I wondered for a moment at the straight-up unfairness the world had to offer. I grew up wishing nothing more than to see my mother's face looking back at me in the mirror. Her full, black hair and pale skin that tanned a honey gold in the Gulf Coast sun. Those big, startling, green eyes, and delicate yet strong elfin chin. If she'd had a tail, she'd have looked just like the mermaids in the stories she used to read to us.

I longed to look like her. To be a mermaid.

Instead, I look like purebred Whalen. Not a breath of my mother in me. Patrick, either. We're both blond with ice blue eyes and porcelain skin. Dolls, those Towners used to call us. The Whalen Dolls. The only thing I had of hers were her hands. Delicate and thin. She loved that we had that in common. She'd put my palms up and make them cup her face, then she'd kiss each of my fingers and fold them shut one by one.

"There's an island just across the bay from where I grew up, did you know that, Bronwyn? I was always afraid of it, just like you're afraid of Belladonna Bay. So I never went. But I heard stories, that over there when mamas do that with their babies, and the babies open their hands, the smell of roses fills the air, and a feeling of love washes over them, making the word *love* unnecessary. Wouldn't that be wonderful, love? If I could give you that?"

There was such sadness in my mother. She never did understand that those light kisses on my fingers gave me all the love I'd ever need.

The very thought of that bit of land behind the Big House, shrouded in a veil of sweet, sick mist was enough to make me turn right around all together.

"You still there, sugar?"

"I'm here," I said, choking back tears. "But I got to run. You tell her I'm coming, okay? You tell Byrd that Aunt Bronwyn is on her way."

Jackson laughed so hard he dropped the phone.

"And what, may I ask, is so goddamned funny?" I asked when I could hear him breathing in the receiver again.

"Look, sugar, she ain't gonna care a lick about you showing up or not."

"Oh, yeah, then if she doesn't need me, why am I coming?"
He was quiet.

"I didn't say she didn't need you, I said she wouldn't care. She's wild like them snakes that hide in the tall grasses, Wyn. You're gonna have to charm her some. Then again, I could be mistaken. I can't tell which way that girl will go. Just like your mama, bless her soul."

I figured that was all I was going to get, so I tried to ask him about Paddy, but he'd dropped the phone again, and my flight was boarding.

One of the problems with taking photographs for a living is you can't just glance at anyone. You have to look *into* them.

The people boarding the plane looked, almost without exception, like each had been disillusioned with life somewhere along the line. But what really got me was the kids. Not like you'd think. They never annoyed me, it was worse than that. Especially the little chubby towheaded toddlers. They hit me like a sucker punch straight to my gut. All of whom, boy or girl, could have been Paddy as a baby.

And there's one of those blond babies on every flight, isn't there?

I flew home to Magnolia Creek by way of Mobile, Alabama, with a little twin of baby Patrick sitting right in front of me the whole way home. Each mile that went by brought me closer to that baby I remembered—and the family I left behind.

Would they even want me back? ran through my head over and over, until I did the only thing I could do. I fell asleep and began to dream.

My bare feet stood on the warm planks of a painted wooden floor. It was a bright, glossy Caribbean blue. A snake slithered slowly toward me out of the creek, but I couldn't move.

I only woke when the plane finally began its descent and the fear of what I was doing moved too close. I thought of Cleopatra, and how she killed herself by putting her arms inside baskets full of asps, and then I looked down at my ring.

Ben? I changed my mind. I'm glad you're going to meet me down here, because right about now the odds I make it through this thing with my head on straight don't look too good.

4

Byrd

Only the children know what they are looking for.

—*The Little Prince*

Jackson had to come lookin' for me to tell me what I already knew, and I didn't need a premonition to see it. I'd heard him on the phone. He'd asked Aunt Bronwyn to come take care of me, and he'd come out of his study to tell me: she was *on her way*.

He walked onto the wide front lawn, as he always did, and let out his yell. "Byrd! Come on home, Byrd! Fly this way, honey!"

When he looked for me, and God knows he was always lookin' 'cause I was always hidin', he never ventured out to the back of our property. Seein' as Jackson is best at avoiding what frightens him most, it makes sense, him only lookin' for me where he wouldn't find me. I suppose it always occurred to him that I *might* overcome my fear of Belladonna Bay and skip on over the creek to explore its misty acres. And he couldn't face that. I told him he didn't need to worry, that it was the *one* rule I heeded. But he knew I was lyin' because it never did have anything to do with the *rules*.

I don't pay no mind to rules. Seems to me, rules are things made up by scared people too afraid to die, so they can't live. Or too lazy to make their own decisions. Rules are for breakin', as far as I'm concerned.

No, it wasn't because of a silly old rule. I never went over there because I never met a mystery I didn't like, and Belladonna Bay was the best mystery of all. Jamie and me, we'd grown up believing all sorts of things about that place. None of which were good.

Anyway, the mystery goes like this: the Old-timers say that those people who came on over from England, the ones at Roanoke that disappeared (and if that ain't the biggest ambiguity of all time, I don't know what is), well, the Old-timers reckon those people didn't go missing after all.

Nope. They just got cold.

So they up and moved. And where do you suppose they found themselves? Right here in Magnolia Creek. Well, it wasn't a creek back then. Back then, it was a wild and raging river. And Belladonna Bay was a tempting piece of forest that sat smack-dab in its center. Why they chose to end up there isn't known, but the Old-timers say there was already a curse on that place. A beautiful, sad sort of somethin' that drew people there like moths to flame.

When the people began to build their new settlement a mighty ruckus started. You see, some of the people wanted to live in the forest like the Indians, all natural like, but some wanted a real village with English houses and *rules*. They fought, and in the end, part of the colony fled. But it was the wild ones who stayed. And then, after a spell, they just disappeared inside that forest and became shafts of light. Ghosts who never died.

And if anyone from the outside comes on over to that place, this mist (or miasma as Jackson likes to call it, always saying it like "my asthma") creeps in their minds and lungs and right into the bloodstream. Makes it so they can't tell what they seen or can't never go back to how they were before.

Miasma. That's one of my favorite words, too.

Every person that goes on over there comes back changed. At least that's what they say. And I believe 'em because I've seen a lot of things that just ain't possible. (And that's sayin' something when you consider the source. Me.)

They say Naomi went over chasing some silly ginger cat across the creek. Skipping over the stones like a ballerina. See, she'd fallen into some kind of mental distress a few months after giving birth to my aunt Bronwyn, and Jackson says that cat kept the sadness at bay. But the animal was drawn to the sick sweetness of Belladonna Bay and ran right over, and Naomi, havin' a bit of magic livin' in her own self, didn't think nothin' of it.

But when she came back she fell deeper into the sad. And no one can recall what came first, the opium or her jaunt across the creek.

My own mama went over there, too. My mama was Italian, see. Not from the country but in her blood. Her last name was Amore. It means *love.* She came down here lookin' for her history and found my daddy instead. She went over there pregnant with me, to find the Belladonna that she expected grew there. My mama had magic in her too, see. It's why I'm *extra* odd, I suppose. She died right when I was born, and I'm sure that little trip had something to do with it.

I miss her sometimes.

And there's story after story just like those. Everyone in Magnolia Creek has a story about someone who defied instinct and fell prey to the mystery. Someone who they loved who came back a different person. All filled up with miasma.

I seen it firsthand. Carter, *he* went over. I saw him crossing back. It was the night they say my daddy did the killin'. The moon was high and I was staring at it out my bedroom window, and there he was, Carter coming out from behind that curtain of mist, his white shirt covered in blood.

I ran outside thinkin' he was hurt.

"Carter, Carter!" I yelled. "What's wrong? Where are you hurt? Why'd you go on over there?"

His silver hair shone bright in the nights light. For a second I didn't think he recognized me, his eyes were so wild. Then he said something I didn't understand.

"Don't worry, honey, everything's gonna be all right. Carter's gonna take care of everything. I been takin' care of this family for years, and I don't plan on stoppin' now. Don't you worry."

He said those words to calm me, but they didn't. Because he said them while he held me too tight, through tears. And not once, in my whole life, had I heard or seen him cry. Not Carter. He's a "man's man" if there ever was one. It makes me almost faint just thinkin' on it.

And later on, when I heard my daddy and Carter talkin', I couldn't make out exactly what they were sayin', but it sounded to me like my daddy, my dear sweet daddy, was tellin' Carter that he did it. *Did what?* I wondered.

Then my daddy said he wasn't goin' to even fight about it. And Carter kept on arguin' with him. I couldn't figure any of it out.

By the next morning everything started to make an evil sort of sense.

And you know what? I blame it on Belladonna Bay and the mist around it. Nothin's been the same since that night. Not one thing. Because that night the miasma crept into all of us.

The next morning, Stick (or Sheriff Croft if you want to get fancy) came round to pick up my daddy as soon as the sun hit the sky. And he was quiet about it, my daddy. He walked out the front door like a prince; his back straight and his golden hair shinin' like a crown. "Come on, Stick," he said. "Take me in."

(Everyone calls him Stick 'cause he's so thin.)

Anyway, Stick didn't want to take my daddy in. They were friends. Hell, my daddy was friends with every Towner. No one didn't like Patrick Whalen.

"I'm sure it's all a misunderstanding, Paddy," he'd said as he put cuffs around my daddy's wrists. I remember he went and carefully rolled up the cuffs of Daddy's starched white shirt. (Minerva sure knows how to make a man look handsome.)

As the cuffs clicked closed, my daddy looked back at me and did the oddest thing. He winked. "Nope, ain't no mistake. I killed 'em, Stick. I was drunk and angry. Now take me in and hear my confession."

"Jaysus, Paddy! Ain't you gonna wait for me to read you your rights? Shit!"

"I don't have no rights. I gave those up last night."

I was screamin' and cryin and carryin' on like a baby. Carter had to hold me back. Jackson was already drinkin' in his study. The air was thick with a secret bein' kept from me.

So Stick put my daddy in the back of his police car and drove him down that long driveway leadin' off our property and straight into town. One straight line down Main Street. The same road my aunt Bronwyn took the day she made her homecoming.

And both days I stood out on the steps waiting and watching. Watching him leave, then watchin' her come, murmuring to myself, "He didn't do it. I know he didn't do it."

My daddy might'a confessed, but it was Carter who was covered in blood. I didn't want to throw blame around like that though. I mean, a girl has to be *sure* of a thing.

And sooner than I wanted, another, more troublin' idea came into my mind. One that shook everything up like a rattlesnake in a chicken coop.

My aunt Bronwyn drove up to the Big House in the shiny black car Jackson sent for her like she was the queen of the world. I stood there frownin'. *You might think you're the queen returning for your crown, only that ain't never gonna happen. I'm the queen of the Big House now.*

I know it was a childish thing to think, but *I'm a child*. Most days anyway.

I came right out onto the front porch and made sure I was three steps above her so I could look her straight in the eye. Jamie always said you gotta look your opponent straight in the eyes. Said because we're human we can't rightly piss on our territory like the animals do (manners were important to my Little Prince), but looking at people straight worked *almost* just as well.

Jamie liked to study the animals. We like nature and outdoor stuff, me an' Jamie. And the day Aunt Bronwyn showed up, I was missing Jamie so damn much I thought my fingers and toes would turn blue.

Then it all went to hell in a handbasket. I was simply not pre-pared for how she looked and moved just like my daddy.

"Hey, Byrd," she said, all soft like cotton. She was wearing a gypsy-style green shirt over faded jeans, and her hair was pulled back, but the sticky hot of the day had set it free, curling it around her face. That Whalen towhead hair has a wildness all its own, and I'm jealous of it. And she had this big, fancy camera around her neck on a colorful strap. Boy, did I want to get my hands on that. I like taking pictures.

My heart melted right away because of her likeness to my daddy, and something else I couldn't quite figure out. I wanted to run to her. I wanted to say all the things I couldn't say.

They say my daddy killed Jamie and his mama. But he didn't. No matter he says he did it. He's liy'n. But my lips wouldn't budge. My hand wouldn't even come out to shake hers. Sometimes I can be more stubborn than I oughta be.

"Hey there," she repeated.

Jackson was watchin' us. Waitin' to see if we'd hit it off or not. Either way, it wouldn't a mattered to him. Nothin' life hands that man, good or bad, can hold sway over him. Minerva calls him an "eternal optimist." Hell, if that's what the bourbon gives you, more power to it. But him watchin' me was annoyin', so I guess I might have said, "I heard ya the first time," or some-thin' a touch rude like that.

Next thing she did was ask me about Dolores. Dolores is my dog. She was at my side like always. And even though Dolores seemed to like her fine, I still couldn't speak to Bronwyn of Magnolia Creek. I could list the ways she'd hurt the ones I loved most. Leavin' like she did. Makin' Jackson and my daddy miss her an' worry over her. But I do have to admit it, she was damn pretty, with a soft bit underneath . . . so instead of just walkin' away from her, as I'd planned, I muttered some kind of answer, I think.

Then she did the strangest thing.

She thanked me for watching out for her brother . . . in *French*. And I thought I'd faint. So I said, "You're welcome" (in French, of course . . . I mean I'm tryin' not to be too rude), and ran off. 'Cause I didn't know what to say next. And nothing, not one thing was coming out right or feeling the way I'd figured it would.

I ran off into the side yard and climbed up into Esther. She's the biggest Southern magnolia in more than fifteen counties. And she's the oldest on our property. I love her.

I sat in her branches so I could watch what would happen next from way up high. Would my aunt turn around and leave again? It's what I'd expected. . . . No matter how much preparation I'd done for her arrival, I didn't think she'd actually *stay*. I figure it's the same for most folks. You plan and you make things all pretty for your guests, but in the end you want them to come for a bit, ooh and aah, and then go on home thinking about how *amazing* you are.

But sitting there in that tree, I changed my mind.

Because everything wasn't fine. And I thought maybe I needed her.

And I never thought I'd feel that way about no one, 'cept for Jamie.

I was relieved when Jackson finally went into the house and Aunt Bronwyn set herself right down on the front steps lookin' off into the distance. She hadn't come after me. Maybe she understood. Maybe she'd be the one to solve the mystery. Maybe she'd love me and stay forever.

These kinds of thoughts I have, that go one way first and then the other so quick I can't keep track, are the thoughts my daddy calls "the crazy fuckalls." I'm not supposed to say it 'cause there's a curse word in there. But it's a good way to describe curvy thoughts.

"Byrd," he'd say—laughing at me because I'd said I didn't want ice cream because I hated it and then I did want ice cream because I like rum raisin and ain't it the best thing ever?—"you got a case of the crazy fuckalls," then we'd laugh and eat a whole carton of rum raisin.

I'd almost forgot his smiling ways and eyes and hands.

My daddy's got the smoothest palms. Rich man hands. Not like Jackson. Jackson doesn't live like he's rich. He did hard work next to the farmhands when he was young and prefers the outdoors—like me. At least he did, until the drink made him escape into the universe inside his chest. That big ol' place where he still lives all twisted up with Naomi. Beautiful Naomi who still dances across the floor of her rooms in the east wing of the Big House. Jackson keeps them locked up, and Minerva cleans them, then locks them up again. But I get in, always have. I go visit her.

Naomi throws fine tea parties. For a dead lady, that is.

5

Bronwyn

BROWNWYN WHALEN.

I saw the sign as soon as I got off the plane, but I ignored the man holding it.

And I'll be damned if he didn't follow me down to baggage claim anyway. Every last person in Alabama seems to know a Whalen when they see one.

Grabbing my bags off the luggage carousel, I made my way to the exit. I could see him roll his eyes and follow me, but I didn't care. I'd been making eyes roll all over the East Coast for fourteen years. BitsyWyn Whalen was surfacing far too quickly for my liking.

Walking into the heat, I felt more than the heavy air. I felt the weight of my memories. The ones I'd hoped would come back slowly—drip by drip, moment by moment—only they weren't cooperating. Instead, they tried to ambush me from behind the air, so I held my breath because I was sure the minute I inhaled, BitsyWyn would wake up and snatch my quiet soul.

The idea that I'd "get my bearings" was laughable. Born out of an orderly northeastern way of thinking about things. *You're off the I-95 corridor now, Wyn.*

Naomi had flown into this airport with Minerva, just like me. They'd waited on a driver sent by Jackson, too, and taken the same road into the unknown.

My mother's unknown began winding itself around mine, and I started to feel the intoxicating love I had for her when I was a little girl. Sorrow is a heavy thing.

"You ready, Miss Wyn?" asked the man sent to bring me back home.

Wyn. He called me Wyn like he'd known me forever.

I decided to take a real look at this escort of mine, so I could get a good feeling for the fellow who'd bring me back to my former life.

He was an older man but not an Old-timer. Not a Towner either. Old-timers were the ones from *way* back. From the time when the Whalens owned every bit of Magnolia Creek. When the lumberyard was the place every man worked, and every woman worried about. When Jackson took over, he closed down the mills and offered all the workers a fine pension. It's those men and their wives (the ones that are left, anyway) who we call Old-timers. The rest of us, the children of all those people, young and old alike (depending on whatever age the Old-timer was when Jackson closed the mill), we're the Towners. But this man wasn't either. He was *new.*

"I seem to be at a disadvantage here," I said. "You know my name, only I don't know yours." I knew I sounded haughty, but I couldn't help it. Sometimes my brain makes my mouth say things to protect my heart.

"Sorry about that, Wyn. My name's Carter. No nickname, no funny sort of pronunciation. Just plain ol' Carter."

"Are you a Towner, Carter? I don't remember you," I said, knowing full well that he wasn't. *Small talk . . .*

"No, miss, you don't know me," he responded, "We ain't never met. I came on over from Birmingham to visit your dad about a job. I don't know, maybe a month or so after you . . . left."

He'd been here, living with my family for almost as long as I'd been alive before I ran off. Time is a blurry thing.

"Heard he was tryin' to cultivate some newfangled 'maters," continued Carter. "And since I know a thing or two about 'em, I came on down, and that's when I met Minerva. I married that woman quick."

Minerva was married. My own great-aunt got married and I never heard about it.

Typical Jackson. He'd written about the hydroponic farm but left out the part where Minny got married.

I smiled and placed a hand on Carter's shoulder.

"Nice to meet you, Carter. I'm sure you've been a big help with Paddy. I wish Jackson had written me about your marriage, I would have come for the wedding." He smiled back at me and moved to put my bags in the trunk of a long, black town car. "Buy American!" Jackson always said.

"No, Wyn. You wouldn't have. But it's mighty nice of you to say so. Now, Paddy's wedding? That one was truly beautiful. That's the one you shouldn't a missed."

Nothing beats a slap of Southern honesty.

"So that's how it's going to be," I said, but I smiled at him as I said it. A truce of sorts.

He opened the door for me, the air conditioner blowing out the "new car" smell. Jackson upgraded all his cars every year. I wondered if he ever got rid of my old car. My love. A cherry-red Mustang convertible. Probably not. Jackson may have liked upgrades, but he was also a collector. He would have kept that car as part of his "Bronwyn the First collection."

I slid into the cool cave of the car and let Carter close the door.

"How's Paddy?" I asked when he'd situated himself in the driver's seat.

"Well now, I suppose he's doin' as best as one would expect, considering. But how 'bout we get you all settled before we open that can a worms."

He drove out of the airport. "You want me to take Ten to Ninety-eight straight on down? Or would you rather we take scenic Ninety-eight? Might give you a little time to reacquaint yourself."

The absence of traffic gave me a second of culture shock. "How much have things changed down here?"

"Not much in the towns, but the interstate is the interstate no matter where you go these days in this fast-food nation of ours. Wall-to-wall convenience. Outlets too, by God."

"I guess we better take the scenic route then," I said.

We drove twenty minutes on the highway, and then we were on county roads. Damn, if the Alabama coast isn't still the best kept secret in America. I watched the trees go by as we drove. Palm trees and crape myrtle bursting with luscious red and pink blossoms. Large, waxy leaves dancing among the magnolias' hundred-year-old branches, their prehistoric and otherworldly pods dangling from the crux of the leaves. And then, the straight-backed pine trees, defiant in their opposition to the twisted trunks of their neighbors.

Trees down south have a difference to them, a subtle, slinking movement, mile by mile—a gracefulness, a swagger. Lanky trees stretching out their wiry thin, Spanish moss–covered branches, moss that sways and beckons . . . *come here, come here,* it says.

"I'm too late for the magnolia blossoms," I said.

"Yep. We're in the green season now. Nothin' much grows in July, as I'm sure you recall."

"Has Esther bloomed since I've been gone?"

Carter laughed a bit and caught my eye in the rearview mirror. "Nope. She's older than dirt. She can't bloom no more."

We passed pecan farms, peanut fields, and grazing livestock. Sweet, little cottages dotted the byways, and soon we were crossing small bodies of water. I'd forgotten how each home had a sign out front with not only the house number but the name of the family who lived there. Calaman, Dumond, Du Puis, Kelsey, Miller, Freehold, Berman, Cooper, and on and on. There's a lot of pride here in the South, and it's so clean. I'd forgotten how clean. As we passed the beach at the town line, our little bit of the Gulf of Mexico, I saw my childhood in the docks, the pavilion, and the stretches of sand where I'd run free from May through November.

Before I knew it, we were making the drive up Main Street in Magnolia Creek.

My mind took pictures. *Click, click, click,* until they all bled together like a choppy Super 8 film. Nothing had changed. I could almost see the sides of the filmstrip, frames bound in black, the negatives showing the dark underlight of it all.

But I could not get drawn back into this place so quickly. It would be easy to drown in its beauty and forget that Lottie was dead, and my brother gone, too. Dead in another way altogether. *Mermaids don't drown,* I thought.

"Want to hear some music, Wyn?" asked Carter, as the filmstrip in my head sputtered and melted off the reel.

"That would be nice," I said absently. Looking out at the windows, I could almost feel myself back on my bike. Me and Paddy, Lottie and Grant, riding like wild children through town. When we got older, Grant and I would ditch them. Kids can be mean. *What if I'd just stayed and married him?* I wondered.

You fill up my senses, drifted from the radio.

John fuckin' Denver. "Annie's Song." It was *their* song. Naomi's and Jackson's personal waltz. This hit so close to my heart that I could hear it beating in my ears. I wanted to jump out of the car and run.

Breathe, I told myself. *It's just a song.*

"You okay back there?" asked Carter.

"Yeah, I'll be fine. That song's haunted me for years, and now that we're close to home, there it is, playing. Doesn't bode well for me, Carter."

Carter laughed a little then, and I hoped it was because he appreciated my candor. "Ain't nothing like that, no spooky hoodoo voodoo about it. Jackson still owns most of this town, and the DJ at the radio station is told he's gotta play it every hour on the hour. And you know somethin'? We don't mind. It's a pretty song, don't you think?"

Come let me love you, let me give my life to you . . .

It *was* pretty, I guess. But the ache it brought on made my throat sore.

It can't hurt you if you own it, try to remember things on your own terms, you can do it, Ben would've said something like that to me, and he held the key to my "calm," so I tried. I closed my eyes and let my mind drift back in time.

The ballroom, mostly empty since Jackson's father held massive parties when the mill was still in operation, made a haunting backdrop for my own mother and father who could waltz around the entire room at any hour of the day. They lived on whim, my parents. And their waltz of choice was to "Annie's Song," which has a distinct "one two three, one two three" rhythm that moved their feet as Paddy and I hid outside, peering in through the windows. I could almost feel them dancing, like I was the wind in Naomi's hair.

I can do this, I thought. *I will do this.*

When the song was over, I felt more confident. I opened my eyes and realized we were already at the twisty iron gates of the Big House, right there where Main Street ends. Paddy and I used to love giving people directions. "Take forty-nine until you run outta road!" Then we'd laugh like crazy.

The Big House sits on what a cartographer would surely call a peninsula. Edged by a forest on the west side, and then the Magnolia River all around the rest. Toward the right, the river dribbles into a creek. I didn't want to look that way as we drove in, so of course, I looked. More out of curiosity than anything else . . . at first.

Memories have a way of playing tricks on people, and I wondered if maybe I'd made up that misty piece of sour land in my mind. But there it was, Belladonna Bay, all shrouded in its signature fog. Then the car veered left and it was gone from sight.

In front of me there was a finer view. Esther. Still as majestic as I remembered. And my mother's garden too, blooming even in the "green season." But Carter was driving straight up to the front of the house, so I had to keep looking ahead even if I didn't want to.

I was acutely aware of the sound of the gravel under the tires as the car came to a stop. I was afraid to look up. Afraid things would be different, and afraid they'd be the same. When I forced myself to glance at the house, I saw her.

Byrd.

Standing on the steps of my childhood home. Flanked by a huge German sheperd on one side and Jackson on the other.

I let my eyes linger on that little girl. I knew her stance. Angry. Scared. Shy.

Beautiful.

Jackson wasn't kidding. She looked just like my mother. Only not broken. Well, not so much. But her frown, and her arms crossed . . . that was pure Paddy. And that combination won my heart before my mind even had a chance to think otherwise.

She was wearing an old-fashioned dress all covered up by one of my mother's aprons. Naomi loved to wear fancy aprons with ruffles and big pockets. She'd wear them over pajamas, dresses, even jeans when she was feeling well and walked out in the gardens with Jackson.

On Byrd the apron was oversized and all tied up like she'd rigged the thing herself. She had a mass of crazy black hair that looked like it hadn't seen a brush in a month and a gaze that dared the world to just *try* and brush it.

I wanted to rush to her and sweep her into a tight hug. But I knew better. I'd been in war-torn countries where children had no choice but to bear witness to terrible things. Even so, I'd have to coax them into letting me take their pictures. In their eyes I'd seen the same sort of despair. The same fearful longing.

She was prepared to hate me but wanted to love me, even if she didn't know it yet.

Jackson came strolling down the stairs. But Byrd stood her ground with her dog (I just knew it was hers) by her side.

"Sugar! Oh, hell. Just look at you! My girl!" said Jackson, opening the car door for me. "What a fine-lookin' woman you make, Wyn! Welcome home, darlin'!" He held out his arms.

The sun was shining behind him, bathing his features in shadow, but I saw enough to be amazed the boozing hadn't treated him as badly as it should have. He was still handsome, charming Jackson Whalen . . . same as he ever was. A bit thicker around the waist, a few laugh lines by his shining blue eyes. Thinner hair, too, but still that white-yellow he'd passed down to Paddy and me. I suppose it never goes silver, just fades to white altogether.

I leaned in for a hug, prepared to pretend everything was just fine. That way I wouldn't have to deal with anything awkward. There's a great deal of power in pretending. But no matter how I tried, my arms couldn't come up around him. He held me for a few, stiff moments and then let me go. He cleared his throat.

"Well, Byrd, darlin', here she is!"

He placed a strong hand on my lower back and began to guide me up the stairs to my niece.

She was tiny for eleven. If I didn't know better, I'd have thought she was no older than seven. It was her eyes that gave her away. Naomi would have called her an "old soul."

"Hey, Byrd," I said, as soft as I could, while holding out my hand. I made sure to stay a few steps below her. I knew she was the queen of this place now, and I needed to let her know I hadn't come to hurt her or to take her place. I just wanted to . . . take her picture. That was all I could think about. I didn't know what we'd be able to create in the middle of the silent, violent storm that was swirling around the people we both loved. All I knew for sure, at that very moment, was that I wanted to make her feel safe.

"Hey there," I tried again.

"I heard ya the first time, I ain't deaf," she said. Her voice was lower than I'd imagined, but melodic. Strong, too. I liked it.

This was no bird I was dealing with. This was a mountain lion. And I liked her.

"Who's this?" I asked, reaching my hand out for her dog to smell.

Byrd put her fingers protectively inside the dog's black leather collar. "Her name is Dolores."

"My," I said, a bit of laughter slipping into my voice, "what a creative name."

"It means 'sorrow,'" she said, her green eyes, my mother's, staring right into me. Daring me to say *one more thing* about her dog or she'd sic it on me.

Then I noticed a book—*my* book—*The Little Prince* peeking out from the top of an oversized apron pocket and found the key to her heart.

"Je suis heureux de vous rencontrer ainsi et je suis heureux d'être à la maison. Merci de prendre un tel bon soin de mon frère."

I watched her eyes soften slightly. A clue that the sharp edge of her guard was coming down.

"De rien," she responded, making a graceless curtsy. Then she was gone, skipping down the steps barefoot, and down the drive,

with Dolores at her heels. She started muttering as she passed me. "We hold these truths to be self-evident, that all men are created equal, that they are endowed . . ."

I turned to Jackson, confused, ready to ask what in the world she was doing, but he was already ahead of me.

"It's like a nervous tic or somethin'. She repeats it whenever she's nervous. Seems your arrival has her a bit undone." He smiled after her adoringly. I fought down an unexpected bit of jealousy.

And then I watched as some redbirds flew down from the trees. Dolores snapped and jumped at them, but they kept flying up and down in loops around little Byrd. Ahead and then behind, a surreal game of tag.

"Please tell me I'm imagining that," I said.

Jackson put his arm around me and laughed a little. "Isn't that a prerequisite of bein' a princess? Birds followin' you all around? Besides, it's been happenin' since the day she was born. That's why we call her Byrd. Used to be Bird with an *i* till she was big enough to change it herself. She revels in bein' odd, that one."

I looked at the apron's muddy hem and her unkempt black hair hanging down as she walked. "That's one unlikely princess, Jackson. Gypsy queen, maybe, or queen of the wild things . . . but princess? I think not."

"You ain't lookin' hard enough, little darlin'. Princesses come in all shapes and sizes." He squeezed my shoulder, and turned to walk back into the house. I knew he was holding back a tugging pain, because it was tugging at me too, making my eyes water.

I'd been his princess a lifetime ago. Not Byrd's kind. I was the tea party, dress-up kind of princess.

"Jackson"—I turned around to follow him—"we really need to talk about Paddy."

He stopped on the steps but didn't turn around. His hands tightened into fists at his sides. "Don't call me that, Wyn. While you're here, you call me daddy. You understand?"

A small, defensive voice came out of my mouth, BitsyWyn Whalen's voice, "You let Byrd call you Jackson."

He stayed with his back turned to me; he never could look at any of us when he was feeling sorrowful. "Byrd ain't my daughter," he said. "And Paddy's in prison. Ain't nothin' we can do about that now."

"That can't be true. I won't believe that. And I'm going to get to the bottom of it, *Jackson*. I swear it."

"Good luck with that," he said, walking into the Big House, letting the heavy door shut with a bang. It wasn't long before I heard the ice clinking in the glass through the open windows of the front study. If my memory served, he'd be incoherent by noon, thank God.

I'd never been able to find a "middle ground" of feelings for my father. It was desperate love or full-on rage . . . interchangeable and triggered by the smallest sigh or sidelong glance.

I stood there not knowing what to do next. Plain awkward is what it was. My ward was gone, and it was too damn humid to look for her. So I sat down on the steps and took a deep breath. It felt good, breathing. "Breathe in, Bronwyn . . . that's it . . . deep cleansing breaths," Ben used to say as he taught me yoga in our old apartment, guiding me gently into each pose.

Thinking about Ben turned on a worry I'd felt lurking ever since I got on the plane in New York. A tiny crack in the calm he'd fostered inside me. I'd grown so used to a steady hand, what would happen . . . who would I be without it?

"Welcome home," Minerva said from behind me. Her lavender and bleach scent hit me before her words did. A comfort from days long gone. She'd always sensed when I needed her, I guess some things never *do* change.

"May I sit by you?" she asked.

I stood up and gave her a real hug. It was so damn good to see her.

She still had her signature red hair. Maybe she dyed it, it didn't matter. I wanted to stare at it forever.

We sat down side by side.

"You look good, Min," I said.

And she did. Older, sure . . . thinner, too. But her eyes were still that same steel blue that always made me think she'd stared at a stormy northern sea too long.

"Congratulations on your marriage." I said, trying to sound light and airy. "Carter seems like a fine man."

That's when I noticed that he'd slipped away at some point . . . quietly, like a cat.

"He's a good egg," said Minerva. "And he's been a godsend for Patrick. I guess you could say he's 'fine' . . . for an old man, and a Southern cracker."

"Oh hell, Minerva, you still fancy yourself a Yankee?"

"Sure I do. Nothing will ever change that. I'm too ornery to be one of these frolicky people." Her eyes flicked to my left hand. I could feel her tense up next to me, but she didn't say anything.

"Yep, I'm engaged. I was going to tell everyone later," I said softly.

"Well, isn't that nice. I mean wonderful! Never mind me. I'm just so happy to see you. We'll talk about that pretty ring and your fiancé later."

"Minerva, are you all right? You seem upset." She'd gotten

colder, further away from me somehow, but I couldn't understand why, when a minute before she'd seemed like the same old Minerva. Maybe she was harboring some anger against me for leaving, and it just found its way through cracks in our small talk.

"Don't worry. I'm just happy to see you. Getting used to looking at your face all grown up. We need to readjust, that's all," she said, patting my arm.

"Minerva?" I asked, taking her hand.

"What, honey?"

"Why didn't you write to me? I mean, I know I didn't write to you, either. But why not drop a line when you were getting married? Or when Paddy first got in trouble? For Lottie's funeral? Or even just to try and convince me to come home after Byrd's mother died?"

I thought she'd pull her hand from mine. No one likes to be accused of anything, but she didn't.

"Well, I should have. So why don't we just chalk it up to 'out of sight out of mind.' I hope that doesn't sound cruel, Bronwyn. I just think my whole family—the Greens—we're wired that way. It's not that I ever stopped loving you or thinking about you. It's just that if you aren't here in front of me, it's hard to remember to sew you into the quilt of the present. No one should understand that better than you, sitting here, right now."

Minerva always had a way with words. And she sure loved the hell out of that quilt analogy. She always told Paddy and me that each new day in our lives was a new story square for the quilt that would be the history of us when we were gone.

I pulled her hand to my face and rested on it for a bit. Sometimes a grown woman needs to feel like a little girl again.

"And anyway," she continued, rubbing my cheek with her thumb, "I wasn't sure you wanted to be found. Or called on, even. You left. Sometimes that's the best thing for a person. No one was going to convince you to come back until you were ready. And now?" She pulled my face up, cupped my chin in her hands, and looked at me. "Now I know you *want* to be here."

"There's so much to talk about, Minny. I have so many questions. What happened that night Lottie was killed? Why did Paddy confess? Was her funeral nice? Did anyone bring sunflowers? Lottie loved sunflowers." My voice broke.

She patted me on the head and rose from the steps.

"Why don't you just sit here for a while, and then, when you're ready, you come in and I'll make some tea and we can have a nice long chat, okay? Lost people always need a moment or two before they decide to be found. It happens *all* the time . . . where I come from, that is."

I nodded but couldn't seem to speak. Reciting the Declaration of Independence was starting to sound like a mighty fine idea.

"I'm sorry that I used to call you names when I was little" was what decided to come out of my mouth. Mouths can be so unpredictable.

"Old and ugly if I recall correctly," she said.

"I was somethin' back then, wasn't I?"

"That's one way to put it. You come inside on your own time."

She went back into the house but didn't let the door bang the way Jackson had. It wasn't her style. We'd had a lot of fights when I was growing up. That woman could yell without even having to raise her voice.

I knew from experience that arguments with Minerva were

like small firecrackers. Fierce, then over in a second. I loved her absolute readiness to forgive. Her loyalty, too.

It was always obvious Minerva missed Fairview. But she wouldn't return. Not even after Naomi died. She'd said, "Her body's in the ground here, so it's by this ground I stay."

It was an angry statement because Naomi wasn't supposed to be buried. She was supposed to be burned. There were an awful lot of rules and regulations regarding the Green family of Fairview, Massachusetts. All families have their traditions, but the Green family's were the oddest I'd ever run across. Especially the one I witnessed the night my mother died.

Most of those strange Green Ways were hard to carry out in a place so far removed, both culturally *and* spiritually.

Though I couldn't remember much of the fight Naomi and I had mere hours before she died, I did recall the scene that took place after she was dead.

It was night, and Minerva thought Paddy and I were fast asleep. She'd given us sleeping medicine (a mix of herbs: valerian root, chamomile, and cannabis) "to calm us," but it didn't work on me. Jackson was passed out drunk, with good reason for a change.

A soft singing floated up the stairs from the kitchen that night. I'll never forget coming down into the dark foyer. I'd never felt smaller. I was seventeen but felt like I was six years old. I crept down the hall and peered into the kitchen. The air was heavy with "you're not supposed to be here."

Minerva had my mother laid out on the long kitchen table. Naomi's nude body glowed, thin and white like a marble statue. I watched as Minerva washed my mother, gently, with a white piece of cloth. She dipped the cloth in a glass bowl filled with cloudy water. Salt water. Minerva had used the same milky water on Paddy and me when we were feverish, as she told us stories about these rituals. *"Chun na farraige,"* she sang as she carefully wiped down each part of Naomi. *To the ocean.* Minerva got a kick out of teaching us certain words and phrases when we were little. I learned them all. I've always been quick with languages.

When she was done with the water, she laid the bowl aside and anointed my mother with pungent rose oil. *"Chun an domhain."* *To the earth,* she sang.

I sat in the shadows and watched Minerva wind flowers into my mother's hair as she sang. Wild roses with leaves, thorns and all.

Gracefully, she wrapped my mother in crisp white linen sheets. *"Chun na gaotha."* *To the winds,* she sang. All the corners of the earth were part of their past lives in Fairview. Only one rite was missing.

Fire.

But there would be no fire.

The traditional funerals of the Green family of Fairview, Massachusetts, demanded that the dead be delivered into the afterlife (or the In-between, as Mama and Minny used to call it) much like the Vikings. Placed on a large pyre and sent floating on a barge of light and never-ending life.

But Jackson wouldn't have it. He asked that she be buried. And buried she was, so Minerva stayed.

I didn't really think Naomi would mind being in the ground.

The ground. The earth itself was a bit of an obsession for my mother. All of the natural world, really.

Besides her garden, Naomi loved trees.

Sitting there, on the steps, steeping in the heat and a tidal flow of memories, I looked out across the sprawling front gardens where the plum trees and oaks leaned together making an inner circle, a barrier of sorts holding back the taller pines. Naomi used to run from tree to tree, crying and holding them.

"Why do the trees make you cry, Mama?" I'd asked her once when I was still little, before I shut her out of my heart. Before I stopped being curious about her strange ways.

"Oh! Can't you hear them, Bronwyn? They're screaming at me!" she'd say.

I was six, or maybe seven, and I'd caught her between trees. I could tell by her frantic, tearing eyes that she wanted to break away from my questions so she could go soothe another one.

"I must calm them or else they get so loud. But it's hard, you know? Because I don't have the answers they want. What do you want?" She'd already turned away from me and was talking to the trees again.

"What are they asking you, Mama?"

"Not just me, darling. Everyone. They're asking everyone. Only I seem to be the only one who can hear them."

"Maybe I can help?" I asked. "Only you have to tell me what they are asking."

"'Why?' That's what they ask, darling. Always '*Why*?' First, they ask quietly, politely, then if I don't answer right away, they get louder. If I still don't answer, they start to scream."

"Why do they ask 'why,' Mama?"

"Why everything! Oh, never mind. You won't ever understand. Just let me go and try to answer them, would you? I wish they'd shut up."

I watched her embrace each tree, murmuring softly to them, one by one. And then the tension in the air eased, their leaves relaxed, and their branches allowed the wind to move them as it wished.

I never *could* figure out what in the world she saw. What kind of 'why' . . . and I never heard the trees scream. But sitting there, staring at those damn trees, with a scream of my own hidden deep inside my mind, I understood.

All the trees were shaped like *Y*s. Their trunks coming up and branches stretching out, asking several different questions all at once. It made so much sense. And with the sense came sadness because I'd never given that crazy, magical portion of my mother much regard once I got older.

I must have sat there for an hour, because the sun was directly over Main Street. High noon.

"Let's get this over with," I said, standing up.

I turned and walked up the wide stairs into the Big House. My childhood home. My mother's gilded prison. My body yearned to throw open that front door and run up the stairs all the way to the east wing and yell, "Mama! I'm home! I saw the why's in the trees!"

But a chill washed over me, a notion that once I crossed that threshold, I'd be walking back in time. It'd be like none of my adult life had ever happened. Just another dream woven in Naomi's magical mind on yet another long, hazy day swirled and obscured by opium smoke. *Maybe it'd be better that way, to go back in time and get the chance to do it all over again,* I thought.

I put my hand on the large brass doorknob and opened it, letting out a scream that could have woken Naomi in her grave.

6

Byrd

Language is the source of misunderstandings.

—*The Little Prince*

I could feel the tugging sadness wash all over me like a sudden rain shower *well* before I heard the scream. And it wasn't the scream that made me come down from my tree, it was the sorrow. Thick and heavy. A sorrow no person on God's green earth should feel. So I did what I had to do. I went to find Aunt Bronwyn to help her get rid of some of that sad she was carryin'.

When I got to the front door, it was hangin' wide open, and no one was there. I walked cautiously inside the house.

It's funny. I don't usually use that big ol' front door. I have all sorts of other ways of gettin' around and wasn't too used to seein' the Big House from that particular angle. I supposed it was possible there was something downright frightenin' waiting for my aunt. I *did* let my mind wander over the fact that she shared a touch of my strange ways, and could have seen a spirit. But Jackson, Daddy, Minerva, and Carter *all* said Aunt Bronwyn didn't have a lot of magic in her, just the ordinary fortune-teller sort of skills, and I believed 'em. And besides, if she *did* have the ways, she wouldn't have been afraid of a ghost even if she did see one.

I tried to figure out what my aunt might have gotten worked up over in that front hall. It's a fine hall. Nothin' too upsetting about the wide foyer or oriental carpets. Two sets of glass-paneled doors stand watch on either side of the reception area. When I was little, I used to try and fog up as many of those panels as I could so that I could draw *B, Y, R,* and *D* in each one . . . but the *B* always faded before I got to the *D.* Frustratin', to say the *least.* Anyhow, ain't nothin' overly upsetting about those doors or the rooms they lead to. On the right they lead to Jackson's study/library/living room/bar. And on the left they lead to a big, fancy-pants dining room that we don't use much.

I use it, though. I like to sit on the table. Right in the middle of its shiny, slippery surface. I light candles and put 'em all around me in a circle. See, there's plenty of room for talkin' to the spirits there. They can all sit, organized-like, on the chairs. It makes it easier. They have a lot to say, and it's stressful. It was funner when I was little and couldn't feel all their woes. Now that I'm growin' into a woman, I can *empathize* and that makes it tiresome.

Empathize is one of my favorite words.

The night after they took my daddy to jail, I came in here. I had to do it, even though I didn't want to. I was scared Charlotte and Jamie'd show up and prove me wrong. Worried sick they'd tell me my daddy *did* kill 'em after all. Worried sick they'd tell me he didn't. . . .

When on earth am I gonna learn to trust my intuition? Jaysus. I can be a stubborn witch. Charlotte showed up all right.

Mighty nervous and scared, so I calmed her down. But she only told me what I already knew. I asked her, "Lottie, did my daddy kill you?"

"Byrd? Am I dead? Is that why I feel so strange?" she whispered.

I fairly rolled my eyes. She's as thick dead as she was alive. I *swear*. But I tried to be nice. "Yes," I said. "You are. But who killed you, do you remember, Miss Charlotte?"

I think the "miss" did the trick.

"No, Byrd. I don't remember. But I know it wasn't Paddy."

I'll admit, my heart soared and fell at the same time.

And I don't know why I even expected I'd see Jamie, too. He's too close to me. Shoot, I can't even see my own mama.

Then Charlotte began awailin' like they all do when they first realize they're gone. It sounds like all the books say banshees oughta sound. Only I ain't never seen a banshee.

"Oooh, oooh, oooh!" she wailed as she began pacing up and down the long dining room. I couldn't help but feel sorry for her. So I asked her the thing I always ask spirits who are just findin' out they're dead.

"You see a light, Miss Charlotte?"

"Oooh, oooh, oooh!" she wailed again, right before she disappeared into the walls. I stomped my feet and yelled after her, "That ain't no kind of answer!"

I can't say I've seen her since. Jamie neither. And I been lookin', let me tell you. They hold the answers, those two. But I can't find 'em. Just thinkin' on it frustrates me.

I frowned, turning away from the dining room. Nothin' scary in there with or without strange ways. Then I looked over at Jackson's favorite room, and there he was, stretched out and snoring on the large, leather sofa, a glass rocking back and forth under his hand as it moved in time with his breath. You ever notice that? That in order to keep completely still you have to hold your breath. We act like waves, and when we hold our breath, we stop all our inner oceans. I spend a lot of time trying to hold my breath. I can hold it for three whole minutes. Jamie's got me by half a minute. But he's bigger.

Anyway.

"Just what kind of father sleeps himself through a scream like that! Damn it, Jackson. That's no way to win back her love," I said mighty loud. He just grumbled something I couldn't understand and rolled over. I left Jackson there asnor'n and went upstairs to Naomi's rooms. I knew Aunt Bronwyn'd go there if she was frightened. All girls want their mothers when they're scared, I think. I didn't have a mama so I don't rightly know. And truth is, mamas seem like a whole lotta worry and then a whole lotta grief later on. Who needs that? When I'm scared I want Jamie. No, scratch that. I'm not scared of nothin' 'cept Belladonna Bay.

Maybe she hadn't gone upstairs at all.

Maybe she went across the creek out of pure sadness. And a feelin' came up in me so strong that me and Dolores fairly ran out the back door. The mist was even thicker that day. I closed my eyes real tight and tried to feel her. But I couldn't. Even Dolores shook her head at me and tried to lead me back to the house, those dog tags shining in the sun and *tink-tinking* together.

Minerva yelled out the kitchen door. "Byrd, for someone who knows so much, you have your head on wrong about your aunt. She'd never cross that creek. She's upstairs. But leave her be. She needs some time, she's lost, Byrd. So lost."

Time, my butt, I thought to myself as I made my way into the house through the east balcony by the ballroom. There's a secret staircase there that leads right up to Naomi's rooms.

There's a legend about the day Naomi died. I've asked her if it's true, but seein' as she don't talk, she can't answer me. She's a true spirit. More like the ghosts you'd think about if you ain't never seen one before. Mournful and lovely, with a mistiness hangin' on her edges.

Story is that everyone in Magnolia Creek knew she was gone before they even found her body. That hundreds, maybe thousands of redbirds flew in over the town, nearly blottin' out the sun, perchin' themselves like a red blanket all over the Big House. It's said that those birds coated the roof from peak to peak, and that's when all the folks in town, drawn by the sound of whooshing feathers, or by pure human curiosity, began looking up toward the Big House, which was fairly dripping with those redbirds, and watched them rise in a hush and a rush, flying up in one big cloud, taking Naomi's soul with them.

People say, that for just a moment, it felt like there weren't no more air in the whole county. That's how they knew, Towners and Old-timers alike, that Naomi was dead.

Jackson said she'd simply had enough of all the roughness of life and went to live with the angels where she belonged. Jackson, unlike most folks who are *right* in the head, preferred believing her death was a choice. He kept on sayin', "Mermaids don't drown, mermaids don't drown."

But Minerva? She tells it right. See, Naomi'd been off that opium for a while. Cleaned herself up for some strange reason or another. And then decided to dip her toe back in. Only . . . she forgot to lower the dose.

Who knows why crazy people do the things they do? Hell, *they* don't even know why. But Minerva's made of rock and salt water. And because she has the same Green blood runnin' through her veins, she knows a thing or two about accidents.

Because accidents happen to everyone, no matter how charmin', special, or loved. But they sure seem to love those of us with Green blood.

But I do wonder why Naomi decided to wade into that mess all over again. What could have made her so sad?

Maybe Aunt Bronwyn would know. If I felt brave, I'd ask her. But I had to find her first.

Secret staircase it was. I love those, they're so dramatic.

7

Bronwyn

A spider. A plain old Southern house spider from the look of it. Paddy used to collect them when we were small. How I let out that scream I'll never know. High-strung, I guess. More Yankee than Southern girl. It fell right in front of me, landing on my shoulder. I screamed and jumped like I was walking on hot coals. When I saw it skitter away, I looked around, embarrassed. "Damn, girl," I said out loud. "Get yourself together."

And then, there I was in the center of the foyer. Jackson was snoring away in his library. A hushed constant twilight fell over this part of the house. And the whir of the ceiling fans echoed throughout the halls with their white noise.

"Minerva?" I leaned up the stairs and whispered her name. I didn't want to wake Jackson and was relieved my scream hadn't already.

I headed up the long, ornate stairway. The pilgrimage I made almost every day of my childhood to "the world upstairs." Naomi's world.

When we were all little, the four of us, me, Patrick, Lottie, and Grant, we spent hours upstairs in her rooms. Playing cards, making forts, and painting huge canvases that she'd have delivered from the artist colony up Route 98. Those were fun days. Laughter layered the walls and clung to the dust mites, making them sparkle like lightning bugs in the daytime.

It didn't stay like that. And even when it *was* like that, sometimes it *wasn't*.

My mother was addicted to opium in fits and starts for almost as long as I can remember, and her illness made her more childlike than a mother ought to be. Eccentric is one thing, incoherent is another. The worst part about her particular kind of sick was it kept her cooped up. Toward the end, she never left her rooms at all. The sweet-smelling smoke plumed under her doorway and crept downstairs like the mist over Belladonna Bay.

It was my father, who loved her more than a healthy amount, who supplied her with that poison. The opium made her fun. The opium made her happy. The opium made her tired. The opium killed her.

"She needs it," I'd hear him say as he argued with the doctor.

"It'll kill her, Jack," said Dr. Henry.

"Nothing can kill Naomi. She's a mermaid. Mermaids don't drown," he'd say, and the doctor always did as he was told. He was an Old-timer, and Jackson is practically God with that clan. How he got it, I'll never know. I don't *want* to know, not really.

The memories crept back with each creak of the stairs as I climbed.

"*Olly olly oxen free . . .*" I could hear Paddy's sweet voice before it changed. *Come play, come play . . .* and pretty Lottie, dead in the ground Lottie, who did nothing but chase both those boys from day one. Lottie who wanted to be a ballerina, but who fell down every time she tried to do a pirouette.

And my brother? I saw him everywhere. Running next to me on the stairs, leaning over the balcony, and making me sick with fear that he'd fall.

Paddy.

I'd gone away and let him fall farther than I'd ever feared.

How had I let go of him? How can anybody forget the things they love most? Tuck them away like old love letters, only to dig them out later and wonder where the hell their life went.

When I got to the top of the stairs, there it was. Naomi's portrait. When I was little, I would sit, cross-legged in front of it, with my hands under my chin just staring at her face. Then I got older and could barely look at it.

Jackson had commissioned it from a local artist down in Fairhope, not long after they were married. It's one of those paintings that's true to life, with just enough whimsy and thick strokes to make more than an elaborate illustration. The artist had posed her outside, on the swing that always dangled from Esther's branches.

He'd captured both the sparkle and the sadness in her eyes. She was just shy of twenty, right before I was born. There they were, those lovely, perfect freckles of hers that Paddy and I used to count when we were small.

"There's thirty-eight," I'd say.

"No, thirty-two!" he'd say.

Esther's leaves dipped down and framed Naomi's head like a halo. Blue skies rose in the back, and red dirt paths led away to the other gardens.

But the real reason I was so transfixed by that painting when

I was little was her smile. I never, not one day that I can remember, saw that particular smile. I waited for it, but it never came. The picture was painted before Naomi's addiction. Drug-induced smiles aren't real. The smile Naomi had in her portrait was *real*.

I reached up and touched her painted lips. Full for such a tiny face, and naturally red. No need for lipstick.

"Oh, Mama," I said before turning and walking down the long, cool hall to her rooms. I had to go there. Those rooms were the keepers of my past, and I knew, deep in my heart, that if I was to unravel the knots of the present, I had to face her. I had to tell her I was sorry.

I don't know what I expected to find. Perhaps there would be layers of dust like the rooms of Miss. Havisham or maybe her rooms would be empty. I think I wanted to see all three of us, me and Mama and Paddy, together again having a proper tea party at the table by the window.

"It's only a set of walls and windows," I said out loud as I pulled on the doors. They were locked.

I smiled a little and went back to the portrait. Right on top of the frame there were keys. I could reach them now on tiptoes. When we were little, Paddy and I had to wrestle his toy box from his room and then a rocking horse, too, so that one of us could teeter, precariously, to reach them.

I went back and unlocked the double doors, swinging them wide open.

It was just how she'd left it. Minerva must have kept it that way. Three rooms connected by large, white pocket doors. A sitting room, a bedroom, and a small library overstuffed with books. There was a massive bathroom off the bedroom area, completely tiled in white, with a deep claw-foot tub. The windows were open, the sheer curtains blew in the breeze, and the pocket doors were open too, so I could see the whole expanse of Naomi's world. The air hung heavy with the scent of roses, lavender, and still lingering there, dense, with no shame . . . the sweet smell of opium smoke.

"How can it still smell like you?" I asked, walking to the bed and touching her soft down comforter. A wave of sight, so strong, passed through me and sent me back in time. I felt dizzy and went to the window for air.

"Are you all right?" asked a small voice from the shadows. Byrd emerged into the dusty light, holding Dolores by the collar.

I found myself struggling to figure out how she'd gotten back inside the house, let alone this room, before me, but remembered this was *her* place now, not mine. Her wonderland. And she knew the secret passageways and shortcuts just as well as I did when I was her age. Maybe even better. I could tell that no one ever stopped *this* little girl from exploring.

"You were remembering your mama, right? Well, not her, exactly . . . the things all around her."

"I was," I said.

"She's right behind you, you know."

"Who?"

"Your *mama*. She's right there behind you."

I stared at my niece, trying to figure out whether she was trying to fool me. She wasn't. Her strange ways were stronger than any I was accustomed to, so I was mighty upset by what that little girl was trying to say.

"I ain't the foolin' type." She glared.

"And you can read my mind, too."

"Mmm-hmmm," she said. "So far, that is."

"Okay," I said, taking a deep breath. "If she's behind me, what's she doing, Byrd?" I asked, not really wanting the answer.

"Standin' there, hovering, reaching out to you," said Byrd, and then she looked down at the floor and placed her hands on Dolores's head, scratching the dog behind her ears. "You don't have to believe me. I know you're new here," she said.

New here.

"Is Naomi talking to you?" I asked.

"No, it's the most doggone frustratin' thing. All the other spirits go on and on. I can't get them to shut up. But Naomi stays quiet."

"Other spirits?"

Now magic, witchcraft, sight, strange ways, shine—whatever you want to call the skill set of my mother's people—that's one thing. But no one, not Mama or Minerva ever said one damn thing about seeing spirits.

Byrd rolled her eyes. "You have no idea. They're so aggravatin' sometimes." She looked up at me again. "I don't normally do this, but I can prove it. I can prove she's there."

"How, honey?

She walked over to the side of Naomi's bed and pulled the nightstand away from the wall. Rubbing on the wallpaper a bit, she found a seam and pulled back the corner, before putting her finger inside a small hole in the plaster beneath.

She pulled out a ring. Grant's senior class ring. He'd given it to me a few months before my mother died.

That ring. It went missing the day after he gave it to me, and I spent weeks searching for it. It broke my heart, losing that ring.

"I don't know the story 'cause she can't talk, but it seems to me, your mama took this from you and she wanted you to have it back. So she showed me where it was."

She handed it to me. I moved it from one palm to the other, feeling its weight. Then slipped it on my right ring finger, where it had been the night he gave it to me.

"Well now, I guess she *is* here," I said.

I watched a light spark up into Byrd's green eyes, the beginning of trust.

I tried to keep calm, but I could practically feel my mother's hands on my shoulders.

"What's she doing now, Byrd?"

"She's hugging you."

I stepped forward quickly, out of the invisible embrace, and started shaking.

I went to the window and said, "I can't stay here. I can't. How can I stay here? This it too much. I wasn't expecting this. I think . . . I think—" I'd never had a panic attack, but I knew I was on the verge of one. And then, there she was. Byrd. Standing between me and the window that I was *seriously* contemplating jumping from.

"Don't worry, I knew you wouldn't be able to stay here. I've made other arrangements. Come with me." She held out her tiny hand.

"Where are we goin', Byrd?"

"Shh," she said, turning and smiling, her black hair falling across her face. "It's a surprise."

I reached out to take that little hand of hers, and when I did, I knew my life was forever changed.

8

Naomi

She's come home. Look at her. All grown up. My baby. See how she touches my picture? Maybe she doesn't hate me so much after all. I never did like the way hate and love walk hand in hand on the earthly plane.

It's such a sad, sour, confusing thing to be a living, breathing person, all cooped up in your body. Never able to break free and see the other side of things. Now that I'm on the dead side, I see a lot of things that I couldn't before. Things I wish I could block out. Who wants to see the way they failed? Not me. But I guess I have to, because I'm still *here*.

I've never been afraid of death. At all. Things might have been different if I was.

The Big House, though lovely, wasn't really my home. I hail from a town off the coast of a northern version of Belladonna Bay. Fairview, Massachusetts. No matter how much I complain about it, I'll admit there are some perks to growing up in a place like that.

Like not being afraid to die.

And watching your hands glow with moonlight when you get excited, fall in love, or need to do some kind of magic. That is, if you're born into a family like mine, or any of the others that share all these "talents." Here they just call them "strange ways." Where I come from, we're called witches.

Fairview is a carnival-like community of the freak show variety. It's filled to the brim with weirdos, psychics, witches, caretakers, and some even say . . . mermaids. Sounds wonderful, doesn't it? Well, it wasn't. Not for me.

When I was born, my mother wasn't ready for a baby like me. So she left. Connie was her name. She was Minerva's sister. Only ever since I was a baby, Minerva's been my Caretaker more than my aunt. She even has the necklace that matches the ring I was given at my birth. So, I always questioned her love. Was it duty? Or was it family? Here on the dead side, I realize those two things were the same. What a waste of worry.

In Fairview we have more than our fair share of legends. And my family, the Greens, figure prominently at the center of *all* the mystery. Some say it's been that way forever. That we're part of something bigger. But some say it's because Coveview, the Green family home, is too close to the island of Fortunes Cove.

The trouble started the second I took my first breath. Minerva says that I simply glowed. I was born with a shroud. Some call it a veil. A bit of skin covering my face. This isn't unusual in our family. Bronwyn was born with one. Byrd, too. Not Paddy, though. What was *unusual* was that before I could even speak, I was affecting people. My sight was strong, and it scared everyone around me. How can a little girl scare a whole family? A whole community?

History. That's how.

Because of who I was, or who everyone thought I'd grow up to become, no one wanted me—except for Minerva.

When I was sixteen, my gran, Catherine, threw me into a mental asylum. It was convenient, as we have one right there in Fairview. One of the last operating ones to this day, I think.

Minerva had to fight to get me out, and then she had to leave Coveview and rent a building in town. We lived there together, she and I. Sort of happily, I guess. We lived in the upstairs apartment and used the downstairs storefront to sell books. I love books. Old ones and new ones. So, I was content, even if no one talked to me.

I think that's why I fell so young, so hard . . . *so fast* for Jackson.

I married Jackson Whalen to run away from the mad nothingness that surrounded me. I spent hours wandering the perfect, cobblestone streets of Fairview, the place my family and ancestors called home. A place can dazzle you with its beauty, and still, you can grow to hate it. It happens that way with people too. No matter how good-looking a person is on the outside, if they have an evil hiding underneath, it seeps out, until all anyone sees is the ugly.

I wanted to love my life, my home, my family. But they didn't let me, so I found every imperfection buried under its quaint beauty and began to hate it.

Except for the sea. I could never hate the sea.

Minerva used to say, "You'd be quite beautiful if you weren't so sullen, Naomi."

I don't know about the beauty part. But I *was* restless. Trapped in a world where I was transparent to everything around me.

Some of the kids even said if you looked at me, you'd turn to stone.

No one dared to look.

It's so funny, isn't it? I spent my early years invisible, yearning to be seen, and then spent my later years trying to make myself disappear. And now? Well, you don't get more invisible than being a spirit, do you?

But Jackson *saw* me. I felt his eyes take me in. He wasn't afraid. He made me feel alive.

I was working at our bookstore when he found me.

Sweet, handsome Jackson Whalen, a young man with a whole lot of old lumber money, was a bibliophile. He told me his entire story right there over the counter in the dim bookstore. He leaned in close, and I could smell the forest on him. He put his hand over mine, and I could see our future together. I saw the biggest tree I'd ever seen, full of flowers that seemed almost prehistoric. The tree, Esther, came through and asked me to be kind to him. Asked me to follow him home. Trees are wise. Who was I to question her?

He told me he'd loved books all his life. He told me he loved the binding, the smell, the pages. And then he told me how as he grew older and traveled, he began collecting books from everywhere he went. That once he started collecting a certain sort of book, he couldn't stop until he'd found the set.

It was this compulsion that brought him from Magnolia Creek, Alabama, to the Rockwell-esque town of Fairview, Massachusetts.

Jackson was collecting witches' books of shadows, handwritten accounts of midwives and witches from the fifteenth to eighteenth century.

"So," he said, smiling at me. "Do you have one?"

I did, and it was special to me, so I didn't really want to let it go.

Trusting my instinct, and believing that Jackson was *supposed* to find me . . . that my magic drew him to Fairview to save me, I decided to show it to him.

I reached down behind my chair and brought the book out from where I kept it, safely tucked away under a stack of books on the lower shelf.

"I'm sort of . . . adding things to it," I said.

"All the better." He smiled.

He wasn't afraid of me.

"Want to get out of here and take a walk? Are you allowed?" he asked.

I laughed then. The sound shocked me. I couldn't remember laughing, not once.

"My aunt owns the place. No one comes in here anyway. Tourists. That's about it." I got off my stool and came out from around the counter, acutely aware that my long hair was tangled, and my sundress, once bright green, had faded to a really soft sage. *He'll think I'm homeless,* I thought. And then realized it didn't matter, because I was.

We closed the shop and I turned the BACK—WHEN I CHOOSE TO COME BACK—AS IF IT MATTERS sign over on the door.

"You've got some moxie in ya, girl. Now, show me around." And boy, did I give him a tour.

As we walked he told me how he'd "stumbled" on the town while looking for that book. He drove right into Fairview without a second thought. Which is odd, because there's that behemoth of an asylum that actually blocks the entire town.

You have to drive around it, in a rotary to see Fairview's beauty. But he wasn't daunted by the ominous building. Not Jackson.

We walked together along those cobblestone streets, and I watched as he gazed in amazement at the picturesque surroundings. It's nice to see something familiar through someone else's eyes.

He marveled at the things I showed him. Things that made him wonder if those books he was collecting didn't have a little bit of truth to them after all. By the end of the day, he was a true believer.

"I've met a witch! A real live witch," he said.

The rooftops of Fairview stretched out across narrow streets, circling toward larger cliffs, and all the homes, especially the large Queen Anne Victorian down by the shore—Coveview, my old home—seemed to shimmer. And the flowers, zinnias of all colors, were enormous.

"It's beautiful here, magical," he said.

"I guess," I responded softly.

"It's all a matter of perspective, right?" he asked.

I just looked at him. And wanted him to take me away.

Was it love? For Jackson there was no question. He told me that mine was the voice he'd heard in the wind but never understood until he met me. He said I filled a longing in him he never thought would be filled.

I don't think I was able to live up to that description.

Besides Minerva, I'd never known love. So I didn't think about it much. When we were settled in Alabama, I felt it. It hurts, love. I wish I'd known.

So while we sat on a large rock overlooking the waters between Fairview and Fortunes Cove, I said, "Take me away from here."

"Why would you want to leave such a place?" he asked.

"Prisons come in all shapes and sizes. I can't breathe here. How's the air in Alabama?"

"Well, it smells like fish after it rains sometimes."

"I don't care what it smells like. If I don't leave soon, I'm sure I'll get sent back there." I pointed in the direction of the asylum. "Or over there," I said, pointing to the island of Fortunes Cove.

He didn't even mention the asylum. How brave he was. Or maybe love *is* crazy.

"What's over there?" he asked instead, following my gaze across the channel to Fortunes Cove.

"No one knows. A strange island full of strange people. I suppose I belong there, only it feels . . . I don't know. Wrong. Don't you feel it when you look over there?"

"Well, I hate to tell you, but I have a misty island, too."

"You have an island?"

"Well, yes. It's part of our land. No one lives there though. Not now, anyway. Not for as long as anyone can remember. It's behind the Big House and across the creek. That's what we call my house, original, huh?"

"What's it like?"

"The Big House?"

"No, the island?"

"I don't know."

"How come?" I asked.

"Ain't never been there."

"But it's behind your house!"

"Sure is. Have you ever been over to *your* island?"

I laughed again and shook my head.

"See? It's probably better for both of us that we haven't had the pleasure of those adventures. Bad things happen to people who visit that type of land."

"And still . . . you ventured here," I said.

"Yes. The way I figure, it's all about instinct. And fate. Thank God I came. Because I found you." He asked, "Marry me?" as night fell and mermaids swam all around us. Or so Jackson liked to say when he told the tale. It made the story finer, somehow. Besides, Bronwyn and Patrick always wanted to hear more about mermaids.

So that's it. My own personal love story. And as Jackson used to say, "It's a hell of a yarn."

Minerva came with me to Alabama. Bless her. I'd have died a lot sooner if she hadn't.

The bond between us was strong. Family or caretaker, or both. My ring was a blue crescent with a ruby tucked in beside it like a dangling fiery star. And she wore her matching necklace as a sign that we were bound together. For life.

When I got to Magnolia Creek, I wanted, more than anything, to be normal. So I took off my ring, and I made Minerva put her necklace away, even though I knew it hurt her to do so. I wanted no reminders of my old life. I wanted to believe that Minerva was there with me out of love, not some magical duty.

There's so much to explain.

I get tired, flitting in and out of reality like this. It's not a bone tired (ghosts don't have bones), just tired like a wind that dies down suddenly. Out of breath.

I tried to hide the ways of my people from my beautiful babies when they were growing up, but they saw things, felt things. And Bronwyn had a touch of magic in her, so I had to answer their questions or lie. And I've never been fond of liars, especially after I became one.

"What's a caretaker, Mama?" asked Paddy once.

"Well, sweet baby, where I'm from there is this strange idea that certain people are born and connected to other people, and that it's their life's job to protect them. Take care of them . . . see? Caretaker!"

"Is it like that for everyone?" asked Bronwyn, combing out a tangled mess of hair on one of her dolls, not looking at me. She was always the one to ask the practical questions.

"No, at least I don't think so, sweet girl. Though I suppose you could call it 'soul mate' or something like that. Only it's not romantic, at least, not all the time."

This made Paddy laugh. "Imagine you and Min kissin', Mama!" he said, rolling around on the carpet next to my bed.

We all laughed. Those were still the laughing days.

What I didn't tell them was the way my family treated me. But I never forgot it and that invisibility haunts me still. You'd think, coming from a family with strange ways, that I would have been accepted fully. Lauded, even. But it didn't work that way. Turns out, I had more magic in me than anyone wanted to believe or understand.

"There's a difference between guessing what a person is think-ing and being able to predict their *exact* time of death, Naomi," said my gran. Having too much magic had hurt our family in too many ways, and she didn't like that I had, let's call them *enhanced* talents. Besides, I'd chased her daughter away. She blamed me for that, too.

"You belong over there," Gran would say, shaking a large knife as she cut stems off nettle or peeled mandrake root. She'd look out the kitchen window of Coveview over the ocean to the misty island of Fortunes Cove.

That was an insult to me, to all of us, because we all knew that crazy things happened on that island. Crazier and scarier than anything ever experienced in Fairview.

We'd seen them come and go, those people who lived there, furtive, secret, strange, sparkly residents.

Everyone in Fairview figured the island was cursed because no one who didn't *already* live there could go there.

There was no rule. Nothing like that. Just a pure, sweet sickness that you got whenever you tried to cross the sea between. So Gran telling me that I needed to live there was really just saying she'd rather never see me again.

I was such a little girl. Who does that to a little, lost girl? And why not love me regardless?

The answers to those questions took me a long time to figure out. I'm still figuring them out, I think.

But I believe I've gone on a tangent. I do that more and more lately, thoughts spinning and veering like birds in the sky, taking formation in one direction or the other. The Whalens call those kinds of thoughts "the crazy fuckalls." A crude saying really, but accurate.

Birds. Back to the birds.

In the Green family we have a lot of traditions. And one of them, my favorite of all, is that when we die our souls become birds. I was kind of excited about getting a chance to be a bird. And when the redbirds came the day they laid me in the ground, I thought they'd take my soul with them. Only . . . they didn't.

They flew away and left me here. Left me like everyone always did. Everyone but Minerva.

Even my babies left me.

Bronwyn left when she was a child. She was right in front of me, but I couldn't find her anymore. One day she was there, her eyes full of love. And the next, they were vacant. She started to hate me. Then she left again when I died. I suppose I wanted her to go, because being caught in a place where you don't belong is a special kind of hell.

Paddy left me when he realized he could count on Bronwyn more than me. And Jackson, dear sweet Jackson, he waltzed me through our happy years, only to leave me for his true love, liquor. See, my husband's addiction was, and still is, as bad as my own.

I've been watching these people I love lose pieces of themselves, bit by bit, year after year. Maybe that's why I'm lingering. Maybe I'm supposed to repair what I broke.

I don't know.

At first, when Stella and Paddy got married, I thought I was sticking around to help Stella with her impossible choice. See, she had her own mysteries and sorrows. She knew she'd die in childbirth, but her own sight had shown her two paths. She could have stayed where she'd grown up, and lived to raise Byrd. But that path meant that Byrd would be trapped in some sort of evil web Stella couldn't show me. Something so dark that she blocked it from her mind. The other path was to leave that place and search for loosely related people to help raise her daughter. But that path meant she'd die, and not get to be with Byrd at all. She was a better mother to Byrd by accepting her fate than I ever was.

When Byrd was born, and so alone . . . I thought maybe I was here to protect her. Turns out she's been more of a comfort to *me*. Figures.

Byrd is the girl I would have been if I'd had more people around than Minerva to love me.

Nothing could explain why my soul lingered—until my first baby, Bronwyn, came back home.

She'd been gone for the right amount of time. Fourteen years. Seems like an even number, only it's not. It's comprised of two sevens. It took her seven years to run away completely, and then seven years to find her way back.

At first, she looked like a beautiful, poised, grown-up woman . . . but the little, wounded blond girl, with a bright red bow in her bouncy curls, was standing next to her. Trying to get her attention. Making her whole soul tilt to one side.

She was in a prison, just like Paddy. A prison she'd created for herself.

And then I saw the magic, and was relieved, because if she could grow her talents enough to see me, I could set us both free.

Because I really thought being dead would be *way* more fun. I'm tired of this game. Maybe there's glitter in the light.

Now I just have to get there.

9

Bronwyn

Before Byrd emerged from the secret doorway, I let my hand touch Naomi's bedding, just briefly. *She died here.* And in that moment, I felt that tingle I used to feel when whatever bit of magic I *did* have would riot up to the surface.

Remembering can be like swallowing glass. Cutting you up from the inside out.

Emily Dickinson said, "Remorse is a memory awake," and I've never met anyone who'd want to wake those types of things up. *Let sleeping dogs lie. Never wake a sleeping baby.* Et cetera. Now, add a bit of "shine" to that remembering and it becomes a cinematic nightmare playing out right in front of you.

There was one big fight Jackson and I had before Naomi died. Sometimes I think if it weren't for that particular fight, I might not have left home at all. I might have stayed.

We were on one of the upstairs porches, the one we used to sleep on when the summer nights got too hot. The Big House porches are not ordinary porches. There are handwoven carpets covering white-painted, wide wooden floors. Massive tropical potted plants live out there in the summer and are moved back inside during the winter months. And ceiling fans line the bead board under the roof, bringing a constant soothing breeze. They were a sanctuary, my own personal heaven—until that fight with my father.

A huge storm was rolling in, bringing an unbearable humid heat. Naomi lazed in her rooms, and Paddy and I ran out onto the large porch and took up our usual spots. Paddy, the hammock, and I, one of the cushioned porch swings.

"You ready, Wyn? It's gonna be a big one!"

"I sure am, maybe it'll take down this whole damn house."

Jackson was walking past the porch doors and heard me.

"That what you want, sugar?"

Problem was, he wasn't drunk that day, he was lucid. And he was *mad*. And I just didn't know how to deal with a mad, sober Jackson. So I did what BitsyWyn did all the time. I fought back, only I never fought fair.

"Yessir, I do. I hope it comes and takes down this place and you and Mama with it."

That made him come right out onto the porch.

He sat next to me on the swing, and I squished myself as far away from him as I could.

Why do you suppose we do that, push ourselves away from those we love right when we need them the most? The whole damn fight could have been avoided right there if I told the truth—that I loved them both more than anything—and just sidled up next to him for the hug he wanted. But if BitsyWyn Walen was anything, it was downright stubborn.

"Go on inside, Daddy. Go on in and check on Mama. I don't need you now. Paddy don't need you. We needed you years ago."

"Don't drag me into this thing, Wyn." Paddy laughed it off, but there was a whole lot of anger all caught up in my chest and brewing up like the storm.

"Oh, here we go. You've been *so* neglected. Jaysus, sugar. You've never wanted for anything. And I love you. You know that. And your mama loves you," he said.

That was it.

"Love? Oh, please. If all this"—I made a wide circle with my arms—"if all this is love, then I don't want it! I don't want you! I don't want any of this! You are *killing* her! You're a fucking murderer!"

Lord, how we sometimes scream out our own prophesies.

"Bronwyn, quiet that vile tongue of yours or I swear to God I will rip it out, and rip it out slow," said my father through clenched teeth.

"Good! Because then I could go into town and actually have some abuse to report!"

"You'd have to bring a pad and pencil with you, as you wouldn't be able to speak." Paddy smiled, trying to get a laugh out of us.

My father grew still. Our brutal words leaving marks on both of us. So I did the only thing I knew how to do. I continued talking, knowing I was hurting him, wanting to cut him deeper than he could ever cut me.

"Ten to one you get up right after this little 'vile' speech of mine and drown your sorrows in that bourbon calling to you downstairs. But how about we have a little wager, Daddy? Tell you what: if you stay here, right here next to me, and watch the storm come in with us, I'll shut up. Forever."

Only now did I realize the trap I'd set. There was no way he wasn't going to need a drink. An alcoholic always chooses escape. But I was sixteen with a heart full of anger, and a whole world to punish.

He left, and I scooted right on back to my spot on my swing.

"Nice job," said Paddy, clapping slowly.

"Screw off. You want some, too?" I said. But I couldn't help but smile. Patrick never made me mad. He knew it. I knew it. Everyone knew it.

He laughed. "I swear, Wyn, you made the storm worse with all that crazy fuckall. Look how much darker the sky is now."

"Shut up and watch," I said.·

The storm crept in, a gangrene god's hand, pointing dead fingers at the swirling clouds. The opposite of a golden touch. More Medusa than Midas.

I closed my eyes, envisioning Magnolia Creek and all its residents.

The children slept, deaf to the trouble brewing above. The adults held each other, silently waiting. Lovers couldn't speak the words waiting on their lips.

Then, when the storm arrived, Paddy and I danced like savages on the porch as the leaves spiraled frantically, bullied by the winds.

We were different from everyone else. A stupid, brave breed.

Then we ran wildly, hollering with mad joy all the way to their house and sat there at their cozy kitchen table. Susan always had something delicious to eat. That night she'd made a big pot of minestrone soup. Steaming, and full of greens, beans, and some salt pork, it warmed my cold soul. And Grant sat too close to me and made me tingle, God love him, as we heard the news about the storm.

All the surrounding towns had a death toll but not Magnolia Creek.

"It's your mama," said Susan in a quiet, solemn voice. "She's failin' fast, and she's creating' all this stuff with her mind. I swear, I don't know if it's God or the Devil in that woman."

"Mama!" scolded Charlotte. She loved Naomi. So did Susan, but my mother had become unkind as she slid into the throes of her last big bout with opium. Susan had grown distrustful of Naomi. And Naomi had fired her from the Big House. That's how bad it got near the end.

Susan Masters. The comfort she gave me. Grant, God, Grant, so handsome. Sweet Paddy. And poor Lottie, gone forever. *I didn't even get to say goodbye.*

The remorse set in. I wanted to slap myself for being such a stupid, selfish girl. But then Byrd emerged, and before I knew it, my mother's ghost was trying to hug me, Grant's ring was back on my finger, and Byrd had offered me her hand.

Emotional whiplash, that's what it was.

"You're hurting a lot, being back here, ain't ya?" asked Byrd.

"I suppose I am."

"Well then, let's take you someplace new, okay? New and old at the same time."

"That sounds like a great plan." I smiled.

Byrd took my hand gently, and that's when it happened.

At first I thought it was sunlight coming through the windows. But it was the wrong time of day, and there were no shafts of light to make dancing, shimmering dust mites.

It was her hand. Glowing warm and bright inside mine. The two of us stared, watching the pulse grow between us.

Love, respect, trust. They all flowed from her hand to mine.

I never wanted to let go.

She held my hand tighter and looked up at me, curious and open. But she didn't let go. Instead, she led me right out of the Big House, taking me out of my past and straight into a future I didn't know I was looking for.

Her hand, soft and small in mine, pulled me down a tunnel-like path crowded over with live oaks and willow branches. A parallel rabbit hole I'd gone down often as a child.

"You know where we're goin'?" she asked.

"Sure I do. My old stomping ground."

"A place you went to feel safe, right?"

"Yes."

And right there, in the middle of what some would deem a forest, there was that familiar grouping of small cottages built for the workers who ran the sawmill. The Whalens kept them up even after there was no more work for tenants.

Most of them were one-room domiciles with kitchens and bathrooms on the outside.

"Minerva and Carter lived in that one over there since they went and got hitched." She pointed at a shack closer to the creek. "But they moved back into the Big House with me and Jackson when . . . . you know."

Fresh paint and a small garden out front told me Minerva still spent some time at her "old" place.

"She seems happier now than she did when I was small," I said.

"Don't let her fool you. She's still just as mean. Now, take off your shoes."

"Why?" I asked.

"Feet tell you a lot about a place. Sharp, soft, safe. You know."

"I don't think I want to let go of your hand, Byrd."

She let go, reaching up to touch my face. "What happened there between us? That glow? It's only ever happened once, and I'm takin' it as a sign. So I'll trust you, Aunt Wyn. That light lives inside of us now, and it ain't goin' nowhere."

She called me Wyn. I took off my shoes.

"Careful for the crawfish holes! It's been dry, and they come all the way up into the mud," she said, skipping ahead of me.

"I *did* grow up here, you know."

She turned around and walked backward as she talked, "I keep on forgettin' that! You were here before I was. But you still never saw things the same way. No one does. Maybe you will *now* though."

"I hope so," I said.

The birds were chirping in the trees. I glanced up. The leaves of the magnolias were shiny and broad. Their undersides varied from red to brown, their big pods, left over from the spring blossoms, spiked and sticky. Alien and otherworldly.

Those magnolias were more mysterious than any sort of magic. You have to love it when a tree can make seeing spirits seem normal.

"Wanna hear my favorite Christian song?" asked Byrd.

Her voice was high and beautiful, pure like the clearest water.

"All things bright and beautiful, all creatures great and small, all things wise and wonderful; the Lord God made them all."

"You religious, Byrd?"

"No, ma'am, I ain't, but I think it's important for people to have someone to look up to. Someone to make them feel all safe and cozy in their souls."

"Who helps you feel that way?"

"Jamie. But he's lost. And I can't find him."

"He's your best friend, isn't he?"

"Yeah. He's a bunch of other things, too. I suppose Jamie does that for me. Jamie's my own personal Jesus!"

Then she shrieked with laughter, running ahead of me.

That's when I saw it. The last river shack on the very edge of our property. The one Paddy and I used as our playhouse growing up. The place we ran to when we needed to escape.

She'd transformed it completely.

Byrd was already jumping up and down on the porch. "Hurry up!" she yelled.

I don't know if it was the way the sun hit the new paint or maybe it was my worn brain, overstimulated from feeling my dead mother's breath on the back of my neck, but whatever it was, Byrd had created my dream house.

"How did you do this?" I asked.

She was grinning at me. "Oh, I suppose I had a bit a help, here and there, you know, with the heavy construction. The Towners helped out, mostly."

"Did you read my mind?" I asked.

"Of course! You're a silly aunt. I couldn't just guess on this. I had to be sure. Can you predict things, too?"

"No, I mean . . . not like this. I used to be able to see a few things other people couldn't, but I haven't used that muscle in a long time."

"Maybe, because we glowed . . . the magic will grow. Then we can be magic girls together! Witches in wonderland. That sounds pretty, don't it?"

"It does. And thank you, honey, for the cottage. I can't wait to see inside."

I took in the pale red metal roof, the pristine glossy white outer walls with light purple hurricane shutters, the color of lavender flowers in full bloom. Naomi and Minerva always used to say that lavender grew better in the rocky, sandy soil up north. Ben did too, when I'd try to grow it on our fertile land in New York State. He'd say, "Lavender's for luck. That's why it grows in the places where it shouldn't, and mostly when you're not paying attention."

Bits of butter-colored, gingerbread trim clung to the small peaks and brackets. And the porch stood solid, coated in a deep, shiny Caribbean blue. I came up the stairs, barefoot, and remembered my dream from the plane. Blue floor. Bare feet.

I'd seen my future. But where was the snake?

"Go on in!" she said, full of excitement. "See it on your own. I'll be right here on the porch with Dolores. She won't come inside yet, not until she knows you. She's a nervous Nelly."

Byrd had created a doll's house for me. I'm sure she knew well the part in *Tom Sawyer* where he got all his friends to paint the fence. I could envision her with a broad smile, sitting up in the plum trees eating one after another while she watched her vision unfold. All the free construction happening while she spat pits on the ground and made her face purple.

As I walked into the newly renovated cottage, the open floor plan and sea breeze colors made me feel right at home.

I wandered over to an old record player and found one of my favorite albums waiting for me. John Coltrane.

As I put it on, and the first strains floated out into the Alabama heat, my mind drifted to Ben's hands. I closed my eyes, and I could almost feel them on me . . .

My eyes popped open in alarm.

She was *still* reading my mind.

"Miss Byrd, you get outta my head! Some things are private!"
I called with only the hint of a smile in my voice.

Byrd came in from the porch, her arms crossed in front of her
chest. She looked ready for a scolding. Dolores refused to follow
her. She sat there whining after Byrd instead.

"Quiet, Dolores," she hushed, and her dog listened quick, lying down after a final whine. Then she turned back to me. "Sex
ain't private. It belongs to everyone, Aunt Wyn. And besides, I
think it's romantic. I can't wait till I'm old enough to do those
things."

I could tell she was scared. She didn't know how I was going
to react. And to be honest, I didn't know *how* to react. I'm not a
mother. So I did what my heart told me to.

I held out my arms and she ran right into them. I picked her
up and carried her onto the porch, stepping over Dolores, hoping we might be able to catch a breeze. I sat us down on a cushioned wicker love seat, and she curled up in my lap just like a
cat. The relief flooded out of her like an electric current.

"Why are you so all fired up to be grown, honey?" I asked,
rocking her a little and breathing in her smell.

"I don't know," said Byrd in a whisper that came from deep
inside. "I just don't know, Aunt Wyn."

I rocked her some more, looking out over the wide porch
railings at Belladonna Bay.

"I hear your mama, Stella, had magic in her, too." I said.

"I don't want to talk about her."

"Why not? I'd love to know more about her."

"She died when I was born, remember?"

I fell silent then. The last thing I wanted to do was bring up the same sort of sorrow inside of her that was lurking inside me. *It doesn't matter, it's already there,* said a voice in my head, one I thought I recognized.

"Aunt Wyn?" she asked.

"Hmm?"

"What does it feel like to be in love?"

"That's a hard question to answer," I said, relieved that she'd changed the subject.

"Nope. I don't think so. It's just hard for you to think on it," she said.

"Well, let's see if I can explain it to you. But keep in mind it's different for everyone. And each love is different, like a house with all sorts of rooms. Like the Big House."

"Each love? How many times you been in love?" she asked, surprised.

I laughed a little. Surprise on the face of someone so clever, no matter how young, is always funny.

"Twice," I said. "But there are a lot of people who think they fall in love way more than that. And, because you asked before . . . sex and love are *not* the same thing."

"Okay, so tell me about these two loves of yours. How do they feel?"

"One was a long time ago, Byrd. And it was . . . furious. Not angry. Just full of fire. I always felt like I was on fire when he was around. Like it burned inside me, and then when he got close enough, the burning went away. If that means anything to such a bit of a thing like you."

Her head popped up. "I'm not a bit of a thing," she said.

"Fine, maybe you're not," I agreed.

She leaned her head against my shoulder again. "So, that was the first love. What was the second like, if it's so different?"

"The second? Well, that's Ben, the man I live with in New York, and it's a wonderful love. Safe. Strong. He makes me feel . . ."

"Whole?"

"No . . . more like—"

"The center of his world?"

"No, Byrd, stop! Let me think . . . he makes me feel . . . different. Less like the person I used to be. I like that."

"I sure as hell don't," she said.

"Why not?" I laughed. "And don't curse, Byrd. It's not ladylike."

She hopped off my lap and leaned against the porch railing.

"Why not? You do. Anyway, seems to me you were fine. I mean, why change who you are? It's kinda sad."

"You didn't know me, Byrd. I was mean and spoiled. I hurt a lot of people. Especially the ones I loved."

"That still don't mean you had to go and change everything. You coulda fixed the person you already were."

"I guess," I said, and closed my eyes, sinking into those soft cushions.

"Who was the person you loved first? Was he from around here?" she asked.

"Grant. Grant Masters," I said.

"No! No, you did not! I can't even believe it. I wish more than anything I could tell Jamie! He'd have a cow! He don't like Grant much."

"Why not? Grant's his uncle, he should love him. I'm sure they've gone out fishing and hunting together for years."

"Not really—and Aunt Wyn? It's a *loooong* story," she said, and then hesitated before asking her next question, "Are you sad? About your friend? I know Lottie was your best friend. Minerva and my daddy told me stories. Seems like you and me are in the same boat."

"Well, I hadn't seen her in a long time, Byrd. But yeah. I *am* sad. And worried about your daddy. I know he didn't do what everyone says he did."

"You're gonna get sadder, just prepare yourself," she said, crawling back into my lap.

"What do *you* think happened to Charlotte and Jamie?" I asked.

"I don't know. Really I don't. I wish I did. I only know one thing."

"What's that?"

"I agree with you. I know for sure my daddy didn't do it. He couldn't kill nobody. He even throws the fish he catches back into the Gulf when he goes out with Carter."

I smiled. Even when we were little, Paddy did that. He had a soft side to him. He'd pull my hair on purpose, and when I cried, he'd hug me as if someone else had done it.

"So, why do you think he got blamed for it, Byrd?" I asked, trying to smooth back her wild hair from her face.

"Can I tell you a secret? I know you'll find out sooner than later anyhow. But I'd rather you hear it from me," she said.

"Of course! You can tell me anything."

"He thinks I did it," she said quietly.

"Who thinks you did what?" I asked.

She jumped out of my lap again and stomped away from me. "Why are you being so *obtuse*? That's my new favorite word, by the way. I look them up every day in the dictionary. And if you look next to *obtuse* in the dictionary you'd—"

"See a picture of me. Yes, I know the joke, Byrd. But I still don't know what you're talking about or why you're so mad."

She ran down the stairs, off the porch, and back up the path. "I don't even care! You'll find out soon. Go'n visit my daddy. He'll tell you!" she yelled before Dolores got up and chased after her. "We hold these truths to be self-evident," I heard her cry as she ran away from me.

Truth was I didn't really know the circumstances of Paddy's arrest, I only knew what my family told me—*nothing.*

My emotional compass was spinning too fast. I'd have to find everything out for myself.

Carter had already brought my bags to the cottage. They were stacked neatly in the bedroom with a little Post-it note stuck to the top.

"Stick is the new sheriff here. Start with him."

Good for you, Stick, I thought. He'd been a strange teenager, nice though, and he'd always wanted to follow in his father's footsteps. His whole life had been about becoming sheriff one day, and now he was.

"Bless your heart, Carter, for pointing me in the obvious direction," I said out loud, before washing my face with cool, clean water and putting on a white sundress. I pulled my camera back on over my head and walked up the path to the Big House driveway, and then straight up the drive until I hit Main Street.

It was damn hot. I'd forgotten how two blocks could feel like ten. The sheriff's office was a storefront on Main Street, and the closer I got, the more I hoped Stick had updated the place with air-conditioning.

"Hey! Wyn!" Stick called out, hopping over the wide front counter to give me a big hug when I arrived. "Carter said you were comin', but I think I only half-believed him. How you doin', girl! Damn, you look good."

"Forget about me, look at you! I'm glad to see you made your dream come true. All those years of pretending to be Dudley Do-Right paid off. And you haven't changed a bit, Stick. Or should I call you Sheriff?"

He was just as I remembered him. Right down to the way he scratched his belly when he was in between sentences. He'd grown into his hawklike face with small eyes and a big nose. He could even be thought handsome, if you looked real hard.

"I'm only Sheriff when people are in trouble or in need of help. Other than that, I'm Stick. It's the best way for me to figure out what hat I gotta put on, so to speak. So who are you here to see? Stick or the sheriff?"

"I suppose I'm here to see the sheriff, but it *is* really good to see Stick, too."

"Well, word on the street says you're gonna stay around for a while, so you and Stick can go out for a drink and catch up. Right now the sheriff is proud to be at your service."

He bowed, and we both laughed as he hopped back over the counter.

"You have a little gate there, you know."

"Where's the fun in that?" he said. Same old Stick.

"I'm assuming you're here about your brother."

"What else would I be here for?"

"Well, I gotta tell you, it's been downright interesting around here lately. I'm about drown'n in calls and reports about things goin' missing. More every day. Strange things. Odd is what it is. Downright odd. And it's not only things goin' missing. There's been strange lights over Belladonna. This job used to be a piece of cake. But now with your brother . . . I mean, excuse me, Wyn. With the murders and now with this crazy stuff going on, I don't even know what to think anymore."

"Well, I could help, why not deputize me? I'd like to go over to the Masters and see the crime scene. Lottie was still living there, right? I remember Jackson telling me that she stayed there after Jamie was born." I didn't realize how much I needed to see where Lottie spent her last hours until I said it.

"Yep. Lottie never strayed too far from home. And, man, I wish I could deputize you, only I'm pretty sure that stuff only happens on the 'boob tube,' as your mama used to call it. All those old westerns Paddy and I used to watch on Sundays over there with the Masters, 'cause with all your money, you Whalens didn't have no TV."

He got quiet for a few seconds and looked past me into a distant, simpler time. Then he cleared his throat. "But you *can* go on over there, I just have to go with you. Those state cops are all finished, but we still haven't found the murder weapon, or Jamie for that matter. I'm at a loss. Have been for a while. Not one clue about where to find Jamie's body."

"Are you sure there's a body to find?"

"Damn sure. There was just too much of his blood. He'd have to be dead."

"What does Paddy say?"

"What do you mean?"

"Well, did Paddy give you any information about it?"

"How could he? He don't know nothin'—he didn't do this damn thing."

I stood very still, listening to the air conditioner blow and rattle in the window next to his desk.

"Stick, if you don't think he did it, why the hell did you arrest him?"

" 'Cause he confessed. But I don't care, I don't believe him. I think he's coverin' for someone."

"You always had clouded judgment when it came to my brother, Stick. Thinkin' he was more than what he was. He was just a teenage boy, like you. I gotta see him. Like, today. Can you make that happen?"

"I sure can, but not today. It's already too late for you to get to Angola."

"Will he even want to see me?" I asked quietly.

"Shit, girl, he's been askin' for ya."

My heart stopped. My poor Paddy.

"Stick?" I asked,

"Yes?" He leaned over the counter like we were still all of sixteen and he was trying for a kiss.

I flicked his big sheriff star with my finger.

"Who do you think he's covering for?"

He straightened up and looked away from me for a long time before saying, "Hell if I know."

And then I realized I'd been gone too long. I didn't know anything. Not now. Fourteen years is a long time. I hadn't even talked to anyone except Jackson. And he never said a word to me about it. I was, as Byrd said, "New here."

If I'd stayed in Magnolia Creek, I'd know who he was covering for. I never would have let him confess. The whole thing probably wouldn't have happened in the first place.

I needed to get to that house and see some things up close for myself. I had to make this whole thing right because in so many ways it was revealing itself as being my fault.

All four lines on his phone started ringing at once.

"You want to be my secretary, too?" he asked.

"Nope."

"Okay, look, if you keep it quiet, I'll let you go on over to the Masters' house without me. Then, first chance I get, I'll call Angola and make some arrangements for you to see Paddy."

"Thank you so much, Stick. Also . . . one more thing,"

"Anything, Wyn."

"Where's Grant?"

I'd been thinking about him since Jackson called me home. Then Byrd got me thinking, too. But I hadn't let myself *really* wonder about him or even remember specific things. Saying his name, here with Stick . . . who used to ride with us and tag along . . . well, it's a damn shame the things we allow ourselves to forget.

The night Naomi died, after I'd witnessed Minerva's ritual, I'd run for my sanity all the way to his house, appearing like a ghost out of nowhere in my white nightgown. Somehow or other he was on the porch waiting, and without saying a word we took his boat out for a midnight ride in the bay.

I gave myself to him that night. We'd been going together forever, but we'd never let it get that far.

And then I ran away. I told him I was leaving just as soon as Naomi was buried. And his words that night came flooding back.

I love you, Wyn. I ain't never loved anyone as much as I love you.
Oh God . . . please don't go. Don't leave me here. Can't I come? I've
got gypsy legs . . . I can come with you. We'll be like Bonnie and Clyde
only we won't get ourselves shot . . . I'll be different if you leave. You'll
take my soul with you, girl . . . they might as well bury me. I'll be
dead.

I must have looked dreamy eyed and lost in thought because
a big, gossipy smile woke up Stick's worried, overstressed face.
"You still interested in him?"

"What? Like, love interest?" I asked.

"Well, you two were . . . you know." Stick blushed. The
phone broke through again.

"Yeah, I know. Of course not. I'm engaged. See?" I showed
him my ring.

"Congratulations," he said, distracted. He began trying to put
what sounded like the whole damn town on hold.

"But really, where is he? I don't feel like running into him
right now."

"Sheriff's office. Hold, please. . . . Not to worry, he ain't around
here no more. I'll tell you what . . ."

An odd mix of relief and disappointment washed over me.

He grabbed a set of keys and threw them at me. "You go
searchin', take some of them pictures you're so famous for, and
we'll talk about all this other stuff later, okay? And call me if
you find anything. Here's my card. All my numbers, home and
office are there. And don't tell no one I let you go there alone.
Swear it."

"I swear it," I said and left the office in search of answers.

Grant and Charlotte Masters weren't really brother and sister. Though they were raised that way. Susan Masters had lost her husband, Kenny, right after Lottie was born. A boating accident near Belladonna Bay, *too* close some think. Kenny'd been livin' with a woman before he met Susan. And that woman had taken off, leaving nothing but her son, Grant, and a note saying she'd never be back. So Ken raised Grant like his own for a whole year before he married Susan.

Because Susan was the cook at the Big House, and because of her friendship with Naomi, the four of us kids were thrown together young and stayed that way. When we were little, we played mostly at the Big House. But then Grant and I started to like each other a little too much, and—that's all she wrote. Naomi wouldn't have any of it. No more visits from the Masters. She cut off Susan entirely. And even though she'd gotten sicker, barely leaving her rooms by that point, she made it clear to Jackson and Minerva that Grant and Lottie weren't welcome.

Susan got sick right around the same time that Naomi fell into her deepest bout with opium. It was so deep that she couldn't get over her own, self-imposed illness to help Susan out with her cancer. To be her friend again. The first few years I was gone, that was the memory that made me the most angry. How selfish my mother had been.

Nothing could stop the friendship between us kids, though. And Susan still wanted us around, so we simply went over to the Masters' house instead. Naomi hadn't thought through her rules very well. Her intention, as always, was to keep us close to her. Her actions pushed us away.

I was thinking so much I passed their street and kept walking straight down Main. When I realized where I was, I had to backtrack two blocks. The Masters lived on Oak Street, second house on the left. A pretty, old Southern cottage. Whitewashed with a proper porch and a picket fence. The outside looked just the same as it did the day I left.

◊

I stood in front of it, snapping photos. *Click, click.*

"It isn't only trouble that comes up behind you, Mama, it's sorrow, too," I said as I walked under the yellow tape that half dipped between two oaks in the front yard.

The tape was old and frayed. I couldn't figure out if Stick was really still investigating a closed case, or if he was a lazy sheriff.

When I opened the front door, I put my camera up to my eyes. A shield between me and the reality of Lottie's death.

Click, click. That house. Small . . . tiny even. One floor, with a peaked attic roof where a circular window let the heat out in the summertime. Two bedrooms only. A kitchen and a living room. That was it. But it held a lot of memories. Too many. And now it was the place that stole the life of two of the people I loved with all my heart.

I'd never get to tell Lottie how much I missed her. How sorry I was that I wasn't around when Jamie was born. I felt dizzy for a second, so I sat down on a chair next to the small entry table.

I looked around. If those walls could talk. There was tape around the kitchen. *So that's where Charlotte and Jamie'd been killed,*

I wasn't ready for that yet. Violence in places you don't associate with yourself is one thing. Violence in a house that embodies your own childhood is another. I got up and walked across the living room instead, to the side hall where the bedrooms branched off. *Click, click.* I walked into Lottie's old room first, but it obviously belonged to Jamie now because it was all blue. There were no toys, and the bed was made. It was a plain room with very little personality; Charlotte had been a messy girl, but she'd obviously stepped up and become more like Susan when she became a mama herself.

I went into Susan's room next. The room that held a thousand stories and a thousand more hairpins, bows, and curling rods. *Click, click, click, click.*

It belonged to Charlotte now. There was less . . . I don't know . . . just less. Less clutter. Less character. Susan always had fresh-cut flowers, even in the green season, but there weren't any vases moldering away in Charlotte's room. And Susan always had a dressing table, messy with pots and potions of all kinds of beauty remedies. Charlotte had the same dressing table, but all it held was a thick layer of dust. She never liked all that fancy stuff.

Sitting on Charlotte's unmade bed, I thought about what a bad detective I made. I didn't even know what I was looking for, and I couldn't even bring myself to poke my head into the kitchen.

So I went back into the living room *(click, click)* where I noticed, next to the telephone on a small table by the worn-out, green velvet sofa, there was a light blinking on the answering machine.

They would have checked it, right?

I know I should have called Stick before I hit Play . . . or at least put on gloves or something. But I couldn't help it.

I pressed Play.

"Lottie?" a voice I knew well, now choked with grief. "Lottie, I know you ain't there. . . . I was callin' to hear your voice and Jamie's too, how he yells in the background? And I wasn't gonna leave a message, 'cause it's silly, right? To leave a message on the phone for someone who's dead and buried. But, Lottie? I miss you. And I'm sorry about that thing with Jamie. And most of all? I'm so damn sorry for that fight we had. I mean, shit. What kind of a brother was I to you? What kind of a man was I? I'm just . . . sorry. I never meant to . . . it was an accident. Oh, God . . . I'm sorry—" The voice went silent abruptly.

Grant.

It sounded like it took him two or three times to hang up the receiver. *His hands were shaking. And the police hadn't checked it because the call was new. It was dated right there in the answering machine message. He'd called weeks after her death.*

"Grant Masters, what have you done?" I asked the haunted walls. Curious and terrible ideas swirled through my mind.

It was time. I stepped into the kitchen. There were still marks and little tags here and there on the floor and counters. It was a small kitchen but one that always simmered with love and good things to eat. Now it was stuffy and all closed up in the heat and lingering violence. I put my camera up to my face again so I could look toward the spot on the floor I'd been avoiding.

A shadow, quick and deliberate, moved in front of the lens. *Click.* I pulled the camera away.

"Stick?" No one was there. I stood very still and thought of Byrd and her ghosts.

"Lottie?" I whispered.

I saw a shadow on the stairs . . .

Nothing.

"Don't be stupid," I said, and focused my camera at the floor. There wasn't any blood. Just a stain. A very large stain on the linoleum.

I felt a tickle at the back of my throat and began to cough, but the words "Find him" came out instead. "Find him? Where the hell did that come from? Okay, I'm done," I said to the house as I left, quickly locking the front door behind me.

I thought about going back to the sheriff's office to leave the keys and tell Stick about the message, but hell, everyone had already screwed everything up. I'd figure it out on my own.

I didn't want to implicate Grant if I didn't have to. Could those hands that once brought me closer to heaven than I'd ever been be the hands of a murderer?

I didn't go back to the Big House but straight to my little oasis of comfort Byrd had created.

She was waiting for me. Playing music on my record player. On her bare tiptoes and, if it was possible, dirtier than she was when I left.

"Jolene" was playing and Byrd had her eyes closed, her head bobbing back and forth. She sang quietly along with the words she knew and hummed the rest.

"I love that song," I said.

She opened her eyes and slowly, like a fox, walked toward me.

"I know, that's why it's sittin' there in your collection."

"You still mad at me?" I asked.

"You can't get mad at people you lo—care about. Don't you know that? We can have a spat every now and again, but then? It's over. That's what family does, right?"

I didn't have the heart to tell her that she was probably right, only that wasn't the way it worked in my own mind when I was younger. No one held a grudge like BitsyWyn Whalen.

Like Jackson used to say, "Right don't mean shit, not if everyone around you is bent on bein' wrong."

"How about this?" I put on some Frank Sinatra and "Fly Me to the Moon" came crooning out all around us. It made me feel lighter than I had all day. Not to mention, I was floating a bit on her unsaid word. *She loves me,* I thought as I walked back out onto the porch with Byrd at my heels. Dolores still wouldn't come inside but was sitting at the edge of the creek bed staring over at Belladonna Bay.

"I went to Jamie's house today," I said. "This music reminds me of Susan, Jamie's grandma he never met."

"I know," she said.

"You'll have to stop playing around in my mind sooner or later, young lady," I said.

"You don't have to worry about that," she said. "Soon enough I won't be able to see nothin' in you at all."

The heat was getting so oppressive; there was nowhere to escape it. But outside was better because there was the slightest breeze from off the creek. The mist, for all its troublesome ways, held a coolness about it that helped out on these desperate hot days.

The music coming out through the windows was muted and scratchy, like in an old black-and-white movie. I sat down on one of the many wicker chairs Byrd had acquired for my little house. Guess we were supposed to have a lot of company. But she stood right in front of me with her arms crossed, murmuring that damn Declaration of Independence through her teeth. It would have been haunting, if it wasn't so funny.

"Are you nervous, honey?" I asked.

"Plenty," she said.

"Why?"

She didn't answer me. Just paced a little "We hold these truths . . ."

"I'd still like to know why you said I was obtuse," I said, hoping to get at what was bothering her the most, at the same time as I knew she was living in a world of stress. It would be moment by moment with Byrd, as it would be with me. It was gathering, like a storm.

She stopped her murmuring and looked at me with softer, pleading eyes.

"What is it, Byrd?" I asked.

And I could feel her about to tell me, but that's when those guests Byrd was expecting showed up.

"Hey there, ladies! So much pretty in one place it should be *illegal!*"

Jackson, with Minerva and Carter in tow, came striding toward the cottage, one hand holding a pitcher of what looked to be his famous lemonade and the other holding a cigar. Carter followed with a picnic basket and Minerva with a tray.

Byrd moved my feet from the small trunk I'd been using as a footrest and pulled out a bottle of bourbon and a bowl of ice.

"Well, my goodness, you don't leave much to chance, do you, Miss Byrd?

She rolled her eyes at me.

"Let the games begin," she said, then whispered, "Don't tell Minny about our glow, okay? I want to keep it safe here in my heart for a little while. You can tell them tomorrow if you want."

"You got it, kiddo," I said.

"Hey, Minerva," I called out, "I sure hope you have some dinner with you, I'm starving."

"Of course I do. What kind of homecoming would it be without some of your favorite things?" she said as she came up the steps, placed the tray on the table next to me, and gave me a hug.

Layers and layers of deep-fried green tomatoes covered in fresh picked crawfish stared up at me. Minerva always tossed the crawfish with some lime juice and some salt. Southern man's lobster. I'd missed the food down here. I never even ate "soul food" up north. It's a fake mess of a thing. Maybe it has something to do with the cooking of it. Like, you have to have high humidity and a certain kind of sarcasm to make it come out *just* right.

Carter began unpacking the picnic basket, setting out big, thick biscuits, flaky and buttery, a bowl of fresh watermelon sliced up and waiting for the sea salt we'd sprinkle over it before eating, and a container of ham, baked especially for me, because I loved Jackson's bourbon-glazed ham when I was little. And a little taste of Fairview too, a nettle salad with mulberry vinaigrette. "Nettles are good for the skin and hair and any type of stomach issues," Minerva used to tell us. The best thing of all was at the bottom of that basket: a tin of Italian cookies glazed with lemon icing and sprinkled with little tiny multicolored sprinkles.

"Those are mine, Aunt Wyn. Don't even touch 'em," said Byrd.

"Stella's recipe. Minny here makes a lot of that food for Byrd. Reminds me of Susan," said Jackson.

"Made ya a fat old drunk, too," said Byrd.

I didn't want to think about things like never meeting Stella, never cooking with her, not even sending a card when Byrd was born. Not being part of Paddy and Stella's wedding, their life.

"Now, sugar," began Jackson, standing at the bottom of the porch steps looking like a preacher about to give a sermon. "Let's get some awkward business out of the way so we can all have a pleasant evenin'. I'm sure you have a lot on your mind and a lot of questions to ask. But not tonight. Tonight oughta be about getting reacquainted, agreed?"

"Agreed," I said.

He nodded with appreciation, and then turned to Byrd. "Byrd! You did a fine job on this ol' shack!"

"You mean she did a fine job coaxing people to help her with it," scoffed Minerva.

"Don't be bitter, Min . . . just because you never thought to paint the floors blue in your old abode," said Jackson.

Their bickering made me smile. They'd always fought. It's something I learned from them. That you could fight and say horrible things and still stay friends. Not that I ever made any friends, not once I moved away. But it always helped with my relationship with Ben. And I always thought it was strange, because those are the things you're supposed to learn from your mother and father. Not your father and your great-aunt/housekeeper/lady-in-waiting. But that's life in an old Southern mansion. Everything's topsy-turvy and right-side up, all at the same time.

Jackson sauntered up the porch steps and settled down into a wide wicker chair across from me, as we all dug into the food Carter and Minerva had laid out.

Sometimes home can live squarely in the taste buds. The salty ham and juicy watermelon. The bursting, perfectly crisp outside of the fried tomatoes. The sweet meat of the crawfish with the bitter lime. I made a sandwich, quickly putting ham and a fried tomato on it. Good food makes people quiet, so after a minute or so Jackson broke the silence. He never did like the quiet. "So," he said, pouring himself a glass of bourbon, "how are you settlin' in, sugar?"

"Well, how could I not love it here? Our Byrd put so much work into this place."

Jackson smiled and then tipped the bottle of bourbon into Byrd's lemonade. I made a face at him.

"What?" he asked, his eyes getting big with laughter.

"Nothing. She's a little young, isn't she?" I couldn't help but let my own smile escape.

Jackson lit his cigar with a grace that comes from years of experience. He used to say, "It's an art form, lightin' a cigar. Separates the men from the boys." And Byrd sipped her drink while Minerva fussed over her. Carter stayed off to the side. Not drinking. Not eating. Just staring off toward Belladonna Bay.

Who is this man? Warm and then cold. Comforting and then distant.

"You were younger than that when I introduced you to the amber heaven," continued Jackson. "Besides, Minerva here told me about your upcoming nuptials. It deserves a toast, don't you think?"

Ben. I'd forgotten to tell him about Ben.

"I suppose you're right," I said, pouring myself a drink.

We all held up our glasses. And Carter walked over and picked up an empty glass to fill.

"To my wayward daughter and her upcoming marriage to a man I've never met," said Jackson.

I sidestepped his sarcasm and took a sip. The bourbon went down with a slow burn as the smoke circled our heads, and all of a sudden—I was home.

"Now tell me, what is the man's name, this man you plan to marry?"

"Ben. His name is Ben Mason," I said.

Minerva dropped her glass.

"You all right, Min?" asked Carter who was quickly at her side.

"Fine," she said.

She was looking at me and about to say something but stopped and poured herself another drink.

Jackson gave his cigar to Byrd and she took a big puff.

"My Lord," I said. "Does this child know no boundaries?"

"I ain't never met a rule I didn't wanna break, Aunt Wyn," she said, a giggle pouring out of her.

"You know, Byrd, drinking and smoking before you're old enough isn't a good thing. The smoking will stunt your growth. Seems to me that's the last thing you'd want to do," I said.

"Didn't hurt you none, sugar," said Jackson, full-on laughing now.

I knew they were trying to startle me, to bring out the uptight Yankee they knew I'd become. But I wasn't biting.

"Suit yourselves," I said, moving to a porch swing and sinking deep into the pillows. I watched the sun try to set through the stormy clouds that were brewing to the south over Belladonna Bay. Even the sick, sweet feeling that island swelled up in me was comforting.

"You've been awful quiet, Minerva," I said. "Kind of like your tight-lipped, silver-haired husband over there." Carter had gone down the porch steps and was looking toward the sky again.

"Well, I can't control these two, and I don't want to. And you leave my Carter out of this. He's been nothing but good for this entire family," she said, leaning against the porch railing, sipping on her lemonade. I could tell she was thinking, and that meant things were about to get serious. Minerva had always been so serious. "You spent a lot of time running, Bronwyn. It's time you settle down, don't you think?" she asked.

"She's BitsyWyn again. Not Bronwyn anymore," said Byrd with her mouth full.

"Hush, Byrd. And don't talk with your mouth full. Jackson and Paddy never did teach you no manners," said Carter.

I took another sip of bourbon and felt the familiar warmth. Glowing hands, crime scenes, memories coming at me every which way. I'd need more than one drink, for sure.

"Well, I don't know if I've become BitsyWyn again, " I said, throwing a wink to Byrd, "but I have to admit, I'm more comfortable than I've been in a long time. At home in my skin. But no matter what I do next, I want to help Paddy. He didn't kill anyone. I know it."

"Now, didn't you just agree that we wouldn't talk about nothin' serious tonight?" asked Jackson.

"We have to talk about it, Jackson. It's important. It's why I'm here."

Jackson pounded on the trunk with his fist, shaking the dishes.

"*No!* You are not here for that. You are here for Byrd. And she don't need to hear about this bullshit. She's heard and lived through enough."

My father was never this insistent about anything. He was hiding something. Carter, too.

"If it's about my daddy, my ears are wide-open, Jackson," Byrd said.

I was quiet for a moment.

"He didn't do it. I know he didn't. And I've only been home, what? Six hours? It's a damn shame that I already know more about this case than any of you."

"Of course he didn't do it," said Minerva with conviction.

"Look, Wyn, we don't believe he did it, but we can't forget he confessed," continued Jackson.

"Then why's he in prison?" I asked, barreling on.

"Lord, Wyn, you can be thick sometimes," said Jackson.

"How do you mean?"

"Look, girl. I did everything I could for that boy. I made sure he had the best lawyers. He fired them. The only thing he'd accept from me was my petition to keep him close. He's up there at Angola. He hasn't let us visit yet, though. Well, Carter. He'll see Carter." There was some bitterness there. But Jackson had to understand by now that he wasn't ever going to win a Father of the Year award.

"See, sugar," he continued, "I think he *wants* to be there."

"That's the most ridiculous thing I've ever heard," I said. "Why on earth would he *want* to be in prison?"

"Maybe you should ask him," Carter interrupted, his voice booming over mine.

If we were up north, I'd be able to speak my mind. Stop everyone and make sure I was heard. But down here? There's a different rhythm to conversations entirely and that extends to declarations.

"Stick rang me up," continued Carter, quieter this time. "Said you were goin' up to Angola. Maybe Paddy'll listen to you. And until then, it seems to me that there ain't nothin' more to discuss."

I liked and didn't like that he felt so comfortable with me. And I had to remind myself that he was more of a member of the family than I was. It had been my choice to leave.

The clouds grew dark as the thunder rolled in low and the breeze fell on us in cool waves. The magnolia and oak leaves rustled together, making a sound so loud you couldn't tell where the whispering leaves left off and the now pouring rain began.

Byrd mimicked Jackson, walking behind him as he went to draw down the bamboo shades so we could continue our drinking on the porch.

"Ain't gonna be too bad," said Jackson. "And we sure do need the rain, don't we, Carter?"

"Sure do," he replied.

These early evening summer storms always reminded me of Grant. Grant had been the most handsome boy in Magnolia Creek, with his dark hair and deep blue eyes, different than Charlotte's and different than mine. Almost violet. "Indigo eyes," I used to call them.

Everyone always sort of figured Grant and I would end up together, and we did. Me and Grant. Paddy and Charlotte.

We'd all drive up and down the Alabama coast in Grant's beat-up pickup truck that he'd souped up so it went extra fast. And we'd feel free. I'd sit up front next to Grant, with Paddy and Charlotte wilding in the flatbed. They'd stand against the wind, yelling at other cars and falling into each other's arms when we'd hit a pothole. Then they'd make out until Grant and I made jokes about them running out of air.

All Grant and I wanted was to go *faster.*

My bare feet on the dashboard, his hand on my thigh.

Faster, I'd whisper into the wind, and Grant, who found my death wish so sexy, would grip my thigh as he drove faster and faster until I thought we might break the sound barrier.

We'd always end up three hours west, in New Orleans. Or at the Beer Cave in Gulf Shores. Stir up trouble and laugh all the way home. One time we made a five-hour drive to the Florida panhandle, ending up in Apalachicola and eating oysters by the dozens. There was nothing better. Nothing felt more real or alive than the ocean in our mouths, and the silver sun setting low. I'd forgotten.

How could things have gone so far off track for all the people I loved?

I'd go see Paddy in prison and ask him for myself. And he'd tell me the truth. He'd tell me everything.

My broken family talked until the rain stopped and the velvet night descended. We talked about Jackson's new hydroponic farm. About Ben, and how we met. About Minerva's marriage. About Byrd's premonitions. And then, when the crickets and cicadas got so loud we could barely hear each other talk, Byrd pointed up into the sky.

"Look, Jackson, there it is again!"

A sort of aurora borealis hovered over the entire island of Belladonna Bay.

"Maybe it's sulfur," I said.

"Don't know what it is, damn miasma. Always making something happen this way or that," said Jackson.

"Had some specialists come by to look at it, but no one wants to cross that damn mist. Tried payin' a fortune to no avail," said Carter.

"It started the night of the murder. The night my Jamie went missing," Byrd added.

Jackson slapped both his knees and got up. "I ain't in no kind of mood to go back over any of that. You ready to git on back home, Byrd?"

"Look at him," said Minerva, "Just assuming we'd be ready to go at the exact same moment he is . . . the nerve."

They laughed together. It was nice, watching them. They were like two peas in a pod. When I was little the two got along, but they always fought over Naomi. What was better for her, what she should or shouldn't be doing.

They all walked off the porch together. Jackson, weaving a bit from too much bourbon, was held solidly between Carter and Minerva. But Byrd hid behind me.

"You coming with us, Byrd?" called Minerva as they left.

"Can I stay with you?" she whispered to me, tugging on my dress.

"Of course!" I said, thrilled.

"I ain't going nowhere with you old coots. I'm stayin' here with my *aunt*," Byrd cried out after them. That aunt came out sounding like "ant" and made me want to hug my brother. Byrd was so much like him in so many ways, but it was her voice, her accent that was just like his. The little girl version.

"Suit yourself, missy," said Jackson as all three disappeared into the night.

Me and Byrd stayed there, quiet, looking up at the night sky.

"I like the dark," she said. "Ain't it just like a big blue blanket wrappin' us up with comfort?"

"That's something my mama used to say," I said.

"I'd like to hear her voice. She's pretty. Was her voice pretty, too?"

My heart broke a little, trying to conjure up Naomi's voice.

"Sure was," I said.

"You don't mind, right? If I stay?" asked Byrd.

We both knew she meant for as long as I was there.

"Of course I don't mind. It feels right," I said, and I walked her into the house. "How about a bath?" I asked her.

"No way!" she shouted. I was a little drunk and too tired to fight. So I did the best I could to wash her face and let her use my toothbrush (which she looked at as if it were an artifact from another world), and then tucked her in to my bed. She quickly fell asleep while I read to her from *The Little Prince*.

I wondered, as I drifted off to sleep, why I hadn't tried to get a hold of Stick by any means possible to tell him about the message on Lottie's machine. Or why I hadn't told Jackson.

Ben always talked about the eightfold path. How the first path was all about uncovering what was real, peeling back the layers of yourself to discover your truth. I could have forced the conversation, but I didn't. Because in my heart I didn't want it to be Grant, either. God, I didn't want him to be the killer. How many sins was I supposed to carry on my shoulders?

That night, with a guilty heart, I had the first of what would be three dreams of Charlotte. It started like a memory but ended with a secret.

〉

The last time I saw Charlotte was the day I left. The same day I watched my mother get lowered into the ground. She didn't come to Naomi's funeral, so I stopped by on my way out of town.

I knew why she stayed away. Because if there was one person I knew better than anyone else, it was Charlotte.

She couldn't say goodbye to Naomi because she loved her. And she couldn't see Paddy cry because she loved him and couldn't bear to see him weak. Weakness was a problem for Charlotte. When we were small, if we'd find a wounded bird, she'd suffocate it with her own hands. Not out of meanness, out of mercy.

My first night home, all snuggled up to my wild and wonderful niece, it all came back to me long after I had already fallen asleep.

Charlotte and me driving down the back roads of Magnolia Creek, with the top down on my convertible. She was leaning forward, trying to light two cigarettes against the wind. We were laughing about Paddy. We stopped by the beach and smoked.

"You and my brother should just get married and have babies," I said.

"Ain't never gonna happen, Wyn,"

"Why not?"

"'Cause even though I love him to pieces, there's someone I love even more."

She put on her devilish smile, and I remember she'd just got her hair cut short, pixielike, and it was dark and shining and modern under the city lights by the bay. She reached in the backseat to get the bottle we'd stolen from Jackson. She opened it, took a swig, and gave it to me.

"Who?" I asked, my mouth full of bourbon.

"Shh," she said. "It's a secret."

"Come on, spill," I said. "You ain't got no secrets from me," I said.

"Not this. This is like, scandalous. Like . . . bad. A sin, even. I don't know. But it makes me shiver on the inside like nothin' ever has."

"Are you in love with the pastor?" I asked, half joking and lighting another cigarette.

"No! Not like that. Anyway, he's married. The pastor, not the one I love . . . I've loved him forever, you know. Forever and ever. And now? I'm thinking I might have a chance."

"Okay, Lottie. Now you *have* to tell me who it is,"

But then she got serious and wanted to go home. I think I even called her a "moody bitch," but that was the person I was then. Part princess, part viper.

And she never did tell me who it was. But right there in my dream I suddenly knew.

She'd been in love with Grant.

Crazy fuckall.

Diggin' Up Dirt

Everyone has a dark side. This is pure *fact*. I can see it
like a shadow behind them all the time.

—*Byrd, age eleven*

10

Byrd

In the face of an overpowering mystery,
you don't dare disobey.

—*The Little Prince*

When the morning sun came sparklin' across my eyelids, I snuck out of Aunt Wyn's cottage. I was confused, see, because I hadn't been prepared to love her. So I left real early before she woke up.

The day before, when I held her hand, I knew I was a goner for sure. It wasn't any ordinary glow that happened. It was even stronger than the one I had when Jamie and I first met. It surprised me, and I don't like bein' surprised. That extra bit of glow? I knew it meant we had a *bond*.

So, I also knew I didn't have a lot of time. Because the deeper I started to love her, the less of her I'd be able to see. Between lovin' her, and her own strange ways growin' . . . there'd be no way to read her mind or any of that stuff.

The night before, she was the kindest person I'd ever known. She just put me in her big bed without a second thought. She didn't even make me take a bath.

I think she looks like an angel. All golden tan.

All it took was one day walkin' through town, and her skin was already brownin' up. It's a wonder she don't burn bein' so pale. But she looked like an angel, tryin' like crazy to talk about important things on the porch, and no one wantin' to listen to her. I wanted to count her freckles.

Before I left her sleepin' there, I kissed her forehead. Firstly, because it looked so damn pretty. And second, because I wanted to get a peek at what she'd found out. Since it was getting' harder to "read" her, kissin' sort of helped that along.

And boy, what I found out . . . she'd discovered something out about Grant! And you know somethin'? I hadn't even considered that possibility. Boy, did I feel good, but confused. Aunt Wyn was wakin' up so many things inside and around me, too. My family, my heart . . . and worst of all, hope. Hope can hurt.

So I did the only thing that made sense. I reached next to her, stole her set of tarot cards I'd been eye'n since she unpacked them. (What? I was gonna give 'em back.) Then I crept out of Aunt Wyn's little cottage (I did a mighty fine job on that, if I don't say so myself) and went on over to the Big House to visit with my friend, Mary.

She always helps me get my crazy fuckall thoughts back in a straight line. It's her best quality, really.

I like walking into the Big House through the kitchen. That way I get to go through Naomi's garden. My garden now. My mama's garden for the time she lived here.

It's where I plant and take care of all the herbs I learn about in Naomi's book.

I add some, now and again, to the earth *and* the book. My mama, Stella, planted new things there, too. She had a little spot all her own that my daddy dug up for her. It's my favorite part of the garden. She must have been a real witch, because she planted things like belladonna, rue, mandrake, and foxglove all tangled up with wild, wild roses.

I know what all those herbs do, and I know how to mix them up. Or, if need be, keep 'em separate. Like rosemary shouldn't grow next to lavender. You can mix those up before they blossom . . . and one means remembrance, while the other means sorrow. That's not somethin' you want to get wrong.

Anyway, that morning I was downright sick with confusion over these feelings I had, and taking a stroll though my garden on the way to visit Mary was just the thing to cheer me up. She's right about my age, Mary, and sometimes a girl just needs a friend her own age to talk to.

I pushed open the screen door, and yep! there she was, stirring the gumbo. I had to make Dolores wait outside, because Mary won't show herself if the dog's there.

I've told her time and again that she's a ghost and that a dog can't bite a ghost, but she said I have to respect her ways 'cause she's dead and I'm not. I suppose she has a point.

She's pretty, Mary. She's got the darkest skin I've ever seen, and her hair sticks out this way and that, tied up in pieces of white cotton. And she's always wearin' this flowered apron, only it fits her. Not like mine. I guess they made aprons that fit little girls back then. I don't know how I feel about that. It's one thing to *want* to work in a kitchen, but another thing altogether if you're *forced* to work there.

So I'm standing there next to Mary, who's stirring her spirit gumbo, and I ask her what I should do.

"Ifn' you love someone, you love 'em. Can't do nothin' 'bout it," she said.

"Can't I put a spell on myself not to love her? A voodoo spell or somethin'?

"Sure, ain't nothing dat can't be fixed or muddled wit juju. But you gotta be careful wit it. Mayhaps you find you fix yourself one way and then can't never love no one again? Dat be okay wit you?"

I thought on it for a bit.

There'd be a lot less missin' of folks who die or leave or just disappoint a person if I couldn't feel love. But I thought I'd start missin' love, sooner or later.

"Nah. Seems like too much work." I said, getting off the chair. "Hey, Mary, that gumbo almost done? It's time for you to cross over you now."

"Dat light be waiting for me, Miss Byrd. Pay me no mind. Gumbo got to be just right. Just riiiiight."

"Can I have a little taste?" I asked.

"You knows betta dan dat, Miss Byrdie. You taste the spirit gumbo, you join us. What you want to do dat fo'?"

I was just about to tell her that she was raised around way too much juju herself and that things like that never really happened, but she was gone. I have to tell you, I really wanted to taste that gumbo. It must have been a mighty fine recipe for her to want to stir it for eternity.

I decided to take some time to think in the very best thinking place of all.

Naomi's outdoor bathroom. Safely hidden there with Dolores, I watched my aunt walk up the path to the Big House. She was lookin' for me. But I wanted to look at her without her knowin'. So's I could get a real picture of who she was when nobody was lookin'.

Her hair was down, and she musta been feelin' right at home 'cause she was still wearin' her nightie. She was barefoot, too. No fancy-pants Yankee clothes, not that day.

Man, I hope I grow up to look like her. She don't even know she's fine. She thinks she needs to be darker. Darker hair, darker skin. Don't she realize she's like the sun?

As I watched her look for me, I realized right away I'd lost her thoughts altogether. It was hopeless. I loved her too much to unravel her mysteries now

So I sat there, in Naomi's outdoor tub (empty, 'cause me and Dolores don't like takin' real baths), petting Dolores just like she loves. I like motherin' her. I thought maybe I'd like Aunt Wyn for a mother if I couldn't *look* like her or even read her thoughts.

But maybe not. It seemed to me, mothers could do more damage than tornados. And they didn't even have to say a word.

Or maybe that's just *some* mothers. Maybe others do the opposite. I get sad when I think about mamas. Especially my own. Makes me start to think that havin' magic is useless if you can't help your own self figure out the simplest things.

❱

You'd think I'd be able to shut my eyes real tight and see the things I need to see. But that ain't the way my strange ways work. Don't seem fair, does it?

So I watched my pretty aunt look for me up and down and everywhere. Then I saw her go into the kitchen. She peeked in through the window first, which made me love her even more. Then when she opened the door, she was gone for a long, long time.

And when she came out, she seemed to know right where I was, but somethin' else caught her eye, that swing on Esther. I love that tree. (I don't let Dolores pee on her, not ever.) Aunt Wyn was starin' at that swing for so long I thought maybe she'd gotten sick. But then she walked through the garden, picked a bunch of lavender, and headed my way.

I got nervous then, because I knew I'd have to tell her the whole *dark* truth. So I recited the Declaration of Independence in my head, until she reached the tub and looked inside.

Everyone has a dark side. I can see it like a shadow behind them all the time.

Some dark sides are more interestin' than others. I like the ones that are complicated. Pure evil ain't interestin'. But take me, for example, I ain't pure evil, but I sure have a dark side.

Mostly I don't notice my darkness.

And I don't worry about it *too* much. It's like dyin', I suppose. We all gotta die, and we all gotta live with the things our dark sides do. People are afraid of their darkness, though. Spend their whole lives so scared of dyin' that they never get to live. Spend their whole lives pushin' down that darkness, until there ain't no light at all.

The only thing that worries me . . . is sometimes I have these *spells,* these pieces of time I don't remember. Like my soul just floats out of me when I least expect it, and when I come around again, I've been doin' all the things I shoulda been doin' only I can't remember any of it.

No one notices. Not Jackson, not Minerva, not my daddy neither.

Only Jamie. Jamie always knew when I was "absinth," that's what he called it.

Well, we were little, maybe five or so, we were skipping rocks on the creek. I remember it got real hot, and then I was sitting at the kitchen table eating pickled okra out of a jar with a fork.

"What happened? How did we get on in here?" I asked him, grabbing for a biscuit on the table because ordinarily I don't even like pickled okra. Call me crazy.

"It was like you were there . . . but not. Like when a kid is out of school, they call it absinth."

I miss Jamie when he was little. All those screwed-up words and tiny lisp. I always felt like I could be a little kid around him, even though I feel like I was born a grown-up in this awful small body.

"Your eyes were empty, like when I come home and the house ain't got no lights on," he continued. "It scared me."

It scared me, too. And it has ever since. But it stopped scaring Jamie. Sometimes I thought he liked fooling me. When he'd see me go, he'd think it was funny to put me in a crazy situation when I "woke up."

In a treetop.

Tied to the porch.

Or, the worst ever? Sitting in school.

And after he disappeared, I went about crazy thinkin' on how I couldn't remember one thing from that night.

You see, the night Charlotte was killed, and Jamie disappeared, I was absinth.

I can't remember a thing. For months and months, I was scared I'd done the impossible. But then, that first morning with Aunt Wyn, when that kiss told me Grant might be another option? The idea that another person might have gone and ruined my whole life, and it wasn't me, was a piece of heaven right there.

But there was something else.

See, I collect things. Things a lot of folks might think are strange.

One of my favorite collections is pocketknives. I like how they click open and shut. I like how some have all sorts of layers to 'em. Forks and knives, baby scissors. All kinds of things. Only . . .

My favorite knife from my whole collection? The one with the mother-of-pearl handle. It was gone. I couldn't find it anywhere.

Lottie and Jamie were stabbed, but no one could find the knife that did it. At my daddy's trial, the Dr. Specialist Whatever Mr. Person, he said that it was a small knife. That's why it took so many cuts.

Dark, dark, and darker.

11

Bronwyn

When Paddy and I were little, all we had was time. Long stretches of time where we simply luxuriated with nothing to do. The recollection tugged at me as I woke up, slow and lazy in my new little house.

I could smell the scent of those days with Mama, Jackson, and Paddy. Soft, loamy ground and bleached cotton. Those were the good days, before she got too sick. When Jackson's laugh rang through the whole house and we'd gather as he lit a cigarette and sat back in one of his old armchairs saying, "Ain't got nothing but time and money. And right about now I'm feeling too lazy to waste money, so let's just sit here a while and waste some time!"

Home is a funny concept. I was expecting a lot of things from my homecoming to Magnolia Creek. What I wasn't expecting was how quickly I'd slip back into my old ways.

When I woke up and found Byrd already gone, I walked

back to the Big House in my nightgown, barefoot like my niece told me I should walk, and went straight around back, through Naomi's herb garden, to the kitchen door. I didn't go in right away, just peeked through the panes of glass at the top of the door.

I knew Minerva would have black tea steeping, and she did. I knew there'd be a bowl of figs on the table, and there was. I knew she'd be sweeping the wide pine-planked floors, and she was. I waited for her to make her way upstairs before I went inside. I needed more time before I saw her and talked to her about the strange things happening with my own shine.

The kitchen of the Big House was always one of my favorite places. Airy and sunny. No modern cabinets or anything like that. Just a room full of windows, set into wise, worn walls.

The long, well-loved table still graced the center of the room. That table was the first piece of furniture the original Jackson Whalen made for his family. Older Hoosier cabinets were there for storage, each with all sorts of hidden compartments and open shelving that showcased all of Minerva's fine jams and pickled things. The kitchen door, painted red from the day Naomi moved in, and a geranium, also red, outside on the stoop, gave the whole area a feeling of whimsy. Something I'd looked for in every place I'd lived since I'd run away. Something I'd never found.

When I walked in through that door, it slammed loudly behind me. I'd forgotten how loose it was on its hinges. "Damn!" I said. "So much for being sneaky."

Minerva hurried back into the kitchen.

"Good morning, seems it didn't take long for you to feel at home,"

"Surprisingly not," I said, reaching for the bowl of figs on the table. I took a nice firm fig, biting the skin away to reveal the stained flesh underneath. It was a childhood habit to eat the soft, purple green skin first, and then the sweeter inside. There were always ripe things in the bowl from the surrounding orchards and forest. Figs in midsummer. Later on, beautyberries and loquats. Then persimmons. Peaches and plums, too.

Minerva went to the fridge and placed a platter of cut, plump figs, wrapped in prosciutto and garnished with lemon wedges, in the center of the table. There was a loaf of thick, crusty bread on the table, too. I pulled off the heel of the bread and held it to my nose. *Susan,* I thought.

"I miss her, too," said Minerva. "She was a fine companion and a wonderful cook. You know, when Stella came, she brought this little recipe book with her, full of food she wanted to make for us. I never had the heart to tell her that most of those recipes were already up here," she said and pointed to her forehead.

"You make fine Italian food, Min. I've lived places where the food is supposed to be better, but nothing compares to the things you and Susan used to make. You really are a chameleon, aren't you? Fitting in wherever you go."

"Aren't we all?" she said, and then she pointed to one of the kitchen chairs, directing me to sit my butt down. She poured tea into two small, dainty cups and sat down across from me, sighing heavily.

"Bronwyn, we can look back to our past later, but right now we have to talk about Byrd and Ben."

I started to ask why we had to talk about Ben, but she hushed me. "First, we'll speak about Byrd. You need to be careful with her. She's a sweet child, don't get me wrong. I love her to pieces. And, as you might have guessed, she reminds me of my people back home in Fairview. Mostly of your mother, but the others, too. The ones that left and had terrible times because of the magic they had. That's the problem." She took a sip of her tea and then placed it with a *clink* back in its saucer. Little cups full of tea were one thing I didn't miss. I wanted coffee. Strong coffee in a mug, something to hold on to with both hands. Something solid. I looked down into my cup as I took a sip and saw the tiny leaves floating in the brew.

"I know you want coffee, I'm sure there's some back at your cottage. In my kitchen, you get tea. Now, pay attention. You know me, Bronwyn. I am the only one left who can even begin to explain the family we're all part of. When you're a Green, no matter where you hail from, you understand there is good found in the bad. Bad things have to happen and there is a certain beauty there. But this . . . almost . . . *medical* side to Byrd, it scares me sometimes, and I don't scare easily."

Jackson sauntered into the kitchen carrying a silver ice bucket. He was a walking oxymoron. A strong-weak man. A right-wrong man. He went straight to the freezer and took out two metal ice trays. Then he began banging the ice out into the bucket.

"A bit early, even for you, Jackson," said Minerva.

"I got a lot of things on my plate today, woman, and I don't expect to be able to do any of them with a clear head. Clear heads are overrated. Like open arms or busy hands."

"Oh, yes, let our minds be muddy, our arms rest closed, and our hands stay idle. That's the way to live," said Minerva.

"If you're rich and lousy drunk in Alabama, there ain't no reason to exist otherwise," he said as he walked back out.

"Now then," said Minerva, "about Ben." She reached into her apron pocket and brought out a ring almost identical to the one Ben gave me, only the one she was holding had a ruby star, where mine was an emerald.

"This was your mother's. There's a matching necklace that we, as caretakers wear. I'm sure Ben has the matching one to yours, if you need some kind of proof. I know his family, the Masons. They're from Fairview. He's your caretaker, honey. I don't know why he didn't tell you. I don't know how he found you. I don't know what it means, either, so don't ask me. He'll be here, sooner than you know, and you can ask him. I'm just as surprised as you are, honey."

What she was saying made no sense and all the sense at the very same time.

"I don't know what to say," I told her, confused.

"Don't say anything, just hold this ring and see what it says. You still have some shine?"

"More than I thought," I said, as she nodded knowingly and placed the ring in my hands.

I thought I'd get flashes of my mother. But instead I saw Ben. Moments when he looked at me when I wasn't looking at him. A nervous, worried Ben who I did not know. The first day we met, as I dealt his tarot cards . . . *worried, confused Ben*. The day we went to look at the house in Upstate New York and I was talking to the Realtor . . . *nervous, anxious Ben*.

"He hid things from me. But why?" I asked.

"Ben's going to have to explain *himself*. There's a reason for all of this, I'm sure of it."

"So, he lied to me. These past seven years have been a lie?"

"Let's not jump to conclusions. Besides, right now we have bigger fish to fry. Just concentrate on Byrd. Make sure you understand her before she works her magic on you. You're already under her spell. I can see it. She's powerful, Bronwyn."

"She sure is," said Jackson, coming back into the kitchen and opening the junk drawer. He clattered things around and came out with a bottle opener.

"Odd, too. You should see where she stays," he said.

"You mean her room?" I asked.

"No, where she *stays*," echoed Minerva. "He's right. Go with him, you might learn something."

Jackson led the way upstairs. I followed him, trying to quell the rage rising inside me. Ben lied. He could have told me, but he lied. I can't stand a lie when it's not necessary.

He didn't deserve my thoughts if he was a liar because Minerva was right, I had bigger fish to fry.

I had to push it aside and take care of the present.

As I followed Jackson down the second-floor hallway, we passed my old room, open and just the way I'd left it. I peeked in, surprised I hadn't wanted to see it sooner. Looking at it, even in a glance, gave me a jolt. I'd shared my mother's taste. My room looked a lot like hers.

And then Paddy's. Now a grown-up man's room, a Southern gentleman's room. Next, there was Byrd's room, which used to be one of the many guest rooms we have at the Big House.

"Is this it?" I asked, peering in. Pink. Very pink. Didn't seem like her at all. Fancy and frilly. A canopy bed. Dolls everywhere. Unopened gifts in the corner. A large, dusty window seat piled with children's books she'd probably read when she was a year old.

"No, I told you . . . where she *stays*."

He walked up the third flight of stairs to the attic. Paddy and I used to play up there. It was a treasure trove of Whalen history. I remembered it with sheets covering furniture, and trunks containing old pictures, clothing, and bits of moldy correspondence.

Now it was a fun house exhibition.

Tables lined the slanted walls and were topped with precariously placed jars of every sort of creature, from spiders to bees to lizards of every size, some floating in liquid, some just dried up.

Piles of Naomi's clothing littered the floor, and Byrd had one large mirror leaning against the wall across from a mattress covered in all sorts of dusty quilts and old down pillows.

Books were haphazardly stacked everywhere, covering subjects from etymology to ancient Greece and even Latin grammar.

One book, open on her bed, was familiar. It was my mother's *Book of Shadows,* the one that brought her here, to Magnolia Creek. Byrd was evidently adding to it by placing dried plants and flowers in-between the pages and making notes in its margins. I loved her more, looking at that book, at the care she was taking with her additions.

She also had a bulletin board on the wall covered with Polaroid photos of the people from town. Taken with my old Polaroid that was next to her bed. Some of the people's pictures had notes scribbled under them. *Mr. Wrong, Medicine? Eating herself to death. Mother ill. . . .*

"What do you think?" asked Jackson.

"What do *you* think?" I asked back.

He scratched his head. "I don't know what to think. She's got strange ways. This is part of all that." He gestured wildly.

"I think she wants to feel loved. To feel appreciated for who she is. I think she wants to feel safe," I said.

"What do you mean? She's *loved*. She's *safe*. Goddamm it, Bronwyn! Why make this into another example of how no one in this family can love?" He started to walk down the attic stairs. Stopped but didn't turn around. "I love her. I love you. I love Paddy, and God knows I loved your mother. You can't measure other's peoples' love, sugar. You best try stopping that particular obsession."

His words hurt.

But who allows a child to live like that? Goddamn Southern hippie rich mayor guy. That's who. Too drunk to notice much.

"Go have a drink!" I shouted after him. Knowing it would cut him, and unable to stop the words from coming out. Old habits die hard. "Grow the fuck up," I whispered to myself, going over to Byrd's mattress. Sitting down, I tried to catch my breath, to make sense of too much information coming at me all at once.

I felt like crying. For half a second.

That's when I saw them. My tarot cards. The deck that never left my bedside. The one connection to my mother that I'd never let go.

My odd, beautiful niece had taken them. I wasn't mad. Not even a bit. I supposed she was trying a little divination for herself.

I took out the cards and shuffled them. It soothed me. There were two missing. I glanced around, and there they were.

The two missing cards taped to the window by the mattress.

Written on scraps of paper fixed right above them were, *Did my daddy do it?* and underneath, the Death card—a card that can be read many ways. And then . . . *Did I do it?* and underneath? The nine of cups—the biggest *yes* of all time.

He thinks I did it, she'd said. Could Byrd really believe she'd done something so terrible?

I took the cards off the board and held them.

For someone so smart, she should have known better. Yes or no questions are the wrong ones to ask. It's a fortune-teller's first rule of business.

The cards are too vague, and if you want an answer to come out a certain way, it does.

But these particular cards were screaming at me, so I needed to talk to someone who could help me figure out how to read them. If only to explain it better to Byrd when I found her.

I found Minerva in Naomi's rooms. She must have been lost in thought because I startled her, and she dropped the blanket she was folding. She was making my mother's beautiful bed with those same white cotton sheets I remembered. Those soft, downy linens embroidered with light blue and sage green, the colors of the sea. Some were embroidered with plain, untarnished white. Naomi spent so much time in bed that it had to be a paradise. And it was, for all of us . . . when we still wanted to be around her.

"Is there something that you need? Are you all right?" Minerva asked once she regained her composure.

"You still change her bedding?" I asked softly.

"I miss her. And it helps me," she said.

I understood that too well

"Minerva, I found something in Byrd's attic,"

"She keeps a lot of odd things up there. Your mother had collections like that when she was a girl. What did you find?"

"My tarot cards. She took them to do a reading about the murders."

Minerva didn't skip a beat. "What spread did she use? Do you know?"

"I sure do."

"She used the yes or no, didn't she? She would have. She's still a child. Impulsive."

"Yes, but it was an interesting combination."

"Come sit with me," she said.

We went through French doors that opened up into a private porch, Naomi's library. The couch there was covered in soft cushions. Her own private heaven.

Naomi would move from one part of her rooms to the other, so each room was an extension of her. But even that was an effort for her by the end.

Minerva and I sat on the cozy cushions.

"These are very easy to read, Wyn," said Minerva, after I explained. "The nine states yes because Byrd probably knows more than she's telling us. Or more than she thinks she knows. And perhaps she even *feels* like she did it, which is a terrible weight she's been carrying. Unless—"

"No, Minerva."

"You're right, of course. She's too small, anyway. Patrick, though . . . that makes sense on the one hand. We all know he didn't do it. But the death card? Now, that's an interesting thing. Does he know more? Was he somehow responsible for it? I'd never thought of that," she mused.

"This keeps getting worse doesn't it, Minerva?"

"Most things do. The less we know, the harder they get. We keep trying to learn lessons, and if we don't, they come right back

around again, even harder to figure out. I worry so much that
Naomi and I coming here all those years ago was a mistake."

"What do you mean?"

Minerva reached into her apron pocket and pulled out a soft
pack of Pall Mall cigarettes. She tapped the pack on her hand and
one slid right out.

"Still smoking, Min?"

"Now and again—it's hard around here not to have some
kind of addiction. Anyway." She sat back with her lit cigarette.

"Have I ever told you about my own great-aunt? Your mother's
great-great-aunt? How she was the reason, long after her death,
that no one would accept Naomi?"

"I think you might have told me some watered-down version
when I was little."

"Well then, you need the grown-up version. Get comfortable.
My great-aunt, Faith Green, was famous, or *infamous*. She was the
one whose history affected all of us. Still does."

"What did she do?"

"It was her legacy, more than any one thing. She'd had the
strongest 'sight and talents' any of the Greens had seen in generations. They called themselves witches, you know. Still do.
Naomi didn't like that, so I never used that term with you children. But if you and Byrd lived there, even today, they'd call you
witches, too."

"Nice . . . we're witches. With caretakers. Go on."

"Well, Faith's talents caused harm. To her and to our family
eventually. But at first she was helpful and everyone loved her.
The entire community. She was the most respected woman in
Fairview. But when she lost both her children to a tragic twist
of fate, everything changed.

"What happened to her children?"

"Her children were my great cousins, Ephraim and Margaret. Ephraim was lured across the sea to our own veiled island. And he was never found. Drowned they said.

"With that, Great-aunt Faith lost her ability to speak and her ability to help the town as well. The problem was, the town had come to count on her. Her healing ways. Her weather predictions. Her sight. She was loved and feared. But mostly? She was needed. Like a drug. And when she locked herself up in that asylum, the people of Fairview suffered a terrible withdrawal.

"Then Margaret, her other child, she ran. Like you. Ran fast and far. Married some Italian. His last name was Amore, like Stella's. Part of the reason Stella came here was to research her past, and one of those family trees led her to us. Anyway, Margaret had to hide away her own 'talents' which brought havoc to her own family. We all started to think the magic would bring more harm than good. Think of it like an aversion. And your mother, Naomi Green, was the first child born with abilities as strong as Faith's. Do you understand?"

"More than you can ever know. Is this 'aversion' the reason Mama hid her magic?"

"Yes and no. She had a chance . . . a choice. She was given two paths. One was to use her gifts and win back a 'taste' for our ways. The other was to hide them. She *did* try that first path, Bronwyn. She tried to make those around us understand. Then she gave up. But there were other reasons she chose to hide it.

"She was plagued with visions about you and Paddy. That damn opium hid all that for her. If you *do* have the magic growing inside of you, Bronwyn, all I can ask is that you don't make the same mistake. Embrace it."

It was then that I decided I'd tell her about the glow when I'd held Byrd's hand, because when I was little, Minerva used her magic more than Naomi liked. I'd find her out on one of our wide second-floor porches late at night, staring up at the moon as if in prayer. Then she would rub her hands together and clap. Just once. And after, her hands would glow, ever so slightly, like phosphorus creeping out from between her palms.

I asked her about it once. I'd had the flu and she'd done the same thing. Rubbed her hands together and clapped. Only then she placed her hands on my forehead and stomach. I recovered quickly after that.

"Does the glow heal people, Minny?" I'd asked.

"Sometimes," she'd answered.

"You love Mama, right?"

"More than you'll ever know."

"Why can't you make the glow heal her?"

"Bronwyn, it's important that you understand, deep in your heart what I'm going to say to you right now. You can't heal someone who doesn't want to get well. You just can't."

"Have you ever even tried?"

"Every day since the day she was born," she answered, and her sadness echoed through me. I never questioned her about it again.

But now, it was time for questions and answers.

"How bright was the glow?" she asked when I told her.

"Bright."

"Well, then. Get ready."

"Get ready for what?"

"The magic . . . who knows, maybe you can bring it back."

"Well, it seems like I can't stop it, Min."

"No, not that . . . maybe you can bring back the wonder, the glorious curiosity that should always accompany unexplainable things. Faith Green lost that for us, the wonder. And replaced it with fear. Witches without wonder are dark creatures."

"I'll do my best, Min," I said.

"I know you will, honey. I know you will."

12

Naomi

Diaspora. The migration of a people from their homeland. The word has haunted me since I was old enough to know what *home* meant and realized I didn't have one.

When I got to Magnolia Creek, I thought maybe I'd found it though. Or something that resembled it at least. Those first few years were the best of my life

Jackson, he was so bright, like the sun itself, but darkness closed him down, so he couldn't ever get mean or mad or even sad. All those things are vital parts of families. Jackson couldn't handle anything but sunshine. He disappeared every time I really needed him. Especially when our babies came.

I suppose most new mothers go through what I did. Fear, excitement, trepidation, worry. But all of that was heightened inside of me because of my sight.

My mind played nasty tricks on me. Made me hold my belly and see the future for my babies. Terrible. Black. Hopeless. Blood. I saw bullies and broken legs. Heartbreak and death.

The images wouldn't stop. Jackson wouldn't listen to me. He wanted to hear more mermaid stories. "Life isn't a fucking fairy tale, Jackson!" I'd yelled, the last night we shared a bed.

He didn't get mad. He said, "It is if I want it to be, and I want it to be. Good night, darlin'," and that was that.

So I turned to Minerva. I remember one talk we had in the garden. Bronwyn toddled all about, just beginning to walk. I was pregnant with Paddy at the time.

"It's happening again, Min, only this time it's worse," I said, trimming back a seedling that was getting too leggy, while Minerva potted geraniums. Red. Always red. A favorite of ours.

"Naomi, now you listen, and you listen good, you know you can't see the right kind of things when you look into the future of the ones you love. It gets all mixed up in worry."

But those premonitions, first with Bronwyn, then with Paddy, slowly broke me.

Still, I tried. Susan was a good friend to me. We were both outsiders, of sorts. She was so brave. I knew the moment I touched her, in the kitchen of the Big House, the day I first arrived, that she'd die of cancer. A kind I couldn't heal. A destined death . . . and still, I loved her.

It was Susan who taught me about bows. We were sitting on the porch, and she was fixing a big red bow in Bronwyn's hair.

"The bigger the bow, the better the mama!" she said.

So, from then on, I'd put big bows in Bronwyn's hair. And she'd laugh and clap. How my darling baby loved pretty things.

Susan talked to me about Jackson. She was the one who noticed his overuse of alcohol first.

"It'll kill him, Naomi," she said.

"Pirates don't drown," I answered.

We were so alike, Jackson and I. He was light and I was dark, but really we were just the same.

I was horrible to Susan before she died.

I fired her from the Big House, even though she'd been my friend and had counted on that job years before I even arrived. I fired her knowing she was sick. I hated her by then.

I was convinced that, as my children grew older, Susan wasn't a friend at all. That she was conspiring to steal my babies. Stealing them with her delicious food, the aroma of garlic and sweet basil drawing them from my rooms and into the kitchen; stealing them with her generous smiles that never seemed to get tired; and stealing my children with the joy she owned. Those kids grew up so close. The opium swirled these lies into my head, speaking much louder than an increasingly faint truth. So I pushed Susan away when she needed us all the most. That was the last straw for my own children. They gave their hearts to her fully then. I don't blame them . . . anymore.

When Susan died she went straight into the light. I hope Charlotte gets to her soon. It's hard for mothers and daughters to be separated.

I should know.

If I'd had a mother who stayed, who wanted to teach me things, maybe I would have understood how to control the magic on my own. Or maybe I was too weak for the gifts I'd been given.

When Bronwyn was born, Dr. Henry gave me morphine for pain.

And that first dose was when I knew. I'd found a cure for magic.

When Dr. Henry didn't want to give it to me anymore, I went to Jackson. I explained how wonderful I felt, how normal.

Jackson wanted peace, so he found a way to substitute the morphine: opium.

It made me happy. It let me mother my children without an ounce of hesitation. I was a good friend, a good mother. For a few years, before the drug took over, I was the person I always wanted to be.

Until I wasn't.

13

Bronwyn

I left the house secretly. Using the passage from Naomi's room to the ballroom and creeping out through the kitchen like a criminal. I didn't want to see Jackson. Too stubborn to apologize, I guess.

The Big House passages aren't the type you'd think about on a dark and dreary night. They're more like inner hallways. Pretty, even.

It's so funny . . . people think that in order for something to be frightening, it has to be dark, musty, and full of cobwebs and secrets.

That's a lie of mythic proportion. The scariest, most unexplainable things in the world happen in the bright light of day. And just when you least expect.

Like what happened next.

As soon as I wandered outside, I realized where Byrd must have gone and slapped my forehead for not thinking of it sooner.

Naomi's outdoor bathroom.

I could barely see it from the garden, but I could *feel* that she was there. I used to hide there when I was little, too. But as I headed in her direction, Esther stopped me short.

Her grand old boughs hovered over Naomi and Minerva's magic garden, stoic and bent with age. But Esther was determined to live forever. A plank board swing large enough for two people at once hung off one of her limbs. Jackson had it checked every year, but it'd been around in some incarnation since the very first Whalens lived on the grounds.

The scent of lavender and bitter nettle hit me and I breathed in deep. Walking through the garden to get to Byrd, I gathered a small bunch of lavender and let the scent linger inside me. When I had a nice bouquet, I gazed at Esther. The air was hot. Heavy. Humid. Not a hint of breeze.

But the swing, dangling there, was swaying. Back and forth, back and forth.

So I looked at it, straight on, with my hands on my hips and my chin squared.

"You'll stop," I said out loud.

Only the swing didn't stop.

It swung higher.

Then I heard her for the first time. *Ben is coming,* Esther said.

Well, shit.

Byrd. I had to focus on her. She'd become the most important thing to me in a single day. And I didn't care if she'd cast some spell, because I'd fallen in love with my little niece. Ben was on his way, and I had to tell him I wasn't going to leave her. And I had to find out why he'd lied and what it meant.

When I reached the outdoor bathroom, there they were. Byrd and Dolores in an empty tub.

Naomi's outdoor bathroom is a splendid thing.

Jackson created it when she first moved in. She'd been taking a basin full of water out to the side yard under an old live oak, its mythical branches creating a natural room of sorts. And she'd wash out there. Only out there.

"What're you doin', darlin'?" he'd asked her all those years ago.

"I like to bathe outside. It's from . . . home. I know it's odd, but we always bathe in the sea. Always."

"Even in the winter?" he'd asked.

"No, silly. But as soon as it's warm, until the day the crickets stop singing their songs, it's in the sea that we bathe."

"Why not bathe in the river?"

"It's a different kind of water. Too warm and placid. I already tried. I was going to try the creek, but it's too shallow."

Naomi said "creek" and that was all Jackson needed.

"Look. Let me have some fellas come over here today and build you a proper outdoor bath, okay? Just don't go near the creek."

And at the end of the day her magical retreat was done. He had builders hang paned windows from the branches with beautiful ironwork chains and an old copper claw-foot tub placed in the center of the space. A mosquito net hung over the tub to protect her while she bathed. There was even a wicker chair and a table to hold a vase of flowers or a book.

Soon, the grass grew over the trenches that were dug from

the Big House to the little paradise, so it seemed that when you turned on the faucets the water came out of nowhere. Like magic.

Byrd sat in that very same tub, fully clothed and without any water. The bathroom was just as I remembered it. Only some of the panes of glass were broken. It made it prettier somehow.

Dolores was in the tub with her. And as that beautiful, regal shepherd watched over her, Byrd tucked little pointy leaves in her collar.

"There you are," I said, softly so as not to startle them. I knelt down and tried to push her hair back from her face.

"I didn't want you to find me," she said.

"Why?"

"I don't rightly know. But now that you found me, I'm glad. You're so pretty."

She reached up, winding one of my curls in her tiny finger. It sprung back as she let go.

"These are for you," I said, handing her the flowers.

"Thank you! But can you just put them on the ground for a sec? I have to finish this up, see?" she said.

"What are you doing there?"

"These here are beautyberry leaves, and if I put them all around her collar they keep the bugs away. 'Specially those damn gnats. Don't you hate those? But you already know about beautyberry leaves."

I smiled. Minerva used to pound the leaves up and slather me with the oils before we went out to play on the nights when the gnats were thick like storm clouds.

"I like the way they make her look regal, all sticking up like that," I said, helping her tuck a few in.

"Me, too. But I think she looks more like a joker than a queen. Maybe next year I can make her a crown. *We're* getting ready."

"Ready for what?"

"For the parade! It's the Fourth of July, silly. Don't you remember the parade?"

"I do. But I think I must have lost track of days . . . that's today?"

"It sure is!"

I did remember the parade in all its Technicolor glory. One of the best days to be a resident of Magnolia Creek was parade day. And we held it on the Fourth no matter what day of the week it was. Not like other big cities I'd lived in where they had to accommodate all the other towns. We take care of our own.

"How about we get Dolores out of the tub, and I give you a real bath? Does the water still work out here?"

" 'Course it does. But I don't like baths."

"That, Princess Byrd, is obvious."

"I ain't no princess, I am a *queen*," she said haughtily.

"Okay, I promise to never call you princess again if you let me have the honor of bathing you, Your Highness."

She laughed wildly, with her eyes closed and her mouth open. A full throttle sort of sound.

"Deal," she said, as they both got out of the tub.

Byrd got undressed without any shyness, and I couldn't get over how quickly she'd grown to trust me.

I ran the water. A little rust came out at first, but then it ran clean.

Byrd motioned for Dolores to get in the tub, too. But the dog and I both shook our heads. Byrd got in when the water was ankle deep and sat down. The dirt started to come off immediately.

"When do you think I'll get boobies like yours?" she asked.

"Oh, soon enough, trust me."

"Did Naomi have big ones? I can't tell because she's all shimmery. I can't get a good, long look, you know?"

"I suppose I'd say they were average size. Smaller than average, perhaps. Maybe you should ask Jackson?" I suggested, laughing.

I found an old, cracked bar of soap from God knows when and took my dirty niece to task.

We both giggled. I can't tell you how good it felt.

"I don't remember much about my mama," she said, washing between her toes.

"Well, you never met her," I said.

"No, but I knew her. I felt her. Aunt Wyn? I need to tell you something. And it's a big, fat secret."

"Go right on ahead, my queen," I said. "I'm a photographer, and what we do best is capture secrets that we never, ever tell."

Minerva was headed toward us with a stack of fluffy, white towels, some shampoo and conditioner, and a comb, thank God. She dropped it all beside me and turned right on back around.

"Okay. Here goes. Sometimes I don't remember things. I don't know why, and it's probably part of all my other strangeness. All I know is that night, you know what night I'm talking about because you don't strike me as no fool . . . well, I'll just say it." She took a deep breath. "Aunt Wyn, I don't remember anything from that night. Not one thing. And I'm afraid I might have done something I shouldn't have. Made a big mistake."

"Byrd, honey, I know what you think," I said. "I found my

tarot cards. I'm not mad. I'll even share them with you if you like. But was that why you thought I was being obtuse?" I lathered her hair and rinsed it.

She nodded.

"Well, if it helps at all, memory or no memory, I don't believe for one second that you did anything wrong. Do you hear me?"

She nodded again, her eyes wide with relief.

"Byrd? Did you know something was going to happen that night?"

"I didn't . . . but the night before I had a bad dream, and I was all alone. I need to pay more attention to my dreams."

"My mother had terrible dreams. She thought they were omens or predictions, but they weren't. That's why she died, hiding her magic. Don't worry about your dreams, Byrd."

"I won't. I don't want to lose my magic. I can't even imagine a life without it."

"I guess she wished she didn't have so *much* of it. It made her lonesome. It took things away from her."

"That's sad, kinda like *you* tryin' to bury up the person you were born to be," said Byrd.

Truth is worse than soap in the eyes.

"But there's something else," she whispered as I put conditioner in her hair and tried to comb it through. What a *mess*.

"Look, there's nothing you can say to me that will make me believe that you did such a thing. You loved them. You couldn't kill them. And I know you wouldn't harm your daddy, either."

"Aunt Wyn, I have this collection of pocketknives. And you know somethin'? I haven't been able to find my favorite one since the night they died. How can you explain that?"

"I'm sure there's some sort of explanation, and I'm going to get to the bottom of it as soon as I can. I was planning on doing some of that work today, but it looks like we have other things to do."

I wasn't worried about a little girl's missing knife. Not then.

I helped her out of the tub and wrapped her in the towels. She smelled so good, like sunshine.

"You ready yet?" called Jackson from across the yard.

"Not yet, Jackson!" called Byrd.

"It's the Fourth of July! We got a parade to attend!" sang Jackson, who was dancing around the yard. Waltzing with his big bottle of bourbon.

"La, la-la-la-la-laaa," He hummed. "Annie's Song."

Byrd broke free from my arms and ran across the lawn.

"You better go get dressed!" she called out. "You're still in your nightie and Ben's comin' off Highway Fifty as we speak! Lawdy, lawdy! You got yourself what? An hour at most to git yourself together? Hurry up, Aunt Wyn!"

I'd known he was coming, I just didn't know he was already in Alabama.

Nervous, I ran back to my cottage to get dressed.

I carefully pulled on a starched, white, button-down polo and a khaki miniskirt and slid on a pair of espadrilles. Then, standing in front of the mirror, I gathered my hair back. All the curls kept trying to pop out, but I wouldn't let them. Ben was coming.

Then I put my camera around my neck—again. My buffer against the world. I was mad, and yet I wanted nothing more than to see him and have him hold me. There was a tightness in my chest that I couldn't identify.

I walked back to the Big House as calmly as I could, went into Jackson's study, and poured myself a drink. Then Carter walked in from behind a bookcase, and I dropped my glass, whiskey and all.

Damn secret passages.

Before I knew it we were on our hands and knees gathering up pieces of glass and ice and mopping up the spill with a cloth he'd had tucked in his pocket.

A gentleman, I thought.

After helping me up, he poured us both a drink.

He was quiet. Just staring out the window.

A strange, quiet gentleman.

"How was your morning?" I asked.

"Fine," he said. He didn't look at me, he didn't even answer with a "How about yours?" He just stared out the windows toward the circular drive. Like he was waiting on someone, too.

Make that a strange, quiet man with no manners.

"So . . . I haven't had a chance to thank you, Carter."

He turned around then, a little too fast.

"For what?"

"Well, for being good to Patrick. For making Minerva happy, and . . . oh, hell, I don't know. I was just trying to make conversation."

I gave up and sat down on the huge leather sofa, sunken in from all the drunken nights Jackson spent there.

"Better watch out, you'll rumple yourself up good. Want to look your best for your fiancé, don't you?"

"How did you know he was coming?"

"Ran into Byrd," he said. "She's mighty excited about the

parade. She's taken to you quick. You might want to pull back on some of that love you're spreadin' on her."

I stiffened. "I don't see how loving a child is a bad thing."

"Look at you," he said, taking in my outfit. "You don't look like you'll be stayin' 'round here. You'll be back up north and then traipsing around the world takin' pictures in no time. And then what happens to Byrd?"

"Now look, just because you're married to my great-aunt does not give you the right to talk to me like that. I don't think anyone has spoken to me that way since—"

"Since what?" he interrupted. "Since you left? Of course they haven't. No one really knows who you are up there. How can they tell you anything honest? You don't even know who you are anymore."

A strange, quiet, mean son of a bitch.

It was all I could do to not throw my glass at his head. I was shaking mad.

"But," he continued, "you're welcome anyway. It's been a joy takin' care of Paddy. And Byrd, too. And Minerva? She's a fine-lookin' woman for an old lady, so we got ourselves a nice little romance."

He began to walk away but paused.

"You know what? You're a girl on fire. And seems to me, you been dousing those flames for years. Let yourself burn a little."

Then he was gone.

"Screw you, too," I muttered.

As if on cue, a rental car pulled up in front of the Big House. Ben. *I hope he's in the mood for a parade.* I thought.

One thing I had never forgotten about Magnolia Creek was the Fourth of July. I always loved it. No matter how hot, people would line the streets. The parade didn't start on Main Street like most. Instead, it began at the town limit sign and wove its way down all the oak-lined neighborhood avenues. There was the requisite fire truck, golf carts decorated with glittering flags, classic cars, and Uncle Sam riding a tractor. But the best part—the part that made it stand out from all the northern festivities—was that each of the parade participants that drove, biked, or even just walked by, threw things into the crowds. Beads, candy, even stuffed animals. The children of Magnolia Creek always brought bags with them to the parade. And when it ended at the small fire station in the middle of town, there'd be a picnic where they all got to compare their treasures.

Paddy and I were "Founders," so we always had to march in the parade, tossing out gifts. It made Paddy jealous, so Jackson made sure he had some sort of present at the end of it. The day always ended with me and Lottie and Paddy and Grant running as fast as we could down to the docks and throwing ourselves, holding hands and fully clothed, into the Gulf. And the four of us would hold our breath, our hair and clothes floating all around us, and the reeds and the sea grass, submerged branches and moorings tickled our feet, making us giddy with fear. We'd come up for air screaming, *"Snake! Gator! Dead body!"*

I could feel the water on my skin, the exhilaration of the fear. The companionship. All gone. Now I was all grown up and sipping a drink in my father's study, watching my fiancé get out of a green rental sedan.

Beautiful Ben, in a white linen shirt and a pair of lightweight jeans, was walking effortlessly up the steps to my home. So confident, so straight-backed.

And all I wanted was to sit down on Jackson's couch and drink myself far, far away. I missed my childhood friends. I wanted my baby brother back. And I couldn't help but think about how Ben had lied to me, had *always* been lying to me.

14

Byrd

> What makes the desert beautiful . . . is that
> somewhere it hides a well.
>
> —*The Little Prince*

I had a lot to think about as I got dressed for the parade. I was up in my attic, where I feel safest of all. So I got to thinkin' about the things I only think about, *really* think about, in that attic of mine. And it is *mine*. I don't care if it's been here a hundred million years.

There's lots of legends about this place, because it's so old. I'm a historian of sorts when it comes to that kind of stuff. I love this old house. And the most interestin' thing about it, is its history. I love history. Jamie's always makin' fun of me 'cause I love learning about how things *were*.

"All you gots to know is how things are, or how they're gonna be. Why waste your time with all that old, dusty stuff?" he said. We were walkin' to school when he said it. I don't go to school. But he does. Well, I go when I want to. When I feel like there's a subject that needs some pontification. *Pontification* being my favorite word at that time. And that day I was goin' because they were teaching the history of the Big House and I wasn't goin' to miss *that*.

"It ain't fair that you get to just come and go as you please, Byrd. It just *ain't*," Jamie complained.

"Life ain't fair," I said as we rounded the bend to the schoolhouse.

That day I walked into the classroom with my head held high. The other kids always get this scared look on their faces when I come in. So I just stared at them with a look that screams: *I know you. I know all of you and your deepest secrets.* Then they turn down their eyes. It works every time.

Jamie was supposed to be in the sixth grade, but they kept him back 'cause he has so many absences. Takin' care of his sad ol' mama.

The teacher, Miss Pimms (like the drink, spicy and elegant, Jackson always says), welcomed me because she knew better than to throw me out.

"Well, hey, Miss Byrd. What brings you to school today?"

Her shaky smile told a world of truth.

"I hear you're fixin' on telling the history of the Big House, and I wanted to see if you got it right," I said.

"I suppose the dog is staying, too?" she asked.

"Why, that's so *nice* of you to invite her, Miss Pimms!" I said, as the class erupted into laughter so hard I almost felt sorry for her. Almost.

I could tell she wanted to give me a whoopin' so I just slid into a chair and scooted up close to Jamie's in the back.

Time after time I'd told him to sit up front. "It makes 'em think you're smart," I'd say.

"I'll leave smart to you, Byrd, and stay back here where I can sleep," he'd say. Lord I missed him and his lazy ways.

Miss Pimms began, "The Big House was bought by Jackson Whalen the First in 1873."

I raised my hand and shook it around. Daddy used to call it "jazz hands."

"Yes, Byrd?"

"Well, with all due respect, Miss Pimms, that ain't exactly true," I said.

Miss Pimms sighed and sat at her desk. She stared out the window for a second and then looked back at me. "Byrd Whalen, why don't you tell this story if you know it so damn well."

The whole class took in a collective, surprised breath. It ain't often a teacher like Miss Pimms will let a curse word out her mouth.

I couldn't wait to tell the story, it's the whole reason I went to school that day in the first place! So I made my way up to the blackboard and picked up a piece of chalk and wrote down, The History of the Big House, Magnolia Creek Alabama. I turned to face the class, clearing my throat dramatically.

"Well, first of all . . . it wasn't called the Big House back then. It was a river shack built out of virgin pine. It had two rooms and a kitchen outside. Jackson Whalen the First, who everyone called 'Big Daddy,' brought his wife and six kids to live there. He was a lumber baron and he'd been cuttin' yellow pine and milling it for a decade before he found the perfect spot to settle down. He built a mill first. And as soon as the mill was operatin' he had to build onto the shack because his wife, Deborah Jane, kept having more and more babies so there weren't no room. He got the best architects from New Orleans to come build. That's why it looks so grand.

"Anyway, Deborah Jane was none too happy about the mist over Belladonna. Not one bit. So she made Big Daddy promise never to go over onto the island to mill any of those trees. He listened. But sadly, some of the kids got adventurous and ran off down there. Who can blame 'em, really? I bet some of you have wanted to go over there too, haven't ya?"

Jamie was holdin' his hand over his mouth, tryin' not to laugh. *Everyone's* scared of the mist.

"None of them came back the same," I continued, making my voice all spooky-like for *effect*, "but it was their youngest son, Farley, who was the most changed. When he was grown, he got drunk in New Orleans and raped a Cajun woman. She was a fortune-teller and mistress of the voodoo, and the story goes that she put a curse on the entire Whalen clan." I gestured wildly with my arms.

"Byrd? Don't you think that's enough, honey?"

"No! Miss Pimms, it's not. Not nearly enough. I'm sorry if you feel it's in poor taste, but the truth is the truth. May I finish?" Miss Pimms sighed, so I thought I might as well go on.

"Anyway, the curse! It's said the curse made it so they'd never be able to have big families again. And that all those children were bound to leave and find lives far away. I guess she figured it was worse to curse the mother of the sinner than the sinner himself. But whether the curse worked or not, in the generations that followed, all the Whalens spread out. And only one or two children were born in each family. My grandpap is the first one to stay forever. I think it's because he closed down that mill. Sort of switched all the destinies around."

Jamie waved his hand like a maniac. "What?" I cried out, half laughing.

"Tell them about the ghosts, Byrd!"

"Well," I said, letting my fingernail screech against the chalkboard. "I ain't sure these kids can handle that."

"That's quite enough, you two," began Miss Pimms.

"Y'all want to hear about the ghosts?" I asked, making my eyes real big.

But really, what kid doesn't want to hear a good ghost story?

Then I did something a little rude. I try to be nice, I swear it. Even if it's only 'cause my daddy gets mad when I'm what he calls "impertinent," but sometimes my worst self gets hold of me and won't let go.

I turned to the lovely Miss Pimms, and I placed my finger in front of my lips. She crossed her arms and got all kinds of huffy, but I knew I had the okay to continue.

"First, there's Naomi Green, my dear old gram. Only she ain't old. She died young. Way before any of us were even thought about. Not even a glimmer in our mama's eyes. Sometimes I think she's the worst because she's caught. She can't speak and she hovers around all murky-like." I shivered there for emphasis. "Some people think the curse young Farley brought upon the family was broken by her. See, Jackson . . . my Jackson . . . he traveled the world. Left the Big House like all the other Whalens. Even after he closed the mill. But when he was up north, he met Naomi and they fell in love." I went all dreamy and made kissy noises with my mouth. Everyone giggled.

"Then there's Janice Whalen, who was in love with Michael DuMond. They'd been in love for as long as anyone could remember. They couldn't have been more than nineteen when they got into a terrible car wreck where old Route Ninety-eight turns into Route Ten. There's still that creepy memorial there, a rotting old cross with drooping flowers all tucked in it helter-skelter like. So the legend goes that Janice lived for a bit on the side of the road, and when the sheriff got there, she told him, 'Tell my mama—*cough, cough*—tell my mama to bury me with Michael. I don't want to be dead without him—*(cough)*!' "

I pretended to be Janice, laying myself half over Miss Pimms's desk and knocking over a cupful of pens in the process.

"Byrd, please get on with this," Miss Pimms said impatiently.

"Janice's mama and daddy, the Whalens of the time, refused to do what she'd asked for. The lovers were buried separately. And now, late at night, you might see the ghost of Janice Whalen in the Big House gardens. Crying and searching, arms outstretched, for the one she loves. Only he never comes."

"Tell us another one!" yelled Jamie from the back of the room, pounding his desk. He was havin' a grand ol' time.

"Okay, what about we move away from ghost stories and talk about demons?" I asked. The class was getting downright antsy now. I had to talk *fast*.

"So, remember Farley Whalen and the curse? They say when he died . . . he didn't die at all. He became a demon who inhabits one child from Magnolia Creek each generation and makes them do terrible, terrible things."

John Fischer raised his hand. He looked a little like Jamie, only not as shiny. "Do you know who he lives inside right now?" I could tell it was a question no one wanted answered. So, I started choking and shaking and made my voice all scratchy-like.

"John Fischer, I do believe the child the demon inhabits is . . . *me!*"

The whole class jumped. And me and Jamie started laughing all crazy-like. Miss Pimms was on her feet. I knew my goose was cooked good.

To make matters worse, stupid Sadie Mathers, a front-row girl, was cryin' by the time I finished.

"*Get out!*" Miss Pimms said, pointing at the door. "Get out and take your nasty dog with you!"

Now, I should have just left and not thought twice about Miss Pimms. Except for being sorry about disrupting her class. Only she didn't need to speak that way about Dolores.

The whole room went quiet. And then I pointed at her. "You like your job, Miss Pimms?"

I'll admit it. That was mean.

But you know what? Everyone has to be themselves. So, I'm mean sometimes.

And that's what I thought when I looked out my window and saw Aunt Wyn walkin' up the path to the Big House. She looked terrible. All stuffy and cooped up. She was hidin' herself and that never ends well.

Now I'd have to get us *both* spiffed up for the parade.

She was dressed like that for Ben. People. I swear. They just don't get it. If you hide from who you really are, you run the risk of gettin' lost for good.

I'd let them have a few minutes alone 'cause Jackson always says, "People gotta work out their own demons on their own time in their own way," so that's what I'd let them do. But then I'd go on and introduce myself. And fix up my aunt's look.

Demons. Like Farley Whalen.

Just a story, really. Trust me on that one. I know what's what when it comes to ghosts and the like. There ain't no demon, and if there was, he *would* live inside me.

I fairly giggled. And thought of that old song, "There Was an Old Lady Who Swallowed a Fly."

"Ah, crud," I said, as I put on Naomi's old wedding veil. "If I'm a demon, I sure do hope I still get my woman boobies. Do demons even *have* boobies?"

15

Bronwyn

Maybe it was because I didn't meet him at the door.

I let Ben ring and knock like an idiot before Minerva, who shot me a look of death as she ran past the study, opened the door to greet him. Whatever it was, he was on edge.

I stood still and placed my drink on a table without looking (thankfully there was a table there, or it would have crashed straight to the ground, making me two for two with the Waterford).

"My, my . . . look what the cat done dragged in. I see you've met Minerva. Oh, wait. You already know her. Ain't that right?" I said, using my best Southern drawl.

"What on earth is the matter with you, Bronwyn?" she asked. She'd have pinched me blue if she was next to me.

I rolled my eyes. Classic BitsyWyn.

"You've got a lot of explaining to do, Mr. Caretaker, whatever that means," I said.

"I missed you," he said, gazing down. Not looking at me.

It was Minerva who saved us. "You two are wasting time. Get this moment over with and just talk it out. People, I swear. Stubborn to the core. Just get on with it."

Her voice was like a bucket of cold water waking me up. This was Ben. My Ben. The man I'd lived with and loved for seven years.

He walked right up to me and held me so tight he picked me up off the ground. "I *missed* you," he whispered into my hair.

"I know," I said. Then I pulled away to look at him, to ask the questions I needed answers to. To make sure he told me the truth. "There's so much I need to tell you, to ask you. Why didn't you tell me about all this?" I waved my left hand, my ring glinting in the light. And then I launched into, "They never called me. They just let him plead guilty! And then there was this phone call, well not a *real* call . . . and it could be Grant, but I don't know . . ." The words tumbled out. Then somewhere between the "I missed you" and the "why are you here?" I started full-on crying.

I'd gone crazy fuckall.

Ben guided me to the couch and sat down next to me.

"Shh, honey, it's okay. Let's take this slow. Look, I'm here early because Minerva called me."

I looked up only to find her still standing in the doorway. She shrugged her shoulders and then went back into the hall and upstairs, yelling, "Byrd! Time to go!"

"Don't be mad at her," he continued, his voice steady. "She knows you need better answers than she's able to give. And she thinks you need help,"

"Help with what?"

"With unraveling your mystery. She thinks you might be onto something with this Grant person, and she thinks there are some other options, too. Things you may not be safe looking into alone. So, I'm here. I'm always here."

He leaned in to kiss me.

"Ahem" came a voice from the doorway.

There she was, my Byrd. And, oh Lord. The way she was dressed. Petticoats, a white ribbed boy's T-shirt, a whole bunch of too big jewelry, and my mother's wedding veil. She was also lugging around a bundle of clothes.

"Byrd, honey? Come here. I want you to meet Ben."

She came right over and sat herself down on my lap like a possessive cat.

"Nice to meet you, I *suppose*," she said, disinterestedly holding out her hand.

"You suppose?" Ben laughed, shaking her hand.

Then she reached up and pulled the pins out of my hair, letting the tight bun loose. My curls tumbled out everywhere.

"That's better," she said, and then to Ben, "I don't know anything about you yet."

"Why don't you read my mind?" he asked.

She was off my lap, and that's when I realized the bundle in her arms was a white, flowing shirt that used to belong to Naomi. She was pulling at my Polo and I didn't even stop her. I just lifted my arms up and allowed her to switch one for the other.

"I already tried. You got magic, don't you, Ben?"

"A bit."

She threw the Polo across the room and then she pulled off my shoes.

"These ain't gonna work, Aunt Wyn. Try this pair."

She put a pair of Naomi's Chinese slippers on my feet. Black and lightweight. They fit perfectly.

She stepped back. "That's better, don't you think?"

And it was.

Then she turned to Ben. "It's not nice to block people from your thoughts," she said.

"It's not nice for little girls to pry," he said.

They were playing a mental game of chess. They contemplated each other, figuring out their next, best moves. Ben broke first. An easy mark.

"Well, all you have to know is that I love your aunt very much, and I'm here to help her get your daddy back home, okay?"

Checkmate. She was smiling.

I held her tight against me, snuggling her and all her layers of lace and bare shoulders.

Jackson came in at that point.

"Well now, what do we have here?"

Byrd got up and raced past him. "See you at the parade!" she yelled. I guessed she was leaving without us.

"Jackson, Ben. Ben, Jackson."

"Well, lookit that," he said. "Ain't you a fine-lookin' fella. I think I approve, son."

"Thank you, sir. It's wonderful to finally meet you."

"I'm sure it is . . . sure it is . . ." Jackson replied, processing. He'd just found out Ben was a black man. And now we were all going to the biggest get-together Magnolia Creek has all year and him being the mayor, he'd have to introduce Ben to *everyone*.

I cannot express to you the childish, spiteful moment of joy that I felt.

I'd spent my whole childhood angry with him for running

away from Naomi's problems. For hiding inside that damn bottle. And now he'd have to stand tall and be present.

"Well." Jackson cleared his throat. "I'm sure you two have a
lot to talk about, but we gotta go. So, come on, and you can talk
when the day is done. Okay?"

"Are *you* okay, Bronwyn?" asked Ben.

"I think so, but you'll tell me everything later, right?"

"Absolutely."

"I'm glad you're here, Ben," I said.

"Well then, if all this welcoming is done, we got a parade to
attend," said Jackson.

I wanted to take pictures, and since I knew I'd be following
alongside the parade, Jackson invited Ben to sit with him on the
grandstand.

He accepted, kissed my cheek, and walked away.

I crouched down near where the parade was starting and began snapping photos.

The parade hadn't changed much, except for Byrd. She marched
in the parade as a lone soul. Jackson explained that when she was
about four years old she *demanded* to march.

Alone.

I watched her, clicking away on my camera. I must have taken
a thousand frames just of her. She wore a driftwood plaque around
her neck with the words "Queen of the Myst" burned into it. A *Y*
in the word like her name. And whereas the other parade march-
ers were throwing out trinkets and candy, our Byrd was throwing
out premonitions and advice.

Byrd was the last person in the parade. The people became quiet, almost reverent when she approached. She seemed to sniff the air, but once she opened her mouth, that damn girl couldn't shut up.

She was wearing Naomi's wedding veil, now torn and dirty along its edges. The flowers at the crown, once alive and vibrant, were now dried, and pieces of them littered her hair like moldy confetti. She'd walk, look for her next "victim," and then make a run for them. Her first target was an overly large woman wearing an ill-fitting dress.

"Mrs. Saint James?"

The woman took a step back, her eyes growing wide.

"Ain't no amount of food in the world gonna glue your sad soul back together again. All it's gonna do is make you fatter. And then you'll die. You want that, Mrs. Saint James?"

The woman shook her head and mouthed the word no.

"I didn't think so," said Byrd. And then she returned to the middle of the street and continued her march. I took pictures like a woman on fire. The camera loved that girl. What a beautiful, haunting, captivating child. She's a spell caster. A lost witch, a creature capable of things one can only dream about. Bad dreams or good.

She stopped next to a small family. The mother and children huddled close together. The father standing separate. His arms were crossed in front of his chest, and the neck of a beer bottle dangled between two of his fingers. His expression made me nervous for her. I should have known better.

She walked right up to the cowering woman.

"He ain't gonna stop beatin' on you. And I swear your girls will grow up thinkin' that's the way a woman ought to be treated.

You want that?" Then she turned to the woman's husband. "You hear me, Mr. *Wrong*?"

And that's when it hit me, his name was Wright. Stephen Wright. I remembered him from school. A bully even then.

"I swear on my father's life that if you lay hands on her one more time I'll find a way to stop you. And it will *not* be pleasant."

"That a threat, sweetheart?" he asked, sarcasm seeping out of him.

"Nope, that's a promise."

She flicked the beer bottle right out from between his fingers and it crashed to the ground.

"Clean that up, Mr. Wrong. Clean it up good or I'll have the sheriff arrest you for litterin'. Ain't that right, Sheriff?"

And as if it were orchestrated beforehand, there was Stick, standing right in back of good ol' Stephen Wright.

"You betcha, Byrd," he said, saluting her. Then he looked at me, winked and mouthed the words, "Come see me." I nodded.

And so it went.

To the druggist: "I know you been waterin' down those medications, you best stop that."

To the little girl on the corner of Main and Oak: "You did well, Hannah! Last year I was concerned you wouldn't stop picking on your sister, but it seems my advice worked."

And then to a man on the street selling little wooden toys, "If you don't get that jigsaw fixed, you're gonna lose an arm."

Next, she stopped at Jane Bradshaw. Another person I grew up with. Her family owned the local soda shop. A fragile, pretty woman with pale eyes and even paler hair. She was holding a new baby. Byrd held her hand out. And Jane jostled the baby to her hip in order to touch Byrd.

"Miss Jane?" she asked, a curious softness in her voice.

Then she looked directly at the baby.

"I'm so sorry for your loss."

"What?" asked a visibly shaken Jane Bradshaw.

I felt my stomach lurch.

"Byrd. Please. What on earth can you mean?" asked Jane.

"Oh, just prepare yourself, Miss Jane. There ain't nothing you can do about it. When the Lord calls, he calls, you know?"

Byrd began to walk away shaking her head a little overdramatically. Jane reached out and yanked on her veil. Byrd turned around.

"Please, Byrd, what can I do?"

"Well, a free lime ricky every once and a while would be nice."

"Fine, Byrd. Whatever you want. Come on, I'll give you one right now."

"Let's go," she said, coming to me and tugging me down the street toward the soda shop. "I could use a pop, you?"

"Byrd, why did you do that to her? Is her baby really in danger?"

"No. It's her mama. I didn't say anything about her baby."

"But you made her think it was the baby. I won't have that, Byrd. We're going over there right now and telling her. And if you think you're getting a free soda, you're crazy."

Byrd didn't even fight about it. Just took my hand and we walked together back toward Jane.

"Bronwyn?" asked Jane when she saw us.

"In the flesh," I said. "How've you been?"

"Better," she said, worriedly giving Byrd a sidelong glance.

"Tell her," I said.

Byrd sighed, before telling the truth. Relief washed over Jane, making her shoulders relax.

"Go on in and get that pop, Byrd," said Jane.

"Jane? Do you think that's a good idea?" I asked, holding Byrd, who was trying to run for the soda shop, by her wrist. "Isn't that like, negative reinforcement or something?"

"Oh, how cute, Wyn! You been readin' up on parentin' in those fancy Yankee books?" asked Jane.

Dear Lord. "Just go," I said to Byrd, who was off like a shot.

"See how happy she is? A little pop ain't gonna hurt her. So, how you been, girl?" asked Jane happily. "I'm so, so sorry about what happened to Lotttie and that dear little boy of hers. I mean . . ."

"It's all right. That's why I'm down here, Jane. To figure it all out. Something's just not right."

"Well, I hope you do figure it out, because we all miss Paddy around here. And we can't believe he'd do such a thing."

"Hey, Jane? May I ask you something?"

"Of course!" she said, shifting her baby from one arm to the other.

"How does this town feel about Byrd? I can't quite get a grasp on it,"

Jane smiled a little too sweetly, as if she was saying, *You don't know much about anything anymore, do you? Been gone for so long . . . come back and try to understand it all in one gulp.*

"Let's see," she said, pausing. "How can I explain this so it makes sense? We love her. We do. Her good and bad. She's done a lot for all of us. I don't know one person she hasn't touched. Healed, warned, all those things. Even me. Sure, she was mean and terrible today. But I had three miscarriages before I had this bundle." She held her baby close and kissed her head. "Then? She just showed up at our house one day with a bunch of dried leaves and a set of handwritten directions. And the next baby? She took."

"So, why don't you ever give her a free soda then?"

Jane shrugged. "I guess it's sort of love and hate . . . no, hate's too strong. She's different is all, follows different rules. Like she doesn't go to school. Also? I swear, she's never asked us. If she'd asked us, we'd have given it to her."

"So you all love her? I don't think she knows that."

"For all she's done for us, for everyone? We depend on her. We feel like she's *ours*. That make sense? We're lucky to have her. She's sorta like a pastor or somethin'. You know how each of their flock thinks that the pastor is speakin' straight from the pulpit to their own heart? It's like that."

"That's a lot of responsibility for a little girl," I said.

"Nah, she loves it. Thrives on it, I think," Jane responded. Then the baby started fussing. "It's the heat," she said. "Look, I'll go into the shop and send Byrd back out to you when she's done with her pop, okay?"

"Sounds good. Thanks, Jane. Nice to see you again."

"You too, honey! We'll get together soon, okay? Have some of that pie Minerva makes. I miss that pie. What was it?"

I tried to stifle the smile. It was shameful really. Every time another kid was mean in any way to Lottie I'd ask Minerva to make a few of her delicious, but tampered with, pies. A little bit of belladonna mixed with myrtle and strawberry leaves go completely unnoticed in a plum pie. But a few days later? Everyone has the flu. Plum pie flu.

"It was plum pie," I said, "And I'll bring some over real soon."

She made the baby wave to me as they walked into the shop. Alone again, I scanned for Ben.

Everyone usually met up at the firehouse for a picnic. I saw Ben sitting with Jackson at a picnic table, laughing and talking with the Old-timers. He waved at me, letting me know I should just go about my business.

Jackson was, of course, holding high court. Being the mayor, and . . . well, just being *Jackson,* he had the prized seat at a picnic table beneath the shade of an enormous silver elm, its scales mimicking those of an alligator. He was already drinking and smoking a cigar. No food necessary for Jackson.

"But you have to do somethin' about it, Jackson!" a man dressed soup to nuts in white linen yelled. A bunch of disgruntled people stood around him, nodding their heads in agreement.

"Bronwyn! The prodigal. Come on over here, sweet sugar, and meet the town board. You musta known 'em when you were little, but you're all grown up. So come say hey, okay?"

I walked over to stand by my father. And, to be honest, felt a little protective of him. "What's all this arguing about?"

Jackson laughed, but the men looked nervous.

"Seems like things are goin' missin' all over town. Pieces of sheds, animals, tin roofs, garbage cans. I'll tell you what, it's strange. But nothing we can't figure out," he said.

"You got the sheriff on it, it's true," said the man in white. "But we only got one sheriff round here, Jackson. Maybe we need more?"

"Fellas, what I need more of is this here bourbon. Follow me over to the bar with your complaints. Ain't it hot, though?"

Typical Jackson. He'd probably take care of the issue, and it was strange for there to be any crime at all here, but he wasn't going to ruin his Fourth of July worrying about it. I felt sort of proud watching him walk off with all those squawking chickens behind him. Ben followed, too, giving me a wink and a kiss on the check as he walked by.

◊

The picnic was nothing much, just hamburgers, hot dogs, and some salads made by some of the older women in town. I got myself a plate and sat under an old oak. Byrd came to sit with me. She eyed the plate with dismay.

"Ain't nothing interestin' on that plate, Aunt Wyn."

I laughed. "Sure ain't."

"You know what? Sam Crocker went out fishin' at four o'clock this mornin' and caught himself a whole bunch of white trout. He's fryin' it up right now at his bar. Wanna go?"

Sam's Place. The local watering hole. Best part about Sam's was the sign outside: COLD BEER: FREE ADVICE. My mouth watered at the mention of white trout. You can't get saltwater trout up north. And you can't freeze it or store it. You have to catch it and cook it. And when you do, there isn't another fish like it.

"Let's do it," I said to my niece. She took my hand and we walked down Main Street.

"Where ya'll goin'?" Jackson called.

"Byrd says there ain't nothin' interesting about this food, so we're heading to Sam's."

"Suit yourselves!" he shouted, "But your Ben is stayin' with me. I quite like him!" Jackson was now clearly drunk. "I *approve* of this young man, and there, see? I've done *saved the South* with that one statement, now haven't I?" Everyone started to laugh. Charming Jackson Whalen. Ben was getting to experience him for the first time.

That spiteful, snarky little feeling I had at the beginning of the day was suddenly gone. I was proud of my father. He'd done well.

I looked over at Ben and motioned for him to come with us. He shook his head. Smiled. He wanted to be there, and I knew why. Caretaker or not, Ben was a writer. And he was doing some *serious* research. My people sure as hell are some *characters*.

Byrd skipped ahead of me into Sam's, the bells on the door announcing our arrival. The air-conditioning was a relief, but the smell of frying fish permeated everything.

Four or five Towners were seated at the dark bar. It's a small place. A few tables, one long bar, and a jukebox. The Towners turned around, smiled, and nodded. A few got up to hug me hello. Byrd went straight to the cash register and hit the bell that was next to it a few times. A few times too many, you might say.

Sam came out of the kitchen and then stopped short.

When we were kids, I always thought Sam looked like Santa Claus. He hadn't changed much. Santa Claus with a "Roll Tide" hat on his head. Got to love Alabama football.

"Why, BitsyWyn, that you?"

"Sure is, Sam. How you been?"

"Same ol', same ol'. What can I get for y'all?"

Byrd answered, "Two orders of your fried white trout, baked beans, and potato salad."

Sam winked at her. "You bet, Lady Byrd. Comin' right up."

"Don't forget the bread like you did last time!" she shouted after him.

We sat at the bar, Byrd spinning on the bar stool while I waited for the next song on the jukebox.

You fill up my senses . . . John Denver.

"Oh, hell no," I said, sliding off the stool with a dollar in my hand.

Byrd came up next to me.

"Let it play, Aunt Wyn. Let it play and dance with me."

"Well, it's hard to turn down an offer like that." I picked her up and she wrapped her skinny legs around my middle. We rocked back and forth and I sang the words into her ears.

Like a sleepy blue ocean . . .

She tightened her arms around my neck. Then she whispered in my ear, "Sometimes we think we hate somethin', only we don't. We're just scared of it. You like this song because it reminds you of the laughing days. But it scares you 'cause it makes you sad. Let it make you sad, so it can make you happy again."

"Oh, Byrd. I'm so sorry I wasn't here to watch you grow up, I wish I'd known you from the beginning."

She pulled away so she could look me in the face. "You want to?"

"Want to what?"

"Get to know me from the beginnin'?"

"I wish I could."

"You can," she said, "But you have to pay attention, because I've learned through experience I can only do this once, okay?"

"Sounds good," I said.

Then she pressed her cheek against mine.

All at once a thousand memories, like still frames came shooting across my mind. *Byrd as a baby. Byrd and Jamie. Byrd sitting on Jackson's knee getting told all the stories of the Big House. Byrd and*

Paddy. Bedtime stories, baths, bike rides. Byrd's fourth Christmas where she got books about magic. Byrd swimming with alligators.

The images ended when the song was over, I let her down. There were tears in her eyes and mine, too. "Thank you, Byrd," I whispered.

"You're welcome." She sniffled.

"What's the matter, honey?"

She didn't say anything. She took my hands and placed one on each side of her face. Then she took them off, kissed each finger, and pressed my hands into fists. When she opened them she blew lightly on my upturned palms and the scent of fresh roses filled that stinky bar, and a feeling of love so big washed over me that I got light-headed.

Sam came out of the kitchen with two to-go containers that he put into a paper bag.

"What on earth?" he said, sniffing at the air. "Smells like a goddamned department store in here. Byrd? How many times do I gotta ask you not to do magic in my bar?"

Byrd grabbed the bag and ran out the front door, "If there's one place that needs magic, it's your nasty ol' bar, Sam Crocker!" The scent of roses streamed out after her.

"I'd say I'm sorry, Sam. But that was pure wonderful. What do I owe you?"

"Nothin'. Call it a welcome home gift."

I nodded and began to leave. Byrd was probably already half-way down to the benches by the beach.

"Sam?" I asked, leaning on the door, letting the hot air outside mingle in.

"Yeah?"

"Do you people love my niece, or are you all afraid of her?"

The other patrons all stared down at their drinks. Sam took a moment before he answered.

"Both," he said. "She's the best and worst of everything, Wyn. And mostly we don't understand her. But if you're askin' me if we wish any harm on her . . . the answer is no. This town needs her like we need air. Only, remember, sometimes the air can carry things on it that are poison. You still have to breathe, though. It's the truth. Plain ol' truth. Careful with her, Wyn. Love can conceal a lot of things."

Cold Beer: Free Advice.

"Well, thank you for that, Sam. But I think I can see things a lot more clear than all of you. Perspective and all that," I said, and left. Let the bells slam hard behind me. I ran a little to catch up with my niece. My magical, misunderstood, lost soul of a niece.

◊

Perspective . . . I'd forgotten about the trees lining the street that ran parallel to the beach. Each one creating a perfect postcard image of the water and shore houses beyond. And I don't know how I could have forgotten that, because noticing it was what changed my future. Naomi didn't like being at the Big House or the property. The mist made her sick. But back before the drugs took over, she had two exceptions. The apothecary for prescription opiates, when Jackson couldn't get his hands on opium, and the sea.

Once, when I must have been very small—because Jackson was proudly pushing Paddy in our old-fashioned pram—we went walking by the beach under those very same trees, as Naomi held my hand.

I loved holding her hands. They always felt so soft, like silk.

I must have noticed the way the trees made frames around the still pictures beyond. Perspective.

Naomi never rushed. So she leaned down to see what I saw.

"Ah, yes! Very good, Bronwyn! You have the eyes of an artist. A photographer even. Doesn't she, Jackson?"

He must have agreed because the very next day I woke up to a Polaroid camera next to my bed. It was my prized possession for years until I moved on to more expensive cameras.

And now Byrd has it, a voice sounded in my head.

Mama, is that you? I thought as I stood there, holding Byrd's hand tight. I couldn't believe I'd forgotten so many important things. I'd stolen away my own past.

It made me feel like a coward.

"You're no kind of coward, Aunt Wyn. You're pretty brave, I'd say," Byrd piped up.

"I thought you couldn't read my mind anymore."

"I can't. You don't need no fancy ESP when someone's hurtin'. You can guess."

"Well, you seem to know more about me and my past than I do, Ms. Byrd. Anything else you want to show me before we go back home?"

"Nah, let's eat. I'm so hungry I could eat a horse!" She rubbed her belly. "Hey, Aunt Wyn?"

"Hmm?"

"Your hands are like silk, just like hers, right?"

"Yes. I was just thinking about that. See, I've spent a lot of time trying to forget her."

"Someday you're gonna have to be brave enough to remember. I think people don't really forget. I think they simply don't want to face things. Face your past, Aunt Wyn."

"Seems to me, young Byrd, you might want to take some of your own advice."

She glared at me, digging into her fish. "I'm too young to have a past."

"Oh, now you're young." I laughed opening my own carton, picking up a long strip of the whitefish and biting into it. It melted on my tongue like butter. There was some barbecue on the plate, too. A gift to us from Sam. Pulled pork, beans, and slaw. And a nice thick slice of white bread to even it out. I bit easily into the tender pork.

Real barbecue is hard, if not impossible to find up north. I wish Ben had come, just to taste. That plate of food was all he needed to know about Alabama.

We made our way slowly back home, walking up Main Street as the sun set. Warmth spread though me like a drug. Byrd, dirty again, and beautiful, kept on talking about Jamie, bending down every so often to pick up abandoned strands of shiny plastic beads.

We caught up with Jackson leaning on Ben for support. And we all went back to the Big House's front porch, where Minerva and Carter were waiting. They took Jackson inside, and the three of us went back to the cottage where I gave Byrd a proper bath, not minding her protests, and tucked her into my bed.

"You've made it real nice here for me, Byrd. Thank you for that."

But she was already fast asleep.

You make her feel safe.

There was that voice again.

"Mama?" I asked. This time, out loud.

No answer.

I went out into the living room where Ben had made iced

tea, took a glass, and stretched out on the couch under the ceiling fan. Heaven equals moving air sometimes. He came over to the couch and tried lifting up my legs so he could sit near me, but I said, "You sit across from me so I can see your eyes when you speak, Mr. Caretaker. I need the truth like I've never needed it before. It's time."

"Here's the thing," he began after sitting where I told him. "You have to know this. I knew who you were, who I was . . . when I met you, it's true. But it isn't why I love you. Caretakers don't have to love the person they're paired with. I mean, Naomi and Minerva weren't lovers."

"A truer statement there never was. Go on," I said.

He sat back, took a breath, and continued. "I'm from a place, one you already know about, one that has its own peculiar ways. And when I met you that day in New York, I knew. I just knew. And I spent the whole day trying to decide if I was drawn to you because of my job or because you were just a hell of a woman."

I couldn't help but smile.

"It was when we were listening to that jazz, and you took out your cards. Do you remember the spread?"

I remembered his hands more than the cards.

"It told me our future, even if you didn't know it yourself. And it told me you were lost. That I needed to stay near you, and to be honest, just being your friend wasn't an option. I wouldn't have been able to not touch you. I can't even stand being across the room from you now."

I stayed quiet.

"I don't know what else to tell you." He sighed.

"Why didn't you just tell me? Right then?"

"Because I knew you were running. I knew that if I made any sort of connection between me and the life you left behind, that you'd push me away. You're good at that."

He was right.

"Why didn't we ever talk about where we were from?"

"Because I always changed the subject, and we made a pact."

"Why would you do that? Why would you misdirect me?"

"Because somewhere along the way I forgot what I was supposed to be doing."

"And what, exactly, were you supposed to be doing?"

"Helping you get home."

We'd been together seven years and he hadn't once urged me to go home. If anything, he'd closed that option right out of my mind. Things he'd said were coming back to me.

When Stella died, I'd thought about coming back.

"I should go," I said.

"Don't you think it would make matters worse? I mean, complicate things for them at a complicated time?"

"You didn't do that . . . you kept me away. On purpose. Damn, Ben, all those things you used to say . . . they're blossoming in my head like an oleander."

He got up and started pacing.

"Well, I started to think that maybe this *wasn't* your home. You know? Maybe you were supposed to live with *me*. That *I* was your home."

"So, you fell in love with me. I fell in love with you, and then you spent the next seven years . . . blocking me? Keeping me blind?"

"It doesn't sound good when you put it that way," he said, sitting back down. Deflated.

There is nothing worse than an awkward silence between two people who've never experienced it before.

So he did what most people would do. He changed the subject.

"Do you think he did it?" he asked.

"Who did what?"

"Do you think Patrick killed them?"

"No," I said.

"Peel back the layers, Wyn. Peel them back. He confessed. What do you really think?"

"Why don't you read my mind?"

"I've been trying. All that's in there is confusion. I can't get your real opinion."

"My opinion. Fancy that. Here's what I think. I think that I don't really care if he *did* do it. I'm going to get him out of prison and back home where he belongs if it's the last thing I do." I said. And saying it that way made me feel strong. Resolved.

Right.

Ben laughed. It rolled out from deep within his chest. Then he came over to me on the couch and held me close.

"You are becoming more like your own people every day, the Fairview ones," he said.

"How do you mean?" I asked.

"We don't ever judge the evil that people do. Bad things are measured the same way we measure good things. Individually. It's a gift, but most people don't understand it. Too much work, I guess, to figure out each person as a whole instead of parts of this and parts of that."

He kept talking, but I was already falling asleep and had already heard everything I needed to hear.

I woke up a few hours later to the sounds of a drunken Jackson banging on my door. Ben had put me in bed next to Byrd. I hastily ran out into the living room, where Ben was sleeping soundly on the couch. He never did wake up for much.

"Shh!" I scolded Jackson, going out on the porch and quietly shutting the door behind me. "They're sleeping. And I don't feel like having it out with Ben again tonight."

He was already getting himself comfortable, lighting a cigar.

"What's this? You and your beau have a fight?"

"No. Just too much truth all at once."

"I hear you. But I came over here to tell you what I should have yesterday. I sure am glad you decided to come home, sugar. And I know it can't be easy."

"I'm just crazy about that girl," I said, sitting next to him.

"I know you are. I saw it in the way you looked at her today. She can be addictive. Makes you feel all warm inside, don't she? Like nothin' and no one can touch you."

"Yeah, that's right. I don't think I could have come home and been this comfortable without her."

"I don't think you would have ever come home at all if I hadn't bribed you with her," he said.

"What do you mean, bribe?"

"Well, looky. There're those lights again, over Belladonna. You see 'em?"

They were beautiful, haunting.

"Jackson, answer me."

When he spoke, he wouldn't look at me.

"She don't need no takin' care of. I do."

My heart sank.

"Are you sick, Daddy?"

"Oh, now I get a 'Daddy.' No, I ain't sick. I'm just . . . tired. The drinkin's catchin' up with me, and I needed you to come home and unravel this mess with Paddy."

"But I thought you wanted to let it be?"

"Well, Wyn, I knew you wouldn't let it rest. And my fear is that if we don't do somethin' soon, poor Jamie's body is gonna turn up. And when it does, there ain't no amount of money or power in the world that's gonna keep my boy out of the chair."

"They'd execute him?"

"You bet your ass they would."

"So you used Byrd as a bribe to convince me to come home to do the work needed to exonerate Paddy?"

"Yep." He sighed, taking a long puff on his cigar.

I'd never seen Jackson need anyone. Except Naomi. And that was a different kind of need altogether.

"Okay. I'll do the work," I said, grabbing his hand and squeezing it briefly.

"It ain't that easy, sugar."

"Why?"

"Well, if he did do it, and he might have, we don't know, we'd have to fabricate a murderer."

"He didn't do it," I said.

He put down the cigar on the end of a little side table and put his head in his hands.

"I shoulda never let him confess. I shoulda never let Stick take him that day without the proper people around . . . I . . ." His voice broke.

"Daddy, you can't blame yourself. What's done is done. Let's just try to fix it, okay?"

He didn't say anything. He talked a good game, my father, but when he was backed into a corner he'd go quiet. Invisible. I wasn't having it, not that night.

"You want the truth, Jackson?" I said harshly. "Truth is, you have a 'give 'em what they want' problem."

He sat up sharply and looked at me. "What's that supposed to mean?"

"Mama wanted her opium. So you got it for her. No matter what the cost. And that price was high, Daddy. Then, when I was too young to know any better, I wanted to run away. So you let me. But not only did you let me, you funded the whole thing! Because that's what I wanted. And then yesterday you were saying Paddy wanted to be in jail. Because he confessed. Because he pled guilty. So, think about it. Maybe you just thought you were giving him what *he* wanted."

My father sat back and closed his eyes.

"What would you like me to say, girl? I'm an old man now. Old on the inside. I'm a drunk, and I hate to tell you, but I'm not prepared to change. So you have to figure out if you want to forgive me and love me like I am, or run away again. Or hell, stay here and hate me. Just . . . know that I love you the best way I know how. I always have. I do the best I can."

I'd never heard such honesty from my father. So I sat back with him and said nothing. Not one thing.

"Want a drink?" he asked.

"I don't think I've ever wanted one more than I do right now," I said.

"That's my girl." Jackson patted my shoulder.

"I want to see Grant," I said abruptly.

"Do you think that's the best idea right now?"

"No, I don't. But I need to see him. I think he might know something about this whole mess."

"I don't know that Grant is in any kinda shape to help us with this, sugar."

"Why? What's he been doing?"

"Well, now . . . Grant's in New Orleans, Wyn. Living the dream. Which should tell you all you need to know about what he's been up to for the last fourteen years. Which is nothin'."

"Thank you, Daddy."

"You are most welcome, my daughter."

That July Fourth ended with my father's arm over my shoulder and a bottle of bourbon we finished off while quietly watching the strange lights play in the sky over Belladonna Bay. The two of us finally realizing that we didn't have to be afraid of each other. That our love could live quietly and without reproach.

It was a damn fine evening.

16

Byrd

It is such a mysterious place, the land of tears.

—*The Little Prince*

I thought long and hard about how I felt about Ben. It distracted me for the whole damn parade.

He had such lonesome thoughts goin' on inside his head. I told him that he blocked me. Which was true. But as soon as he was convinced I was done trying to read him, he let his guard down. It's so easy to make grown-ups do the things you want 'em to do.

I like him. Don't get me wrong. He's one of us. And he's hand-some and not sweaty. I don't like people who sweat too much.

I could tell how much he loved my aunt. Too much.

And he was *worried*.

And I could feel her. Even if I couldn't read her mind any-more. I could feel her pulling away from him. Or bein' torn, at least.

And then later? They thought I was asleep, but I was listening to their conversation.

There were three things I noticed.

ONE: There was no hankey-pankey. (Later, Ben slept on the couch and Aunt Wyn slept with me.)

TWO: Ben was havin' trouble understanding that he'd broken her trust. And trust is downright important. How can you even begin to enjoy a person if you don't trust 'em?

THREE: Well, actually, there wasn't a third thing. I just can't stand even numbers.

Then I started thinkin' 'bout Jamie and crawled back into my aunt's bed 'cause I got lonely all over again.

I know babies aren't supposed to remember things, but they do. Normal babies remember it deep down in who they are. Because I ain't normal, I remember everything right up front. Even bein' inside my own mama's belly, God rest her gypsy soul.

But what I remember best is the first time I saw Jamie.

He don't recall it like I do. He remembers things like normal people. He felt a tug toward me. He don't remember how it felt when our hands first touched. But I do. And boy, was I frustrated with that baby body of mine that couldn't just get on up and play with him. I'd been so lonesome without my mother, without her heartbeat whooshing in my ear. And that's what happened when I touched my hand to his. I heard his heart beat. And you know what it said? "Byrd, Byrd, Byrd, Byrd, Byrd."

I found my safe place. And it was inside of Jamie.

But now Jamie's gone. Luckily I found a whole other safe place inside of Aunt Wyn. It's scary, to love like that. I already knew what it felt like to lose all the safe around me.

Loving my aunt like a kid loves a mama was starting to look better and better.

A child can't simply go through life with *no one*.

And though I liked Ben, I wanted to tell him that he could go straight on home to where he came from. And that he wasn't gonna take her.

He'd have her over my dead body.

❖

The mornin' after the parade, I got up and shook Aunt Wyn awake. She looked a mess. Ben was still asleep on the couch.

"You been drinkin' with Jackson?"

"Sure have," she said, squinting at the morning sun.

"I'll close the blinds," I said.

"Thank you, sweetheart."

The "sweetheart" made all the worries come right on out of me.

"If I didn't do it, and my daddy didn't do it, who could it have been? " I asked in a rush.

That sure as heck woke her up.

"Shh! Baby! I don't want Ben to hear. These walls are thin and he's only just on the couch! It's ridiculous. Let it go. You didn't do anything, and your daddy didn't do it, either."

"Do you really think it was Grant?"

"Did I tell you about that?"

I shrugged.

"I guess I did, even if I didn't, right? Well, it's possible. That message he left on Charlotte's answering machine was strange. But I'm not too crazy about that idea, either, Byrd. To tell you the truth."

She didn't want it to be Grant. I could *feel* it. But he was the best way to get my daddy out of jail.

"Him and Charlotte had some sort of parting of ways a few weeks before she was found . . . maybe . . . maybe she told him something that upset him. So, even if he didn't do the killin', maybe he knows something about who did?"

"They had a fight? What about?"

"Jamie."

"Why would they fight about Jamie?" she asked.

"Got me," I said, but I knew. Sort of. Only that information belonged to Jamie. I'm a loyal friend.

"Well," she said. "That settles it. Time to get up. Jackson and I had a good long talk last night, and I have to get busy today. I'll go see Stick, then your daddy, and then I'll go find Grant."

The smell of chicory coffee, bitter and strong, wafted in from the great room.

"Ben's up, I guess." I muttered.

"Do you like him, Byrd?" she asked.

"Sure! I think he's great. A nice fellow." *He just ain't takin' you anywhere.*

She laughed. "Has anyone ever told you you're a card?"

"Nope. Mostly I just get called crazy."

Then she grabbed me and tickled me right down into the pillows. "You are, you are, you are!" she said. "And I wouldn't want you any other way!"

We laughed like loons, then we caught our breath there, together all wound up around each other.

"Let's get up," she said. "I need some of that coffee. It's gonna be a long day."

"I'm comin' with you," I said.

"No, Byrd, this is grown-up stuff."

"I'm comin'!" I felt a rage well up inside of me. I stomped around the words and huffed and puffed.

"You done?" she asked. And you know somethin', she didn't look mad or frustrated or nothin', she looked downright amused.

"What's so damn funny?"

"You. *You* are funny. You remind me of your daddy." She came to me and put her arms around me. She felt like a harness, a safe one. Like when Dolores gets upset and I have to hold her tight.

"I have an idea," she said. "Since you have to stay here, how about I give you my camera, and you can take pictures, however many you want, all day long."

"Really?" I'd been wantin' to get my hands on that fancy camera. But I didn't steal it. Which should prove how much I loved her.

"Deal," I said.

"I'm gonna figure this whole thing out, Byrd. Don't you worry, okay?"

And I told her "okay," but I *was* worried. Because facts is facts and I still couldn't remember that night or find my knife.

She got up to go have some coffee. I could hear her talking quietly to Ben, but I couldn't hear what they were sayin'.

When I came out of the bedroom, they told me their plan.

"Byrd, Ben wants to come with me. I know I told you that you couldn't come, but I really need the support. It won't be easy seeing your daddy like that. So don't be mad, okay?"

Ben was dressed. He held his coffee gracefully in one hand.

He looked like he'd walked right out of one of those *GQ* magazines my daddy reads. Classy.

I didn't answer. I just put the camera up to my eye and took their picture.

It's a funny thing that happens when you look out from behind a lens. It's like there's this wall between you and the rest of the world. I liked it. A lot.

I left them there, taking pictures all the way out of the house. I took about a hundred of Dolores. She was on the porch. Gettin' closer and closer to going inside. She's a good dog, but she likes to hide from things she doesn't know too well.

I wondered if that's how come Aunt Wyn stayed away so long. Because she was hiding.

I took picture after picture of my garden until Minerva came out with some ice-cold sweet tea.

"Have a drink, Byrd. You'll get dehydrated in this damn heat."

I took the glass and walked over to Esther. She's the shadiest spot in the whole place. I sat up against her trunk and gazed up into her branches. Me and Jamie were right here not seven months ago, havin' a terribly interestin' conversation.

We'd just come back from his house where we'd been watching movies.

"I think it'd be neat to be Hannibal Lecter's little girl," I said. *The Silence of the Lambs* is our very favorite movie.

And he said, "Why you wish that? You want him to eat you?"

"No. That's exactly the point. I think it would be a really nice feeling to be close to someone who ate people, only they didn't eat *you*. Like, you'd be special to them. The *specialest*."

"I think I understand," he'd said to me. "Like, you could

be the one thing that was different in a person's life. The one thing that made them say, 'Nah, I love this person too much to eat 'em.'"

"Something like that," I said, and then tagged him so he'd have to chase me. I loved it when he chased me 'cause sometimes I'd let him catch me and then we'd fall down and almost kiss each other, only not really 'cause we're too young. But it's good practice. A girl should be prepared for her first kiss.

Sittin' under Esther all alone, I put my fingers on my lips. Who would be my first kiss now?

I just couldn't imagine it ever bein' anyone but my own little prince.

"I swear," I said to Esther. "If they find him dead, I'll wear black for the whole rest of my life, and I'll never, ever love another boy again."

Esther stayed quiet, but I could tell I wasn't alone anymore.

Charlotte Masters was back and I'll be damned if she wasn't swingin' on my swing.

She's the one who told me *where* to take the pictures. I didn't see anything then, but when a ghost tells you to do somethin', you do it. Period.

17

The Whalen Dolls

Truth be told, I was glad Ben was coming with me. The thought of seeing Paddy in prison orange was enough to make me sick.

I had to see Stick first. That was the easy part.

But then I'd go straight to Angola because I had to see Paddy. *Had* to see him. I'd been away from my brother too long. And hopefully I could hold him and try and figure out why he put himself in this predicament in the first place.

Then, Grant. Bringing Ben with me to see him would be another type of difficult. Colliding past, present, and future together is a dangerous endeavor even when nothing precious is at stake. I'd have to keep my head on straight or my brain would go all crazy fuckall and I wouldn't be able to help anyone.

Grant could cloud my mind with one glance from the very moment I started thinking of him as more than a friend. We were eleven, Byrd's age, when my heart first leaped for him.

Susan had given him a small boat. Nothing fancy, just a fish-ing boat that had been Kenny's and sat rusting in their backyard for years up on blocks. She told him when he fixed it, he could go wherever he wanted with it. She didn't know he'd have that baby up and running in a month. Paddy and I went down to the docks as soon as it was in the water.

"Shoot, Grant. She's a grand ol' girl," said Paddy, only ten and itching for his own key to freedom.

"Take us out!" squealed Lottie, jumping up and down next to him, making the dock bounce.

"Nope, this maiden voyage belongs to BitsyWyn," he said.

I could feel the disappointment trickle out of Paddy and Lot-tie as I got on that boat, Grant started the motor and we took off.

"Faster," I said as the water splashed up around us and Grant walked here and there like a pirate looking for treasure.

I never wanted us to go back. I wanted to sail off into the unknown with that boy who had somehow become a man in all of five seconds.

"You and me," he said. "When we get older, Wyn . . . you and me are gonna take the world by storm. If I can manage to find some treasure, will you marry me? Like, not now, when we get big."

"Back in the old days, girls got married when they were thir-teen. I'm only about a year away from that, you know," I'd said, exaggerating just a little.

"Does that mean yes?" he asked.

I thought of saying something funny and maybe mean too because he was making my heart hurt with his attention. He was getting too close to me, and I'd already tried shutting off my heart to anything. Naomi's gift to my troubled tween years. Only I could never do that with Grant, because he was born inside my heart already.

"Grant Masters, of course I'll run off with you someday. And you don't need no treasure, either. Money kills people. Let's just be poor and live off the land. Now shut up and make this thing go *faster.*"

He did, and the faster he made that boat go, the faster my heart opened to the idea that it would be Grant who would save me. His magic was real. He could do anything.

Only he couldn't save my mother, and he couldn't save his.

I'd thought he failed me, somehow.

Someone should really try and bottle up teenage righteousness and sell it for a fortune.

◊

Ben and I walked back up to the Big House to ask Minerva if my car was still around.

"Sure, but why not have Carter bring you where you need to go?" she responded.

"I—"

"Want to be in control," she finished for me. And she was right. Partly. And I didn't trust Carter anymore.

"I'm driving," I told Ben when Carter brought the car around.

I saw Ben's eyes get big. Bronwyn drove a Subaru. Not Bitsy-Wyn. BitsyWyn Whalen drove *this*.

Lord, I loved being back behind the wheel of my old Mustang. Cherry-red. I'd named her Cherry. (Sixteen-year-old Wyn might have been a spitfire, but she wasn't all that original.)

It only took a hot minute to pull up in front of the sheriff's office. Ben bounced forward in the passenger seat.

"Bronwyn, these cars don't have air bags. Be careful."

"Shit, Ben. Live a little. Oh, and stay here."

"Why did I come with you if you want me to stay in the car?"

"Moral support?"

"Fine."

I walked into Stick's office.

"*You* never came to see me yesterday,"

"I got . . . caught up."

"I figured as much. It wasn't important. Just wanted to tell you I liked your fella. Also wanted to tell you that I made arrangements for you to visit Paddy today. The Fourth would have been next to impossible. Does that work for you?"

"That's why I'm here, Stick. But, there's one more thing . . . now, don't get mad . . ."

"Oh, no. What did you do? I swear I am up to here with the shit goin' on around this town. Now I got people missin' garage doors! And lights and all sorts of crazy things."

"Well, see . . . when I went to Lottie's house . . ."

"What. Did. You. Do?" asked Stick.

"Well, I . . . okay. There was a blinking light on the answering machine. And I sort of . . . played it. Don't be mad. Because I think I've figured a few things out,"

"Who was the message from? It must be new because we checked it."

"Right. See? Yes. It was new. And it was from Grant. And he was going on and on about how sorry he was. Did you hear me? *Sorry.* I know he's in New Orleans, but I thought you might know his exact location. I'd like to pay him a visit."

"He didn't do it, Bronwyn," said Stick, his face dead serious.

"I don't want him to have done it, either. But he might *know* something. Where is he?"

Stick scratched his stomach, and then sighed.

"He's bartending on Bourbon at a place called the Frosty Tooth. But, trust me, if you're lookin' for him to see if he did it, he didn't. Now, if you want to, you know, catch up with him, go right ahead."

"Why are you so sure he didn't do it, Stick?"

"Instinct."

"Well, I got my own instinct, and I'll bet you your firstborn child that mine is better than yours."

I took Route 10 to see Paddy. It was the quickest, and I wanted to stay focused. It felt good to drive. But I knew if I'd taken Route 90, I'd be looking at the Mississippi coast wishing every second I'd brought my camera and not used it to bribe Byrd. The casino boom had made every inch of that area a photo waiting to happen.

Once we arrived, Ben decided to stay in the car instead of the waiting room. It had air-conditioning and he'd brought a *New Yorker* to read. Arrangements were made for me to see Paddy alone, and he knew it.

Stick had arranged it so I could see Paddy in a room, not behind glass like a regular visit. I looked at him through the door before the guard opened it. He had his head resting on his arms. Just like when we were kids.

Time turned inside out as tears welled up in my eyes.

When he'd be naughty, Minerva would punish him and make him put his head on the table. She'd say, "Don't you move, Mr. Smarty-pants. You move and you'll see nothing but the inside of the pantry for the rest of the day."

He always paid attention, but he'd roll his eyes and play with whatever was there on the table while her back was turned.

I called it "defiant submission." He'd let her go on and on, and from the back it seemed like he was listening, but he wasn't. He was *waiting*. The thing about Patrick is that he's patient. More than anything, that boy has always been maddeningly *patient*.

My cheeks damp with tears, I realized I'd seen my beautiful brother before he saw me.

He looked older, but not by much. I wondered for a second if he might have got some of Mama's magic, too. But he didn't. If he did, he wouldn't have been where he was.

Doors buzzed and slammed open and shut.

He saw me and stood up, fast, then slow when he got a stern look from the guard.

"Wyn," he said, his voice cracking. "Wyn . . . oh, my God."

It was a desperate cry, the sound he made when we were told our mother was dead and never coming back. It was me he cried for that day. Me he wouldn't let go of. And now in this moment, he sounded just the same.

You can feel it when your heart breaks. It's a stabbing, ripping kind of pain. And all the air you have comes out.

And my heart broke, but I went to him. I looked at the guard, but he nodded.

I put my arms around my brother and I tried to soothe him. Hushed him. Let him cry. Let him be a little boy again, if only for a minute or two.

We held on to each other long enough for the guard to feel we'd had enough and start banging on the windows.

Then we sat across from each other, clasping each other's hands on the wide particleboard table, just like in the movies. But he didn't waste time getting to the point.

"Look. I know we have a lot to say to each other. All the 'sorries' and 'should haves and could haves.' Let's agree to get those over with some other time, okay? We don't have a million years to catch up, Wyn. But I have to tell you somethin'. Just listen, okay? Don't talk. It's a hard thing, the thing I have to say."

"Anything, Paddy, tell me anything,"

"Byrd did it, Wyn. God help me, it was Byrd. And you gotta stop diggin' and let it be. Carter came and told me, and you gotta let well enough alone."

"No, Paddy. You're dead wrong and too close to it to see clear. She couldn't have done any of this."

"Evil comes in all shapes and sizes, Wyn."

"You know what's evil? She thinks she did it, too. Did you know that? She thinks it because she can tell *you* think it. So you better have a damn good reason for thinking it."

He took a deep breath, and boy, did I want to shut off my ears when he finally started talking.

"It was those animals that follow her around. Sometimes I'd find them dead and mutilated in the yard. And at first I didn't think it was her, but it was."

I shook my head. "No. *No.* How can you even be sure?" I asked, trying to stay calm. *Dead animals.*

" 'Cause she told me so. And then there was the dog."

"Dolores?"

"No. The dog *before* Dolores. Didn't you ever think Dolores was a strange name for a dog?"

I smiled, remembering that first day. "Not really, she said it meant 'sorrow.' I think it's clever."

"Whatever. Well, get this: Her first dog was named Dog. Not so clever. And one day . . ." He paused. He didn't want to tell it, and I didn't want to hear it. But we had no choice.

"Paddy, look, nothing you can say can change the way I feel about her. You've done good by her, little brother."

He squeezed my hand.

"Well, one day that dog bit me. I was playing with Byrd, chasing her around the house. And she was screaming with delight. God, Wyn, I miss her. And I think Dog was just old and confused. Thought I was hurting her, so he bit me. Here."

Patrick rolled back the orange sleeve of his prisoner's jumpsuit to reveal a large ugly scar.

"Jesus."

"And then the next day the dog was dead in the yard, and Byrd was digging a hole with a shovel much too big for her. 'What happened here?' I asked her. And she just cried, 'I killed him, Daddy, I killed him because he hurt you.'"

"But how does that connect to . . ." I trailed off.

"See, Charlotte hurt me, so she killed her. Just like the dog."

"What were you even doing fooling with Lottie anyway, Paddy? That's been over for an age, and even back when we were kids, you guys fought like cats and dogs."

"Charlotte came on by one day with Jamie on her hip. She set him right down next to Byrd, who Minerva had put in a Moses basket next to me. I was just so torn up about losing Stella, you know? I loved her so much."

"Paddy, I'm so sorry I never came back. I wish I'd met Stella. I've been so selfish."

"We don't have time for all that right now, Wyn. Let me finish."

"Okay, go on."

"So Charlotte and me got to talkin' and our babies did the strangest thing. Byrd reached up with her tiny hands and Jamie placed his palms against hers. And that glow, you know the ones Minerva has? It lit up their hands. That's when I knew Byrd had the strange ways and those two began their own little love affair.

"She'd cry and cry unless Charlotte dropped him over.

"And as soon as she was big enough, she just walked out the front door and down the road to find him. Like she had some kind of internal GPS.

"That's how Charlotte and me got together again. At first it was nice, then it was just, I don't know, toxic. We never could get it right. Fought all the time.

"Charlotte broke it off with me the night before she was killed, Wyn. And there I was crying like a baby to my little daughter with the strange ways, crying about how hurt I was, how it was all Jamie's fault, and that I wished they would just disappear."

"Oh, Paddy, you didn't."

"I sure did."

"And the next day, they were dead."

"That doesn't mean she killed them. I still don't believe it, Patrick."

"I wish I didn't believe it."

"But why would she kill Jamie?"

He stayed quiet then. The chatterbox. *Hiding, he's hiding something.*

"Did she say she killed them?" I continued.

"No."

"But she said she killed the dog, right?"

"Yes, but—"

"But nothing, Patrick."

"Look at me, Bronwyn," he said seriously. "Look at me and know what I know. Try to conjure up some of that magic Mama passed on to you. Yeah, I know, Carter told me that, too. Look, I'd never think the worst of Byrd unless I was sure it was true. And now your job is to convince her that she's innocent because if she thinks I'm in here for life for something she did . . . she's gonna do it again. And I can't live with that."

"You mean to tell me that you think you raised a serial killer? And that I have to fix her?"

"Yep."

"That's just crazy fuckall. Look, Paddy, she's just too physically small."

"But she has the ways of Mama's people. And then Stella. I knew she had strange ways, too, but I loved her so much . . . I wasn't thinkin' about the kind of kid we'd make when those genes collided. Who knows what kind of strength is in that girl? Not to mention, the curse. I mean, between the magic, and the demon of Farley Whalen, we have a few scenarios we can't ignore."

I'd totally forgotten about Farley Whalen.

"That's a load of crap, something we were told to scare us into being good, and you know it. Besides, there's something you *don't* know."

I told him about Grant's message and about the fight Byrd said he'd had with Lottie.

"Holy shit," he breathed out.

I sat back for a minute. "Paddy, who's Jamie's father? Is it you?"

"Of course it ain't me! I didn't take up with her until after he was born," Paddy said defensively.

"Well, who is he then? It seems to me someone should find him and tell him his son is missing."

"Well, if that ain't the twenty-thousand-dollar question."

"Really, Paddy, this is important. He may know something. She must have told you or hinted. *Something.*"

"Nope, she never said a thing. But I'll admit, I never really pushed her much about it. We had enough trouble."

I remember her wide-open smile as she talked about why she wouldn't marry Paddy, not ever. Because she loved someone else more.

And that message. *"I'm sorry . . . what kind of brother . . . what kind of man . . . .*

"Well, I think I know," I said. "Though I don't want to know it."

"Who?" he asked.

"I think you already know. I think you just put two and two together the way I did."

"Grant?"

"I know, it seems crazy, but what else explains that message?"

"Wyn, I know Grant always felt protective of her, like a brother, nothing more. I mean . . . he loved *you,* Wyn. It devastated him when you left. It almost killed him."

"I thought we weren't going to talk about that now?" I said.

"You're right, we're not," he said. "But you know what? Shit. The more I think about this, the more it makes sense!" he said. "When Lottie got pregnant, Grant took off to New Orleans. Never came around again. Why else would he have done that? He would have stayed and helped her out. Goddamn! He never would have let her raise a child alone unless he was full of shame."

"What if they were fighting over custody? What if Grant wanted Jamie and Charlotte said no. Then he goes to the house and gets mad. Kills Lottie in a rage and steals Jamie! Paddy, did the cops look into that possibility?"

Paddy stared at me, stunned.

"I'm sure—I mean, they'd have to have, right?"

And what I knew in that very moment was that my single-minded, stubborn ass of a brother had not ever entertained the possibility that it was anyone other than Byrd. He'd been so sure it was *her* that he'd taken all the blame without even considering anyone else.

"He didn't take Jamie," he said.

"How do you know?"

"I just do, don't ask me anything else. But I'd never considered him a killer. I'd never thought about it for a second. It *could* have been him. Except . . ."

"What? Except what?"

"Byrd's knife."

The knife. That damned knife.

"What if she lent it to Jamie? And it was there and easy for Grant to get? And even if he didn't do it, and we both know I hope that's the case, it's a really strong reasonable doubt. It could get you a new trial. Or an appeal. You could claim you were crazy, Jackson would help, then you could get a new trial and introduce Grant as a possible suspect. Maybe neither of you would get any time. Maybe it would cause just enough doubt for you to cancel each other out."

I saw the wheels turning in my brother's mind. He had finally realized he made a mistake.

"Wyn," he said, tears in his eyes, "you got to get me out of here."

18

Naomi

Before my gran put me in the asylum, I spent days upon days alone at Coveview.

Eventually I looked too long out my window to that misted Island of Fortunes Cove, and I decided to make my grandmother happy. To just go there.

I didn't know that when I dove into the waters off the cliffs by our house, that Minerva was watching me. Always watching me. Like a good Caretaker should.

When all was said and done, the authorities, as well as good old Grandma Catherine, decided I'd tried to kill myself. I didn't argue. So I was sent to the Fairview Mental Hospital.

It's not such a bad place. Fancy. No one harmed me there. Just a quiet sanctuary. I've wondered so many times if I should have just stayed, but Minerva didn't want me to give up on my life. So she got me out, for better or worse, and we moved into the village.

But still, even with Minerva's attentions, I was alone. Alone in my childhood, alone in Fairview, alone in Magnolia Creek. Always alone.

What was my purpose? Why was I born the way I was? My thoughts would swirl. Nothing ever stopped them. Until, I found opium.

Lost witch, wife, mother. I had to live and act like I was alive. And for a while, I did it. Minerva helped. The children, too. But when you're *really* lost, you can't be found. Jackson couldn't help me, because after we'd lived and loved for a while, I realized he was as lost as I was.

There's this rule, that when you get lost in the woods you're supposed to just sit there and wait for people to find you. To save you. Well, how do you sit and wait when the forest is calling to you? When getting even *more* lost seems like the best decision? Losing myself completely was always a hidden intention of mine. And I can say that if I never succeeded at anything else, I was a success at hiding myself so well that no one could find me.

"Who am I without you?" I'd ask my darlings, kissing their sweet faces, while smelling the tops of their heads. That's a pretty big thing to ask a child. The more I watch Bronwyn with Byrd . . . the more I see the mistakes I made with my children.

But when they were babies, I believe I was a good mother. It was easier then. The drugs were always there, but at that point, they were still helping me. The people closest to me, Susan, Jackson, Minerva . . . they'd ask me why I couldn't stop.

"What is it about that stuff?" asked Jackson, brave on bourbon and a hypocrite to boot.

And the kids. My babies. When they were old enough to understand that I was sick, they'd ask.

I tried to explain it. But nothing came out the way it should have. *It makes me happy,* I'd say. Which left them feeling as if they couldn't make me happy. I know that now.

It was also a lie.

You see it all clear, standing on the dead side of life, you can see everything for what it really is, was, and will be.

Once, when my sweet, darling Paddy was about twelve and the spitting image of his father, he got real brave and came into my rooms for a talk. I was reading on the sofa in my library.

"Mama? May I come in?"

I put down my book and held my arms out. He always came to me. Wyn had stopped hugging me when she was ten or so, but Paddy never stopped. He even hugged my dead body when my spirit was hovering above it. Broke my ghost heart.

So he came to me and I held him close.

"What do you need, my love?" I asked him.

He started to cry. I could feel the tears go straight through my nightdress. He took the pipe out of my hand. I remember being worried he'd shake out the last bit of opium. I was more concerned about that than I was about him. That's the truth.

"Why do you smoke this, Mama? Wyn's too afraid to ask, I think. Or maybe she just don't care. But I do. I miss you." He didn't look at me. Couldn't. Just kept his head buried against me so that his voice, changing at the time, was muffled.

His request was so sincere that I tried my best to answer him.

"Well, now. That's a big question, isn't it?" I said. "One that I don't even know if I understand myself. But let me try, okay?"

He nodded against me, still crying.

I took the pipe back, relieved to have it in my hand again.

"When I smoke this . . . medicine, I feel a wave of warmth

rush through my body. And there are no worries. No cares. Everything melts into the edges of life. And I don't feel the magic so much. No sight. Nothing. It's better that way, Paddy. I don't like to see the future."

He pulled his head up, wiping his eyes. "Can't you control it some other way? In science we learned that the brain has chemicals in it, and that we only use part of it. Can't we just retrain your whole brain, Mama?"

It was a good question. But I didn't want to do that. I wanted to use the drug, and I wanted everyone to leave me alone. So I kept explaining the unexplainable.

"But, baby, I can still do things . . . well, at first I could. Everything was so beautiful. And quiet around me. And even if you don't remember, I was a better mother during those early days. I played with you. I ran around the yard. Danced with your daddy. Made meals with Minerva, and . . . Susan. But the problem is, the drugs build up in your system and soon—"

"You can't do nothin' anymore." he finished.

"Yes, that's right. This medicine and, Paddy, believe me, it *is* medicine . . . it builds up. Then I need more in order to feel that way again. And taking more just makes me sleepy. I don't mind, though. Feeling sleepy makes me warm and happy."

"We learned about that, too," he said. "It's called addiction." His words startled me.

"I guess you're right, my smart boy."

"Don't you want to change?" he asked, desperation dripping from his voice. I couldn't tell him I didn't want to change. He'd be devastated.

"Of course! And you know what? I'm going to try. As a matter of fact, I have your daddy looking for something else that can make the things that bother me go away. But until we find it, this is just how it is, Paddy. I need that peace, honey."

I fed him a shit lie, and look what I lost.

He left the room then. And I had to get Jackson to support that lie. He wasn't looking for anything else. But I knew Patrick needed something to hold on to. And I wasn't brave enough to make it the truth.

I was a terrible mother.

My children never knew what mother to expect, so they stopped expecting me to be anyone. In time, so did Jackson. I was "sick." Minerva was the only one who truly understood.

One night, while I was writhing in sweaty sheets trying to come off of a particularly long binge, she held me. I wouldn't let her take the pains away. I wanted to punish myself.

"But don't you understand, Naomi? Whether you're smoking the opium or coming off of it, the only thing you're thinking about is opium. You have successfully saved yourself from ever actually thinking about your own life. Your longing, your fear, your magical ways."

"Well, then, what do you propose I do, O mystical Caretaker?" I spat at her.

"I've never told you what to do, and I'm not starting now. I'm here to love you, not boss you, so I propose you do what you need to do to get by."

So I did.

The night I died, Bronwyn's words cut deep.

We'd been arguing about Grant. I wasted so much time worrying about that boy when it was me who pushed her away. She still carries the words she said to me that night. She blames herself for my death. I know it now.

I was on the stairs and she was walking out the door, ignoring my request that she stay home. Finally, I'd just muttered at her, "Do what you want. I'm tired of fighting with you and need to rest." *Rest* is the word they all knew meant "I'm closing my bedroom doors and smoking myself into oblivion."

"Oh, poor you. Poor *baby* wanting a break from the voices in your head. I'm so sick of hearing about it!" she screamed as I walked back up the stairs. She had so much rage, and she was right to feel it. But back then I just wanted to be high. To get away from her. And I'd been clean for about two weeks, so I figured it was time.

"That's right! Run to your rooms!" she screamed. "Close those doors and don't pay any attention to the world around you. And just so you know, while you're up there I'll be out on the boat fucking Grant. Do you hear me, Mama? Go get nice and high and I'll be out making my own life miserable because that's what you taught me to do. Sometimes I wish you'd just die already, so I wouldn't keep worrying about it."

I knew she was lying. She was just saying that to hurt me.

That's when I realized what deep scars I'd created.

She hated me. And with Jackson's distance and Paddy's fear, I understood I was more alone in Magnolia Creek than I'd ever been in Fairview.

Was it an accidental overdose? I don't think so. I think I knew I was making a decision to go to sleep for a very long time.

I never thought Bronwyn would live with the guilt of my death on her conscience forever. That she'd run away and never come back. I was too selfish to realize that.

If only I could find a way to tell her, I'd take the rightful blame. And wash her clean of all the dirt I'd buried her with since she was born. She choked on the earth I covered her with. But I never noticed.

I told myself I'd never leave them. But I was gone all the time. You can't leave anything if you were never present in the first place.

Liar, liar, liar. Go to the funeral pyre.

19

Bronwyn

Leaving Paddy would have been harder if I wasn't so motivated to find Grant. Paddy'd be home in no time if we could cast doubt on the whole thing.

Ben played down my theories and ideas in the car. Tried to stay calm.

"Why are you trying to take this away from me?" I asked angrily.

"Eyes on the road, Bronwyn, please."

"But answer me! I have a solid idea on how to get Paddy out of that place, and you keep telling me all the ways it might not work."

"I'm just trying to keep you from being disappointed if it doesn't go the way you want. Dear God, do all the roads have seventy miles per hour speed limits down here? Makes everyone do ninety."

A few days before, I'd have loved that. Wanted it. Craved it.

Keep me safe, clear-minded, clever, sober, and responsible. Yes, Ben. Do that. Make me drive slow.

But not now.

Coming into New Orleans, no matter which route you take, is always an experience. There is no other city on earth where you can measure a mile by district and be in such completely different worlds. One block the wrong way and it's like another country all together.

"I love it here. I used to come here and write," he said.

"You did? I never knew that."

"That pesky past of ours," he said.

I went straight to the French Quarter and parked in a lot near Bourbon Street.

No matter how many times I visit that part of the city, I'm always amazed. The architecture alone is dizzying. And the people. Dear Lord. Everyone is happy in the French Quarter. Sure, they might be drunk, and maybe even miserable, but they're happy nonetheless. Misery clings to those that are the happiest, it seems.

"I always forget how beautiful it is," said Ben.

"Me, too. I wish I had my camera."

"We can get you a disposable," he offered.

I rolled my eyes at him.

"What?" he said.

"You really think I could take pictures like that? That's like me telling you I can get you an old slate tablet for you to write on," I said.

He was quiet then. I don't usually talk back to him like that.

Silently, we walked past beautiful courtyards blooming over with plants and flowers. *Abundance* is the best word to describe New Orleans. Abundance of poverty, abundance of wealth. Abundance of fine music, food, and liquor. Abundance of history.

I didn't expect to find Grant at that bar on Bourbon where Stick sent us. I thought I'd leave a message and come back.

But there he was.

I could see him drying glasses through the open-air front of the Frosty Tooth. He wasn't seventeen anymore, but even from a distance I could see that he looked just how I expected him to. Minus the stupid T-shirt that had the bar logo on it.

It was the bar itself that surprised me more than Grant all grown up. It wasn't a blues joint or a fancy place. It was a chain, a franchise, that seemed to sell mostly frozen drinks and Jell-O shots. A place that, in the old days, we would have avoided.

He saw me at almost the same time I saw him. Shock washed over his face, but without hesitation he turned and yelled to his partner, "Take my shift, Angel. I got an old friend to see."

He hopped over the bar and grabbed me, picking me up off my feet and spinning me around as Ben took a step back.

Grant.

God, the memories I had of him. I'd loved him with no safety net.

"Where you been all my life?" he said. He slurred a little and it was only then that I realized he was drunk.

"I thought you were bartending, not partaking," I said.

A shadow fell across his eyes. He had a quick temper that matched my own.

"Yankee girl gonna be a monkey on my back, or do you wanna catch up proper? Lost your manners up north, I see."

Ben cleared his throat.

Ben. Shit.

He held his hand out politely to Grant, who shook it. Solidly.

"Ben Mason," he said.

"Grant Masters."

They shook hands for a second too long and a touch too firm. A pissing contest.

Men. I swear.

"I'm a friend, from up north," said Ben.

"Must be nice."

"Look," said Ben, "I'm going to go a few blocks over to Cafe Du Monde and get my fill of coffee and beignets. I don't know when I'll be back down this way again. And you guys can get caught up, "

"You sure?" I asked.

"Very," he said, walking away.

I turned my attention back to Grant. I knew the way to get to him was to be sweet as pie, so I smiled a big, warm smile. And for reasons only the heart can know, secretly slipped my ring off my finger and dropped it in the pocket of my jeans.

"Do you have some time I could borrow, handsome? It's been too long," I said.

That did the trick.

"Come on in and I'll get you a drink on the house. Still a bourbon girl?" He didn't wait for me to answer. "Angel! Get me a Maker's on the rocks. Make it two, okay?"

"Sure thing," she responded. When I glanced at her, I saw who I might have become if I'd followed Grant's path. It was uncanny, the resemblance. Pale, with soft blond features. But she had her eyes outlined in black kohl and her hair was a mess. She was sexy in that goth kind of way and wearing a black ribbon around her neck, with tattoos inked up and down her arms. She hummed and twirled as she made our drinks, and then brought them out to where we were sitting at a dirty little glass-top table. She leaned into Grant as she put down his drink and he grabbed her ass.

"Give me some sugar, you sexy thang," he said.

She leaned over and I could see her panties through the ripped black fishnets under her jean miniskirt.

She kissed him. Long and hard. BitsyWyn would have punched her.

Her lipstick left a bright red smear across his mouth that she unsuccessfully tried to wipe off.

"I'm Angel," she said, holding out a thin hand embellished with permanent black henna tattoos and chipped black polished nails.

I shook her hand reluctantly. "Nice to meet you."

She smiled with cigarette-stained teeth. "You bet it is. Just so you know? He's mine. I have his name tattooed on my ass and everything."

"Just so you know," I replied, "you look just like me. Go check it out in the bathroom mirror the next time you need to get your fix of whatever drug you take that makes your eyes wiggle. You're a poor man's version of me, that's all."

"What the . . . she's crazy," said Angel as she headed back to the bar.

I wanted to slap my hand over my mouth. I couldn't even believe I'd said that.

"Shit. I'm sorry, Grant. That was about the bitchiest thing I've done since I've been back. Should I go apologize?"

Grant lit a cigarette and pushed back his black hair, a little too long . . . but still shiny and gorgeous.

Then he laughed.

"Well, damn, girl. It's good to see you. No worries here. I was scared you'd come back prissy and uptight. Guess I was wrong. Besides, she's got six of me on the side anyway. And she lied about the tattoo."

Laughing, we looked at each other, and I swear that cloudy feeling I had around him when we were younger came right back. *You're in trouble,* I thought.

Grant took a long sip of his drink and offered me a cigarette. I took it, ready to inhale my teenage life.

"She ain't you, by the way."

"Nope. Me she ain't."

Angel shot us a glare.

"Let's get out of here and walk these streets like in the old days, whaddaya say?" Grant winked.

"Sounds like a plan."

He offered me his arm and we began our journey through the twisted back streets of the French Quarter. It's a strange place, but not for reasons that visitors could ever define. Not because of drunks or ghosts or even voodoo. It has all that strangeness, but also something more.

Each building in the French Quarter has a garden of sorts, as well as a stone alley that leads there. Some are private, but most are connected. So, if you explore *behind* the city, not just the facade, you get the real deal.

Arm in arm with the man I'd lost my virginity to, who I was happy to see, and who I thought might have killed my best friend, as well as his own son, I couldn't help but wonder about the strangeness of life.

The human heart is a mysterious place. Love comes in all shapes and sizes, and I'd loved Grant. Hard.

"You hungry?" he asked. "I think I need some food to soak up the liquor so you and I can have a proper conversation. They got the best muffaletta sandwiches down at the market."

"Better than your mama's?" I asked.

"No, nothin's better than her cooking, but they're close."

"Sure," I said as we made our way through the streets to the market. Grant ordered and we found a table.

The sandwiches were huge and stuffed full of imported meats and cheeses and sprinkled with pickled vegetables.

"That's better," he said after he'd eaten about half of his in two bites. He wanted to be clearheaded for me. Which, coming from grown-up, drunk Grant, was a wonderful compliment.

"Grant, I'm happy to see you. Maybe too happy . . . because I need to ask you a few questions that are going to be hard."

He sat back and sighed a little. Then went to his pocket for a smoke, but there were "No smoking" signs posted everywhere.

"Can't say I didn't think this was comin'. But not here, okay? Let's wrap these up and find somewhere quiet."

"Sure," I said.

It's funny how patterns become talismans of comfort. Grant and I were doing the most normal thing in the world. Having lunch, wrapping up the sandwiches, asking for a bag to carry them with. Only we fell back into a natural rhythm. I went for the bag as he condensed the food onto one plate. We'd done it a thousand times before. We were always impatient, yet mannerly. *Thank you, may we have the check, a bag please, yes, no the food was fine . . .*

The fast retreat we made from the market felt more like a homecoming than anything else had so far. But I shouldn't have been surprised, because Grant had always felt like home.

As we walked, the smell of him damn well intoxicated me. Part of me just wanted to take him to bed. Do not pass Ben. Do not get Paddy out of Jail. Do not collect the truth. Just sink back into the past and luxuriate the days away with Grant. Even with his newfound rough-and-tumble exterior. Possibly because of it.

Grant was all man now.

We went into a quiet, public courtyard and sat on a bench at the base of a statue.

He offered me another smoke.

"No, I need to just say this," I said. I had to get to the point or I'd never leave. "What I really want to know is what you were fighting with Charlotte about before she died. And why you left that crazy message on her answering machine after she'd died. And, well, what you were doin' the night she was killed."

He laughed tightly. "Really? That's why you came to see me? No 'how you holdin' up with Lottie dead?' no 'haven't heard from you in fourteen years and how you been?'"

"Or even," I hesitated, "how do you feel about your son being missing?"

Grant tensed up beside me.

"Shit. You know. Who told you?"

"No one had to. Well, Paddy and I sort of put it together today when I went to see him."

"You saw Paddy? Damn, how is he? I've been meaning to go, too. Really. I just . . . well . . . it's hard."

I grabbed his hand and squeezed gently, "Do you think he did it, Grant?"

"Hell no," he said.

"Did you?"

"Dammit, Wyn! No. I could never—" His voice broke a bit.

"So, will you help me then? Just answer a few questions. That's all I need. We have to get him out of there, right?"

"Fine. Ask away, I'd love to help Paddy. I'd do anything to help fix this mess."

I paused and took a breath. "You don't happen to have Jamie, do you? If you took him, or even if he ran away that night and came to you, Jackson could help get you out of trouble for hiding him. If we can find that boy alive, we could scratch the electric chair off our list of worries."

He stood up, leaning against the statue so I had to turn to look at him.

It was the statue of a man kneeling at the feet of a woman, but she wasn't just an ordinary woman, she was Cajun. And I could feel the magic all around her. The plaque on the statue read: NEVER UNDERESTIMATE THE EVIL THAT MEN DO

The historical society must have added the smaller, less ornate plaque next to it: THE CURSE OF THE WHALENS OF MAGNOLIA CREEK, ALABAMA: PORTRAYED HERE: FARLEY WHALEN AND THE CAJUN WOMAN HE RAPED. CIRCA 1900.

"Well, look at that," I said. "I've never seen it."

"What?" he asked, looking up.

"This statue."

"Damn! I never did either. You'd think I planned this."

"Did you?"

He gave me a look. "Of course not."

"So, how 'bout it, Grant?" I asked softly. "You going to help me out?"

"I'm not hiding him, Wyn. Lord, I wish I was. I'd give any-thing to see that boy again. And I swear I didn't do it, and I can't believe you'd even think for a second I did." He sighed. "I thought maybe you just wanted to linger around in our past a little bit. I even sobered up, started to feel the sun on my face the way I haven't since you left."

"I know, I'm sorry, Grant. I just . . . have to figure this thing out. You should have seen him today. He's broken, Grant. My baby brother . . ."

"Listen, do you still have that . . . shine? I mean, maybe you can read those cards of yours and figure it out that way."

"Funny you should ask. That part of me seems to be growing stronger the longer I'm home. Only, the backwards part is that we can't see anything close to us."

"We?"

"Me and Byrd."

"Ah, Ms. Byrd. I always loved that kid, but the last time I saw her she was in diapers. She always reminded me of you, though. And Naomi. She's an odd one, in a good way. Why don't you try? Hold my hands or somethin', maybe you can see I didn't do it. I don't want you to think I did this thing, Wyn. That'd kill me for sure."

"Okay." I breathed out. "I'll give it a try." I reached over, grasping his hand and lifting it to my cheek. My whole body tingled. Then I breathed in sharply as I remembered. It came to me just as strong and in full color as the memory I'd had in Naomi's bedroom.

But it wasn't about Paddy or Charlotte. Or that night.

We were sixteen, Grant had one of his crazy ideas. We'd take his truck and drive all the way to Daytona Beach to watch the

Enduro races. The cars that run the tracks round and round bumping into each other until one lone car is the winner. Only we'd need four days. Two days to get there, two days to get back.

So we ran away.

We drove the back highways in his broken-down truck. And because the radio didn't work, we sang every Steve Miller song we could think of. Laughing. "This here's the story about Billy Joe and Bobbie Sue"—then we'd clap—"two young lovers with nothin' better to do."

Then we moved right on through Johnny Cash and Patsy Cline. All the good old country music we were raised on. My feet hanging out the window. His hand never leaving my thigh.

We stopped off in Apalachicola for the night. Ate oysters and got a motel room. He was such a gentleman, letting me sleep on the bed while he slept on the grimy carpet. We hadn't slept together yet. That would come later on the saddest night of my life, and I'd be gone before we could talk about it. But that night I figured, why the hell not? It was Grant who'd said no. That he wanted it more than anything, but that I wasn't ready. And that it wouldn't be in a place like some seedy motel. "I'd never ask you like this, Wyn. You and me? We'll be outside in the high grass under the stars. That's how it'll be."

When we got to Daytona, we had the most amazing time. So much laughter. And friendship. The kind of friendship you can only have with someone you've known your whole life, the kind that makes romance that much sweeter. He even won me prizes on the boardwalk.

When we got back, the scolding from everyone, the worry we'd caused, none of it mattered, because we'd had that moment. Together. One we'd never forget.

Only I did.

"Anything?" he asked as his hand left my face.

"No," I said.

"Then I guess we're done here," he said, starting to walk away. I got up and tried to follow.

He turned around and put his hand up. The universal symbol for "Do not come near me."

"Grant, please. What about that message you left for Lottie? The fight you had with her over Jamie? Anything you know could help raise a reasonable doubt and maybe get Paddy out of prison. You have to tell me."

"Go on home, Wyn. If you're tryin' to insinuate that I had any-thing to do with killin' my sister and my"—his voice broke—"son, you're crazy." Then he was gone.

I sat back down, confused for a second, wondering what he was talking about, and watched him walk away.

Before I left, I gave a kiss to Farley Whalen.

"You got a bad deal, Farley. You probably didn't do it, either. And I could kill you myself for all the times I had to hear your tale as a warning when I was little. But it would be a lot easier if you were a real demon. Byrd and I could vanquish you with our magical powers and solve everything."

Another couple had come to sit on the bench, and they looked at me like I was crazy. I felt crazy, so I said, "Boo!" and they jumped a little.

I had to get out of NOLA.

I walked in the direction of the cafe, but all I could think about was the one thing I didn't want to think about.

That girl with her red lipstick kissing on Grant. Who the hell did she think she was?

I'd officially lost my mind.

I was so frustrated I didn't even realize I was already standing in front of Cafe Du Monde. I put my ring back on.

Ben was sitting at a table, wiping powdered sugar off his lips. He could tell I wasn't in the mood, so he paid his check and met me outside.

We walked back to the parking lot in silence.

Once in the car, I put the air-conditioning on full blast. I needed air. I needed to breathe.

"He was the one, wasn't he?" asked Ben.

"What?"

"When I asked you, all those years ago in Rocco's pastry shop. He's the only other man you've loved. I'm right, aren't I?"

"So what? That was years ago, Ben."

I started the car and backed out, fast. I drove, weaving in and out of traffic until we were back on the highway.

"You don't have to drive fast to make a point. All you're do-ing is proving me right," he said.

"I already said you were right. Yes. *Yes.* I loved him. Then I left, and like everything and everyone else, I failed him. Some people can quietly leave where they came from and are never missed. I leave, and everyone suffers for fourteen years. And no one tells me. And I don't ask. And why don't I ask? Because of *you.*"

"I was only with you for seven of those years, remember that," said Ben. Calmly, but with more anger than I'd ever heard from him.

"Right. You. Are. Right. Let's make it all about me. Let's pretend you didn't do anything, and I didn't kill my own mother. Let's just—"

"What did you say?"

"I don't know . . ."

"You do know. You just said you killed your mother. I think we may be getting closer to something important here, Bronwyn."

"Will you fucking stop calling me that! Jesus. I hate that name."

"I would like to get out of this car," said Ben.

"Screw you, we're going home. I'm not letting you get out."

That's when he got really angry. I'd pushed him too far.

"Do you think this is easy for me? Last week you were mine. We were happy. I was seeing little kids of our own running around. Last week you looked at me with love. You wanted to touch me. *Last week I was happy.* Now? Who are you? I don't even recognize you. And the worst part? I know you, and this you? She's happy! Here I am, realizing for the first time that all that joy I thought *we* had was *mine.* I created it. You were just sitting there letting it happen. Fuck me."

I pulled over onto the shoulder and began to yell back. Mean things. I don't even remember what I said. But as soon as I banged my hands hard against the steering wheel, everything stilled.

The glow came out from my hands and filled up the car, only Byrd wasn't around. I'd done it myself.

That's when we stopped fighting.

By the time we got back to Magnolia Creek, it was dark. And Ben and I hadn't spoken since the glow.

As I pulled into the driveway at the Big House and parked,

I looked up at it, with its lamps glowing through the windows out into the velvet black night, and thought maybe now that I had glowing hands, Naomi'd be there waiting for me. That I'd see her ghost. I wanted all of it back. My brother. My childhood. My laughing father. My friends. Just thinking about it started a panic inside of me that I can't quite explain. A sort of desperation. Like I was at the bottom of a deep, dark hole and I could see the people I loved shining in the sunlight up above me, but I just couldn't climb out.

They were all sitting on the front porch: Jackson, Byrd, Carter, and Minerva.

All of them just sitting around, laughing, like nothing was wrong.

How could they be laughing and carrying on when the whole world was falling apart?

"Should we get out of the car, Br—Wyn?" asked Ben.

I couldn't even answer him.

I sat there in the car. Not moving. Thinking that what I was really mad about wasn't Ben's behavior but my own. All the things I'd said to him were my fault. Not his. I'd left. I'd carried on without a second thought. I'd missed out on a life-long friendship with Lottie. I'd missed watching my brother grow into a man. I'd missed Byrd being born and meeting Stella. I'd missed everything. And why? For all those years, I thought I understood my reasons. But now? Mud. My thoughts were *mud*.

Carter got up and came down the steps. They were all looking at me now. Watching me like a zoo animal. *They all want something different from me,* I thought. And none of them were brave enough to come get it. Maybe *brave* isn't the right word.

Maybe they were all just smart enough to stay away from me for a little while.

"Is it okay if I get out of the car?" asked Ben.

I nodded yes and he got out, making his way up the steps.

That's when Carter came.

He tried to open the door for me, but I quickly pushed down the lock. I put my forehead down on the steering wheel. He rapped lightly on the window and motioned for me to roll it down.

I cracked it open slightly.

"Wyn, come on out now, honey, it's been a long day. You come out and I'll put the car away."

I looked at him and I tried to speak, but there were too many words in my head.

When I was younger, I read this article in a science journal of Jackson's about how there's this transmitter in the brain called glutamate, and it allows us to process information. Only, when we get too much information, it makes our brain stop functioning altogether. Glutamate. That was it. I was having some serious glutamate problems.

"Look," said Carter. "I know I'm not your favorite person right now. I'm an ornery fool sometimes and my love for this family gets the better of me. But, Wyn, you're part of this family, too, so I got to get you out of this car. Come on, darlin'. Whatever crazy fuckall thoughts goin' around in that head of yours, they need to get straightened out. It was a hard day, I can see that. But now it's over. Your hard day is over, Wyn."

Carter. *A strange, kind man.*

I unlocked the door and he placed his arm out, like a true gentleman, to support me.

"You'll be just fine," he said. "Listen to your heart and mind together, that's the trick. Not one or the other, both."

I smiled at him, deciding right then that I *did* like him. Maybe.

Jackson got up to greet me, swaying a little too much.

"Let's go inside, Jackson. You've had one too many . . . again," said Minerva, leading him in.

"Daddy wait, I have something important to tell you. I saw Paddy today and—"

He waved his hands at me. "Not now. Not now."

"Oh, fine. Tomorrow then. Come on, Byrd. Let's get you to bed," I said, picking her up. I needed to be close to her. It was like being close to Paddy.

Ben began to come down the stairs, too.

"Ben?"

He stopped.

"Do you think it'd be all right if you stayed here tonight? I feel like . . . God, if this isn't the rudest thing. I'm sorry, but I need to be alone with Byrd."

"No, no. I understand. I get it," said Ben.

"Come on, Ben," said Carter. "I got a guest room all set up for you."

"Of course you do," he said.

❧

That night, curled up next to Byrd, I had my second dream.

Only this time, it wasn't a memory. It was a warning.

We were standing on the beach late at night and the waves were wild. Lottie was dressed in a white gown and glowed brightly. And when I looked down, I saw I was dressed in a gown, too. Only mine was black, the converse of hers.

"Find him," she said, staring out at the sea.

Then I heard a giggle. Jamie and Byrd were playing near us, chasing the waves and doing cartwheels. Their faces flushed with love.

"Look, Lottie! He's right there," I said, trying to point. But my hand was heavy. I looked down and I was holding a large stick; it looked like a cane.

"No. He's not there. He's somewhere else. Find him. *He* is the answer. Find him and you can save them all. Find him and bring him back to me."

When she turned her gaze my way, her face. Oh, Lord. Her face was on fire.

20

Byrd

What's the definition of torture? I'll tell you what it is. It's when someone you can't stand to be parted from leaves you to go figure out a mystery that you yourself have been tryin' to solve . . . and they leave you behind. Nothin' feels worse than bein' left behind. After I took a zillion pictures, I felt all lonesome again. My eyes began to burn and my heartbeat went all fast. *I am dyin'*, I thought.

But then I noticed the wetness on my face. No, I told myself, you ain't *dyin'* you're *cryin'*. And it was a very, very, very hot feeling.

One time, me and Jamie were watchin' TV over at his house. We might have all the money in the world, but we ain't got no TV. Minerva and Naomi had somethin' against them. Do all Yankees hate TV?

Anyway, we were sitting on the floor in his bedroom watchin' this show about Incredible Things on the Discovery channel.

I have to be honest with you, most of the shows on there ain't got nothin' to do with discovery. More about looking into people's minds and hearts and naughtiest thoughts. If everyone was magic like me, we wouldn't need no TV at all. I mean, all I have to do is walk through town to get entertainment.

So there was this show on and it was talkin' about when people just *burst into flames*. Like . . . *whoosh*! Burned up from the inside out.

"Can't be real," said Jamie.

"Why not?" I asked.

"Just can't."

"I think it would be fun to watch, though. Don't you?"

"Yeah!" he shouted, laughin'. Then, starting with his mama, we went through the whole damn town thinking of things that would make them burn right up from the inside out and makin' up fun stories about where they'd be when it happened. Like the produce aisle at the market. Or the bathroom. We laughed so hard I could barely breathe!

But when I was all mad at my aunt for not takin' me with her. I was so mad I thought I'd combust for real. And that wasn't funny. I was so mad I could *spit*. But instead, I took more pictures. Mostly of the gardens and the house, but also of the mist over Belladonna Bay.

I didn't much like bein' alone. Funny. Before she came, I didn't mind at all.

I swear! A child needs *guidance*. Sometimes I think they're all afraid of me. But not her, her eyes stayed soft from the moment I met her.

And when she finally came back that night, she carried me

back to the cottage and read to me from *The Little Prince*. Then when she thought I was fast asleep, she said the most beautiful thing I've ever heard.

"I don't care if you did it, Byrd. I wouldn't love you less. I'd move heaven and earth to protect you, just like your daddy. And that's the God's honest truth. I'm never going to let anything happen to you."

That's when I knew I'd never let her leave me.

Ever.

21

Bronwyn

I woke up the next morning with too much on my mind. I had to find Jackson, tell him about Grant. I had to find Ben and apologize for that terrible fight. Then I'd go see Stick and make him do his goddamn job. But it was Sunday, and I knew Stick would be at church for a good long while.

I gently untangled myself from Byrd's arms and legs and crept out of the room, shutting the door gently behind me. The dream was loosening its grip, but I knew I had to figure everything out soon or I'd lose my mind.

I started the coffee; hoping Ben would wander back from the Big House when he realized Minerva would only offer tea in tiny cups. Ben appreciated his morning coffee even more than I did.

But first I needed to see Jackson. He had to hear my plan about getting a new trial for Paddy first, before I went into town to tell Stick. I wanted him to know that I was doing as he'd asked. I wanted him to be proud of me.

The Big House was quiet, so I went in through the kitchen thinking I'd find Minerva.

Instead, I found a little girl standing on a chair stirring the best-smelling gumbo I'd ever smelled.

"Good morning," I said.

"Good mornin' right back, ma'am," she said. "You lookin' for Minerva?"

"Yep, or Jackson. Either one."

"Well, miss, today is Minerva's day to herself. She 'n Carter. And they be at church, as you should be too ifn' you don' mind my sayin'. And Jackson's gone to the farm. He thinks good thoughts there."

"Thank you," I said. "What's your name? Are you friends with Byrd?"

"My name's Mary, ma'am. And Byrd and I are real friendly-like."

"May I taste your gumbo?" I asked.

"Oh, no, miss. T'ain' ready yet. I'll let you know when it is. There's figs, though. I like 'em wit salt. You ever eat 'em like that? You know, all the salt in these here parts got a little o' the bay in 'em."

"How do you mean, Mary?"

"It's from the mines, don't you know," she said. And then, "Ma'am? Be careful today. Today is full of bad juju."

Jackson used to tell the story of how the Confederate army dug salt mines up and down the bay during the Civil War, so that when the tide came in and then out, they could scrape out the salt deposits left behind. It was a saving grace for the South, since there'd been so many embargoed goods.

"They still mine salt, Mary?" I asked, grabbing a fig.

She didn't answer me. I turned around and she was gone. The gumbo, too.

It can't be, I thought, going to look for her.

Little girls are fast. But . . . *how does a pot disappear?* I thought maybe I was still asleep and having a very odd dream.

I went into the main hall as a lady in black walked down the stairs. "Well, I thought you'd never come!" she said.

"I'm sorry?" I asked.

"Aren't you the seamstress from New Orleans?"

"No, ma'am."

She shook her head and sighed, walking back up the stairs.

"I don't know what to do without help. I need to fix up these dresses for my girls!"

I left the house fast then, through the kitchen and into the side garden, where a pretty, redheaded young woman paced back and forth in a tattered dress.

"Can I help you?" I asked.

"Yes . . . have you seen my . . . have you seen . . . I'm supposed to be with him. Please . . ."

"Who?" I asked. But she was walking away from me, wringing her hands. The sadness and worry all around her sat hard in my throat.

Bad juju indeed.

I was seeing spirits, like Byrd. I'd known it when I turned around and saw Mary's pot had left the building with Mary, but it took three of them to convince me. And it took the fourth one to help me understand that spirit seeing, though unnerving, can make visible the invisible line that hovers right above our instinct, showing us the moments we might otherwise have been unable to alter.

A beautiful woman, wearing a light pink dress, stood barefoot in the center of Naomi's garden. Her long, curly black hair framed her face and fell in layers over her shoulders. She was pointing at Esther, and though her mouth was open, she didn't make a sound. Instead, small, sparkling bits of light came pouring out each time she tried to speak. Like stars.

Stella.

"Are you Stella?" I asked, walking toward her. Her feet hovered an inch above the belladonna planted there.

She made a face at me then, looking so much like Byrd I knew I was right. Her face said, *"You already know who I am, and I'm pointing somewhere, and you are walking in the wrong direction. . . . What's the matter with you?"* Which, you could say, was exactly the same thing as being obtuse.

"Okay, I get it, you want me to go to Esther," I said.

Lord, how I wanted to know her. To sit with her, laugh with her, tell her how wonderful Byrd was. But I'd lost that chance years ago. And Stella probably already knew her daughter was a magnificent little girl.

I went to the tree, placing my hands gently on her trunk. Then I felt a whisper of a breath from above. Stella was lounging on one of Esther's lower branches, looking pleased with herself and pointing down at the base of the tree.

"Dig?" I asked. I'd never been more mortal and clumsy. Even my thoughts felt as heavy as my limbs. Any fear I had of my own death disappeared in that moment, as I dug in the ground, a clumsy oaf of a woman, with Stella, her dress draping and her eyes filling up with stars, watching me.

I dug into the soft, mulched earth with my hands, but I didn't have to dig far. Half a foot down, I uncovered a round tin.

I pulled it out and looked up again, only Stella was gone.

I sat back and leaned against the tree, wiping the dirt off the container, and realized it was a candy tin. Lemon drops.

I opened it and found a letter sealed in a plastic bag. The note was from Stella, and it was addressed to me.

Dear BitsyWyn,

If you're reading this, you've taken the path I saw for you. The sight is fickle though, and our futures are always changeable. I hope—at the same time as I don't—that you've found your way home. You see, the path you're walking is one that holds great danger for my daughter, Byrd. I don't know that you can save her, but at least I can give you a head start. Now, if you hadn't come home at all, she either wouldn't be in dire straits or she wouldn't have the chance to be saved. I don't like those odds, so I'll hope that I was right.

She's always been my light, that girl. I came here, to this glowing, safe world of Magnolia Creek, to find my past and my future. I come from a darker place, Wyn. One so dark that it kept my family captive for too many generations of Amore women. When I finally figured out that I had a choice: Leave my own home and allow the next child to grow up free of our dangerous history, or stay where we've always lived and have her grow up in the shadows like I did. I chose to leave. One path, the darker one, would have allowed me to raise my baby. The other allowed me to see her thrive, even if it meant my life.

We can change anything if we are brave enough to make hard decisions.

The Amore family and the Greens have been intertwined for

hundreds of years. The Masters, too, though they were originally La'Maestras. You know that already because of Susan. I wish I'd known her.

I wish I'd known you.

I used my lineage to track down other branches of my family, so Byrd would be raised in a place that didn't question her shine. I knew she'd be born, no matter what, but loving Paddy so fierce was a bonus. Jackson, Minerva, and Carter, too. I loved everything about it here, Wyn. And when I saw how you would come back and love my girl as much as any mother could love her child, I knew I'd made the right decision. Thank you, sister.

Here is where your path diverges. You will have the choice to act or not. And if you can't find the strength to alter the course, I can't promise that any of you will be safe.

Byrd is in serious danger, Wyn. Her body, mind, and very soul will be tested. And soon. You have to help her. Please.

Now, do as I say, BitsyWyn Whalen.

Run

Run

Run!

I looked back up at the branch, hoping to catch another glimpse of her, but she wasn't there. Instead, a snake, the one from my dream on the plane, was curled up in her place. It raised its head to strike me but instead struck out in the direction of my cottage.

That's when I knew. And that's when I ran.

I got to the end of the path, just in time to see Byrd walk straight into the mist over Belladonna Bay.

I kept running, screaming her name, and I must have screamed help because I heard Jackson and Ben calling from behind me, their footfalls growing close.

"Wyn! Stop! You don't know what you're doin,'" yelled Jackson.

"You don't know shit about shit!" I yelled back and dove straight into the mist after Byrd.

Only, I found Charlotte instead.

It All Comes Out
in the Wash

Evil and good walk hand in hand, like hate and love.
You can't have one without the other.

—*Byrd, age eleven*

22

Byrd

Then if a child comes to you, and if he laughs,
if he has golden hair, if he doesn't answer
your questions, you'll know who he is.

—*The Little Prince*

Why is it that just when we think we're free of trouble, it comes
up behind us and hits us in the back of the head? I'd been lookin'
for trouble since I was a baby. Carryin' the weight of everyone's
sorrows and fears. And the mornin' when my own worst fear
was realized, I had no thought of it whatsoever. I woke up and
went out onto the porch to find Aunt Wyn. That's when I took
a good, hard look across the creek at Belladonna and noticed
somethin' peculiar. The mist had lifted . . . just a bit. But that
bit was enough to let me see a familiar shadow movin' back and
forth on the island itself.

Well, hell . . . just when I was startin' to feel normal.

So, I took a deep breath, squared my shoulders, and ran straight
across that creek. I don't think I was afraid. Not really.

When I crossed over, I was ready for the mist to be sweet and
clingy like buttercream. But I wasn't quite prepared for the nau-
sea and complete joy that hit me all at once. Pretty soon there

was nothing but mist all around me, and I couldn't help but start thinkin' on Naomi.

I wondered if she'd hopped, skipped, and jumped across the creek or if she'd taken her time. I reckon she just ran across not thinkin' 'cause I don't think she did much of that. Thinkin', that is.

Then I wondered whether or not this feeling washing across me, all wonderful, horrible, and wonderful again, wasn't something she felt when she did those drugs. And something Jackson felt when he was three sheets gone, something just so delicious that I'd want to stay inside it forever and ever. I had to fight it 'cause I started to understand all those stories of people not comin' back at all, or not comin' back the same. But then I thought about Carter. You know when somethin' really important happens and the whole thing just melts out of your damn brain? I'd been so worried that I killed my Little Prince and his mama, and all filled up with guilt over my daddy in jail, that I'd forgotten about Carter. He'd gone into the mist. He'd gone over and come back, sure . . . he was covered in blood, but he'd come back. And he hadn't changed.

So maybe the mist didn't do nothin' at all?

A person can go from terrified to brave real fast.

And you know what? The second I wasn't afraid . . . that mist was *gone*.

Also, I'd figured everything out. And I couldn't let myself get all sweaty with fear. I had to come back from Belladonna in one piece. Because everything rode on it.

I had to save them all.

So I needed to be brave. Too brave. You might be askin' yourself if there's such a thing as too brave. Well, there is.

When that mist cleared, I was standin' there on the Bella-

donna's banks, bein' all brave, lookin' right at my very own Little
Prince.

Ever been on a roller coaster and you're at the top, right about
to go over and straight down?

That's what it felt like. Standing there, looking at him. My
heart dropped straight down into my toes.

"Damn, girl. It sho' took you a long time to git on over here,"
he said.

"Are you a ghost, Jamie? No foolin' with me!"

He smiled big. "I ain't no ghost! I'm as real as you are. Pinch
me if you wanna."

"I didn't know you were over here . . . I didn't . . . oh, Jamie!"

Jamie. I ran to him, up the small sandy bank and toward the
tall pines that seemed to go up for ages. The sunlight shone silver, diffused here by the mist, still lingering above the island like
a bubble.

He picked me up right off my feet, and I realized he'd gotten
taller. I touched his face and his arms and his nose to my nose.
Jamie. He smelled good. Like sunshine and love and the deep
red dirt he'd been livin' on.

If love has a smell, it's Jamie.

"What took you so long, Byrdie? I missed you."

"You know as well as I do that I can't just see things when I
want. Especially you! Who's closer to me than you? No one, that's
who."

Jamie looked down, away from me.

"I'm real sorry about your daddy, Byrd. I wish he hadn't confessed to anything. He didn't do nothin'."

"How do you even know what's been happenin'? You've been
all cooped up over here, right?"

"No . . . I mean . . . I just want you to know he shouldn't be in prison."

"Well, hell, Jamie! You better come back on home and tell everyone that! Do you know who did it? Was it Grant? Aunt Wyn thinks it's Grant one second and then she goes all crazy fuckall—"

"Don't curse, Byrd. It sounds terrible comin' out of that pretty mouth of yours. Time you learned some manners, don't you think? But, nah, it ain't Grant. But I wish it was. I wish it *was* him in the kitchen that night. I hate him and wish he was dead."

We sat down next to a small fire he'd made in the sand out of pine mulch and needles and twigs. It smelled so strong. If you eat pine and don't die, it makes you forget. I hoped that just smelling it wouldn't make me or Jamie forget anything because I needed to know all the things he knew. And my heart was *singing.* My daddy hadn't done it! And Jamie was alive!

"What's your trouble with Grant?" I asked. I'd only met him once. But I'd liked him. He seemed lost and broken. A deep sadness lived inside Grant Masters. And he was handsome. I like pretty, broken things.

"You know what I found out?" Jamie's voice got real hard just then. "Not two weeks before . . . you know, she died . . . I found out that he ain't my uncle. He's my daddy. It's sick! They're brother and sister!"

Well, now . . . maybe we are a bit backwards, I thought, but didn't want to give him more fuel for the fire burnin' inside him. "Not really. Not by blood," I said.

"Sure are . . . by the way they grew up and all, raised like sister and brother. And what's worse? My mama'd loved him her entire life, till it finally took over her whole self. She got him real drunk one night, and he fell for it. They both got wound up in the worst kind of weakness, and used it against each other.

"So they did what they did, and my mama got me. Only she didn't get him. Because he felt tricked and sick. Lied to. I'm a living lie, Byrdie. And then he wanted to see me, and my mama was yellin' at him on the phone. That fight I told you about? Well, I was too dang embarrassed to tell you the whole reason why . . . me bein' a lie and all . . . but he wanted to see me. And she was screamin' and cryin' and tellin' him that she wouldn't let him near me unless he'd love her, too. Can you imagine? She was more desperate than a pig on the way to bein' bacon. He'd left me for all my years with that crazy piece of work. I hate him for leaving me. I'll hate him forever."

I knew right then how angry Jamie musta been. He'd spent his whole life tryin' to figure out who his daddy was. The only thing we ever knew for sure was that it wasn't *my* daddy because we'd asked and asked when we were little. And I know Jamie'd had a hard spot on his heart ever since he finally believed it. Because he'd have liked to have my daddy, who wouldn't? Only I wasn't upset about it, 'cause then we couldn't grow up and get married and have babies like I thought we would. Which made me understand just how mad Jamie was, and just how desperate Lottie must have been. I loved her right then, Lottie, because I could have turned out just like her.

It was damn messy.

"A foul business for sure, Jamie," I said, leanin' forward to push some of his hair out of his eyes, my hands glowing from just from bein' near him.

But still. He knew what happened, so I had to ask. Only I

shut my eyes tight when I did because I was afraid of the answer. It had to be bad, bad enough for him to hide out here away from me.

"Did I do it, Jamie? I did, didn't I? I did it and you came out here to either get away from me or to protect me. Right? That's got to be it. You been stayin' away so's you could protect me."

He didn't say anything, so I opened my eyes.

He'd stood up and started walking around in circles. He reminded me of a peacock the way he was puffing out his chest. He kept tryin' to say things, but he couldn't get nothin' out of his mouth.

"I'm like the moon," he started, "the hidden side of the moon. Not seen because it don't want to be seen. Everyone knows ther's is shadow there, but no one looks. It's like that with me, Byrd. I'm part illuminated, part in shadow—and that part that shines is all you ever wanted to see. But it kept getting smaller, and now it's dark. I'm a new moon now, Byrd. All there is, is shadow. Can you still see me? Do you still love me?"

He was talkin' crazy. And I couldn't talk at all. I tried to make words and they wouldn't come outa my mouth either. He noticed and got even more worked up. He hadn't answered my question. What did that mean? And I thought about my book, *The Little Prince,* and how at the end, before he died, he got to talkin' crazy, too.

"I swear it, Byrd. I got home that night after we'd been fishin'. It started with that weak little tree in the front yard. I'd told her and told her to get the guy over who could fix it. But she'd been lazy and never called.

"I had no intention of killing her until I walked home and saw that tree all bent and broken. And I thought to myself,

'Damn, I better just cut that sucker down, because nothing so strong should ever display such weakness.' And then I walked into my house and there she was, leaning up against our dirty, worn-down counter, sipping a glass of wine. Lookin' old.

"For the first time, I saw her, *really* saw her. Her gray hairs. Her roundness. She was old, Byrd. Like, all of a sudden.

"'What you starin' at, Jamie?' she asked me. 'You still mad I won't let you go over to NOLA to see that broken man of a father?' Seemed she'd had too much to drink already. I put my hands in my pockets and realized after fishin' I never gave you your knife back. So I grabbed it and . . .

"I killed her."

Sometimes, there are no words.

Jamie didn't like nothin' weak, I knew that.

But that wasn't enough of an explanation. A dead tree, some mean words? There had to be more.

"But, Jamie," I asked, "can you tell me *why* you did it? It can't just be 'cause she looked old. Did she come at you first?"

His answer came out so calm that I had to believe the thing he'd said about the moon. He'd gone dark.

"She was all tired from work and sat down at the crummy kitchen table. Same one she probably sat at when she was a kid. And lit a smoke. Asked me to take off her shoes.

"'Take off my shoes, Jamie boy. Do you mind? Mama's been on her feet all day,' she said.

"And her feet, Byrd, you know how they smelled? Used up, that's how. Weak, sweaty working feet."

"She *does* work hard, your mama," I said. "I mean . . . did."

"Lemme finish. So I asked, 'Mama, you want a pain pill?' And I knew she'd say yes, but I gave her one from last year, where the dose was high 'cause she was eatin' 'em like candy, remember? She took it with her wine, got all groggy, and . . . Bydie? Why did it have to be like that? Why couldn't she be like you and Jackson? All smellin' of flowers and money. I'm like you, not her. She made me sick. And then I thought I'd kill her, like I kill all those animals when they ain't no use to nothin' no more. I told myself to stop thinkin' that way, that it was sick with a capital *S*. But when she asked me to rub her feet, I don't know, I just—"

He broke off, cryin'.

I can't stand to see Jamie cry. It ain't normal. So I held him, because no matter what he'd done, he's still my prince.

"How'd you get over here, you run?" I asked him.

"No. It's kind of a mystery to me. I was so crazy when I saw my mama there on the floor and seen what I done. I tried to cut my own neck, see?" He showed me a small, ragged scar on the side of his neck.

"But then I must have passed out, straight on into the glass door by the dining room. I had glass up and down my backside. And when I woke up, I was here in the cottage I built when I was little and a fire was goin' and I felt a little better. Only I don't know how I got here."

"Jamie," I asked, "you've been over here, without me? For years? I thought you were afraid of this place."

He shifted his feet a little and looked up into the sun, squinting like he was tryin' to figure out how to weasel himself out of the biggest lie of all time.

"Well, Byrdie . . . a boy needs a place of his own. And I love you. More than anything. But sometimes I needed to be alone. And I didn't want you followin' me neither, so I lied."

He sounded sorrier to have lied to me than he was about killin' his mama. Such a strange boy, my prince.

"We have to tell someone," I said when I felt he might be
calming down.

"Who?"

"I don't know. Anyone? You're a little kid, you'd get off. And
then my daddy could get outa jail. You can't let him stay in there
for what you did. Not if you really love me."

A look came into his eyes at that moment that I won't ever
forget. Worse than a shadow, a stranger.

"Let's forget all this, Byrdie. Let me take you to my castle. I've
been making it, working night and day, building it for you." His
voice was hollow. There was something very wrong with my
prince after all. And my instinct, God love it, finally kicked in.

I went with him because I knew I didn't have a choice.

23

Wyn

It feels like the island itself is right there over the creek. Step on five or six large stones and you'd be there. That's how I'd always imagined it. It wasn't like that at all.

Most of the time we imagine things wrong, so it's stupid to even try to prepare yourself. Like, you can't prepare yourself to see a ghost. Especially one you knew alive first. It hums in your head, and there's a quick beat of fear, and then it just is what it is. Most people see them, you know. Only they don't want to, so they get a funny feeling on the stairs, or some air on the back of their neck. I'd blocked them out my whole life. But I couldn't do it anymore.

And there she was. Lottie.

She was balancing on a rock, with her arms stretched out for balance. I watched as she placed one foot on the side of her leg and lifted her arms up, turning her head to the sky. I'd forgotten how long her neck was. Then she did a pirouette.

A perfect one.

Lottie loved ballet. We used to make so much fun of her. But looking at her now, I realized too late what a wonderful ballerina she would have made. If we'd supported her, would she still have quit?

"No," she said, her voice soft. "I wouldn't have. I may have even gotten out of Magnolia Creek."

"I'm sorry, Charlotte," I said. I didn't know what else to say.

She moved toward me, we must have been halfway through the mist by then. Meeting in the middle like we always had.

Meet you halfway . . . halfway to the church, the beach, even school. Meet you halfway in friendship, too. Only I didn't meet her. She always held up her part of the bargain, and I was always late.

Her image crept lower the closer she got. The water was up to her calves, and her long gown, colorless yet glittery, was wet along the bottom.

"Come closer to me, Wyn. I won't bite you," she said.

"I have to pass you, Lottie. I'm sorry. I have to move past you. Byrd is over there. You know her, right? And she's . . . well . . ."

"You love her." Her voice hovered over the word *love,* dragging it around and hanging it inside the mist. Not an echo . . . a layer.

"Yes. I do. That's why I need to go to her."

Charlotte raised herself up again, levitating for a moment before sitting down on a larger rock in the center of the creek. She patted the spot next to her. "Come sit by me for a little bit and let's us have an old-fashioned chat," she said.

"Lottie, I have to go. I'll chat with you on the way back,

okay?" That's when I tried to pass her, but I couldn't. I took two steps forward and felt a squeezing around my heart that wouldn't let go. *I'm having a heart attack.*

"No, you aren't," she said. "I won't let you by. You can try for hours. On all different sides of me, but I won't let you. You'll have to sit a bit and listen to me first. Or else that mist? I'll make it go right into you and you won't be able to breathe. Not one bit. Don't make me do that, Wyn. I don't want to make any more mistakes. I've made far too many already."

I sat down, the pressure around my heart easing.

She took a long pause before she started speaking.

"Remember when all we did was sit like this, side by side? On your porch or my porch? Or the docks or—"

"The swing," I finished.

She laughed, more watery sounds.

"Was that you? On the swing that day?" I asked.

"Yes. And it was me in my kitchen, too. But you couldn't see me yet. I wasn't sure you'd ever get up the courage to accept yourself. See, that's the key. I've just learned it myself. Dead and all. Just learned that in order to be free, we have to allow ourselves to be . . ."

"Is that why you can't cross over?"

"Maybe at first, but not now. Now I know what way to go. I see my path." She looked to her left, longing filling her eyes. "I'll get there soon enough. I've seen it, you know. It's beautiful, Wyn. Really. But first I have to help my baby, and you have to help him, too."

"How can I help him? I don't know him, and I don't know where he is."

"And whose fault is that?" she asked, snapping her head

around, seething. "*You* left. *You* ran away, leaving us all here to wade around in the chaos. It was like quicksand. You left Paddy all alone after you promised you'd never leave him. And Jackson was even more lost than ever. He still is. Not to mention Minerva. She shed a few tears, too. Does that surprise you? It shouldn't. But the worst? You know what the worst part of all of it was, Wyn?"

"What? I'm so sorry. I wish there was a bigger word. I didn't even realize . . . I ran, but I was lost, too."

"I don't give a shit about that right now. Let me finish. The worst part was that you left Grant. And you left me. And I swear, though I missed you, damn did I ever . . . I was happy you'd gone. Because, I'm sure you've figured it all out, I wanted Grant to myself, and I thought if you were gone, I'd have a chance.

"But you took him with you, didn't you? Took his heart. That's when I started to hate you. I suppose I should ask you to forgive me for that. Who knows? Maybe it was my hate mixed up with your guilt that made some kind of alchemy, a witches' brew of staying away forever."

"I'm starting to believe in all sorts of things, Lottie. I don't doubt a person can put up a wall around a place or a person and not let them inside," I said.

"Well, hell. You just figured out this mist, didn't you? More than that, you just figured out your mama."

Naomi.

"Have you seen her? She's here, isn't she?" I found myself looking wildly in the mist. Her presence was strong, close.

"Yes. I have. But that's another thing for another day. Today, I'm gonna take you down memory lane, and then you're gonna do me a favor, okay?"

"Okay," I said quietly.

"Here we go: you're fifteen, and I'm fourteen. You've run off in the middle of the night after a fight with your mama. You're in that white cotton nightgown, you remember? You came up to my window and knocked at it. Looked like a ghost yourself."

"I remember," I said, and I did.

Naomi had come into my room and woken me up. She wanted to "talk," this happened a lot as she used more and more. She'd get these "amazing ideas" and need to share them. I don't know if she only chose me, or if she made the rounds in the family, but that night, I wasn't having it.

"Get out of my room!" I'd screamed at her.

She put her hands over her face and said, "I'm not really a person at all, Wyn. I'm a ghost. I'm living in-between the walls. Not in the passages, in the plaster. I'm under the plaster. I can't see you, and you can't see me and I can't . . . talk because there's all this dust . . . in my throat." She scratched at her throat, leaning against my door. This was the moment where I'd usually help her back to bed.

But not that night. That night I'd had enough.

"*Get out!*" I yelled again and reached out to my bedside table and took the crystal water glass that had been there since I was born, with its matching fancy water decanter, and threw it as hard as I could, straight at her. It shattered next to her head.

We were both shocked. Naomi's eyes got wide, and then she ran. She ran away from me, which is what I wanted all wrapped up in what I didn't want.

So I left the Big House and ran to the Masters. I wanted to see Lottie. And Susan, only I knew Susan would be sleeping, because . . . damn . . . she was sick, too.

Charlotte put her spirit hand on top of mine. And the chill brought me back from the past, back into the mist.

"I always wondered why it was my window and not Grant's that you came to that night, Wyn,"

"I needed you, not him. I needed my friend. And you loved Naomi. I wanted someone to be mad at me. To tell me I'd behaved badly."

Fourteen-year-old Lottie had pressed her face against the screen. "What's the matter, Wyn? Everything okay?"

I just shook my head, crying.

You were crying.

Young Lottie took the pack of cigarettes by her bed and a lighter, too. Then she climbed right out of the window in her pajamas. White with yellow flowers, I remember.

"Come on!" she said, grabbing my arm, and we started running.

The two of us ran free and laughing into the night. Up Main Street and out onto county road 10 until we were smack in the middle of a red dirt road, illuminated by the full moon. The pecan trees ahead and the soybeans with their low green leaves covering the ground on either side of us.

We sat in the middle of that road. Neither of us able to wash that red stain out of what we were wearing again. We smoked and talked.

"I love you," she said.

"I love you, too," I said. "You saved me tonight, Lottie. You always save me."

We got up, attempting to brush the red dirt off.

"Yeah, you owe me for a lot of things. Things you don't even understand."

Fifteen-year-old BitsyWyn never knew what she meant.

But I understood now.

She'd let me have Grant and still stayed my friend. I couldn't even imagine how hard that must have been, watching us all those years.

Then after I was gone, she was never able to get him to love her the way she wanted him to.

"You owe me one, remember?" said spirit Charlotte.

"I know."

"Then go. You solve this whole thing. You have to figure out who killed me, and bring me my son. You have the rest of today and all of tomorrow. After that, I can't change fate. Do that for me, and then I can cross. You owe me."

"Lottie, don't you remember who killed you?"

"Maybe I do. Maybe I don't. Maybe I just don't want to remember. *You* have to figure it out."

"And you'll let me back over when I do?" I asked.

"I'll either let you back over or kick her butt back out, it don't make no difference to me. Now, at least."

"Lottie? Why does it have to be so quick?"

"Because if it ain't done soon, Byrd won't be able to stay alive, you hear? There's things I already know, but you have to confirm them. I'm trying to save little Byrd, too. Get it straightened out in the land of the living so I can get it straightened out here on the dead side," she said and then turned away, pirouetting back across the rocks until she was lost in the mist.

I made my way back out, but all I could think of was Byrd.

She felt so far away. *Is she cold? Does she feel safe inside? Does she walk knowing she's loved? Please don't die, please don't die, please don't die.*

24

Naomi

That old magnolia, Esther, knows all my secrets. She watched me from the moment I set foot on the Big House property. She saw me change and then slip away. I love that tree. She never asks questions. She's the only tree I ever met who already knows the answers.

I watched my own funeral from her branches and noticed my family's absence then more than any letters or packages they never sent. Minerva always told me, "You can't measure love by the post office."

Everyone wants to get rid of their pain. Smart people know they need to face pain so they can make good decisions. Pain is like a map, I guess. But I found a shortcut on my "map of the heart." Shortcuts always take longer, don't they?

I always assumed I'd be the kind of mother I saw on TV. Grandma Catherine and the rest of the family purchased a television set for me when it became evident I wouldn't be able to participate much with anyone. So, they went off to school, parties, annual picnics, and I stayed in my room watching game shows or reruns of *Donna Reed*.

I couldn't identify with anyone on those shows, and I couldn't lose myself in the entertainment, either. I began to hate it, television.

When I moved to Magnolia Creek, we got rid of them all.

My thoughts, they wander . . . aprons. Yes.

I wanted to be an apron-wearing, knowledgeable mother. Capable of all things domestic. I gave it a try. The only thing that stuck was the apron. I loved my aprons.

My grandmother used to wear them. I could have loved her, if she let me. Minerva said they were all *scared* of me. I believe that now. I was scared of my own children, and that's why I ran away from them.

Irony is becoming exactly who you told yourself you'd never be, and not knowing it until you're dead. My apron-wearing, mean-spirited grandmother's eyes were the most expressive I've ever seen. And she was terrified of me. Afraid I'd end up wielding the same kind of control over Fairview that her own aunt, Faith Green, had. More than that, though, she was afraid of loving me. Terrified that she'd lose me and not willing to take a chance. I did exacty the same thing with my children.

She used to say, "We've just come out from under all the tragedy that woman and her ways brought down on the heads of this family and this town. I'll be dead in that cove if it happens again. You keep your ways still. You hear me? Control them. Tamp them down. It's a bad, bad thing."

And when I was little, I'd argue with her. Kind of like Byrd.

"But you have talents, and so do others in this town. What's the matter with mine? What makes me different?"

"You're a distorted version of who we're supposed to be, Naomi. And that's all there is to it. Harsh or not, it's the truth. If you don't listen to me, I promise you'll bring hell down on those you love. You already chased your own mother away by being born. That was my daughter, *my daughter.*"

Minerva would usually come in and defend me, but I still heard my grandmother in my heart. It's one of the reasons the drugs took hold, they helped me create a wall, and the voice would go quiet.

My bond with my children when they were babies was entirely different. But when they got big, around three or four, I used to look for them. I'd find these bigger, independent, sticky little people and think, *Where did my babies go? Who took them?*

For a long time I blamed Grant for taking Bronwyn. And I feared his deep affection for her. I could tell, especially when I was coming off the opium and could feel the thoughts again, that his love for her was extraordinary. Once in a lifetime. And I didn't want that for her. She'd drown in it.

But I was wrong about my children. I was wrong about everything.

No one took them from me. I left them. Like my mother left me when I was a baby. Like my gran left me to rot in that asylum. Like Jackson left me when he drank too much . . . which was all the time.

But because I couldn't see what I was really doing, I blamed them, my children, and all who loved them. I threw the blame around like mean confetti, when it was my fault all along.

Oh, why couldn't I fly with the birds when I died? Why did I have to face all the truths when I had no way to fix them?

Instead of flying, I climbed up inside of Esther and moved

my hands over her old, aching branches. I perched there and watched as my family fell apart.

Esther told me if I waited till the lights over Belladonna Bay turned a silver pink and shone in the daytime, that I'd be set free. That if I waited, was patient, I'd find whatever my spirit was waiting to find, and then be able to cross over into the light of the in between.

"You can't help her until she asks for you, Naomi," she'd whispered.

I'm tired, Bronwyn . . . so tired of lingering here with no voice, and reliving a past I can't change. Help me, sweet girl. Help me find my way home.

Forgive me, BitsyWyn and then ask for me . . . .

25

Wyn

You don't promise a ghost something and then go back on it, you just don't.

Ben and Jackson were waiting for me when I came out of the mist. It felt like I'd been gone for days, but they told me it was only a small stretch of minutes.

"I tried to go after you, sugar. I did, but that mist was choking me. Ben here pulled me out. Why'd you go there?"

"Jackson, I need you to be calm," I said. "Byrd's over there. I went to get her."

He looked at me with that sort of confusion that comes over you when your heart doesn't want to hear whatever someone is saying into your brain.

"Did you find her?" he asked.

"Yes and no. You have to trust me, okay?"

I looked at Ben, who was staring off toward Belladonna Bay. Not even looking at me. Something was confusing him, too. I wanted him far away. I knew it wasn't fair; he hadn't brought any of this trouble. But I needed to be angry at someone, and he *was* the easiest mark.

That's when I read Ben's mind, and my heart went haywire.

I didn't know this would happen, she's not safe. I've been so selfish. This is my job, why am I not doing my job? Forget you love her, forget you love her . . . help them.

His feelings had muddled up his instincts about everything. I was furious.

I turned to Jackson.

"Come on, Daddy, we gotta talk."

"Now? Have you lost your mind, Byrd's out there," he said.

"Daddy, if you'd let yourself feel anything real for once, you'd know I wouldn't be back without her if I'd had a choice. I can't get to her until I've solved this mess. At least, that's what Lottie said."

"But she's . . . oh. Now *you* see them, too. Okay," he said, sort of breathless, "Okay. But Jaysus, I need a drink first. I haven't been this sober in forty years, and it ain't right."

He turned to Ben as we walked up the short path to my porch steps. "Don't take your eyes off that mist, young man. Byrd could need us at any moment."

"I know, sir. I know," said Ben.

I wanted to drop-kick him all the way back to New York. Because I was done playing with all of that righteous, brave bullshit. I had a job to do, too.

You'll get it done, I have faith in you, he said, right into my mind.

Strange ways could give a person a serious headache. "Get outta my head, Ben Mason!" I shouted. He didn't turn around.

"What's that all about?" asked Jackson as we settled on the porch.

"Trouble in paradise," I said, flipping on the switch for the fans. The white noise helped clear my head. Then I poured us both a drink, morning or not, and told him what Lottie had said. Only I left out the "she might die if I don't solve this thing soon" part, because he'd run over there himself and get his breath taken, too. And I loved him. So that wouldn't do at *all*.

"So you have to find Jamie," he said. "Shit, darlin' . . . we seem to be trapped in a box of sorts. If we don't find his body, we lose Byrd. If we do find him, we lose Paddy to the electric chair. It's a Solomon kind of decision, don't you think?"

My father. I knew what he wanted to do more than anything. He wanted to go back to the Big House, grab a fishing line, two cases of beer ('cause beer's for fishin', don't you know), and forget his life entirely. I couldn't let him do that. Not yet.

"If there's anything you know that you haven't said, Daddy, tell me now."

"What are you hinting at, sugar?"

"Did you know Grant was Jamie's father? You had to have known. No one's born here without your damn *permission*."

"Yes. I knew. But how does that help us? I was tryin' to keep a secret that belonged to a dead woman. I ain't lost my chivalry yet."

"But what if he did it, Jackson? What if he killed them? I swear I don't want to believe it, either."

"In all honesty, Wyn, that boy couldn't have done it. I believe it just like I believe Paddy couldn't have. I know them both, inside and out. He just didn't."

Jackson took a long sip and seemed to get his thoughts together, "There's a fine line between right and wrong and good and bad. And it's blurred all the time. You should know this better than most. Heroes come in all shapes and sizes, Wyn. You can be a hero and not be healthy. Grant was always tryin' to be something he wasn't after you left."

My stomach soured. I didn't think Grant could have done it, either. But I needed to get the case reopened.

So I told him everything. I told him about the fight between Grant and Charlotte; about the message on her answering machine, about my plan to use that evidence as some kind of probable doubt.

"I knew you'd think of somethin', sugar. But don't it feel like robbin' Peter to pay Paul? And I'm not sure it's enough to get the case opened again. It's sealed tight right now. We'd need a witness, a murder weapon . . . all that forensic bullshit."

"All I know is that I have to find Jamie, and I have to find him fast. Once I do, a brand-new trial will open up, and then we have . . . Grant."

"It's a sad day, ain't it, darlin'?"

"For sure, Daddy. But I have to try and protect everyone at the same time. So, can you think of anyone else who might be able to help?" I asked.

Jackson finished his drink and poured himself another. "Stick. I know, I know . . . he's a little lazy and scratchy, but he might know more than he thinks he does."

"You're drinking too much, Daddy," I said.

"Always," said Jackson.

He sighed. The sun played across his blue eyes, showing the sadness. Everything stilled for a moment, and I held him. We rocked on the swing, together again.

There's a particular type of magic between fathers and daughters. I'd seen it in photographs I'd taken. And I felt it when I was little. A golden bond. Innocent and free. The purest sort of love. But it comes with a price. If the love is abused, there is no greater abuse. But right then, I knew that Jackson had done his best. He'd let me go, and he'd taken care of me at the same time. Somehow, through all of my nonsense, he'd protected me even when I didn't know he was there. He hadn't ever forgotten about me. He'd thought about me every day for fourteen years. Blame can make a person so damn blind.

Minerva and Carter showed up while we rocked and paced with quiet worry.

I was the only one who knew we were running out of time. I snuck away while Jackson told them what happened and called Stick at the sheriff's office but got the machine. I turned his card over and tried his home phone, no answer there either.

I burst back onto the porch, letting everything around me slam. Patience may have been Bronwyn's best trait, but BitsyWyn Whalen had none of it.

"I'm going into town to find Stick," I said.

"No, you are not," said Minerva. "Today is his day when he goes to see his mother in Mexico Beach. He stays over. It's a five-hour drive. You can see him first thing in the morning."

First thing in the morning might not work because I'm running out of time! I wanted to scream but couldn't seem to say much. Then I looked at Carter, who couldn't make eye contact with me. My opinion of him wavered again. And a thought as clear as anything occurred to me.

Carter. He knew something. That's why he'd been trying to push me away and pull me in, all at the same time.

Cup holders. *Damn cup holders.*

I'd driven my Subaru in upstate New York for two years and the only thing I didn't like about it was there were no damn cup holders. One day, Ben was driving and we stopped for coffee. He pushed a little button next to the radio and *poof!* Cup holders popped out from the dashboard. I was astonished.

"You always overlook the things in front of you, Bronwyn." He'd laughed. We'd laughed together that day.

Carter. Standing in front of me. If you looked up the word *obtuse,* my picture *would* be next to it.

I was going to find out what he was hiding if it took all night. For me, for Byrd, for Patrick. What had that foul man done?

The day dripped past us slow. I tried several times to get Carter alone, but he's a clever son of a bitch. I tried to read his mind, but I could Feel Minny in there, protecting him. Not for any other reason but pure love. I respected that. I made a quick dinner with Minerva, pasta puttanesca, a favorite of mine growing up. Fresh tomatoes, olives, capers, garlic, and onions. All fried up in olive oil and then tossed together with pasta. The smell of it cooking was rich and decadent. But none of us had much of an appetite. As soon as the sun set, we all wanted to turn in. No one seemed to be going back up to the Big House. A big, solemn slumber party was unfolding. Byrd would have loved it.

"I'll sleep on the porch," said Ben.

"Fine with me," I said.

Jackson was passed out in an armchair, his legs on an ottoman. Minerva had the couch pulled out, putting linens on it for her and Carter.

"Carter?" I asked straight out, tired of trying to coax him into anything.

"Yes?"

"I want to speak with you."

Minerva looked at me, a quiet suspicion in her eyes.

"Don't look at me like that, Minerva," I said. "I'm not gonna kill him . . . yet."

Carter looked around for an escape, but Minerva motioned for him to follow me. So he did. We went into my bedroom, and I closed the door.

"Tell me what you know, Carter. I'm sick of playing cat and mouse with you. Sick of it."

He sat on the edge of my bed.

"Look," I said. "I know Paddy thinks Byrd did it. Hell, Byrd told me she thought she did when I first got here. I kept her secret, you know. I can keep them. Tell me. I know Paddy was lying about something yesterday. And you know what that is, so tell me now or I'll knock your teeth out."

"Wyn, there's nothing I can say."

"But you don't have to protect her anymore, if that's what you're doing. I know she didn't do anything. So just tell me. Goddamn it, Carter. I need to know. It's important."

"Look," he said, "I made a promise to Paddy. I love him like he's my own flesh and blood. And I've seen, firsthand, what broken promises do to that boy. I won't say one word unless I'm damn sure we're wrong about Byrd. So you can go ahead and knock these teeth out if you want."

And he left.

Broken promises . . . he'd been talking about me. About my promise to always be there for Paddy.

I was out of arguments.

◊

"Bronwyn!"

I woke to Ben yelling in the silver light of early morning. I ran into the living room. Jackson had already jumped up out of his chair. I looked for Minerva and Carter, but they were nowhere in sight.

My father and I ran to the creek to see Ben giving mouth-to-mouth resuscitation to my little niece, who was as blue as a still-born baby.

"Move, Ben!" I shouted.

He moved away from my still, beautiful Byrd, who seemed even smaller than she usually appeared.

"Work, please work," I whispered, rubbing my hands together, praying.

They felt a bit like sandpaper. I clapped, once, and there it was, the glow. Born of sadness, of fear, longing or frustration. Whatever, wherever it came from, I didn't care. It was there. I laid my hands on her head and chest, like Minerva used to do when I was little.

It didn't take but a moment. Byrd coughed, sputtering out water. She jolted up, her eyes stricken with terror, which frightened me because I'd seen a lot of things on that girl's face, and terror wasn't one of them.

"You okay, honey?" Jackson said, picking her up and rocking her in his arms. Tears ran down his face.

But she couldn't say a word. Not even the Declaration of Independence.

Ben looked at me with haunted eyes. And for the first time I wondered if maybe I'd been the worst thing to ever happen to him. But the thought didn't make me any calmer.

"What the hell is going on here?" asked Minerva, walking up behind us, Carter by her side.

"It's all gone to hell in a handbasket, Minerva," said Jackson, carefully passing Byrd from his arms to mine. "And I don't wanna know any more about it. Give me a holler when she's talkin' again, Wyn. And don't bother me until that time comes, you hear?" Jackson took a flask out of his back pocket, drank a large swig, and walked, shoulders defeated, back to the Big House. My broken father. "She'll be fine," I heard him mutter to himself. "Mermaids don't drown."

That sentence scared me more than anything.

Ben tried to console me. But I pushed him away.

"I don't even want to look at you," I said.

"Why? What did I do?"

"You kept me away."

"Come on over to the Big House with us, Ben. Let's give Bronwyn some time with Byrd," said Carter.

"You used your hands," said Minerva, who came to me and pushed the hair out of Byrd's face.

"I did."

"Good girl," she said and followed behind Carter.

Ben didn't say a word. He just followed them.

That's when Minerva stopped, turned around, and yelled, "I swear to Christ I leave for five seconds, for breakfast of all things, and this family falls apart."

"Apparently so," I said, carrying my little Byrd into the safe haven of the cottage. She'd built it for me, but now *she* was the one who needed it.

And then I stopped short.

She found him. Byrd must have found Jamie's body, because if she hadn't, Lottie wouldn't have let her cross back over. Blue or not.

She'd come face-to-face with her biggest sorrow. I wanted to scream for a thousand years.

◊

Minerva, Carter, Ben, and Jackson came back like ants to a picnic to check on her not half an hour later. Min even brought a carafe of *coffee*.

"Don't be angry with me, Bronwyn," Ben pleaded, after we tucked Byrd into my bed.

"I don't understand you. I don't understand a lot of things," I said, looking down at my hands. Hands that had taken millions of photos, hands that had saved Byrd.

And then I walked away. I needed to clear my mind and find the truth. Until Byrd could talk, she wasn't out of the woods. And I wouldn't have her death on my conscience along with everything else I'd done. So I went to find Stick.

"Let me come with you!" yelled Ben.

But I kept on walking. I didn't even turn around. I was being rude, I know. But it's part of who I am. Rude, entitled, vain, loyal, and passionate. How on earth had I forgotten who I was?

Didn't matter. I had *things* to do.

◊

I walked down Main Street with a purpose. So much had happened in the last twenty-four hours, I couldn't quite grasp it. I stopped, every so often, to lean on the trees that lined the street.

"I still see them, Mama. I still see the why's in the trees. But now I understand. I'd just like things to be quiet. Just for a moment. So I can catch my breath. Is that how you felt?"

The wind kicked up. A *not at all* usual thing to happen on a humid July day. It swirled around me, and I heard Naomi's voice. *Yes.*

I took off running down the street and didn't stop until I was in front of the sheriff's office. My reflection in the glass was distorted and sweaty. A Bronwyn I didn't recognize. Hair sticking out, curls flying everywhere. Thinner. The realest version of myself I'd ever seen. BitsyWyn all grown up. That's who she was.

Walking into Stick's air-conditioned office was like getting ice water thrown on my face.

"Wyn! What's goin' on? You're all flustered!"

"Why, thank you, Sheriff!" I said, as Southern as I remembered passive-aggression to be. "Now, if we are done with commenting on my physical appearance, may I ask you a very important question?"

"Sure thing. Anything. You know that."

"Is there *anything* you know about this whole case that you are not being completely honest about?"

"What do you mean? There's a whole lot of questions, that's for sure."

"How do you know Grant didn't do it?" I asked. "Besides the fact that you all used to be friends. How are you so sure? You better tell me or I swear, now that I'm back in my daddy's good graces, I'll have you fired so fast you won't know what happened to you."

He paused, but not for long.

"Well, we were together." Stick was looking down, unable to look me in the eyes. And he was scratching at his damn side. "So, I'd say I have a pretty good reason."

"Why didn't you tell me? Do you have any idea . . ." I panicked for a bit, thinking about what holes his confession could poke in my theories.

"Look, I didn't want you to know I wasn't here. I mean, the biggest crime in our town's history happens, and I take the night to go to NOLA and party with Grant? I was embarrassed, Wyn. Plain and simple."

"Okay, I get that. Everyone deserves to let off steam," I said, even though I wanted to slap him. I wanted to slap everyone. "But you didn't investigate Grant because you were embarrassed?"

"Oh, come on, Wyn! He didn't do it. You know it, I know it. He couldn't have done it. It's like believing Paddy did it. It ain't right."

"So if Paddy didn't do it, and Grant couldn't have done it . . . why is my brother in jail instead of Grant?! Seein' as how they're both innocent!"

I paced. If that wasn't the biggest fuckall of all time.

"Look, if you really want to figure this out, start with Byrd, Wyn. She knows the truth. She has to. She knows everything."

"First of all," I said, pounding on his desk, "Byrd is not the caretaker of this town and she does *not* know everything. You people. Really. And second? Right now, Byrd is at my cottage in my bed unable to talk. She's been over to Belladonna."

"Damn," he said, resting his elbows on the counter between us and rubbing his temples. "Okay. Byrd might not be able to talk, but think like a detective . . . her things, the stuff she surrounds herself with. Start there. As the Old-timers say, 'Thems that's closest to us ain't nothin' but moonshine and shadow.'"

"First things first, Stick. Now that you've come clean about Grant, I want to know more about Carter. After that, I want to find the damn murder weapon. As a matter of fact, let's reverse that. I'll go back and look through Lottie's house, while you find whatever information you gathered about Carter during the investigation."

"Well, Wyn, see . . ."

"Of course. You didn't do any of that, did you?"

"Paddy confessed, Wyn. What part of that don't you understand?"

"What part of *you didn't believe he did it,* don't *you* understand? I mean, hell, Stick, weren't you even curious?"

He just looked at me, not able to say anything else.

"Oh, forget it. I'm goin'."

"Do you need the keys?"

"No, Stick. I never even gave them back to you."

I could feel Grant there even before I saw the yellow lines of caution tape in the yard were taken down.

I heard him breathe in and out, in my mind, before I noticed the cut lawn or heard the sound of the wet saw coming from the porch.

And if I'd been smart, the smart Yankee I'd learned to be

during all my years away, I'd have simply turned around. Because I didn't need to see him again. At least I thought I didn't. *Our minds and our hearts do battle inside of us every day.*

I stood at the end of the flagstone path that led to the front porch and waited for him to notice me.

He was standing there, leaning over the saw and cutting what looked like tile. He wore no protective goggles, and he had a cigarette hanging out of one side of his mouth. He was always able to do that—smoke without having to pull the cigarette out between inhales and exhales.

Some thought it odd. I found it sexy. The ultimate in multitasking. He finished cutting the piece of tile and stood up straight as he saw me. He took the cigarette out of his mouth and put it out in an ashtray, precariously perched on the railing.

It took him a second to say "Hey," but just like always, I waited. It's always best to give a Southern man a second to get his bearings. Things work slower here, conversation happens in a much more practical way than up north. I was starting to realize that all that "fast conversatin'," as Byrd called it, was simply a wash of words. Because how do you find the things that really mean something in a fountain of words?

"Hey," he said. But he didn't come down off the porch. I could tell he wanted to. I could almost feel the strain of his body working to keep still.

"How come you're here?" I asked.

"I don't know. Maybe your visit made me realize a few things."

He sat down on the porch steps, and I walked slowly up the path, trying hard not to step on the grass that grew in between, like we used to do as kids

"Where's the Angel of Death?" I asked.

He'd taken a sip of his sweet tea and spit some out with a fast laugh.

"Yeah, I guess you'd think like that about her. And you ain't half wrong neither. I had to get outta there, Wyn. Hadda get home and start facing . . . hell, I don't know." He took a pack of cigarettes out of the pocket of his T-shirt and shook one out.

"Want one?" he asked

"Sure," I said.

I took one, and he searched for a light, bumping into me as he did, making us both laugh. For a second I felt free, like nothing bad had happened and we were there under normal circumstances.

"A lighter would help. I'll get one," he said. "Want some tea? I'm goin' inside anyway. And I fixed the porch swing and fan if you wanna sit down up there and have a talk."

"That'd be great. You sure were busy this morning," I said as he walked inside. My voice held an awkward flirtation that made part of me cringe.

Hadn't I come here for facts? Hadn't I come here to find proof that put more blame on him than Paddy? Didn't it seem strange, maybe a little more than strange, that directly after he knew that I was thinking of him as a suspect he comes back and cleans up the place? Alibi or not, Stick could have been wrong about the time of death.

He'd been wrong about everything else.

But I didn't care. All I wanted to do was sit on their porch and smoke a cigarette, drinking some sweet tea, just like when we were kids, hoping he'd sit real close when he came back outside.

My ring felt even heavier on my finger. Oh, Ben. What was I doing to you?

When Grant came back out, he balanced a clean ashtray, a lighter, and two glasses of iced tea as he pushed the screen door open and let it slam.

The way that door slammed.

It used to slam twice . . . once with Charlotte and me running out. And once with Grant and Paddy following along after us. All of us free. All of us sent out to play.

Free. Free to do and be and play, free from the future. The horrible future that I think, now, we all felt pressing on us.

Out of breath and halfway to the beach, we'd stop.

"Wanna play hide-'n'-seek?" said Paddy, always. It was his favorite game.

"Nah," said Grant one day. We were thirteen at the time, Grant and me. Charlotte and Paddy were twelve.

"Aw, you just wanna go work on your boat engine," said Charlotte, who usually lost all interest in playing if Grant wasn't around.

"I say we play hide-'n'-seek backwards," he said.

"How do you mean?" asked Patrick, his amazing, open face completely ready to be duped.

"Me'n Wyn are gonna team up, see, and you and Lottie you go on and hide. But you have to stay there until we find you. No runnin' for base if you can't see us, okay?"

"So we stay together?" asked Patrick, already liking the idea, because he already liked Charlotte.

"Yeah, you got the picture, now . . . go!" he said, sending them both off running before he even had a chance to count.

"Come on over here with me, " he said, taking my hand.

"They ran off that way," I said, pointing in the other direction.

"You really think I wanna play that fool game? I want some time alone with you, Wyn."

My heart beat so fast I thought it would explode. That I'd die right there.

He led me to a bench by the beach. We sat there, staring at it, but he didn't let go of my hand.

Is there anything else in the world that compares to the first time a boy you like holds your hand?

"You gonna kiss me, Grant?" I asked.

That's when he laughed, his great big old laugh that sounded like he was much older than thirteen. Sounded like it should belong to a man that lived a long and wise life.

"Ain't you direct?" he said.

"Well, I simply wanted to know because, well, if a girl is going to have her first kiss she should be prepared."

He leaned in and tilted my face with his finger on my chin, and that kiss—the kiss all first kisses are made of: cotton and hot summer days—left me thick with new sensations. Waking up parts of me that I didn't know I had.

A girl's first kiss. In one kiss, climbing a tree will never be the same. Music will never sound the same. One kiss. That first kiss changes everything for everyone. But I couldn't help but feel, that day, with the breeze off the Gulf and Grant's strong mouth pressed against mine, that I was special. That no one had ever had a first kiss quite like that.

"Well," he said, pulling away from me. "How'd I do?"

"Fair," I said, and then pinched him on his upper arm and ran away. Ran all the way home. Not because I was scared but because I wanted to be alone and remember that kiss. Make it last in my mind.

So I ran, leaving Grant to find Paddy and Charlotte. And when I got home, I went in through the kitchen and straight up the stairs, determined to lie on my great big bed under the ceiling fan and stare into my memories for a while.

But Naomi was standing at the top of the stairs. I was so surprised to see her up and about that I almost fell backwards.

Instead, I tried to get past her without touching her, I didn't want to be touched by her. I didn't even want to make eye contact with her. But she held her two stick-thin arms out, blocking me.

"Where have you been?" she asked me.

I decided to push past her anyway. And as I did, she fell limp against the hallway wall.

"I am talking to you," she said.

I turned around. That rage I had as a child held no bounds.

"Now? You want to talk to me now? I haven't even *seen* you in a week!"

"It's not my fault, Wyn," she said. But she used that voice, that soft, weak voice that made me cringe. The one that she used when she needed attention.

"It's not *your* fault! What are you even talking about? Who smokes that poison into their lungs, Mama?"

"Where were you?" she repeated.

"I was out playin' with Paddy and Lottie and Grant, okay? May I go now?"

"Why don't you kids hang around here anymore? I miss you all so much."

She walked toward me and put her arms around me and smelled my hair. I used to love that when I was little.

"Because you told us we couldn't! Now stop touching me, Mama," I said, pulling away.

"You've been kissed," she said.

I turned around and headed to my room, fast.

"You are too young to be kissing!" she screamed after me. And she continued screaming and screaming incoherently. My door was shut, my eyes were shut, my ears were shut, and I could still hear her. And then Minerva must have come, or Daddy, because the world went quiet again.

And then, as if nothing happened, I stared at my ceiling as I'd first planned and remembered the feeling of Grant's lips on mine.

The screen door slammed and I was all grown up again with more on my mind than kissing. Because it slammed only once. Lottie and Patrick weren't around to make it slam again.

"What are you thinkin' on?" asked Grant, jolting me back to the present.

He didn't sit next to me, just leaned against the railing and handed me a glass of tea and a lighter for the cigarette I was still holding.

"So I see you're fixing up the place." I ignored the question, placing the glass of tea on the ground and lighting my cigarette.

"Yeah, I figured it was about time I came on back. You know. Face stuff."

"So you said. What are you facing, Grant?"

"Demons, I guess. Mistakes. Seems to me, you're doin' the same thing."

I laughed, because he was right. And because he always made me laugh.

"I suppose so," I said. "Only I'm not cleaning up a crime scene."

"Stick told me I could. Told me it wasn't considered an active crime scene anymore."

I just looked at him, standing there all solid and handsome. I noticed the bloodshot eyes were gone. I noticed that he seemed less rough than he had in New Orleans. He cleaned up quick.

"Well, I was just coming on by to check it out for myself. I know there's a murder weapon around here somewhere."

"What you want it for, Nancy Drew?"

"Because it might have prints on it. I have to figure this thing out, Grant. There's not much time left."

"Maybe whoever did it wiped it clean."

"Maybe they did," I said, eyeing him.

"You really think I did it?" he asked.

"I don't care." I lied. "But I do know Paddy didn't do it. I know it like I know the back of my own hands. Anyway, Stick just gave you an alibi."

He put out his cigarette and went back to the wet saw.

"Look, I'm tryin' real hard to get myself back on track. I quit drinkin' and got a job over at Sam's. Barback, but it's a start. I don't need this shit from you. And you know what else?"

"What?' I asked, getting up and snubbing out my own half-finished cigarette.

"You never could see past your own self. You're so sure Paddy's innocent. But you don't even know him anymore. You may think you know him like the back of your hand, but my mama always had a saying that I think is more appropriate for you right now."

"Oh, yeah? What was that?"

"Can't see the forest for the trees. You're blind to what's closest to you, Wyn. Just like all you Whalens. Just like all of us, I guess."

I felt the anger in my throat tighten into a knot. I walked

over to him and poured my sweet tea over his head. Then I punched him hard. In the arm.

"Fuck you," I said icily, walking down the porch steps. I took one at a time. Waiting for some retaliation.

There wasn't any.

"Don't bother calling me, you son of a bitch," I yelled from the main road. The saw started up again, only I heard him yell after me anyway.

"I never said shit about calling you."

Damn. He hadn't. Had he?

26

❧

Byrd

One sees clearly only with the heart.
Anything essential is invisible to the eyes.

—*The Little Prince*

My prince had created a castle out of all the things that had gone
missing since he killed his mother.

These were Jamie's prizes: corrugated rooftop shingles, trash
cans, plyboard, even half of a garage door.

He had built me a junk castle and a junk garden, but it was
beautiful. Half in a tree, rambling down to a ground floor. He
was a regular Robinson Crusoe.

"Come live with me and be my love," he said. "Or princess
of the alligators, you like that title, right?"

How could I still love him? It don't matter, I just did. *Don't
trouble yourself anymore about it, just keep on listenin' to the story like
you been doin'.* But my infernal mouth took over.

"I don't want to stay here, Jamie. I want to go back home and
put everything back to the way it was before."

"We can't do that, Byrd. If'n I go back, they'd put me away.
Somewhere for crazy people. Like in that movie *One Flew Over*

the Cuckoo's Nest, a place like that, only for kids. They might not even let me out when I git grown. They could just keep me."

I stood still, crossing my arms. But I have to admit, the castle was really interestin' and I wanted to explore it some. But I knew I had to stand my ground.

"I wouldn't let them do that. I'd be on your side the whole way."

"Don't you care that I killed her, Byrdie? Ain't you scared of me now?"

"No, I ain't!"

I meant it. But that didn't matter. I needed to get back so I could tell someone what he did so I could get my daddy outta jail.

"There has got to be some way that we can *all* get what we want," I said.

"I want you to stay here with me. It's nice here. Quiet. We could live here together like in *The Blue Lagoon.*"

"You know what I think? I think you an' me spent too many Sunday afternoons watching junkola movies in your room, that's what I think."

"Please, Byrdie. I'm so lonely. And sometimes I feel him rising in me, and I don't like it."

"Feel who?"

"Farley! I'm possessed by him, don't you know? How else could I have killed all those little animals? How else could I have killed my own mama?"

He was getting upset.

"I was there when you killed those animals, you did it because you were savin' them. 'Cause they were all sick and weak and dyin'. It was a good thing, not a bad thing."

"It wasn't always the case, Byrd."

"What?"

"Sometimes, when you weren't with me. I'd take one that was just . . . fine. And kill it. I don't know why. It's Farley. I know it. I'm full of him up to my eyes."

Jamie. My Jamie. He could kill his mama . . . and I'd understand. Sort of. He could put my daddy in jeopardy, and still, I was willin' to forgive him. But animals? Ones that weren't even hurtin'?

My blood turned to ice, I swear it.

"Farley's not real. Jamie. He's made up. I know it and you know it. And if it *was* real, I'd be the one to bear it, not you. It would travel in the blood."

He knew I was right.

"Don't say that! I *have* to be him!"

"Why?"

"Because if I ain't, then it's been me this whole time bein' evil. And I don't want that to be true. I want to be the me *you* see, Byrd."

"Then you are," I said. But I was thinkin' something different. Evil comes in all shapes and sizes. Like princesses and princes. Also I was thinkin' that love sure as hell *is* blind.

"I'm hungry, Jamie," I said, a plan of sorts taking shape. "If you want me to stay here, I better get us somethin' to eat. I don't fancy squirrel."

"What if you get lost?" he asked.

"I will always find you," I said. And I looked him straight in the eyes so he knew I was talkin' true. It's something we do, me and him.

"You won't run away, will ya, Byrdie?" He was peelin' a stick and poking it into the sand. Jabbin' it hard.

"No, I would never do that, Jamie."

That's when I did a thing I thought I would never do.

I was walking in the woods of Belladonna and suddenly, there she was. Lottie. And she was showing me what I had to do. Even though I was already on my way to doin' it.

But the thing I did? It broke my heart.

But you know what broke my heart more?

The thing I hadn't thought of while he was busy confessing, cryin,' and showin' me our new home. Sure, I get why he didn't come back to save my daddy. But he must have known I blamed myself. He must have. And he knew how much I missed him, too.

And still, on all his trips stealin' this or stealin' that, he never once came and told me he was okay. He let my heart ache.

I couldn't forgive him for that. Besides, I wasn't gonna be no princess of alligators. He didn't know me at all. I'd be the queen. Love lies.

So I did what I had to do. Aided by his dead mama. Belladonna Bay, it turns out, is a fair and true name for that island.

It was pure luck that the berries were ripe. When it was done, I held my breath and dove back into the mist. Only I couldn't quite get my breath back when I was on the other side. Sorrow has a soft edge around it, like feathers in one of Naomi's fluffy pillows. A soft edge that can suffocate you when you ain't lookin'.

27

Wyn

Walking back to the Big House, I'll admit I was at a loss. There were no files on Carter. Grant was home, blocking me from searching his house for the knife. And though I tried to conjure them, there were no apparitions in magical gardens leaving me clues. Byrd had been right, sometimes these ways can be downright frustratin'.

"*Start with Byrd,*" Stick had said. And seeing how I was out of time and ideas, I listened.

I went straight up to Byrd's attic.

I'd like to say I was respectful, but I wasn't. I tore the room apart. Clothes and papers went flying. I worked up a sweat looking for something I couldn't even imagine. But then I spied a Polaroid of her and Jamie at what could have been last year's Fourth of July parade. I grabbed it, thinking I could use it to coax her to speak again. I knew it would be hard for her, but Jamie was the key. I had to get her talking again. I needed her help. I ran down the stairs like a teenager and stopped on the landing where my mother and father had framed pictures I'd taken when I was younger.

My camera.

I'd seen this boy before.

I remembered going through my camera to look at the pictures Byrd had taken while I was off on my trip to Angola and the Big Easy.

There had been a little boy who looked just like this, peering out through a drugstore window. . . . Couldn't be . . .

He wasn't dead at all. There'd be no body to find. Byrd had found Jamie. Alive.

I ran so fast I was out of breath by the time I got to the cottage. I ran in, past Minerva, Ben, Carter, and Jackson, all sitting on the porch, and threw myself on the bed next to Byrd, bouncing us both a few inches into the air.

"Damn, girl, you best wake up because I need your help."

Nothing.

I picked her up and brought her out to the living room and sat her on my lap.

It had to be Jamie. It was the only logical answer. An awful, logical answer. I pulled my camera from the side table and scrolled through all the pictures. And there he was, only it wasn't just in the pictures that Byrd took.

There was Jamie behind the trees in the pictures I took driving up to the Big House. And there he was, watching the parade from a second-story window above the drugstore.

And there he was in so many of the pictures she'd taken that day. Standing just inside the mist of Belladonna Bay. He'd been there; he'd been watching us.

"Byrd . . . I want you to look at these pictures. Do you see anything here?"

That's when she got off my lap, stood up with her hand over her ears, and started screaming.

Jackson, Minerva, and Carter came rushing in. Not Ben. He stayed just outside the threshold with Dolores.

"All of you get the hell out of here! Now!" I said.

I have to give them credit. They did. They left.

When she finally ran out of noise, she whispered, "He was there. I found him."

I hugged her tight and gave her a million kisses. "Byrd! Listen to that voice! I'm so relieved. Did he hurt you?"

"No. But I'll tell you one thing," she said.

"What's that, honey?"

"Jamie certainly ain't no Jesus. I was wrong about that."

"Did he kill his mama?" I asked softly, so softly I could barely hear myself.

She nodded, the tears streaming down her small face.

"Anything else happen over there?" I asked. But those tears only came down faster.

I held my Byrd for a long time. Because whatever had gone on over there had broken her. Then I set her back on my bed and made some tea with honey for her cracked voice. As I waited for the kettle to boil, I thought out loud.

"It was all so simple. It was Jamie. The body they never found. Why didn't anyone suspect him?" Too close, I supposed. The forest for the trees, like Grant said. I made the tea and brought it back to her.

She was still crying.

"Okay, magic girl or not, you need to sleep. But, baby, now

that we know you saw Jamie and that he told you he . . . you know, we need to call Stick . . . he's not much, but he can probably solve a case that's already been solved. I should tell Grant we found him, Byrd. And we need to tell Jackson, so he can call the lawyers. You'll be asked a lot of questions."

"Can we wait until tomorrow?" she asked. "There's gonna be a lot of sad mixed up in this. I'm too tired to feel anymore today."

"Sure we can," I said, not sure we could but not willing to upset her anymore. I sang her to sleep. "You fill up my senses . . ." Then I made a cup of tea for myself and went back out onto my porch to look over at Belladonna Bay. What was that boy doing over there? He could run away and we'd never be able to prove what he did. Was I crazy to listen to her? Every bone in my body screamed *no*. There was something happening that needed to happen.

I did it, Lottie. I found out for you . . . though I don't know if that information is the stuff to help you cross over . . . but for better or worse, your son killed you. I don't know why or how . . . yet. But I kept my promise. And I love you.

The lights in the sky were brighter that night.

When I finally went to sleep, curled up next to Byrd, I had my final dream about Charlotte Masters.

We were little again. Sitting on her front porch. Byrd's age. And Grant was inside playing his music way too loud.

"He's dreamy," I said.

"He's my brother, don't be weird," she said.

"I think you think he's dreamy, too."

She was quiet.

"He's my fate. Good or bad. It's in my bones."

"I don't know what the hell you're talkin' about, Lottie," I said.

And then everything shifted and we were back on that lonesome beach. There was a bonfire, and Jamie and Byrd were no longer there.

"Let me tell you about Jamie."

The fire crackled as I listened.

"Jamie, my love . . . a strange boy. The good almost won out in him."

"How can you say that?" I asked her. "He killed you."

"He would have done worse . . . thank you, Wyn. Thank you for coming back. I think I can leave now." She walked away, but just before she left I saw her look to the side, smile a big "good news" Lottie smile, and then run toward whatever she'd seen. Fast. Then she was gone, and I was alone.

He would have done worse. Those words echoed in my head as I woke and night faded into day.

28

Wyn and Her Mama

It's funny the way things that are all tied up can get all undone in one moment. I remember once when I was little, Jackson was tryin' to prove a point to Minerva that he actually knew how to use the vacuum cleaner. The cord was in this incredible knot. It seemed impossible to get undone. Both of them were yelling at each other and taking turns trying to get the cord straight.

"What in God's name did you do to it, Jackson?"

"Really? You think I did something to it? What about you? You're the only one who uses it. Those other cleaning folk bring their own. So you musta just cursed it. Woman, I swear! Fix this thing!"

"You think I'd waste a good curse on a goodfornothing-sonofabitch?"

And so it went.

But then, just like now, Jackson shook the knot out of frustration and the thing just . . . unraveled. Easy as pie. Almost like it was telling us we should have all left it alone in the first place and it would've worked itself out.

◊

That next morning I called Stick and told him I'd meet him at the Big House because I had news.

Byrd and I shared a quiet breakfast of biscuits and mayhaw jelly that Minerva'd left on the front porch. Dolores was with us, finally not afraid to come inside. She was at my feet, her head resting against my ankles.

I looked at Byrd from across the small kitchen island. She was quiet. A little solemn.

"I'm sorry for whatever happened over there with Jamie, honey. But you're strong. You'll be able to work this whole thing into the quilt of your life. It might be a dark square, but it only adds to the amazing woman you'll grow up to be. Big boobies, too. I can see it now."

She put down her biscuit and came around the corner to put her arms around my waist and bury her head into me. "Thank you," she said.

That child. Dear God. I'd known it for days, but I felt it strongest right then. You'd lie for her. Steal for her. Kill for her. You'd die for her. All the love she evoked in everyone around her mucked everything up. Like developing film in a lit room. Overexposed. You can't see a thing.

"You know somethin'?" I asked.

"What?" she said, still holding me tight, her eyes closed.

"I was thinking that maybe you and me could both add things to Naomi's book. Would that be all right with you? How about we work on something together, like . . . say . . . something to convince Esther to bloom again?"

"I love you" was all she said.

I felt a pain, deep in my heart that was like joy, only bigger. *This is how it feels to be a mama,* I thought. It hurts; it's full of worry. No wonder . . .

That's when I heard my own sorrow.

Mama? I want you. I need you. Where are you? I forgive you. Will you forgive me?

After breakfast I gathered everyone, including Stick, at the Big House on the wide side porch, the one facing Belladonna Bay. Byrd and I stood in front of them and we told them what happened. How Byrd had seen Jamie. How he'd confessed to Byrd, and we had all the photos, too.

"So you're sayin' Jamie did it?" asked Stick. "But there was so much of his blood . . ."

"He tried to cut himself across his throat. Only it didn't work. It healed up somehow. He even showed me the scar," said Byrd.

Carter cleared his throat, coughing a little.

"Well, we'll have to get a search party . . . bring him in. You know. All that."

"You won't find him," said Byrd.

"How can you be sure of that, sweetheart?" I asked her.

She shrugged her shoulders and looked out over the creek. She still wasn't back to normal, and that scream of hers was still ringing in my ears.

"None of this will hold up in court, you know," said Stick.

"What would you need?" asked Carter.

He was just standing there, leaning on a banister, his arms folded in front of his chest, wearing a strange look on his face. Guilt. Relief. Love. All mixed together.

Stick was just about to answer when Byrd's voice rang out loud and clear. A little thin, too. Like she was worried, or curious, even.

"Ben?" asked Byrd.

"Yeah, honey?"

"Look over there, you see it? The light turned rosy pink, and it's the daytime, too. Is that what you were looking for?"

Ben nodded at her, turned to me, and placed a hand on each of my shoulders.

"It's time. Go there, Bronwyn. You've got to go see her, or else you won't ever be truly home. I've been waiting for the sign, and now it's here."

"See who?" I asked

"Obtuse," said Byrd, shaking her head at me. "Go see your mama. She's waitin' on you."

Mermaids don't drown, mermaids don't drown, mermaids don't drown, I said as I walked into the mist.

It didn't feel thick like it did when I saw Charlotte. It felt like regular old mist, leaving tiny droplets of water on my arms and face. It was like walking through a cloud. Tight on the skin. Almost like salt water when it dries. Sticky but natural.

I hadn't seen the other side of the mist on my last visit, and I thought it would end in a lingering sort of way. But it didn't. As soon as I crossed the creek, it was just—gone. And the sun was shining on the island of Belladonna Bay. The island I'd grown up next to but never seen. The island that haunted my childhood dreams. It was lovely. There was a wide riverbed, with grasses and submerged tree limbs. And smaller shrubs, all flowering out of season with bright red azaleas and deep purple beautyberries.

A small inlet of water, surrounded by waist-high wild belladonna, was off to the side.

A wonderland.

I had an urge to explore. To try and find our elusive Jamie, to climb a tall tree or two. To linger for a little, living and breathing in this place trapped in time.

I didn't get the chance. Because the ghost of my mama, Naomi Green Whalen, appeared not ten feet away from me. God, she made a beautiful phantom. It made a perfect kind of sense.

"Mama?" I called to her.

"I'm lost, I think." She began to make her way toward me, gliding across the tall grass.

"I'm looking for something, someone," she said, coming to a stop in front of me, and looking from side to side. The smell of roses clung to the air around her.

"Who, Mama? Who are you looking for?" I reached out to touch her face. It didn't feel like skin. It was the warmth the skin leaves behind.

She leaned into my hand and reached out her own. I felt the shimmer around her begin to enfold me.

It was as if she finally saw me.

"Bronwyn, look at you, my gorgeous girl."

"Mama, please . . . I'm so sorry," I said, the tears streaming freely.

"Don't cry, Wyn. Don't cry, my love."

"Mama. I'm sorry I said those awful things to you. I remember it now. I never wanted you to die."

"I know, I know . . . it wasn't you or your brother. Or Jackson. God, how I loved all of you. It was me. I pushed you away. Do you understand? I'm the one to blame. The best mothers let their love echo all around their children. They pour it down, with no expectation of return. They're so brave, those mothers. I couldn't do that. So everything that burdens you, belongs to me. You have nothing to be sorry for."

"I love you" was all I could say.

"I know," she said, then looked around again.

"Who are you looking for, Mama?"

"You, I think, only *not* you . . . you and your brother." She looked around, past me and through me.

"I'm right here, Mama."

"No, not *now*. Then. When things were better, you know? I need to find my way back. I think I'm supposed to be doing something. I can't go. Not until I know." Naomi ran her hands through her glimmering hair. Sparkles shimmered down around her.

"What do you need to know, Mama?"

"I need to know that you knew. I need to know . . . until, you do, I can't . . ."

I'll admit that right then and there I was at a loss.

Consider it for a moment. You've crossed into the badlands of your childhood, and you are standing in front of the ghost of your mother, and she doesn't seem to be making sense.

And just before I was about to run from the pain that her sweet wide-open face.—*thirty-eight freckles, no, thirty-two*—was inflicting on my soul, I saw them. Two little towheaded children that looked like the most beautiful china dolls you'd ever seen. Whalen dolls. *I'll be damned, it's me and Paddy. How?*

"Are you looking for them, Mama?" I asked, pointing to where they'd emerged.

Naomi turned, leaving a trail of energy in the air behind her.

Then she turned back to me. The worry and confusion was gone. She wore that real smile, the one from her portrait.

"Those are my babies," she said.

"How can that be?" I asked, sinking to my knees as the air left my body. There was no room for anything but ache.

"Time, you know. The past, present, and future, it all runs side by side. See, those are my babies. *Those* are my *babies,* they need me."

"They do," I whispered. My throat was tightening and felt hot. Soon no words would come. I understood why Byrd had come back mute.

The children, holding hands, stepped tentatively out from the shadows of the dripping Spanish moss and on to the riverbank.

"Mama?" they asked in unison.

Naomi turned away from me, holding out her arms. And those children—her babies, me and Paddy from another time and place—came running, open-armed and openhearted in the way only children can run.

They closed their eyes, more than content in her embrace. Not a trace of disappointment.

A million moments came back to me.

Paddy on his way to a birthday party with Minerva and not his own mama: "But why can't you be like other mothers?"

Me shouting from my bedroom about books she said she'd read only didn't have the energy once bedtime came around: "I hate you! I hate when you promise to do something and don't do it!"

But she was right. These children she held, they were still little. Too little to care about what she could and couldn't do. All they wanted was her love.

Naomi loved us.

The three of them were so peaceful. Breathing together, fluttering hands and eyelashes. I wished I could hold on to her, too, but you don't get do-overs after death. You only get to remember things differently. And that's what she'd needed. For me to see how much she loved me. For me to quit questioning that. All I could hear were the three of them murmuring to one another: *Where were you? Right here! I looked and I looked, you are good hiders! We love you, Mama. You are the best, prettiest mama. I love you the universe. I love you bigger than that. I'm so lucky to be your mama. Shh. Thirty-eight freckles, thirty-two . . .*

Completely enfolded now, it was getting harder to tell where she left off and the children began.

I thought she'd kiss them and then blow into her hands to make the rose glow she's always dreamed of . . . but that isn't what happened.

Instead, she burst into starlight.

Thousands of pieces of Naomi taking flight.

My mother was free. She'd been the light in the sky.

Thank you, darling was a whisper in the air as I stumbled, aching, back across the bay.

29

Wyn
(Carter Tells a Tale)

After I got back, Jackson picked me up like a baby and put me in a wide chair on the porch. Everything went fuzzy for a while.

I heard muffled voices and felt Byrd's soft kisses. "Time to wake up," she whispered. And I did. Just in time to see Jackson coming out onto the porch with Carter and Min and a whole bunch of food.

"We made your favorite, Wyn. Shrimp and grits. Byrd stirred the grits for the whole time they cooked," said Minerva.

"You gotta keep on 'em and give them love, else they won't love you back in your mouth," said Byrd.

The shrimp were pink and coated in golden butter. Ben handed me a bowl, He was quiet, but I wasn't mad at him anymore. Just glad he was there. He'd given me a gift. I knew that now. He did, too.

"All right," I said. "What the hell happened when I was gone? Everyone's so calm and peaceful. We have an innocent man in prison. Did we forget?"

That's when it all came unraveling like the vacuum cleaner cord.

"Well," said Jackson, "a funny thing happened when we were making this here meal. And you were making peace with your mama." His eyes flashed for a second, as if he wanted to say, *Did she ask for me?* He cleared his throat and went on, "Seems Carter's been holding out on us."

"It's a confession of sorts," said Carter.

"Tell me, Carter. Tell me how you can help fix all this," I said.

Stick put his bowl on the railing and stood up slow, smoothing out his sheriff uniform pants.

"Well, Carter, it seems Wyn is about to make you do this all over again, so why don't we go down to the station and make it official. If you're ready, that is," said Stick.

Carter nodded. Hands in his pockets now. He'd come clean, this strange, quiet, loyal gentleman. Finally.

"I'm coming," I said.

"I didn't think I would be able to stop you. But only you, okay? The rest of you," he said—waving his finger around at Ben, Jackson, Minerva, looking sadder than I'd ever seen her, and Byrd—"you crazy lot better steer clear until I get this sorted out."

"Well, I'm taking Min to Sam's," said Jackson. "We need to be at a bar after all this, I think. Ben, you want to come?"

"Sure, that'd be great," he said.

"Byrd, you can come with me if you want. I don't care what this fool says. I don't want to leave you alone," I said.

She shook her head, but she never turned around. She stood there, looking over at that damned island and pushing her grits back and forth in her bowl.

"Leave her," said Minerva. "She'll be fine. She needs—"

"You people, I swear!" I shouted. "She needs, she needs . . . dear God. What about what's right and what's wrong? It's damn wrong to leave her here alone with that boy out there."

"Fine, stay here then," said Minerva, who knew I wasn't going to let Stick interview Carter without me present.

"Nope. I'm going," I said. We'd never be the family that lived by right and wrong. Our moral compass was shot to shit. But at least I knew, finally, that there was love.

I held my arms out to my niece, who came without hesitation.

"Byrd, listen to me, if you're scared or you feel alone, you come right on down to Stick's office, you hear? And don't even think about crossing that creek. I mean it, you haven't seen me mad yet."

"It's okay, Aunt Wyn. I kinda want a little solitude anyhow. And if you think I'm gonna venture on over there, you're being all *obtuse* again."

That girl. I swear.

The whole story unwound exactly where it should have the night it all happened—in the sheriff's office.

"Sit down, Carter. Try and make yourself comfortable. You want anything, a coffee or something?" asked Stick.

"No, sir. I'm fine. I just wanna get this whole thing over with."

"I'm gonna record you, so Wyn here needs to be quiet, and you need to refrain from speaking to her as well." He turned to me. "Not a word, you hear? This recording has to hold up with the district judges. Not even a deep breath, okay?"

I nodded my head and pulled my fingers across my lips.

He cleared his throat and pushed Record: "Interview with Carter Simpson: Magnolia Creek. Sheriff Bill Croft.

"Carter, would you like me to ask you questions? Or would you prefer to simply tell the story of the night Charlotte Masters was killed?"

"Well, Sti—I mean, Sheriff, I suppose I'd like to tell my story. How about you just interrupt me when there's somethin' that needs clarification?"

"Sounds good, Carter. Start whenever you're ready."

"Well, I suppose we need to start at the beginning. Paddy 'n' Charlotte. What a pair. Both of them getting more and more tired of life as it wore on, you know? And each tryin' their absolute best to raise their children up right. And Byrd and Jamie? They weren't a pair who took kindly to bein' raised. So it was only a matter of time before Charlotte and Paddy just sort of fell in with one another. Only, they didn't get no comfort. They got more, I don't know, full of sorrow. That's what it was. And they drank too much together. Other drugs, too.

"I tried to warn Paddy. Tried to warn him many times that Charlotte and him were a toxic sort of combination. And Jamie? He hated Paddy trying to get 'fatherly' with him. I suppose I had a little to do with that, too. I urged him to try. I mean, everyone needs a father, don't they? But the more Paddy tried with Jamie, the more Jamie pulled away from him and Charlotte, too.

"Anyway, they'd had a big fight. And that weren't no surprise. Toward the end they were always fighting, those two. Fighting about how they felt toward one another. Fighting about the kids. Fighting about what color the sky was by the end of it.

"And the night Charlotte was killed, Paddy was on his way over there with fire in his eyes. I stopped him in the hall. Had a talk with him. Convinced him to come with me to Sam's before he went over there. Figured I could stop somethin' bad before it happened. But I was wrong about that. If I'd let Paddy go straight over, he could have stopped the whole thing.

"Those damn best-laid plans.

"So there we are, a little drunk, walkin' back up Main Street when Patrick decides he's going over to talk to Charlotte anyhow.

"'I'm goin' with you then. You're in no shape to handle yourself right,' I told him. And he didn't mind. He just wanted to see her, I think. Try to convince her to stay with him.

"When we got there, the house was dark, all except the kitchen. And the front door was wide open.

"'What do you thinks goin' on here?' I asked Paddy. 'Maybe we should call Stick first?'

"'Nah,' he said. 'Nothin's goin on. Charlotte never locks her doors. Hell, no one does round here.'

"But I could tell. I could feel something bad had happened. And all we could see once we got inside were Lottie's feet in a pool of blood. Patrick ran in there so fast he slipped in the blood and skidded into the cabinets. He was on her and cradling her in his arms before I could stop him. I knew immediately he'd be one of the suspects, so I wanted to keep him as clean as possible. But then I realized neither one of us would ever be clean again. There she was, stabbed—damn, Stick—how many times?"

"Fourteen."

"There was so much blood," continued Carter. "That's when

I really looked around. To see what could have possibly happened.

"Paddy and I saw the knife at the same time. He let out a wail that I thought would bring down the whole house. It was Byrd's knife. Her favorite one.

"'Oh, God, Carter! We gotta get rid of all this! We gotta make sure she ain't held responsible,' he cried at me, covered in blood."

Stick interrupted at this point. "Carter, why did Paddy think Byrd did it?"

"Well, see . . . there was this incident a few years back with her old dog. The sweet thing killed it because it bit him. And then there were all those dead animals we found. When he asked her about it, she just said she and Jamie did it. So, I guess he was scared she'd lost her mind with all those strange ways and simply killed Charlotte for hurting him like she'd killed the dog. Hell, Stick, I don't know. All I know is that once the thing was in motion, it rolled away from us like a rock down a slope."

"Okay, go on," said Stick.

"That's when I noticed young Jamie. He'd been pushed, it seemed, through the glass doors that went into the dining room. And there was all this glass stickin' in him where it shouldn't have been. He'd lost a lot of blood, too, and there was a small knife mark on his neck.

"'He's still alive,' I said.

"And Paddy sat there, nodding like a fool. 'Yessir, he is. Because she wouldn't have killed him, not if she came to her senses. Looks like whatever happened to him was an accident. Like he came in, and she just pushed him away before she knew what she was doin'.'

"'We got to get him to the hospital, Paddy. We got to call Stick. Now.'

"'Can't we take him somewhere and help him ourselves? He'll tell on her when he wakes up. He's just a kid. He won't know what to say to all them folks. We need to help him and figure out what to tell everyone.'"

"'How we gonna explain it when they find him?' I asked.

"'I can't think about that now. Just . . . just take him some-where. Somewhere no one can find him. Then we'll get him well and tell him what he can and cannot say. Once he's better, he won't turn on our girl. I know he won't.'

"I don't know why I listened to him, Stick, I swear. But the whole situation was crazy. We were there, mourning Lottie. That sweet lost girl. And looking at a seriously injured child. All the while thinking our Byrd was the killer and we had to protect her. That's what families do. So Paddy told me, 'So, you take him, okay? Take him. And take the knife, too. Do something with it. I'm gonna leave my hands all over this place,' while he's still holdin' on to Charlotte. Still cryin'. Moving his hands around in the puddle of blood on the floor. Broke my heart.

"I folded up Byrd's knife and put it in my pocket.

"So that's what I did. I picked up Jamie who was still breath-ing, but just barely. I had no idea how that kid would survive. But I made that choice.

"Then it hit me. The only place no one would look was over at Belladonna. So that's where I took him. There's an old shack in the center of that dammed island and I took him there, laid him down, and made a fire."

"How'd you know there was a cottage there, Carter?" asked Stick.

Carter laughed. "I'm not from here, remember? I never believed those stories. So the first thing I wanted to do after Minerva and me got back from our honeymoon was to explore that
place.

"And it ain't much of a place. But there is one small cottage
sort of a ruin. But when I saw it again that night, it was livable.
Looked to me like someone had been there a bunch. Kept it up,
you know? I didn't know then what we all know now. I didn't
know I was bringin' Jamie to the exact place he wanted to be.
His own place. Guess he'd been going there for years. If'n you
can have 'years' when you're still only about eleven. Anyway, I
got him settled on a cot and covered him up with a blanket that
was left there. Then I ran on back over the creek to get some
first aid supplies.

"But there was Byrd, in her white nightgown. Holding her
arms out to me. Her eyes so big and wide and full of fear. I
knew right then that she'd done it and that she didn't remember
doin' it. Paddy had made me so damn sure, I couldn't even think
past the idea."

"It's called loyalty, Carter. It's okay. Just keep goin'. Why were
you so sure, right then that it was her? Besides the fact that Paddy
got the idea stuck in your head?" asked Stick.

"It was the look in her eyes. I could tell she'd had one of her
'blackouts.' Those damn strange ways of hers. It's a curse. So I
picked her up and told her everything was gonna be just fine.
That Carter was gonna fix up everything just so. And I put her
back to bed."

Carter stopped there for a second and took out a handker-
chief. His eyes had welled up, and he was trying not to cry.
Strong, older Southern men crying is the most awkwardly beau-

tiful thing on this earth. I wanted to hug him just then, but he continued.

"Then I got some supplies and went out back across the creek to fix up Jamie. Only he wasn't there."

"What do you mean, he wasn't there?" asked Stick.

"Exactly what I said. And now we know the truth. But back then I was sure he'd crawled off somewhere to die. So I looked for him. I did. I swear it. But there wasn't even a trail. And I'm a half-decent hunter.

"I figured I'd go back in the morning. I made sure the fire was nice and warm in case he made his way back. It soothed me, makin' that fire. Made me feel better. Like I wasn't doin' something terrible. Even though I was.

"I walked back into the Big House and washed my hands good in the sink, and then made my way upstairs to check on Patrick. I was relieved when I heard Patrick in his room. I knocked on the door and he let me in. He'd taken a shower. He seemed way too calm and clearheaded. I'd not seen him so sharp in a long time. 'I called Stick,' he said.

"'Oh hell, Paddy, you didn't. What did he tell you? What did you say?'

"'I called him and told him he needed to get to Lottie's in the mornin' and to come here right after. He was half asleep. And he don't know the hell he's gonna face in the morning. So I'm sure I have tonight. Stick ain't never rushed anywhere in his whole life.'

"'What are you gonna do, Paddy?'

"'I'm gonna confess. What else?'

"'But you didn't do it!'

"'No, but we both know who did.' He put his hand on my

shoulder and squeezed it hard. 'Look, Carter. I'm not gonna say this twice. I'm not ever going to let one hair on her head come to harm. It aint her fault she's the way she is. It's my mama's fault. It's all our faults. And I'm gonna have to ask you to do one more thing.'

" 'What's that, Paddy?'

" 'No one will know what we saw. They can guess, but they can't ever *know*. Okay?'

" 'You could get the chair, Paddy. How'm I supposed to sit back and let you die?'

" 'Maybe I will, and maybe I won't. But it don't matter. Because she's worth it. You understand me?'

"I just shrugged. I couldn't shake the vision of Paddy in the electric chair. My boy. I'd raised him up since he was sixteen. He was combing his hair like a dandy in the mirror, all clean and neat and to one side.

" 'Did you take care of Jamie?' he asked.

" 'Yes. Only when I went back, he was gone.'

" 'Gone, like dead?'

"I thought about telling him the whole truth, but I knew he needed to be free of worry to do what he needed to do. So I just nodded.

" 'I hate to say it, Carter. But that might be the best thing. Did you take care of the knife?'

"The knife. I'd forgotten about it.

"I took it out of my pocket.

" 'Shit! Carter, we gotta hide it.'

" 'Where?'

" 'You decide. But don't tell me about it. Don't tell no one.'

" 'Okay.'

"He hugged me then. Hugged me like he hadn't since he was a boy.

"'I'm not scared, Carter. I feel better than I have in a long time. I feel, useful. And now I'm gonna crawl into bed with my little girl and hold her like I did when she was a baby. You hide that knife and get some rest. You're gonna need it to help with Byrd come tomorrow.'

"So what was done was done. And when I went to the cabin on Belladonna the next day, Jamie was *still* gone. I looked for hours. Not a sign of him. So I thought he was dead, for real . . . and eaten up by an alligator or something."

"Where did you hide the knife, Carter? That's gonna be important," asked Stick.

Carter laughed. "You wanna know? Here you are: it's in the kitchen of the Big House in the junk drawer near the back. I wiped it, though."

"Carter, you could have left it at the bottom of the creek and we'd still be able to lift prints off it. Don't worry."

Stick pressed Stop on the tape recorder.

"I'll need you to write it down, too. And then sign. That all right with you?"

"Anything we need to do to get this whole mess straightened out," said Carter.

"Come on, Wyn, let me walk you out. You better get home now, there's a storm comin'."

When we were back at the front of the office, I turned to Stick and said, "Look here, I'm going to ask you something, and you're going to comply, okay? I'm not going to throw out any threats or tell you how you fouled up this whole thing. I'm just going to ask you a favor."

"What, Wyn?"

"You go back in there and record that confession again. And you have Carter take out any mention of Paddy. You tell him to say he'd done the whole thing himself thinkin' Paddy did it. Covering for him. I know it's a lie. But it's a good one. It will save a lot of people a whole lot of pain."

"I can do that. I shouldn't. But I can."

"Good," I said. And I knew Carter would be more than willing to fix it up for Paddy. He loved him with a real sort of love. The kind that doesn't ask for anything in return. The kind of love I was just learning about.

"Can Jackson do anything with whatever charges Carter will face?" I asked.

"Sure he can. And he will. Paddy will be home in no time."

"How long is 'no time'?" I asked.

"Soon, Wyn. And man, that's gonna be something."

"Sure is," I said, and then, "Hey, Stick?"

"Yeah?"

"I consider you a friend, and I'm grateful for what you're about to do. But really? You're a shitty sheriff."

Then I left.

30

Byrd and Wyn

It was night by the time I got home.

Byrd was rocking back and forth on the front porch of the Big House. She ran at me so fast I thought she'd project herself right over the railing.

"Hey! Hey there, slow down. Are you trying to fly or something?"

That's when she burst into tears and threw herself at me. I almost fell backwards down the stairs. I sat hard on the top step instead.

Weeping. My girl was weeping.

"Shh, honey. It's all over. It's all over now. Your daddy's comin' home. We've solved all the mysteries."

"No, Aunt Wyn . . . not all of them. I . . . please. I can't talk about it. I need you to try and read my mind." She put my hands on her head and shut her eyes tight.

"It doesn't work that way, honey, we just love each other too much. And even if I could, I can already feel this thing you need to tell me is hiding so deep inside, you'd block it away from me anyway. Like a dam, right?"

She nodded, hiccupping with sobs.

"A girl can try, can't she?" she cried out, wailing again.

"Lord, Byrd, what is the matter?"

"I want to tell you something. But I can't tell you. So you need to see it and I can't figure out how to get you to see it!"

I understood. There was one more piece.

"I have an idea," I said.

Her head popped back up. "What?"

"Well, why don't you go back to the cottage and get my tarot cards. I'm pretty good at using them. Maybe if I read your cards I'll figure out your secret and you won't have to tell me anything,"

She jumped from my lap and ran toward my little house.

"They're next to my bed!" I shouted after her.

"I know!" she yelled back.

"Hurry up! It's already starting to rain!" I shouted louder, because she was farther.

"I know!" she yelled out over the thunder that rumbled, shaking everything around us.

The Big House was empty. A large, empty house is always a scary thing. Your mind can play tricks on you.

I went to the kitchen and turned on the lights, but they flickered and went out. It would be one of those quick, violent storms. I felt around for the candles and matches Aunt Min always kept on the windowsill over the sink and lit a bunch on the kitchen table.

"This is a good place," I said to the dark room. I would do her reading on the table that had seen more than its fair share of Whalen triumphs and tragedies. We'd be able to put things in perspective that way. More voices could come through the cards.

"A good place for what?" asked a voice from the shadows.

"Ben! You scared me, I thought you were with Jackson and all them at Sam's."

"I was."

I could hear the grandfather clock in the hall. Tick-tock, tick-tock . . . silence.

"You've never been a winter sort of person, Bronwyn," he said.

"What's that supposed to mean?"

"Think about it," he said. "Winter. It explains, precisely, the difference in personality between someone who hails from the North of this country or the South.

"When you live through winters—true, deep, dark, snowy winters—you can hibernate your soul. You can pretend to be quiet. You learn how to shut yourself off. You've done that for too long. I allowed you to live a Yankee life, a true northeastern life for so damned long you shut yourself down. Completely."

His words resonated.

The South. It seeps out and thaws a person so quickly. If it's in you, it comes right back as soon as you accept who you are. And it was Ben, out of all the people and out of all the things that happened that summer, who taught me this lesson. Birthed it out of me through our contrasts. Allowed me to see the truth.

Be who you are.

If you're broken, be broken. If you're crazy, be crazy. If you're opinionated, yell your opinions from the rooftop. If you have strange ways? See it as a blessing, not a curse.

He sat me down at the kitchen table as the rain poured down outside.

"I'm going back to New York." he said.

"I know."

"And you're not coming,"

"I know," I said softly.

"I will ship your things. Don't worry about me; I realize, now, that you *can't* come back, Wyn. See . . . even I'm calling you by your true name now. You love it here. You belong here. And there's something else . . ."

"What?"

"You love Grant. You loved him when you were small, and you love him still."

You know when you look at someone in astonishment, only it's not really astonishment at all, you just need something to say because you've been caught with your hand in the cookie jar? That's what I felt like. So I came up with the only thing I could think of. "You are *crazy*. You've gone and *lost your mind* in this heat and this storm."

He smiled a knowing Ben smile.

"Bronwyn, you have to let me go and let him know how you feel. If the way he looked at you in New Orleans when you weren't looking is any indication, he'll walk on clouds when you tell him."

"I'm so sorry, Ben."

"Babe, you and I were over the second you got on that plane.

I know it now. And don't misunderstand me. I wish I was wrong. I wish you loved me and wanted to go back to our life together. But I can't have that, so I'm letting you go."

I started crying. From relief and pain so intermingled I didn't know what was what. Then he took my hands and switched my rings. Put Grant's on my left, and his on my right.

"Can we still be friends?" It sounded so pathetic in my own ears I could have slapped myself. But it was true. I didn't want to lose all of him.

"Always."

Just then, Byrd came bouncing in through the kitchen door, soaking wet, with my tarot cards held close to her chest. She looked at the two of us, confused for a moment, but just a moment.

"I reckon I'd tell you I'd give y'all some space, but I don't think neither of you want none of that. So while you say your goodbyes I'm gonna set up this table so Aunt Wyn can work her magic. Okay?"

"It was good to know you, Byrd," said Ben.

"We hold these truths to be self-evident, that all men are created equal . . ."

"She's going to miss you. That's what that means."

"I know. But we'll see each other again soon. I can feel it in my bones. Kiss me one more time and then I'll be gone."

I wrapped my arms around him and felt his strength. His solidity. I kissed him full on the mouth and wondered if I was making a huge mistake.

He pulled away first. "No, you're taking steps back so you can move forward. But thank you for the kiss, I needed that," he said, walking out the door into the rain and out of my life.

But even as the minutes passed, I could still hear him in my heart.

"Thank you, Ben," I said, my eyes closed, hoping he'd feel my words as he drove down those dark, lonely, country roads.

"You can still hear him? In your mind?" asked Byrd.

"Yeah," I responded, shuffling the cards.

"You know what that means, right? Or do I gotta explain it to you?"

"No, I get it now. I can hear him because he's far away from me."

She nodded her head, as if suddenly she'd become very old, and the day that had just occurred was already a part of her memory, long forgotten until stormy nights like *these*.

The past, present, and future live side by side . . .

"Hey," I said, clearing my throat, "before we get started, and just in case this reading turns up things we don't really care to know, you want a drink?" Like I said, no moral compass whatsoever.

I put some ice in a glass and filled it with lemonade, splashing some bourbon on top before handing it to her.

Aunt of the year.

She got right up, poured some off the top of her glass, brought the bottle to the table, and topped off both our drinks. Significantly. "I do believe we might want to get a bit silly, Aunt Wyn. I got a *bad* feelin' about what these here cards are gonna tell us.

"Wait! My favorite song is on! Let's dance too, Aunt Wyn. Just for a bit, one song before we sit and read these *evil* cards," she said, even though there was no music playing. She pulled a wooden stool over to the refrigerator, where an ancient radio sat perched on top.

"The electricity's out, darlin'," I said.

She scoffed, rubbed her hands together and then switched the oversized knob to On. Just like that, Patsy Cline came pouring out of the radio.

Crazy, I'm crazy for feelin' so lonely . . . . I'm crazy . . . . crazy for feelin' so blue . . .

We danced together all over that big country kitchen. Its huge windows black against the rainy night showing our reflections. We sang at the top of our lungs, letting our lemonades splash onto the floor as we twirled, twisting and dipping each other. And every time Patsy sang, "Crazy for lyin'," crazy for tryin'," Byrd shook her hair back and forth with her eyes closed. My gypsy queen.

As soon as the song was over, she turned off the radio.

"Why not leave it on, honey?"

"This ain't no time for music. Time we got serious. Okay?"

"Okay," I said, sitting at the table. I lit a few more candles and gave Byrd the cards to shuffle and hold. "Give them back to me when you feel you've told them the whole thing, okay?"

She took it seriously. She must have told a thousand stories to those cards. Her eyes were closed, tears silently falling.

When she gave them back, I took one of her hands and held it as I placed my other hand on the deck, connecting us both to the cards.

"Are you ready?" I asked.

"I am, but remember. I'm not going to talk. So you'll talk and you can ask me yes or no questions, and when it's over? I don't want to talk about it again. *Ever.* Okay?"

"Deal," I said, laying the spread of cards on the table.

I did a full twenty-one-card storyboard. Those are difficult.

But as each card turned over, I saw the truth. Three cards in particular were all I needed to know about what happened. The
others colored in the gray areas, telling me how terrible she felt.
But those three cards were clear as day.

The beginning: the priestess

"So you went into the mist and you were happy, but confused, right? And you saw many different ways you could try to
help Jamie and everyone else."

She nodded.

The middle: the alchemist

"But something happened. Didn't it, Byrd? Something happened that led you to believe that you needed to do something
right then and there to keep everyone safe. And it had to do
with mixing things together."

She nodded again, her lip quivering

The cards that came between were the saddest and most confused set of combinations I've ever seen. My heart was breaking
for her. But when I turned over the last card, I knew why she'd
been so adamant about never speaking about it.

The Ten of Swords. The card of intellect, and creativity. In
this case, a bad sort of creativity. The card of winter. Death. The
card of air and spirits. The card that told me she'd killed him.

"You made him something to eat. Something with belladonna in it . . ."

She nodded yes as she took a shuddering breath.

She'd poisoned her prince.

"You were afraid he'd hurt other people, too."

She nodded, moving across to my side of the table and sitting
on my lap, her small body shaking with silent sobs.

"I love you, Byrd. And I bet that Jamie knew what he was

eating. He knew that island too well, so don't beat yourself up forever. Some people need a reason to hurt themselves. You didn't kill him, honey. You gave him permission to kill himself."

We were quiet after that, and I just held her tight as the storm raged around us. Sometimes what's right is wrong and what's wrong is right. And we have to figure it out as we go along.

It was done, and the only thing that mattered to me was in my arms.

The old-fashioned phone on the wall in the kitchen rang, at the same time the lights came back on, startling us.

"You jumped first," she said.

"Uh-uh. You did," I said.

We laughed a little, both knowing that our solemn, magic evening was at its end.

"I'll get it," said Byrd. She was sounding like her old self.

"Hello, this is the Whalen residence, *whom* may I ask is speaking?"

"What the hell is that?" I said, looking at her funny.

"I'm tryin on a new pair of manners. I'm growin' up and I think I need some."

"Good luck with that," I said.

"Anyways, it's for *you,*" she said, almost teasingly. She held the receiver out to me and then, when I took it from her, said: "Don't do nothin' I wouldn't do."

"Hysterical," I said to her, then put the phone to my ear.

"Hello?"

"Wyn?"

My heart stopped dead.

Grant.

He'd called me after all.

◊

It wasn't a long conversation. He asked to come over. Said he was broken up over Jamie. "Well, I'm kind of in the middle of something," I said. But Byrd was shaking her head like a madwoman and already gathering up the cards.

I held the phone to my chest. "You sure, honey?"

"I think we both know this is the best it's gonna get . . . it is what it is. Plus, the storm's over. So there's that."

She shrugged at me, finished gathering up the cards and was gone.

That damn girl. "I guess it's fine," I said.

"See you in a few," he said.

I hung up the phone and banged my forehead against the wall a few times.

Do what feels right, I thought, and went out onto the front porch to light candles and the lanterns. The ones Naomi used to love, all strung up, colorful and warm. *Oh, Mama. I miss you.*

He didn't drive. He came walkin' up the stairs just like he always did. Like fourteen years hadn't even gone by. And he was soaked through, too.

"You okay?" I asked.

He didn't answer me.

"Want to stay here or go to my cottage? Byrd fixed up my old playhouse."

"Walking sounds nice," he said. "I got the lowdown at Sam's. I needed some air."

"Seems you've already had a good walk. Maybe you should dry off . . ."

He knows his son is dead. He knows.

"I'm okay," he said. "Better now. Just lookin' at you always made me feel better."

He was nervous. His hands tucked in his jean's pockets. His shoulders up to his ears, like he was ready for someone to hit him.

I held out my hand and he took it.

Jumping in the ocean off the docks, just us. On a day when Paddy and Lottie weren't taggin' along. Running like the wild things we were. Running against time. We jumped so, so high and then held our breath for so long amid all those reeds and weeds and brackish grasses. "In all the world, there ain't never been a love like I feel for you, Wyn."

The memory was a feeling more than anything else, a warmth that spread from my hand to his.

"It wasn't you, Grant. It wasn't ever you. I—it was my mother. And not just her death, the day she died. Remember? I told you a little bit when I ran to your house that night. I understand now why I left and never came back. I was hiding. And I found a wonderful, safe hiding place. To be honest, I could have probably lived there happily for the rest of my life. Only I never would have really lived at all, I guess."

"Did you really think I did it, Wyn?"

"All I wanted was Paddy out of prison. You have to admit, you were a great suspect. If I'd traded him in for you, I would have been obsessed with getting you out next. I know it."

"I know it, too," he said.

We walked farther along the path toward my cottage. Still holding hands.

"I never got to know him, Wyn. My own son. Maybe it's my fault. Maybe if I'd taken responsibility for him, he'd have turned out different."

"You tried, Grant."

"A day late and a dollar short, I tried."

"Sometimes we just have to accept what we've done and forgive ourselves. Byrd's teaching me that. Sometimes people are just born bad. Not a thing you can do about it. And sometimes bad things happen. They just happen. And that's the way you can tell when really lovely things happen. And they are—"

"You always talked too much," he said, pulling me to him fast, and then pushing me up against a tree, kissing me like we were seventeen again.

Every cell in my body opened to a new sort of oxygen. I was alive for the first time since the night my mother died. I didn't die with her. I came back to life right then and there with that kiss.

"I died when you left, you can't leave again," he said, pulling away breathlessly.

"Let's get outta here," I said, trying to shake off the passion building inside of me.

The moon, set free from the storm clouds, was full and misted over, framed by the magnolias. The lightning bugs dotted the landscape.

He stopped me again and held me close, Spanish moss swayed above our heads. "Let's stay here a second, Wyn."

"It's beautiful, isn't it?"

"You're beautiful, Wyn. As if you'd swallowed light."

He cupped my face with his hands and leaned in for another kiss. A sweet, long kiss that could have ended with one of us pulling away again, but didn't. A kiss that grew into a frenzy of kisses, our arms entwined, my fingers tangled up in his hair.

His hands moved down under my cotton shirt, finding their rightful place on my breasts. I couldn't stand it.

"Now, Grant, please," I gasped, and he set me gently on the grass, pushing up my skirt.

Sex is a word. It doesn't mean anything. There are some things that don't have words. They're only experiences. Language-less. Grant and I didn't have sex under the wide green leaves of the magnolia. We did something that has no words. But we moved together, forgetting everything around us, all our troubles, sorrows. Arm over arm, legs entangled, thoughts clear . . . Grant, Grant, Grant, like a heartbeat. My body glowed next to him as it should have been from the beginning, now it was.

"I love you," he said.

"I love *you*," I said. "And I'm never leaving again."

"Do you think we can make it to the cottage, or are you gonna molest me again in the grass?" he asked.

"No more grass," I said. "I have mosquito bites where they ain't oughtta be. Let's get inside."

◊

We made love all night. "Makin' up the lost years," Grant said. But I was living in the moment, without worry, without fear.

As the sun rose, we went out onto the porch and saw, for the first time, the entire island of Belladonna. Forested and lovely. No mist at all.

"He's not there. I know it. You don't have to say anything, but nod if I won't have a chance to get to know him," he said.

I nodded.

He looked off at the rising sun for a bit.

"I can't reconcile it in my heart," he said. "Maybe I won't ever be able to make it right."

"Right and wrong are two sides of a coin, Grant. Flip it over in your head. If you can't forgive yourself, who will?"

"Damn, girl, what happened to you? You're different. Nah, that ain't right. You're you, only . . . the best possible you. I want to learn how to do that. How to become the best possible me. You're gonna teach me, okay?"

"How?"

Byrd and Dolores came bounding up onto the porch. Dolores ran inside the cottage, surprising all of us. Byrd curled up in between me and Grant on the porch swing.

"You're gonna do it like you did it with me, Aunt Wyn. You're just gonna love him like crazy."

A week or so later, Stick drove up to the Big House with Paddy in the backseat.

We'd all been eating a late breakfast together on the side porch and not one of us could believe our eyes.

When Stick got out of the police car and let Paddy out, Byrd ran like a girl possessed and threw herself into her daddy's arms.

I don't know how long they stayed like that, but it didn't matter. The rest of us were watching a miracle. We were watching two people heal right in front of us.

He carried her up onto the porch and we all took turns hugging him, welcoming him home.

"Stick, you son of a bitch," said Grant, laughing. "How the hell did you manage this so quick?"

"Well, we got a man here," he said, giving a nod at Jackson, "who knows a shitload of people in this state.

"Son, it's good to have you home. I—I'm sorry I even thought for a second you did this thing."

"Daddy? You don't have to worry about nothin'," said Patrick. "I felt it was my fault. And in a way? It was. I'm still cheatin' if you look at it. Carter lied. I was there that night."

Everyone looked at me. "What?" I said.

"What nothin', Wyn," said Paddy. "It's a good thing that old man ain't gonna serve too much time because I woulda told the whole truth and nothin' but if he'd gotten a second more."

Minerva leaned over Paddy's shoulder and kissed his cheek. "You're a good man, Patrick. He's fine. Trust me. Your mother would be so proud of you."

Later, Paddy asked if I'd walk with him, show him the cottage. We needed a moment alone.

I held his hand. And there it was, for just a second. The glow.

When we got to the cottage, we sat on the steps. We were always step sitters when we were little. Easy to run from, easy to get back to. Like base during a game of tag.

"So it's true, you have a full-blown case of Mama's magic. Amazing," he said.

"*Peculiar,* I think, is a better word,"

"Thank you, Wyn. Thank you for fixin' this whole thing.

Thank you for comin' back, for takin' care of Byrd. For believing in her."

"Paddy, anyone in your position would have thought what you thought. Don't beat yourself up. And I'm to blame as well. I should have come back sooner. Maybe we'd all be here. All of us."

"Have you gone?"

"Where?"

"Have you gone to Lottie's grave?"

I hadn't. I hadn't even thought about it.

"No. I can't believe it, but no."

"Let's go. We'll go together, the three of us. Me, you, Grant. Okay? Let's go and tell her how we feel," said Paddy.

"Yes, we will. Let's go get Grant and pay our respects. Say goodbye. Say sorry and mean it."

"And then, you know what I'd like to do?" he asked.

"Anything, Paddy,"

"I'd like you and me, Grant and Byrd to get in the car and drive to Apalachicola. I've been dyin' for some oysters. Can we do that?"

"I can't think of a finer idea," I said, smiling.

He leaned over and hugged me hard. "I love you. And I want you to know that I was never mad. That I never felt like you left me. When I really needed you, you came. That's what good sisters do."

I started crying, a million pounds of guilt coming off my shoulders.

We got up and walked back toward the Big House.

"Hey, Wyn?"

"Yeah?"

"Your eyes. Did you notice? They changed color. It's the damnedest thing. They've gone green. Like Mama's."

31

Byrd

For she did not want him to see her crying.
She was such a proud flower.

—*The Little Prince*

So here we go. Hold on to your hats 'cause we're comin' up close to the end of this tale. Right after Aunt Wyn made her way back over from Belladonna and had her reunion with Grant, things started turning all kinds and colors of curious.

And my daddy came home. But I can't explain that feeling, because sometimes there are no words.

Anyway, a mighty strange thing started to happen once all the dust had settled down. The mist moved. I swear. It just lifted up and we all thought, for half a second, that it was gone. But it wasn't. Just like those colonists the Old-timers used to yammer on about, it moved. It moved over us like a cloud and settled in full around the border of Magnolia Creek proper.

I kid you not.

Kinda like that ring in *The Cat in the Hat Comes Back*? Yep. Just like that. Seems like we didn't cure the town of no kind of curse. Seems like we made the curse, well, worse.

But *curse* is a funny word, ain't it? I mean, back in the old days ladies who got their periods called 'em curses, right? Only those curses brought life. So I looked up the absolute definition of *curse* in the dictionary and look what I found:

Curse: The cause of great harm, evil, or misfortune; that which brings evil or severe affliction; torment.

So, like I said. It's a funny sort of word. I mean, if you take the word *curse* outta the definition above and replace it with *love* it means the same damn thing, don't it? Let's try.

Love: The cause of great harm, evil, or misfortune; that which brings evil or severe affliction; torment.

See?

Now let's try another one, because it's what I'm gettin' at.

Fear.

Fear: The cause of great harm, evil, or misfortune; that which brings evil or severe affliction; torment.

See, that's what happened, though it took me longer than it shoulda to figure it out.

The mist over Belladonna was made of fear. And as soon as we fought that fear, it lifted.

Only not everyone fought it.

So, I figure, the scared people left Magnolia Creek and the brave people stayed. Simple as that. And those scared people stayed scared of what we did here, fightin' off all that evil and comin' to terms with our own loves, curses, and sorrows . . . it scared them so much that they left the mist all on the outside of the town.

Don't get me wrong, there's still some fear here now and again. But we puzzle it out and get to the rotten core. Kinda like pullin' a bad tooth.

Ain't it funny how things work out? Life can be so *interestin'*.

The thing is, losing fear doesn't make you feel less lonesome.

I was real lonesome after the mist lifted. Even with my daddy back, even with Aunt Wyn lovin' on me every second.

I wanted Jamie. Still.

I tried searching Belladonna Bay now that it stood there shinin' in the sun, open for all to see and explore.

But he wasn't there, and our castle stood empty.

Jamie realized I'd tricked him. That I wasn't going to stay with him forever. And then he realized *the thing of which I do not speak*. That's when he told me he would never forgive me. He cursed at me, too. Said terrible things.

That's why I was screaming when I found my voice.

But I was sure he'd get over it and I'd be able to find him and fix it. Ain't nothing broken that magic can't fix. At least, that's what I thought. I think I've been wrong about that.

I've been wrong about a lot of things.

So my heart stood empty. Just like our castle.

I've wondered, more than once, if I shouldn't have just stayed there with him. Evil boy or not, he was *my* boy. Seems to me that what he did might have been a mistake more than anything.

Aren't we all allowed a few of those?

And if it was a mistake, then I made a bigger one. I can't think on it. I just won't. And you can't make me, even if it makes this story make sense. I won't ever say.

I was tossin' all those thoughts around early one morning, lyin' out on the grass and lookin' up at the sky. It didn't take too long for Aunt Wyn to find me. She's good like that, always keepin' her eye on me, but not aggravatin' me with it, either.

"Hey there, Byrd," she said.

"Hey."

"What are you doing out here all by yourself?"

"You got a baby in there," I said, poking her stomach as she leaned down.

"I know," she said, smiling. "How do you feel about it?"

"I think the better question is how do *you* feel about it? I ain't the one gotta push a watermelon outta my body."

She laughed so hard then that I laughed, too. Then she got down next to me to look at the clouds.

"That one's an elephant eating a boa constrictor," she said.

I love her.

"How do you feel about all these people comin' and goin' in our town, Aunt Wyn?"

"Change is good, I think," she said. "And the worst thing that can happen is that we have a really boring Fourth of July parade."

I rolled over and curled up in the crook of her arm. "Can't have everything, I guess."

Epilogue

Wyn

After I had had my baby, Byrd came into my big bed, and she snuggled up so that the baby was cradled between us. Grant and I had taken up residence in the Big House and now called Naomi's rooms our own. It was midspring and the Southern magnolias were blooming everywhere. A lemon-vanilla heaven with a touch of spice that you can only recognize if you smell it in person. All the windows were open and the breeze was blowing all kinds of pretty air around the rooms. The bed was made up in Naomi's old favorites. White and cream with bits of lace and pretty swirled embroidery.

"Know what?" I asked her.

"What?"

"We're callin' him Jamie."

Her eyes got wide and filled with tears. She didn't need to say anything. Her hands were glowing.

We smiled at each other, and each took one baby hand

and held it to our cheeks. Then we both kissed each of his hands.

Byrd did the counting, "One, two, three . . ."

And we blew. I could tell you that the room smelled like roses, only it didn't. It smelled of cotton and lavender and hot sun. It was salt and water and honey. It was persimmons and figs and loquats. It was the forest and the pine. It was Naomi's and Stella's garden. And weaving over and under and in between was the scent of the magnolias.

That year, Esther bloomed for the first time since anyone could remember.

Later that same night I walked quietly down the hall to check on the baby.

Byrd was with him and she was speaking to him softly. Both my loves. I listened by the door.

"Now, let me tell you another story altogether. Let me tell you the secrets in my heart that I didn't even tell Jamie the first. I'll share Aunt Wyn with you. Because in my heart she's my own mother now. A mother is a person who'd lay their own life down on the railroad tracks for you. She'd do that. And you know what else? You'll be my Caretaker and I'll be your queen and maybe, when you're older, we'll search for him— that other Jamie, again . . . over there on Belladonna Bay. Just you and me."

I didn't disturb them.

Later, I went to little Jamie's crib. I picked up my darling boy and nuzzled his peach fuzz head. I sang to him and told him stories, and just before I put him back into his crib, I pressed my lips against his baby ear.

"Stay," I whispered.

Byrd

I found him, you know. Just not the way you'd expect. I don't know where the other Jamie went. My first Jamie. I'd thought he'd come to me in spirit. That he'd show himself and forgive me. And then I could forgive him, too. I forgot how close we were. I forgot the limits of my own magic.

Maybe he did like those crazy colonists and disappeared right into the trees, the soil, the land itself. And I like that idea, I sure as hell do. That way I can feel him all around me.

I found him in baby Jamie. When *he* grows big enough, he'll help me. We'll be a team. And I'll try to explain that evil and good walk hand in hand, like hate and love. You can't have one without the other. No matter how frustratin' it is.

I will always have Jamie. It's like my favorite little bit of writing in *The Little Prince*. A passage I'd loved even before all the trouble started. When I read it now, I realize that all of us are the Little Prince. Not just Jamie . . . me, too. Everyone. We should all turn into stars when we die. Maybe we already do.

And you'll open your window sometimes just for the fun of it . . . And your friends will be amazed to see you laughing while you're looking up at the sky. Then you'll tell them, 'Yes,

*it's the stars; they always make me laugh!' And they'll think
you're crazy.*

See, that whole time while I was learning to love my aunt (a
real and honest love), I finally read those words true. We gotta
let people go, don't we? If we hold on to them with all that anger, resentment, love . . . whatever, we strangle them. Spirits
can get strangled, too, that's what makes 'em linger.

So, I realized something that broke my heart and glued it
back together at the same time. My mama's name was Stella
Amore. *Stella* means "star" in Italian. The world is an awful odd
place full of coincidences, and magic . . . even if you can't read a
person's mind. Sometimes all you have to know is their name in
order to understand them.

Every single night I go out into the yard and look up at the
stars. "Forgive me, Jamie?" I ask. And then I tell him the most
important words in the dictionary (if you truly mean them
when you say them, which I do). I say, "I'm sorry." Maybe he
hears and maybe he don't, but at least no one can say I don't have
good manners. Anymore.

That'd be just terrible.

Anyways, it seems to me, that whatever a person does, they
should have a second chance at happiness and redemption. As
long as they remember it ain't about other people. It's about forgiving yourself from the inside out. Like Jackson and Naomi,
Grant and Aunt Wyn, Charlotte and my daddy. And me and
Jamie, too.

And damn, if *redemption* ain't my new favorite word.

1. Some of the most complex characters in this book are children. Jaime and Byrd are drawn to each other and both have a light and a dark side to them in ways that the adults do not. Why do you think the author chose children to demonstrate the good and the bad in human nature?

2. Naomi is a person who looms large over this family and yet she's not physically present. Explore how Naomi's absence has affected her own family. Would her family's outcome be different if she were alive? If so, how?

3. The family seems frightened of Byrd's magical potential and yet loves and protects her. What is it about Byrd that draws her family to her, despite all the doubt they feel about her actions?

4. Bronwyn and Byrd have a special connection. Do you think the absence of their mothers is what draws them together? If so, why? In what ways do you think this has made them different or similar? In what ways do you think Naomi has affected them? How do they reflect her? Discuss.

5. Byrd says her favorite word is "obtuse," that is, slow to understand. While she seems to dislike when other people are being obtuse, could she just be talking about herself? She knows, or thinks she knows, what is going on around her even as she pretends to turn a blind eye. Discuss.

St. Martin's Griffin

6. Naomi says Jackson's alcoholism won't kill him, that "pirates don't drown." That's an interesting juxtaposition with her as a mermaid, the siren. Who leads who astray?

7. At the beginning of the novel, Bronwyn is scared to revisit the person she was when she was growing up. Have you had any experiences where you had to revisit bad decisions in your life in order to move forward?

8. The theme of forgiveness is front and center in the narrative. Why is forgiving the people who have hurt us most so crucial to living a peaceful life? Do you think before forgiving one another all the characters ultimately had to forgive themselves? If so, why, and how does this play an important role in allowing them to move forward together?

9. Bronwyn consistently says things such as "Time lies." How do these moments in the novel reflect the transformative power of honesty?

10. How does the setting of the novel influence the narrative arc of the story? The author creates "characters" out of architecture as well as nature. Would the dynamics between the family members be as poignant if this novel were set somewhere else? Discuss.